Back to Life

BOOK YOUR PLACE ON OUR WEBSITE AND MAKE THE READING CONNECTION!

We've created a customized website just for our very special readers, where you can get the inside scoop on everything that's going on with Zebra, Pinnacle and Kensington books.

When you come online, you'll have the exciting opportunity to:

- View covers of upcoming books
- Read sample chapters
- Learn about our future publishing schedule (listed by publication month *and author*)
- Find out when your favorite authors will be visiting a city near you
- Search for and order backlist books from our online catalog
- Check out author bios and background information
- Send e-mail to your favorite authors
- Meet the Kensington staff online
- Join us in weekly chats with authors, readers and other guests
- Get writing guidelines
- AND MUCH MORE!

Visit our website at
http://www.kensingtonbooks.com

Back to Life

Wendy
Coakley-Thompson

DAFINA BOOKS
KENSINGTON PUBLISHING CORP.
http://www.kensingtonbooks.com

Acknowledgments

Before I do anything, I must take a moment to thank God for watching over me and for giving me innumerable blessings, even when I proved ungrateful and undeserving. I truly believe now that I have everything I will ever need in order to survive and to thrive.

If it truly takes a village, as the old African proverb says, then I would like to thank all "the village people" who contributed to this novel. It was with their help and encouragement that I was able to carry on in the face of many trials and tribulations.

Franca Fabbri patiently helped me with the non-Jersey slang Italian translations during sometimes unintelligible phone calls. Tordis Coakley provided the Swedish translations, pointing out that there is a world of difference between Web translators and the way people *really* talk. Irene Vartanoff indicated where I strayed with characterization, story, and other things of that ilk, all couched within war stories of the New York City publishing scene as we remembered it. Robin Matthew Esq. let me play devil's advocate with the legal issues and had precedents at the ready even when my scenarios seemed far-fetched. I also want to give thanks to Angie Thompson, my Ideal Reader, who enlightened me from the perspective of my potential audience. My editor, Karen Thomas, helped me shape my work and find the words when they escaped me. Any errors in translation and interpretation are mine and mine alone.

I also have to thank my agent, Janell Walden-Agyeman, for nurturing me and being patient through this exciting and new experience. Additional kudos go to Sean and Gina Tepper, who pushed me onto the Information Superhighway with their design of my Web site that defies description. Check it out at *www.wendycoakley-thompson.com*.

Forever the researcher, I checked my facts, even though

I lived through the political context that permeates the book. I found both the John DeSantis book, *For the Color of His Skin: The Murder of Yusuf Hawkins and the Trial of Bensonhurst,* and the 1991 *Frontline* episode, "Seven Days in Bensonhurst," infinitely helpful.

Lastly, this book is for my mother, Marina, who is beautiful of both heart and spirit, and for my wonderful family and friends who believed in my dream and encouraged me to keep my eyes on the prize, especially my sister Chrissie "Krissy Luv" Thompson-Russell (a.k.a. Moonbeam). Much love and many thanks.

Prologue

Bryan stood in the kitchen doorway like he still lived there, dressed in his chinos, loafers, a plain white T-shirt, wire-rimmed glasses, and his ubiquitous imperious air. Lisa marveled at the brothah's unmitigated gall. "What do you want?" she demanded.

Bryan smirked, looking down his cherished white-boy nose at her. "What, no kiss for your better half?"

Lisa stretched her arm across the doorjamb, clearly indicating he was no longer welcome. "I'd let you kiss me, Bryan, but I'm too tired to bend over."

Unfazed, Bryan eased under her arm and into the all-white kitchen. He looked around, arms akimbo. "I see you're in a great mood . . . as usual," he said tersely.

The fucking nerve! Lisa slammed the door so hard that the sound crashed against the silence in the kitchen. "When you asked for a divorce two weeks ago, Bryan, you gave up any right to comment on my moods. Now, what do you want?"

Bryan crossed the kitchen in five long strides, and Lisa followed behind him. "You can take that stick out of your ass, Lisa. I just came for the rest of my stuff."

Lisa felt her blood pressure begin to thud in her ears. He made her feel little, powerless, even in her own house. "You don't live here anymore, Bryan. There's an invention called the telephone. You could've used it to call to tell me that you were going to disrupt my Sunday afternoon."

Bryan gave her the once-over, and Lisa remembered that look all too vividly . . . lusty, dirty, like he'd visually opened her white terry cloth robe, spread her legs, and fucked her right there on the floor. "Oh, that's the special robe you wear when the Kennedys come over for brunch."

Bryan extended his territorial stride to the living room, and Lisa followed frantically behind him. He looked around at the wooden furniture and the Persian rug on the hardwood floors like he still lived there. He moved to the state-of-the-art entertainment system against the near wall under the framed Romare Bearden lithograph and began carelessly flipping through her CDs. Lisa had had enough. "I want your keys," she declared.

He didn't even look up. He turned on the stereo, picked out Stevie Wonder's greatest hits, and popped it into the CD player. "I don't think so," he said, perusing the liner notes. "I keep these keys until the house is sold."

"No, *I* don't think so," she shot back. "This house was bought and paid for with my father's money before we were married—it is mine! Before you leave, you will give me those keys."

"Yeah, right, and monkeys'll fly out of my ass."

She steeled herself. "I want those keys. Or else . . ."

"Or else what, Lisa?" he demanded. "You're going to sick your big Ubangi dyke of a lawyer on me? Ooh, I'm shaking in my loafers, Lisa."

"I have told you what I want, and that's the way it's going to be."

"Is this the part when you jump up and down and hold your breath when you don't get your way? God, you're such a spoiled little rich bitch, aren't you?"

Lisa stared incredulously at him, this man she had given the best years of her life to, now this mewling, bratty ingrate so undeserving of her affection. "*I'm* spoiled?!" she cried. "How fucking laughable is that? You're the one who suckered me into supporting your ass while you got your precious Columbia MBA. The ink wasn't even dry on your diploma before you asked for a divorce!"

No remorse in his beautiful hazel eyes. Just entitlement. "Look, the sooner I get my stuff, the sooner I'm out of your life."

"And not a moment too soon, either."

"Can you look and see if we still have those boxes in the attic?"

"Fuck you. You go look yourself."

Lisa stormed out of the living room.

"I guess it would be too much trouble for you to make me a cup of that coffee I smell," he called after her.

"Yeah, right," she whispered.

His presence seemed to suck all the air out of the house. She heard him tooling around in her space and tried to ignore him and everything he meant to her. She ran the broom over the floor. She filled the sink to wash the dishes. Still, though, she couldn't ignore the fact that he was there in the house. They'd built a life there. Their first night in that house, they'd made love in every room. She'd made him dinner while he studied at that kitchen table. She'd juggled the bills at that table so that he could have his dream. She wondered how he could just so suddenly fall out of love with her and reject everything they'd built together. She looked down at the mug in her soapy hands. His New York

Giants mug that he loved so much. So she wasn't the only part of his past he'd discarded.

She watched as Bryan rolled a swath of clear packing tape onto the last of the five cardboard boxes in the living room. Stevie's "You Will Know" played in the CD player, the music filling the room. *So this is it*, she thought, part wistful, part relieved.

Lisa approached him, carrying his New York Giants mug filled with coffee. Bryan sat on one of his boxes, watching her like a predator. Begrudgingly, she handed him the mug. "Here," she said. "It's your mug, too. Take it with you when you leave."

Bryan took the mug. "Mmm, chocolate hazelnut," he said, then sniffed it and smiled. "And not even a trace of bitter almond smell."

"Very funny. If I wanted to poison you, I had many opportunities to do it long ago. And saying 'Thank you' never killed anyone."

He laughed, and Lisa remembered just how much she'd loved to hear him laugh. She used to take pride in her ability to make him happy. "You're wrong," he said. "There was this one guy in Germany . . ."

Reluctantly, she smiled. "Boy, you're in rare form today. Eddie Murphy had better watch out."

Bryan drank deeply, and Lisa watched. For a second, he was her husband again, funny, sweet. Then she looked around at all the boxes. "Look, are you almost done here?" she asked. "I'm having dinner at Nina and Tim's, and I have to get ready."

He rolled his eyes. "Nina," he scoffed. "Poor Tim. That white bitch is his cross to bear. I bet when you two put your heads together, Eddie Murphy's not the only man who'd better watch his ass."

Lisa flushed. "Please!" she protested, a little too strongly to be real. "You men are the last thing either of us talks about."

"Yeah, right," he said. "That's why my ears have been spontaneously combusting lately."

"If I'm thinking of anything on you spontaneously combusting, I'm thinking further south."

Bryan smiled deviously. "Just can't get me off your mind, can you?"

The blush deepened under her milky brown skin. "You need to check your ego."

From his vantage point on his perch, Bryan stared pointedly at the fold in Lisa's robe, between her legs. "Hmm ... I see London, I see France ..."

Lisa self-consciously covered the fold. "Stop that! Besides, there is no London and France. I was just about to grab a shower when you burst in here."

A lusty expression blanketed Bryan's handsome face. He raised and lowered his eyebrows suggestively. "Oh, really?" he chuckled.

Lisa vehemently shook her head, long, brown, relaxed hair softly brushing her face. "Oh, no, buddy!" she cried. "I know that look. You have fucked me in every way for the last time."

Her stance didn't seem to have the desired effect. Instead of shrinking away, Bryan drained his coffee mug. "Come here," he said, his voice like honey velvet.

His mack daddy voice. Lisa gulped. She could feel her resolve waning. "Why?" she weakly demanded.

He laughed, that same silken laugh that used to precede stepping out of his briefs to proudly sport his massive erection. "I can't believe you're afraid of me," he said, then extended his hand. "Come here."

"I said no," she stated, even weaker.

Bryan got up off the box and walked toward her. Lisa's heart thudded in her chest. He took her hand, and she let him lock his fingers in between hers. He pressed her close against him, and they swayed to the music. Her sense memory traced every inch of muscle and sinew of his body. She closed her eyes and sighed, thousands of memories flooding her feverish brain. The all-too-familiar erection pressed against the soft flesh of her thigh protruding through her robe. She caressed the back of his neck. His hair spilled through her fingers. His breath came hot and labored against her neck. "Damn, you feel good," he groaned.

Her vagina flooded and throbbed. Right then, she wanted nothing more but to feel him inside her, thrusting deep to touch her soul, like he used to. She ached for his legs and arms to be wrapped around her, pulling her close. She wanted him to explore her with his tongue, suck her full mouth until she felt as though she'd die from the sheer ecstasy of it all. The motherfucker always knew how to knock it out.

Gradually, though, "You Will Know" eased into "My Cherie Amour," as if seamlessly. Suddenly, Lisa's heart squeezed painfully. Her throat constricted. Tears welled in her eyes. Slowly, she extricated herself from Bryan's grasp. "Look, you need to go," she whispered.

Bryan was on a slow burn, sexually thwarted. "What?"

Lisa blinked, and the tears spilled down her face. "I'm just remembering the last time we heard this song together," she said. "Do you remember?"

He thought for a minute. "No. When?"

She wiped tears from her face. "It was playing that afternoon two weeks ago. On the jukebox in the diner." She laughed wryly. "When you said those magical words to me. 'Baby, I want out.' "

"I didn't know," he said quietly.

"Of course you didn't, Bryan. You were busy thinking about *your* needs."

A mask of anger descended on Bryan's face. He abruptly turned around and furiously kicked the nearest box across the floor. The box slammed against the stereo cabinet. The song skipped back to the beginning. "Goddamn it, Melissa!" he roared.

Lisa jumped. She was used to his little manly tantrums and knew how to handle them. This time, though, she sensed she was in store for a whole lot more. "Oh, grow the fuck up, Bryan!" she commanded.

"You always fucking do this! All I wanted was to come here, get my stuff, and say good-bye . . ."

"So, say good-bye and get out!"

". . . but you had to take that away. You fucking drama queen! Taking my manhood away from me wasn't enough for you, was it? What would you want, Lisa—my bronzed balls on your mantelpiece, next to the picture of your dead father that I was never able to measure up to?!"

Another body blow. "Leave my father out of this. This is about us!" she cried. "Don't cry to me about your alleged lost manhood. I gave you my heart, and you ripped it out of my chest, and showed it to me. If you have an inferiority complex and you want to know who to blame, look in the fucking mirror, Bryan! That's where you'll find the only person you ever loved!"

He grabbed her arm so roughly that pain shot down the length of it. "I hate you!" he hissed.

She yanked her arm away. "Get over it. You wanted out? You're out. Now get out and leave me the fuck alone!"

She didn't even see it coming. By the time she realized her husband had turned rabid, he'd reached out with lightning quickness and struck her across the cheek. It felt like he'd steam-pressed his fingerprints into her flesh. She went down, sliding on her back across the shiny, hardwood floors. Stunned, she lay there in shock, an airconditioned draft blowing from the floor vents across her bare crotch where her robe had opened. She opened her eyes, and his hateful face swam above hers. Her heart echoed in her ears. His emotions had run the usual gamut during their marriage, but he'd never been violent with her. Until now. "Get up!" he shouted.

Her entire face ached. Her head swam. Fear throbbed through her, paralyzed her.

"I said get up, goddamn it!" he yelled louder.

Before she could will the motor functions that would make her legs work, Bryan reached down and dug his fingers into her throat, slowly closing off the air to her chest. Her eyes bugged out of the sockets. Bile crept slowly up from her stomach. Sparkly dots began to float in her gaze, fixed on his face contorted with fury.

He yanked her to her feet. "You fucking bitch!" he rasped through gritted teeth. "This is my house. I leave when I want to leave. Everything in this friggin' house is mine, including you!"

He relaxed his grip slightly, and Lisa gulped a little more air through her constricted throat. With his free hand, Bryan untied her robe. Through the sparkly haze, Lisa realized what he wanted to do to her. She cried out, shaking her head. "Bryan . . . I . . . can't . . . breathe . . ." she gasped.

With the same hand, Bryan unfastened his trousers and pushed them, along with his underwear, slowly to the floor. He stepped out of them, revealing his bare bottom. "All right," he said softly against her wet cheek. "Now, I'm going to let go, and you're going to be my good little wife and not scream, right?"

Lisa nodded through the sparkly haze. As he promised, Bryan relaxed his grip on her throat. The air and bile hit Lisa's throat full on. She began a coughing fit, sucking air into her chest. Bryan leaned in toward her. She could smell the coffee on his breath. "You know what you're going to do for me?" he whispered. "You're going to suck my dick, just the way I like it."

Lisa looked up at her husband in disbelief that he was capable of this . . . that she was capable of falling in love with a man who was capable of this. "No!" she sobbed.

"Yes," he said, practically salivating at the prospect of a forced blowjob. "You're going to suck my dick and you do anything stupid, I'll snap your neck like a fucking twig."

Bryan guided her to her knees in front of him. Profound sadness and abject helplessness overtook her, and all she could do was cry.

"Shh!" he commanded. "You're spoiling my concentration."

As if being forced to take a bitter medicine, she closed her eyes and took him into her mouth. She used to love giving him head, loved the taste of him, the smell of him, how he tensed at the moment of maximum joy. Now all she felt was nausea and disgust, as if no amount of retching and mouthwash would get the stench of him out of her throat. He pressed his hands against her head, clutching her hair through his fingers. "Aw, shit, baby . . . just like I like it," he groaned, his voice quavering and thick.

"My Cherie Amour" ended. Silence enveloped the room, magnifying the sickening sounds of sucking, her sobs, and his moans of unadulterated passion.

The yard at Rikers Island Prison bustled with midday activity, despite the May sun baking the concrete, casting shimmery, silvery shadows. Convicts in drab street clothing—T-shirts, jeans, and the like—milled around, either solo or conversing with other inmates or flexing to conceal their fear at being locked down in one of the nation's most notorious prisons. Marc wore a white T-shirt and jeans, too. Poor attempt to blend, be inconspicuous. Regardless of what he thought about his parents and their strange way of raising him and his brother and sister, it was testament to them that he'd gone thirty-eight years without having served a day of time. If you believed popular culture, every Italian was a jail-hardened mobster. *Just get the fucking interview and get out.*

Maybe this wasn't the best time to write this book. Maybe he needed to concentrate on his marriage, rather than on his craft. He'd had another fight with Michele last night. No matter what he did, she just didn't seem happy anymore. And he certainly didn't understand her lethargy, her mood swings, and her chronic fatigue. Was she sick and keeping it from him? They didn't even have breakfast together that morning, like they usually did. He'd awakened this morning to find her gone, her side of the bed ice cold. He was losing the only woman he'd ever loved, and he didn't know what to do.

Focus, Marco. He remembered where he was just then. This wasn't the place to drop your guard for one millisecond. Lost concentration led many a man to his grave here.

Suddenly, through all the detritus of manly New York criminality, he saw the target: Vito Morali, a nervous, squat, aging inmate dressed in jeans and a cut-off cotton shirt. Vito was low man on the *Cosa Nostra* totem pole, about to be dropped from the *capo's* radar screen. From his research, Marc knew that Vito was one night in jail away from flipping. Marc figured he'd try to beat the feds there.

Vito was staring up at the cloudless sky like he was wishing he were a bird. Marc approached. "Hey," he said with a wobbly smile.

Vito regarded Marc with contempt. "Fuck off," he tersely commanded. "I got nothin' to say to nobody."

Try humor. "Actually, using a double negative in that sentence really means you have something to say."

Vito's eyes narrowed to slits. "What are you, a fuckin comedian?!"

Marc shook his head, looking up at the blue sky. "Apparently not," he murmured.

"Then what . . . a cop?" Vito questioned. "I don't talk to cops."

Marc leaned in, and he could smell fear oozing from

Vito's every pore. "Look, I'm not a cop," he said. "I'm a writer. I write books."

"Yeah?" Vito challenged. "Like what?"

He couldn't believe he was auditioning for this mobster. Vito didn't seem like he spent many days at the library. "Like *Benny Blues*," he said.

Vito scoffed and Marc felt his face turn red. "*Benny Blues*?!" Vito laughed poisonously. "What kinda fuckin' faggot name for a book is *Benny Blues*? What's that about, some bitch with a pill habit?"

His own wife was a stranger to him; what he knew about women certainly could not fill a pamphlet, much less a hardcover book. *Don't be defensive, Marco; this is an opportunity to educate this man.* "No," he replied. "It's about people from the north of Jersey who go down the shore in the summer. A benny is someone who's quote-unquote 'seeking the beneficial rays of the sun.' " Vito's face remained blank. "Get it?" Marc implored, coaxing. "Benny's short for 'beneficial.' "

"Hey, don't talk to me like I'm some kinda fuckin' moron!" Vito sniped.

Don't get the mobster mad. After all, Vito had punished many skeletons in his day.

"Sorry," Marc said.

Vito nodded with a shadow of confidence, like he still had the power to flex. "What else did you write, Mr. Book Writer?"

"*When Irish Eyes Are Crying*. It's about . . ."

Vito's washed-out brown eyes lit up in recognition. "Yeah, I know that one!" he said excitedly. "I bet you thought I never read a book, didn't you?"

What was he, a mind reader? "Naw," Marc lied, shaking his head. "Did you like it?"

"Hated it," Vito declared. "I stopped after page 20. Who wants to read about a buncha micks dying on some peat bog? They're killin' Italians right here in the fuckin' United States of America."

This isn't going well.

"So, what's MarcAntonio-fuckin'-Guerrieri doin' in jail, man?" Vito asked. "Whadid you do—whadda they call it—'plagiarize'?"

Marc laughed heartily. "No!" He leaned in closer. "No. I'm doing a book about . . . you know . . . the family . . . *La Cosa Nostra* . . ."

Instantly, the nervous, twitchy Vito returned. He moved away from Marc, frenetically examining his surroundings. "That kinda book could get you killed, Mr. Book Writer," he said, his voice shaking. "You and me both."

Marc knew he had to calm him, first and foremost. "Hey, it's okay," he said quietly. "Look, we have a mutual friend on the outside . . . Joey Lacitignola, you know, Tiggy? He said to see you if I needed some information . . . like Gotti stuff."

Far from being calmed, Vito was so agitated, he looked like he would have a seizure at any second. "Tiggy and his big fuckin' mouth!" he said through gritted teeth, opening and clenching a fist. "They don't call Gotti the Teflon Don for nothin'! You and Tiggy could go fuck yaselves—you're both *pazzo*. Call me crazy, but I like breathin'."

"No one has to know that you said anything to me," Marc assured him.

"Look," Vito pleaded, "you look like a smart kid. This ain't somethin' you wanna fuck with. Trust me on . . ."

Vito looked over Marc's shoulder and instantly clammed up. His dull brown eyes filled with abject terror. Marc turned to see a dark, wiry man behind him. Under slick, greasy hair, steel eyes glinted menacingly; the man's skin was slick with sweat. He possessively cradled his right arm against his body. Icy fear bit at Marc's gut.

"Wow!" the hoodlum said sarcastically. "Looks like you two are talking about some real important shit."

Vito opened and clenched the fist faster. "We ain't talkin' about nothin'!" he squeaked.

Stay calm, Marco. "Vito, you know this guy?" Marc asked, his eyes darting around the yard for a potential escape.

"Jesus-fuckin'-Christ!" Vito cried. "How many times do I have to say it? I don't know nothin' and I don't know nobody!"

The hood's eyes hardened further. "Unfortunately, Vito," he said icily, "the people I work for can't be too sure that you're gonna stick to the party line."

"I don't know what you mean," Vito laughed nervously. "There ain't a more loyal guy than Vito Morali."

Marc's eyes scanned the crowd like blue lasers. So typical of New York; where the fuck was a guard when you needed one?

The hood's sinister vibe did nothing but frighten Vito and make him twitchier and more nervous. "You're old and tired, Vito," he declared matter-of-factly. "Nobody knows what you might say to get outta here. Nobody wants to take that chance."

The hood showed the inside of his thin right arm to reveal a homemade shank, crudely fashioned out of wood and steel. The metallic point glinted in the afternoon sun, in stark contrast with the hood's knobby, venous flesh. Marc's eyes widened. *Oh shit!*

The hood lunged toward Vito, who was petrified, scared shitless. "Vito, look out!" Marc cried.

Some superhuman, arcane instinct took over, driving Marc to push Vito out of harm's way. An evil combination of fate and physics propelled the hood along his same path, though. Before Marc could retreat, the hood's shank plunged into Marc's stomach. He expected to feel pain; he didn't. It felt like he'd been punched really hard. Reflexively, his hands flew to the point of contact, and he felt a sticky, warm wetness. He slowly looked down and saw his own blood staining his white T-shirt.

"Holy shit!" Vito sobbed hysterically. "Ya killed him!"

From somewhere far away, Marc heard an alarm sound, saw a crowd encircle him, Vito, and the hood. He suddenly felt so tired. He eased down to the ground. He just wanted to sleep. Michele was leaning over him, kissing him. "I love you, Marc," she whispered.

Her angelic face fought against darkness swimming before his eyes until the blackness swallowed her up.

1

August 1989

The party raged in the Simons' living room. People dressed in all their summertime finery were either chatting or off dancing on the enclosed patio to the funky, blistering sounds of Soul II Soul's "Back to Life" blasting through the speakers. Caron Wheeler's mellifluous voice floated on Jazzie B's fat beats and the sweaty, sexually charged air. Caron sang, and bodies gyrated in an arcane groove.

Lisa stared at all the people from her vantage point: a stool at the bar. She was wearing her best elegant black party dress and black pumps. Her face was beat to near perfection. And she was convinced everyone was digging the fete but her. She turned to Tim—tall, black, handsome, mid-thirties—who was pouring a concoction into a tall glass behind the bar.

"How can someone be in a crowded room and still feel alone, Timothy?" she asked, bobbing her head to the music.

"You're not over Bryan yet?" Tim offered. "Even though you guys split up over a year ago."

Lisa scoffed. "I'm over Bryan like the sky," she declared, then looked out at the couples kissing and slow-dragging on the patio. She couldn't even remember the last time a man touched her like that, so lovingly carnal. "It's just hard," she sighed. "Being alone after five years."

"Nina and I have been married for nine years, and I couldn't imagine one second without her," he said knowingly.

Lisa forced down the nagging instinct, the irrational sensation every black woman felt when thinking about a black man with a white woman, particularly the trophy blonde. It was even more irrational, since Lisa's own grandfather was a big white Englishman with an ocean of love for her. "That's sweet," she said sarcastically. "I think I'm getting a cavity."

Tim laughed. "I'm trying to be that sensitive, post-eighties guy." He handed her the glass with a frothy tan liquid over crushed ice. "Madam, your Long Island iced tea," he said with an affected British accent and a quick head bow.

Lisa took a sip. It tasted cold, sweet, and lemony. "You're like Tom Cruise in *Cocktail.*"

He laughed. "Thanks, but I'm not throwing shit around. That's just plain showing off!"

"And we all know that men don't show off!" she giggled.

Slowly, though, the laughter died. The CD changed, and the first few beats and the breathy, come-hither vocals of Guy's "Baby Don't Go" came through the speakers. Slow-dragging on the patio began in earnest. Lisa stared at them, sucking on a bitter combination of melancholy and envy. "You're going to have to hose them down," she laughed bitterly.

Tim touched her arm. "Hey," he said in his classic everything's-gonna-be-all-right, Tim Simon voice. "Forget

bout Bryan. In three months, he'll be ghost, and you'll
e free to get your head on straight."

She forced a laugh and raised her glass. "To New
ersey no-fault divorce!"

Tim looked past her. "Aw, shit," he whispered. "Here
omes my wife the pimp with some suit-and-tie dude."

"Damn!" she cried. "Is it too late to run?"

Tim cleared his throat and faked a smile. "Honey!"
e exclaimed. "There you are!"

Lisa turned and saw Nina, working the low-cut red
ninidress on her statuesque frame. She had a model's
reat looks, and with her long, flowing blond hair, she
ooked like a refugee from a shampoo ad. In tow, she
ad an attractive, nervous-looking black guy in an Italian
uit and glasses.

"Tim, are you taking care of our little Lisa?" Nina asked,
nd Lisa marveled at how strange her accent was, be-
ause she was Swedish but raised in Britain.

"Yup," Tim assured her. "Mixed her a good, stiff drink."

"Perhaps she could use a good, stiff something else,"
Nina snickered, elbowing Lisa in the ribs.

Tim and Nina and the suit-and-tie dude laughed like
hey'd heard the world's greatest joke. Lisa didn't laugh.

Adding fuel to the comedy of errors unfolding be-
ore her, Nina pushed her friend forward. "Lisa, this is
ance Killingsworth," she said. "He's a lawyer in the City."

As if on some polite reflex, Lisa and Lance shook
ands. He had a limp handshake. Lisa could only guess
vhat else was limp. "Hi," she said, warily sizing him up.

"Nice to meet you," Lance said, and almost instantly,
Lisa could see the glint of an ambulance-chaser in his
lark eyes. "Nina tells me you're going through a divorce."

"Yes. I have a lawyer, though. Jaye Barraclough."

Naked admiration replaced the ambulance-chaser
ook. "Oh man, she's good!" he laughed. "She'll have
our husband shaking in his shorts and will take them
ff him when she's through."

Lisa smiled brilliantly. "Cool."

A smile of self-satisfaction played at the corners of Nina's mouth, as if this was evidence of a love connection. "Maybe we should leave these two alone, Tim," she suggested.

The prospect of being trapped for the rest of the evening with yet another bland fix-up with a flaccid handshake was more than Lisa could bear. She rocketed up off her stool, almost spilling her drink on the bar. "Actually, I've got to go . . ." she said hastily, then her brain cramped. *Go and do what?* " . . . powder my nose. Nice to meet you, Lance."

Lance looked confused, like a man who'd been promised a sure thing and then had been unpleasantly surprised. "Yeah," he mumbled. "Same here."

Lisa rushed away, convinced she could feel the eyes of Lance, Tim, and Nina boring into her back.

She picked her way through the four corners of the Simons' house, looking for a moment's peace. It seemed, though, that in every corner, people were talking, or smoking, or making out. Drunken, smirking men rubbed up against her under the guise of passing through the hall. Their women gave her catty glances and snatched their men away. Right then, all she wanted was to peel off her entire party facade and curl up in bed with her cat and flannel pajamas. "Fucking parties!" she swore under her breath.

When she saw the next inebriated guy headed her way with his gaze on stun, she ducked through the nearest door, shut it, locked it, and leaned against it. She sighed, looking around her. The room was comfortable and inviting, filled with stuffed chairs, a sofa, glass coffee table, pictures of Nina and Tim and their children, and trophies from trips abroad. An ad for *Lethal Weapon 2* played at a low volume on the big-screen TV in front of the sofa.

Suddenly, Lisa realized she wasn't alone. Seated in

one of the stuffed chairs, a white guy, rocking the spare black tee under a black suit, held a telephone receiver to his ear. He nodded and smiled periodically. He must've realized that he wasn't alone, either, because just then, he trained on Lisa the bluest eyes and the whitest smile she had ever seen and waved hi.

Lisa didn't usually go for white boys. In her experience, they only looked at black women when they had a brief taste for the antidote to that whiny, white-girl sense of entitlement. They went back to their side of the fence when they realized that black women weren't biologically different from their white counterparts. They usually didn't have the stomach for the path of most resistance. That aside, she could certainly appreciate a tall, hard body and striking blue eyes set in a ruggedly handsome, tanned face.

She made a phone sign with her hand to her ear. "I'm sorry—you're on the phone," she whispered. "I'll go."

He shook his head and waved her in. To the person on the phone, he said, "Yeah, I'm at a party at a friend's house."

Lisa tentatively approached the couch and sat, all the while watching him watch her. He watched her, all the while carrying on his conversation. "Make my day, Linley— tell me how'd *Goombah* do on the first day on the shelves," he said, all the while smiling at Lisa. *Nod, nod.* "That's great. Isn't it a little early, though, to be thinking book signing?" *Nod and laugh.* "Okay, okay, keep 'em on, Lin. I won't even pretend to tell you how to do your job." *Nod, nod.* "All right, pencil me in." *Naughty laugh.* "I'm always a very good boy for you, Linley."

Lisa looked away at the TV and rolled her eyes in disgust. So, he needed an audience to be a player.

"Okay," he said finally. "I love you, too. Sleep well."

With that, he hung up the phone. "I saw that," he said.

"Saw what?" she asked.

"That perfectly timed rolling of the eyes."

"Look, I didn't mean to eavesdrop on your conversation, but you were laying it on a bit thick, weren't you?"

He came over and sat next to her on the couch. Instantly, she threw her guard up. "Maybe," he conceded, "but Linley loves it, and I aim to please."

"Who's Linley, your wife?"

He laughed. "Linley's a sweet, fifty-year-old, Southern black woman."

"You're Evasive Man, aren't you?"

"When it's called for, I can be quite direct. Like now. I think you're hot. I also think the way you wear that dress is making me dizzy. There. That wasn't evasive at all, was it?"

She looked at him, disgusted. "So you're Smooth Evasive Man."

He laughed. "Linley's my agent."

"You're a writer."

He nodded.

She knew that each and every one of the Simons's friends had an interesting story of how they met them. She wondered what his story was. "How do you know Nina and Tim?" she asked.

"I'm an assistant professor at SCNJ Montclair. Nina and I work together."

Interesting enough. "Oh. I'm taking a class there this fall," Lisa said. "I thought you just said you were a writer, though."

He leaned in; on reflex, she leaned away. "I'm allowed to do both," he said. "I'm sure you've heard of 'Publish or perish.' "

Dick! "My experience may not be as vast as yours, but somewhere in there, I've heard about 'Publish or perish,' " she said tersely.

He moved away. "You could be nicer."

"Look," she said, pissed. "I've been here for almost

our hours. Nina thinks my divorce means I'm chum for
every single guy in the room. I've been pawed by
drunken yuppies, and my feet are killing me!"

"Aha," he said knowingly. "Pavarotti Woman."

"What does that mean?"

"Me me/Me me/Me me me," he sang, operatic fashion.

She wanted to laugh in his face. "Oh, please!" she
cried. "Who could be more self-obsessed than you?" She
affected a sleazy, smooth manner. "'I'm on the phone
with my agent.' 'I'm a writer.' 'Linley loves it, and I aim
to please.' Give me a break!"

He laughed sheepishly, shaking his head. "I thought
I was being as charming as hell," he said. "Chalk it up to
performance anxiety . . . overcompensation . . ."

She softened. "Overcompensation for what, lack of
sexual prowess?"

He feigned wounded macho pride. "Hey, I'm Italian.
That's for other guys."

They laughed, relaxing. He extended a hand. "I'm
Marc," he said.

She shook the hand. "Lisa," she said.

"Give me your foot."

"What?!"

Marc patted his lap. "Your foot," he prompted. "I
give a mean foot massage."

He looked harmless enough. Still leery, though, Lisa
kicked off her shoes, exposing soft, manicured feet. She
wiggled toes with square, red-lacquered nails, and eased
her right foot in Marc's lap. "My mother would have a
hissy fit if she knew I let a stranger give me a foot massage," she said.

"I just told you my name," he reasoned, "and you already know I'm a friend of Nina's. That means I'm not
a stranger."

"Male logic in action," she said sarcastically.

Marc laid his hands on her bare foot. Lisa closed her

eyes briefly, savoring the feeling. He then expertly mas
saged her right foot, her aching heel, her painful arch
the top of her feet where her sandal straps had cut into
her flesh. His touch was warm but firm, innocent bu
sensual at the same time. He worked his thumbs agains
the reddened ball of her foot. The last time a man's
touch felt that good, she was naked under him. She
moaned involuntarily.

"Good?" he laughed.

"Very," she shuddered.

"Pretty feet."

"Nice touch."

Inane TV white noise filled the moment for a few
minutes, until the urge for someone to say something
became palpable. Finally, Marc said, "What I mean
about overcompensation? I've been out of the game for
a while myself."

A kindred spirit, united in heartbreak. "Divorce," she
guessed.

He nodded. "A little over a year."

She let out an exasperated sigh. "No one seems to
have the right perspective on how to get through this
Nina and Tim are so fucking cutesy together. To my
mother, all men suck. My lawyer looks at Bryan—that'
his name—and sees dollar signs."

"Sorry to say this, Lisa," he said, sounding quite like
the old sage, "but divorce is like any shock-to-the-system
first-time kind of experience. It's different for every
body. What worked for one person won't necessarily
work for you."

"Well, what worked for you?"

He sighed, massaging and avoiding her probing, ques
tioning gaze. "Well, the first three months, I was pretty
sick, so I was trying to recover from that. The next eigh
months, I . . . 'dated,' for lack of a better word, a lot o
women, finished my book, stayed drunk, and was gen
erally an asshole to anyone who had the misfortune o

meeting me. The past month or so has been pretty
slow."

What woman would leave *him*? "Sorry," she said.

His smile was pained. "Don't worry. She's in the next
book." He touched her knee. "Left foot."

Obediently, she slid her left foot into his lap, and he
worked at massaging her foot like it was another job.
She looked down at his head, which was framed with
short, dark waves. "You're good at this," she laughed
tentatively. "I should take you home with me."

"Tease!" he chuckled. "Your turn to share."

The last day that Bryan came over to visit flooded
her mind. She felt every muscle in her body painfully
clench. "He moved out after he decided that 'til death
do us part was a bit too confining for him. But he'd in-
vent reasons to come over for . . . you know . . ."

His blue eyes were glacial. "Great," he remarked.

"So I got a cat, I moved into a studio apartment, and
I put the house up for sale."

"Being okay with the hand you've been dealt is the
best revenge. That's what worked for me in the long
run."

She stared incredulously at him. "As simple as that,"
she concluded, disbelieving.

"Yup," he said confidently.

"Yeah. Sure."

On the TV just then, the theme music from Channel
4's *News at Eleven* came from the television. After the signature, amped-up opening of the show, replete with dra-
matic music and swirling chyron darting across the screen,
an attractive, black, intelligent-looking anchorwoman and
her classic, anchorman counterpart appeared on the
screen at the theme's final crescendo. The chyron flashed
the date—August 23, 1989—at the bottom of the TV
screen.

Lisa laughed. "Let's see if your little revelation made
tonight's news."

"It's the talk of the tri-state area," he said, tongue firmly in cheek.

The TV camera cut to a close-up of the anchor-woman's very grave face. A graphic of a gun with a flash exploding from the barrel was perched over her left shoulder. Her green eyes looked almost sad. "An East New York teenager is dead and three others injured after a racial incident in Bensonhurst tonight," she announced. "The teenager, identified as Yusuf Hawkins, was fatally shot after he and three friends were attacked by thirty to forty white teenagers. Let's go to team coverage for more . . ."

Reflexively, Lisa swung her feet from Marc's lap. They both stared at the TV as if in a trance at the images flashing across the screen . . . the bloody spot on Bay Ridge and 20th Avenues where Hawkins's body had lain . . . the parade of white teenagers being led away into police custody . . . Hawkins's distraught parents. The images and the narration led her to an all-too-familiar conclusion. This young man, all of sixteen, was minding his own business, and these ignorant white assholes smoked him for no apparent reason. Other than he was black. Ignorant white assholes who had inadvertently created another statistic and snuffed out a bloodline. Arcane anger boiled in her stomach. Too pissed to speak, she sucked her teeth, shaking her head. She shot a glance at him, dying to see his reaction, wondering how he felt to see his own kind being escorted away.

Moist, shocked blue eyes scanned the TV screen. He sighed, hands on his head. *"Déjà vu,"* he murmured. "Just like when Michael Griffith ran across the Belt Parkway in Howard Beach three years ago."

Talk about revisionist history! "Ran?" Lisa scoffed. "More like chased to his death. By another gang of Italian men. The only difference is, this time, it's Brooklyn, and that time, it was Queens. Damn it, what is it with us and them?"

Instantly, the climate in the room shifted. Mentally, they went to their corners, with her as the representative for "us" and him in the icy Siberia of "them," as they watched the news in silence.

2

The late-afternoon sun bathed the campus in warm, abating rays. It was the end of August at the State College of New Jersey, or SCNJ, at Montclair, second only to Rutgers University as a jewel in the state college system. Between the construction finishing on the new library and long lines for everything from late registration, to books, to infamous pizza at The Rathskeller (affectionately called Rat Pizza), the campus predictably came back to life after a sleepy summer in which only the ultramotivated or the slackers reeling from the previous semester's failures occupied the buildings.

Only this August was decidedly different. Angry fallout from the Hawkins shooting had made its way across the bridges and tunnels from Brooklyn to Montclair, a town less than twenty miles outside of New York City. It wasn't surprising. Montclair was populated mostly by transplanted City dwellers who wanted all the culture and magic of the City, without the crime.

The fallout, too, made its way to the activist element on the SCNJ Montclair campus. Ordinarily, the demonstrations would have gone on until students realized that activism was all well and good, but their parents had sent them there to attend class. That was what happened when the activists who were barely old enough to remember the sixties turned out in the quad in front of the Student Center to plead for divestment from South Africa. A flurry of protests in the face of a blissfully disinterested faculty and chancellor dissipated into so much smoke. The quad cleared, and students returned to class.

This time was different. SCNJ was on the verge of becoming a university. The powerbrokers had spent taxpayer money and revved up an awesome public relations blitzkrieg in preparation for the influx of out-of-state students and out-of-state dollars. The college's chancellor, Donald Swift, possessively oversaw the transformation of his fiefdom into a kingdom and suffered gladly no one who was a threat to his mission. How was he to know that the murder of a sixteen-year-old black kid miles away in Brooklyn could potentially derail the SCNJ's move to university status?

Derailment came in the form of the campus's fringe activists, awakened by the helplessness and anger felt in the wake of the senseless shooting. The racially mixed group of students protested in an ever-growing circle in front of the Student Center, a mammoth white trophy of concrete-and-glass modern architecture. "No justice, no peace!" they chanted loudly, the voices reverberating four floors, through the glass on Pidgeon Hall.

Marc watched them from his office window. His office was small but he used space efficiently. On his desk, there was a personal computer, IN and OUT boxes, framed book reviews, and a ten-year-old photograph of his family. A guest chair was propped next to the stuffed-to-bursting bookshelves, and a stereo box on one corner of the desk. The sounds of Nina Simone's "Mississippi Goddamn" playing on the box inside the office commingled with the muffled shouts of "No justice, no peace" coming from the quad outside.

Marc moved away from the window and plopped down in the chair behind his desk. He looked down at the "No Justice, No Peace" button in his hand, put there a few minutes ago by a black guy in an African cloth hat as he picked his way through the quad on his way to his office. He never could understand this thing with his people and black people. He certainly had never seen in his house in Fairfield any of the racist shit he heard from his school friends when he was a kid, or any of this stuff going down now. Even though Fairfield was one of the whitest enclaves in Essex County, the same county in which the overwhelmingly more diverse Newark was the county seat.

But then again, by the time Marc came around— MarcAntonio Pasquale Fiore, the third and last button on Daniel and Rosalie Guerrieri's coat—his parents were tired. They pretty much left him alone. He spent more time with Adam, his older brother by four years, than he did with his own father. It was Adam who introduced him to books, and soul music, and art. It was Adam who took him to get his hair cut, who showed him how to throw the perfect, spiraling pass, who told him about girls and how to use protection. On the other hand, Marc and his dad had an uneasy alliance. Daniel was the father; Marc was the cultured son who had out-achieved practically everyone in the family. That was the vibe he and his dad had. It didn't leave much time for them to malign other ethnic groups.

Marc clipped the button onto his denim shirt and eyed *The Clarion*, the school newspaper. "SCNJ's Bid to Become a University on Track," the headline announced. In the delusional Swift kingdom, the demonstrations were unworthy of mention.

Just then, distraction, in the form of Nina, stuck its blond head into the office. "Hallo!" she said.

She always managed to brighten his day. "Yo!" he laughed.

Nina breezed in and plopped down in the guest chair. "Haven't got long to chat," she said. "I'm up for tenure this year, so I have to meet with the old Promotion and Tenure ponces to find out which flaming hoops I must jump through."

"God, do you ever come up for air? How do you talk so fast?"

"Comes from winning arguments with Tim. Did you have fun at the party?"

He remembered those minutes he spent with Lisa and smiled. "Yeah, I was having a great time." The smile faded. "Until the news."

Nina shook her blond head, like she'd just heard the news that minute and the disbelief was just as new. "Tim knows one of the camera chaps who taped that ghastly scene. First Howard Beach, now this."

"Makes me proud to be Italian," he said sarcastically.

Just as suddenly, Nina's concentration shifted. Marc sensed she had the attention span of a med fly. She raised and lowered her plucked brows suggestively. "Saw you with Lisa."

He shook his head, feeling the trap snap shut. "Yes, Yenta," he said. "I was with your friend Lisa."

"There I was," she mused, "introducing her to every other man in the place, and you found her just like that."

"My dumb luck."

Nina glared at him as if he were a willful child. "For someone who just made a love connection, you could be happier," she stated.

"Whoa!" he said. "I said I liked her. That doesn't translate into us picking out china patterns." *Grasp at whatever straw you can find, Marco.* "Plus she needs time to get over that Bryan guy."

"That's cack!" Nina insisted. "They've separated for almost one-and-a-half year."

" 'One-and-a-half year,' " he teased. "You're so mad at me, you're sounding Swedish."

She slapped his hand. "Oi!" she cried.

He tried hard to stifle a laugh and failed. "Sorry," he said.

She began her sales pitch. "Why do you say she's not over that arsehole Bryan Livingston? You and Michele were apart for almost the same amount of time. You're over her, aren't you?"

Okay. Sore spot. Michele, his Italian-American princess . . . until she decided that she didn't want to be married to him anymore and ran off to her beloved California. The defenses sprang up. "Call me wacky, but I could've sworn we were talking about someone named Lisa," he declared.

Her grey eyes lit up, like she'd suddenly touched on the answer. "You're still in love with your ex-wife!" she said.

Defenses on acid. He tried to play it cool, but he felt his face flame hot. "Is my part in this script, 'Am not!' And you say, 'Are too!' until one of us gives up?"

It was Nina's turn to tease. "Someone in this room is not in touch with his feelings . . ." she singsonged.

Confess, Marco. After the party that night, he and Lisa kissed good night as they went their separate ways. From that moment, he couldn't stop thinking of her. And the attraction was not just intellectual, but animal, magnetic. He sighed. "Okay. Here's the deal," he said. "I liked your friend Lisa. She was articulate, and kind, she had a nice pair of feet . . . no corns at all. And man, that black dress she was wearing made my BVDs feel two sizes too small."

"But . . . ?"

He ran through the litany of excuses that he pondered that day after the party, but he had to stretch. All he could remember was massaging her feet, her happy laughter, her brilliant conversation, and her quiet strength in the face of all she was going through. But he knew it was doomed, particularly in the current context. Plus Michele . . . what was going on with his feelings for Michele? "She's a little young . . ." he said weakly.

"She's twenty-nine," Nina insisted. "She's going to be thirty in January. That doesn't exactly make you Vladimir Nabokov, does it?"

"I'm ten years older than she is."

"Everyone knows that women mature faster than men. One issue of *Cosmopolitan* could tell you that," she argued.

"Point well taken, but you can't explain away her husband," he persisted. "I don't know what he did to her, but man, she's bitter."

Nina was solemn. "He treated her horribly. And she's not bitter. She's lonely and maybe a little bit horny. I'm sure you remember what that's like."

"Those expensive clothes and shoes she was wearing? She's got steak tastes," he said, and even to his ears, he sounded whiny. "Obviously, she comes from money. I'm just a blue-collar boy from Fairfield."

From the look in her eyes, he could tell she thought he was full of shit. "Bullshit!" Nina scoffed. "You've got more money than God. You're going to fault her for having professional parents? You're not fooling me. Why don't you just come out and say it? It's the black-white thing."

Marc saw the anticipation in her face. She was practically begging him to prove her wrong. But he knew she was also a friend and could understand where he was coming from. Cautiously, he said, "Okay, yes. To a certain extent, it is the black and white thing."

Unvarnished hurt stared back at him. "Well, Marc-Antonio Guerrieri," she said. "In all the times we've hung out together, all the times you've shared meals with me and my husband and my children, I never would have suspected you were a racialist."

When in doubt, make light. "In American, we say 'racist,' " he laughed.

She looked away. "Whatever," she said, pissed.

God, he was almost forty; when would he ever be good with women and anticipate their needs? He took her hands and locked his fingers between hers. He looked down at them, at the short, manicured nails, the blue veins snaking under her pale skin. She was right; she had extended those hands to him in friendship. She'd cooked him delicious meals and applauded all his efforts. What an asshole he was to trivialize her feelings. "Nina," he began. "I can't assure you enough that I'm infinitely less of a racist than Steven Curreri, Pasquale Raucci, Keith Mondello, and whoever the hell else had a part in what went on on that Bensonhurst street corner on that horrible night when Yusuf Hawkins was shot. You're just gonna have to take my word for it."

"I wasn't implying you're homicidal."

"I was a teenager in the sixties. Twenty years ago, I was in the mud at Woodstock. Not for nothing, but I've slept with women of all shapes, sizes, races, creeds, and colors."

"So you've fucked around. Bully for you!"

Get to the point. "At this stage in the game, Nina, any relationship I get into has got to have great potential for success. I like Lisa. If it were worth it, I think I could like her very much. But fundamentally? I'm Italian, and she's black."

"But Lisa's not like that," Nina insisted.

"Maybe not, but society is," he countered.

The CD ended, and the office was silent. Muffled shouts of "No justice, no peace" intruded, as if to punctuate Marc's point. Then Nina glanced down at her watch. "I'd better go," she said, and Marc relaxed his grip on her hands. "Can't keep Les Grantham waiting."

He forced a sad laugh. "Les Grantham—Super Dean!"

he said, knowing full well she'd see the irony. Les Grantham was an asshole.

They got up, and Marc was truly afraid that he'd revealed too much. "Hey, are we cool?" he asked, this time he was begging her to prove him right.

In response, she gave him a hug. He smiled, burying his nose in her fresh-smelling hair. For a nanosecond, he envied Tim. "I didn't mean to call you a racialist," she said in the expanse of his chest.

"Racist."

"Whatever."

Nina kissed his cheek. "Give me a pen," she said.

He reached over and snatched a felt-tip from his desk. Nina took his right hand and scrawled something in blue on his palm. "To hell with society!" she mischievously exclaimed.

She breezed out of the office on an air of honeysuckle and perfume. Marc curiously looked down at his hand. In fluorescent navy blue ink he read LISA—555-0603. He ran a finger over the ink. What would he say if he called her? What would she say if he asked her out? Between college and his adult experiences, he had met his share of black people. But it was an unwritten rule that blacks and Italians didn't get along. Recent news reports reinforced this. "I must be out of my mind," he murmured.

Lisa rushed into the crowded bar, the favorite happy-hour hangout of Fidelity Data Processing employees on the Eisenhower Parkway. Yuppies sucked down liquid lunches, sitting in leather booths and on stools at high tables in the middle of blood-red velvet and pictures of dogs playing poker. She saw A.J. perched on one of those stools, with her flashy houndstooth suit, perpetually anchored to a Marlboro Light. At the stool next to her was Ione, tall, dark, statuesque, with braids down to the middle of her back.

She rushed up to them. "I'm sorry, I'm sorry, I'm sorry," she said breathlessly. "I had to mail the certified check for Jaye, check with the property manager on the house, and buy some books for school tonight."

A.J. took a healthy sip of her frozen margarita. "Yeah, right," she scoffed. "Your ass is always late!"

"That's not true!" Lisa protested, despite the fact that she was indeed perpetually late.

"I hate to say it, but Miss Wood is right," Ione sighed. Lisa loved her, because she was so Brixton; Lisa's mother was so posh London. "She can't help it. It's the West Indian in her. West Indian Time is ten minutes past C.P. Time."

Lisa hopped up on the third stool. "Traitors," she remarked.

"Just don't be late for that class tonight," A.J. said, signaling for a waitress. "I'll treat your late ass. What are you drinking?"

"Diet Coke," Lisa said.

A.J. looked at her like she had a third eye in the middle of her forehead. "I'm sorry, what?"

"I don't know what you two do over in I.S., but I have to go back to work," Lisa said.

Reluctantly, A.J. called the waitress over and ordered Lisa's Diet Coke. "What are you, twelve years old?" Ione asked.

A.J. dragged deeply on her cigarette. "You stay right there, Miss Straight Arrow. This is why Bryan's tapping your ass in court right now."

She had to admire A.J.'s flair for making everything a conspiracy. "Me not getting zootie-banged with you two has nothing to do with my fuckhead husband. I did my share of drinking when he left. I'm trying to get healthy. I even started running again."

A.J. and Ione stared at her . . . their weird, almost-divorced friend. "What?" she asked. "I used to run in college."

"It's official," A.J. declared. "You need some booty."

The waitress reappeared and set the Diet Coke in front of Lisa and chardonnay in front of Ione. "I didn't order this," Ione said, puzzled.

The waitress pointed to a white yuppie at the bar, gazing at Ione with hangdog, basset-hound blue eyes, like he appreciated her very existence. "He sent it over," she announced.

A.J. shot the yuppie an overtly disapproving glare. "Well, send it back," she commanded.

No man had looked at Lisa like that since before Bryan had fallen out of love with her. "I think it's cute," she said.

"You would," A.J. said. "Bourgie, rich Montclair girl."

Lisa's face stung as if she'd been slapped. But this was vintage A.J., best ignored. "All right, Miss Blacker-than-thou. Let Ione decide what to do with the drink."

"I'll take it," she laughed shyly, waving at the yuppie.

The waitress disappeared. "Just another white boy liking chili sauce," A.J. remarked.

"Hey, some people make it work," Lisa said. "Look at Tim and Nina."

A black man with a white woman. A.J.'s disapproval meter dipped into the red. "That self-hating brothah and his cave bitch," she spat. "A marriage made in heaven."

Ione sipped her chardonnay and smiled sweetly. "I like Nina, even though she's right Sloaney," she said. "Besides, everyone could use some love."

"Or at least some Vitamin F!" A.J. giggled, obviously enjoying her margarita buzz.

Lisa laughed bitterly. Nobody focused on the dark side of love, the physical and emotional abuse, the lawyers, the betrayal. "No, thank you," she said quietly.

A.J. was clearly in her cups by now. "Aw, come on," she slurred. "I know Bryan's a full-on dickhead, but he's not the be-all-end-all to manhood."

Lisa's mind flashed back to Marc, from Nina's party. He was sweet and articulate, handsome and self-deprecating. Even though there was no way that they'd ever be together, he left her with the realization that not all men sucked. "I know," she said, "but I've sworn off them completely."

"Not every man on the planet is a greedy, degenerate rapist like the man you married," A.J. reminded her, uncharacteristically tender for one second. "Suppose all that was standing between the death of the species was you giving the last man on earth some booty?"

She associated that with Bryan's hands around her throat, squeezing the air from her chest, forcing himself into her. "Then the species is going to die," she said.

Ione sucked her teeth. "She's just saying that. You watch—next year, she's going to be married and preggers."

Lisa laughed in her face. "Not bloody likely," she said, affecting Ione's accent.

Just then, the yuppie in the Brooks Brothers suit sidled up. He looked harmless enough. "Ladies," he said, all goofy and sheepish. He focused on Ione. "Hi. I'm Matt."

Ione slapped on a million-watt smile, tossing her braids like a white girl. "I'm Ione," she giggled, then turned to her friends. "This is A.J. and Lisa."

"Hi," Lisa said.

"Welcome, Matt," A.J. laughed.

Matt gave them a half-assed wave and a look like he'd heard the pun more than once, then turned his naughty attentions again to Ione. "You're English," he said.

A.J. leaned in toward Lisa, and she got a whiff of A.J.'s smoky breath and a glimpse of the red capillaries in her hooded eyes. "Sharp as a fucking tack, this one," she whispered.

"Shh!" Lisa cautioned, laughing.

Matt leaned in so close to Ione like he wanted to fuck
er right there on the table. "Let me guess," he said
oftly. "You're from London."

Boy was talking those drawers off. Ione's eyes lit up.
Brixton!" she squealed.

Matt laughed seductively. "David Bowie's from Brixton,"
e said.

A.J. leaned in again. "Okay, I'm putting a stop to
his." She cleared her throat. "So, Matt, you got a thing
or big black dykes?"

Poor Matt turned three shades of pale. "Pardon?"
huddered from his lips.

Obviously, A.J.'s devilish sense of humor escaped
oor, sweet Ione. Confused, she looked to Lisa. "What?"

Lisa had to turn away and snicker. "A.J., stop it," she
aid.

The penny dropped for Ione. "We're not . . ." there
vas a sharp thump under the table, and her face con-
orted in pain. "Ouch!" she cried, eyes wide.

"A.J.!" Lisa cautioned, swallowing a laugh.

Matt went from pale to brilliant red in three seconds
lat. "Umm . . . I guess I'd better go," he murmured.

"Yeah," A.J. agreed, glaring triumphantly. "I guess you'd
etter."

Matt walked briskly away. "Thanks for the drink!"
one called pathetically after him.

A.J. looked satisfied. Another mixed coupling foiled.
Once Matt was safely at the other end of the bar with
is suit-and-tie friends, A.J. burst out laughing. "Oh,
ord, forgive me!"

Ione pushed her, and A.J. nearly fell off her chair.
What'd you do that for?!" she whined. "He was nice!"

Lisa couldn't help but laugh. Sure, A.J.'s antics were
orderline prejudiced, but the shit was funny! "A.J.,
ou're evil," she said. "Not all white boys are after some
ss."

A.J. dragged deep on her cigarette. "Yeah, right, don't

believe the hype," she declared. "White boys are after the same shit they were after 200 years ago. Only difference is now, they have to bring over a drink and ask nice first."

Again, Lisa thought about Marc. He wasn't asking for anything from her but conversation . . . human companionship. "That's not true," Lisa said.

"They don't all marry us like your grandfather married your grandmother, Lisa," A.J. said. "He's the exception, not the rule."

"Who says I want to get married?" Ione protested. "I just wanted to talk to him."

Lisa stared at A.J. and wondered just when she'd gone from distrustful of white folks to downright bigoted. "Can we just have our drinks and give the revolution a rest for now, A.J.?" she asked.

But A.J. was distracted, looking over their heads toward the bar. Both Lisa and Ione followed her gaze, their eyes coming to rest on the TV over the bar. The Reverend Al Sharpton, permed and rotund, had a consoling arm around a black man who looked like he was struggling like only a man could struggle to keep away the tears. "Turn it up!" A.J. called.

The same waitress who'd served them their drinks cranked up the volume. The chyron—*Moses Stewart*—appeared magically in the lower third of the screen. From all the press, Lisa knew he was Yusuf Hawkins's father. A profound sadness blanketed his strong features. He was mid-sentence, when suddenly, his voice caught and Sharpton squeezed his shoulder comfortingly, like he empathized.

The unseen director kicked it back to the news crew in the studio, who began their sanitized prattle. But Moses Stewart's deep grief was all the story they needed. A deathly pall fell across the table. Lisa sighed. This was getting worse by the minute. "Damn," she said softly. She suddenly wanted that drink.

A.J. turned to Ione, her eyes flashing. "You still want to be some cave boy's sexual field trip?" she spat.

Ione averted her eyes, looking guilty and ashamed. And Lisa, because she understood the guilt all too well, hated A.J. for making Ione feel that way.

At Fidelity Data Processing, Inc., or FDP, Lisa rushed through granite-colored cubicles until she arrived at her own. Her home for eight hours, replete with grey modular furniture, a desk, file drawers, and an overhead compartment. No photos of family, nothing personal. As a graphic artist, her weapon of choice was her Macintosh computer with a 20-inch monitor. The harsh fluorescent lights above her made everything look washed-out, including her. Lisa plopped down in the blue swivel chair, peeled off her sneakers and socks, and was about to switch on her computer when Rick Farrelly, her boss, materialized. He was salt-and-pepper, baby-boomer office *GQ* chic, with a friendly demeanor and twinkling grey eyes. "Long lunch?" he teased.

Cold busted! "Umm . . . I was abducted by aliens?" she laughed.

He leaned in and sniffed her suit. "Yeah, aliens who smoke," he said.

Change the subject . . . "Enough about me—how many days 'til the year-end report deadline?"

He covered his heart with his hands in mock sincerity. "You dare to speak the words 'year-end report' without genuflecting?" he gasped.

Lisa played along, doing a quick bow. "What was I thinking?"

Rick applauded. "Just the right touch of sycophantic realism—120 days and counting. It has to be perfection, as always."

"Ask my shithead husband," Lisa said. " 'Perfection' is my *first* name."

"Oh, yeah, sounds much better than 'Haley,' your other first name," he mocked.

Genie appeared with characteristic stealth, and Lisa and Rick started. People joked that someone should put a bell on her. Before anyone would realize it, the dowdy secretary, looking much older than her mid-thirties, would be on top of you, scaring the shit out of you. She handed Lisa a pink piece of paper. No hello, no small talk. "Phone message for you," she stated tersely. "I guess you have better things to do than to answer your phone."

"Thank you, Genie," Lisa said, attempting to draw her out with a sweet smile.

She should've known better. Genie turned and walked silently away.

Lisa watched her go. "Folks are so nice 'round here."

Rick dismissed her with a wave of the hand. "Don't mind her."

Lisa read the message and smiled. Finally, a break! Despite her tenuous relationship with Him as of late, God was definitely good.

"What?" Rick asked impatiently.

"My realtor, the one you recommended," she laughed. "Someone bid on my house!"

Rick looked genuinely happy for her. "That's great," he said. "First day of school, and now someone wants to buy your house. You're on your way, kiddo."

She thought for a moment, and for once, she believed that to be true.

As the sun painted the blue sky in pinkish orange, Lisa rushed like mad through the huge throng of protesters in the SCNJ Montclair quadrangle in front of Pidgeon Hall, the brown brick building which housed the School of Humanities. The chanting was near deafening and added exponentially to her level of frustration. She was late, and she was lost. A man wearing a

Kente cloth hat and matching shirt approached her. *Salvation.*

Before she could realize what was happening, he pinned a "No Justice, No Peace" button on the lapel of her jacket. "Thanks for joining the cause, my sistah!" he shouted over the din swirling around them.

She grabbed his sleeve and looked down at her schedule. "Is this the Humanities building?!" she yelled.

"Yeah!" he yelled back, and the crowd swallowed him up.

"Fuck," she spat.

Hopelessly, Lisa entered the maze-like building, consulting the schedule, looking around, and then looking at her watch. She was almost twenty minutes late for her six o'clock class. "Where the hell am I?" she cried.

She heard footsteps and grabbed the harried young earthy-crunchy redhead as she passed by. "Hey, where can I find the Fiction Writing class?" she asked.

"Follow me," the redhead said. "I'm going there myself."

"Thanks," she sighed with relief.

They wended their way through the labyrinthine halls, Lisa practically giving chase as the redhead's long-legged stride ate up the distance at a good clip. *Damn, can I have half of what this bitch is on?* The redhead waved a stack of pink papers. "He's got phone messages from all these people," she complained. "They just won't leave the poor guy alone."

"Who?" Lisa asked.

"Your fiction prof," she answered, irritated. "I'm Merilee, his GA. You really should try to be on time for his class, though. He hates it when you come late."

Lisa held up three fingers. "Next time, I swear."

Lisa and Merilee finally arrived at the orange door to the white, cinder-block classroom. Lisa peered in at the eleven other students—five male, six female—who sat in desks arranged in a semicircle. Then her gaze shifted to the teacher's desk at the mouth of the semicircle, and her heart lurched at her rib cage. Seated Indian fashion and in denim splendor on the top of the desk was none other than Marc, the expert foot masseur from the party. *Jersey is way too small!*

"This class will challenge you," he lectured, and all eyes were front and center on him, the men with admiration and most of the women with lust. "You will work hard. But if you're diligent, you'll experience writing that can free your soul."

Suddenly, the blue gaze behind trendy specs shifted, and Marc saw her. He graced her with a confused, lopsided smile, and she remembered again how fine he was that night at the party. "You're here to see me?" he asked.

She realized she was staring. "Umm . . ." she looked down at her schedule ". . . you're the professor? You're MarcAntonio Guerrieri?"

"I am," he said simply.

Get your shit together, girl! Lisa came forward, waving her schedule. He took the schedule and examined it. Meanwhile, she checked him out. The denim shirt made his eyes seem even bluer. The glasses made him look more intelligent. She realized he had a mole on his smooth-shaven cheek. She gazed at his impressive arms, with the muscles moving under the denim as he moved. She became acutely aware of the heat surging through her body. Then she realized something. For the first time in over a year, she was actually horny . . . for this white boy sitting in front of her no less!

She had to say something . . . anything. "Umm . . . my friend A.J. Wood and I picked up this class last week in the gym," she explained, tasting the salty sweat forming above her top lip. "I swear I didn't know you'd . . ."

Marc, however, remained focused on the schedule. " 'Haley Melissa Martin.' " He looked up. "That's you?"

"Yeah," she said. "Long story."

Marc gestured to A.J. "Well, your friend's here. Why don't you have a seat next to her."

A.J. looked at Lisa while holding up a copy of the *New York Times*, partially to shield her face in mock shame. Her mouth, though, bore a teasing smile that read, *Oh, you're in trouble!* The students stared as Lisa made the short walk of shame and sat at the empty desk next to A.J. Merilee and Marc began talking in hushed tones, and she gave up his messages.

"Girl, you're a shitty example," A.J. whispered. "Talking me into taking this class, and you're late?"

"First Guerrieri, now you?" she whispered back.

"This is slammin' . . . having him for our prof," A.J. whispered. "I hear his shit is way correct." She tapped the newspaper with a red acrylic fingernail. "*Times* review says his book is hot shit."

Lisa's eyes searched the headlines. "What's the latest on Yusuf?"

"They're still looking for that fuckhead who shot him, and those boys in custody won't say a word. Ain't that like white boys?"

A.J., resident activist. No nuances of doubt there. In the world according to A.J., all white boys were inherently violent. This was just another way that such violence manifested itself.

Merilee left in a haze of gingham, Birkenstocks, and patchouli, shutting the door behind her. Marc tossed a stack of paper on the first desk in the semicircle. The nearest blond coed in a sweater tighter on her than it probably was on the sheep eyed him suggestively. He smiled politely. "I'm sorry, what's your name again?" he asked.

"Carlette," she breathed, as if one second away from an asthma attack.

"Okay," he said. "Carlette is passing around the syllabus for this class. In it is my address here on the fourth floor, my phone number, and my office hours, which you will need to grovel to me if you don't have your assignments done. It's simple—everyone leaves this class having written a hundred pages. The first twenty are due next week."

Groans of disapproval filled the room. "Oh great," A.J. murmured. "Billy Bad-Ass."

He was right. The class was hard and challenging, but for Lisa, the time passed like she'd blinked. They wrote sample paragraphs, they worked in dyads, they listened to Marc's words of wisdom. Just like that, it was three hours later, and students were filing out of the classroom, talking amongst themselves.

"Dag!" Lisa cried. "I'm feeling every one of those seven years I've been out of Fordham."

A.J. packed her papers into her briefcase. "It was decent."

"Go on, lord your master's over me."

"Girl, I'm too tired to lord. When I get home to Brooklyn, I'm gonna make myself a G&T, throw on some Luther, and hop into the shower."

"A G&T'd hit the spot right now. Listen to us. FDP's turning us into a bunch of alcoholics."

"Ain't that the truth!"

Lisa realized that she didn't want to go home. "Want some company?" she asked.

A.J. snapped her briefcase shut. "No offense, girl, but this is the first week I'm not straightening out some shit at an FDP region. I'm enjoying this alone."

From behind her, Lisa heard Marc ask, "Lisa, can I see you for a second?"

A.J. leaned in. "Plus you're in trouble with the teacher," she whispered, teasing. "Peace."

She breezed out, leaving Lisa and Marc alone, awkwardness and sexual tension swirling around them. She laughed nervously. "How's this for coincidence?"

What a difference a context made. Where he was warm and engaging the night of the party, tonight he was cold and businesslike. "Let's talk in my office," he stated.

Lisa stewed in the elevator ride up to the fourth floor. He said nothing to her, nor she to him. She guessed he wasn't much for small talk. The elevator lurched to a stop, and they stepped out into more labyrinthine halls, a carbon copy of downstairs, only higher up. A few feet later, Marc ushered her into his office, lit only by an architect's lamp on the desk. She checked out the decor. Crowded literary chic, she determined.

Merilee cornered Marc in the doorway. She handed him more pink slips of paper. "Doc, messages from your publicist," she announced, harried. "She says *Good Morning America, Today, CBS This Morning,* and MTV want you. You've got to call her, like, yesterday."

"Thanks, Merilee," he said gratefully. "I'd die without you."

Merilee smiled coquettishly, the controlled efficiency gone. *The effect this man has on chicks!* "You better believe it," she giggled, like a schoolgirl. "Umm . . . I'm going home now."

"See you tomorrow."

Marc shut the door, then put a CD in the stereo box. Lenny Kravitz's "Sitting On Top of the World" instantly played at subtle volume. *Boy's got taste.* "You got the new Lenny Kravitz CD," Lisa said.

He nodded. "His sound takes me back," he said.

"I thought it wasn't coming out 'til next week, though."

"My agent scored me an advance copy."

Boy's got taste . . . and juice. She stared out the window at the lights in the distant quarry used for student parking. "Great view."

He waved at the guest chair. "Sit?"

Whatever was going to hit her, she was going to be ready. "I'll stand, thanks."

He seemed to melt some, giving her a fleeting, appreciative once-over. "You look great," he said, and she detected a slight, husky catch in his voice.

She smiled, looking away. *God, am I shy in front of him?* "You, too."

"How've you been?"

"Fine. My feet are another story. You?"

He exhaled through pursed lips, running his hands over his dark head. "Crazy," he said. "Promoting the book."

"The *Times* loves you."

He melted a bit more. "I enjoyed the party. Us. Together."

She remembered that he made her laugh, made her feel safe and protected. She missed that from a man. "Me, too," she said.

The businesslike demeanor popped up immediately. "But you're in my class now," he reminded her.

She sighed. *Here we go again.* "Look, I didn't know," she explained. "I told the guy at late registration I wanted Fiction Writing. He told me they'd added another section. He didn't tell me who the prof was, and I didn't ask."

"I'm not implying that you knew."

This was turning ugly. "I didn't say you were."

"Look," he said. "We're both thrown by this thing."

"Hello!" she nervously laughed.

"I mean, I don't usually massage prospective students' feet."

"I think we both agree anything that happened that night is best left there. In the past."

"You're right. We were both romantically vulnerable that night, but our heads are on straight now." He hesitated. "Right?"

She was sad, for some reason. "Right," she agreed.

Marc opened the office door. "Now that we're clear, I've got a million phone calls to return," he said.

Negotiated flag on the sexual tension play. "See you in class, then," she said.

"Try coming on time from now on," he suggested.

The sarcasm wasn't lost on her. She did a mock salute. "Yes sir, Dr. Guerrieri!" she laughed.

His smile seemed to light up the entire room. "Cute. See you next Tuesday."

Lisa stepped into the long corridor, lit with fluorescent lights, and flanked on either side by offices. Marc closed the door behind her. She glanced over her shoulder at him through the glass in the door. He was hunched over the telephone on his desk, vigorously punching at the numbers. Well, that was that.

One of the other doors opened, and Nina, briefcase in hand, entered into the hallway. Lisa immediately brightened. "Nina!" she called.

Nina looked up from locking her door with a fistful of keys. "Oi!" she laughed.

Lisa caught up to her, and Nina hugged her. After the day she'd had, she needed that hug desperately. "What are you doing here?" Nina asked.

Lisa beamed. "I had my first class," she said, her tone cryptic. "You wouldn't guess who my professor is."

"Lisa, I've just rolled around with the Promotion and Tenure committee. I haven't got the strength."

"Your friend Marc from the party," she announced, like a cat that just ate the canary with a healthy dose of Tabasco.

Nina's grey eyes lit up. "Oh, you suddenly got you some energy now," Lisa laughed.

"Oh, my love, do tell all," Nina eagerly implored.

Lisa looked point-blank into Nina's anticipation-filled face. She was going to enjoy this. "No," she said simply.

Nina was taken aback. "No?!"

"No," Lisa repeated. "You're too nosy."

She then headed for the doors to the stairwell. She smiled as she heard the manic click-clacking of Nina's heels behind her. "You might as well tell me now," Nina stated. "I'm going to find out anyway."

Lisa laughed. Nina was right. Eventually Lisa would tell her everything. She always did. For now, though, she was going to have as much fun as she could letting Nina stew in her own matchmaking juices.

3

What the fuck is wrong with you?
That question led her on a mission to discover why she thought about Marc Guerrieri every second since she met him at the party. God knows she wasn't looking for anything. Bryan's soul-destroying departure had scorched her; only recently had she found the courage to leave a therapist's couch to test the life strategies she'd found there. Plus, even though she'd been surrounded by white boys in her sheltered suburban existence, she'd never had the inclination to go that route. She'd found them corny . . . bland . . . too curious about what she had under her skirt. Light-bright-damned-near-white Bryan was the closest she'd come to crossing the color line.

So what the fuck was her problem? What was the deal with the erotic dreams about Guerrieri? The curiosity about him as a person? Her wondering if he was losing similar night rest thinking about her?

Her morbid curiosity led her to the media room at SCNJ's newly refurbished Lawrence K. Hughes Library, which was part of Chancellor Swift's Faustian bargain with the state to make SCNJ a university. She sat at one of the computer terminals, typed MARCANTONIO GUERRIERI into *The New York Times* Index program, and watched the listings scroll up the grey scale screen.

Moments later, Lisa pulled up a copy of *The New York Times* from 1978 and read in a whisper the review of *Benny Blues,* next to the review of Bruce Springsteen's *Darkness on the Edge of Town* album. Her eyes scanned the title of the article. "Two Fresh New Jersey Voices," she whispered. "MarcAntonio Guerrieri, The Voice of Italian America."

She searched on, coming to another section of *The New York Times* from 1978. "Author Weds NYU Literature Scholar," the title read. Lisa suppressed a stab of envy as she studied the accompanying photograph. The NYU scholar was tall and willowy, with long, blond hair and cat-like green eyes, her simple ivory dress enhancing her tanned skin. Marc, quite the paradox, wore an elegant black tuxedo which clashed with his bushy, hippie beard. They both looked deliriously happy. She read on about the nuptials, that the scholar was named Michele Aulisio from Los Angeles, California. Lisa smirked. "So, that's the kind of women you like, Guerrieri, Malibu Barbie dolls," she mused.

Undaunted, she flipped through the database . . . reviews of *When Irish Eyes Are Crying* . . . accolades . . . until she came to a copy of *The New York Times* from 1988, the headlines of the New York section reading "Writer Stabbed at Rikers." Lisa read on, riveted, an expression of horror on her face. She examined the picture of Marc being lifted on a gurney into a helicopter. "Stabbed by an inmate who was shot while eluding guards," she whispered, then remembered back to the party . . . his comment about his first months of divorced life. " 'Pretty sick,' huh? Understatement of the year."

In a later paper, the dissolution of the Guerrieri-

Aulisio union read like a whimper on page 16. "Poor guy," she murmured.

So what kind of literature could come from such pain? she asked herself. A search of the stacks revealed that all copies of Marc's books were checked out. So she endured beastly parking lot traffic and throngs of bored teens at Willowbrook Mall to purchase *Benny Blues, When Irish Eyes Are Crying,* and *Goombah* from Waldenbooks. She spent the better part of the week in her cluttered, neat but lived-in studio apartment. She curled up with Wisteria, her calico cat, beside her on her futon, listened to her new Quincy Jones CD, and read as Marc used words to paint pictures in her mind. He took her to the Jersey shore, to occupied Northern Ireland, to Little Italy. He showed her all the manifestations and the ambivalence of the human condition. Mostly, he drew characters to which she could relate, even though their experiences were radically different from hers. The man truly had a gift.

After reading his work, she knew anything she could come up with as a first draft for his class would pale by comparison. Next to him, she was just a tourist, someone who figured that her mother must have imparted some writing talent through her placenta to her. How could she even compete? She anguished, typed, discarded, typed some more, discarded some more. Nothing seemed to be right. Either the characters were wooden, or anything resembling a plot was hackneyed, contrived. *God, you're such a failure, Melissa!*

She couldn't feel any worse, so she decided to try her first run. At Brookdale Park after work. She, in grey sweats and Reeboks and with a Walkman on her head, jogged tentatively around the track like a beginner. More seasoned joggers zipped by her as if she were standing still. And the shit hurt! She hadn't done any kind of focused, rigorous exercise since college. She cranked Al B. Sure's remix of "Off On Your Own, (Girl)," as if the slamming beat would take her mind off of the burning in her lungs as she gulped in air like she was dying. She had to stop or she'd collapse. She staggered over to the track's grassy center, bent over, and sucked more air into her chest.

Suddenly, she felt hard arms snake around her waist from behind, as if someone was interested in very public doggy-style. She could hardly muster a frightened gasp and swat her headphones from her ears. "Are you okay?" the concerned man behind her asked.

She looked up. It took a while for her eyes to focus in the fading sunlight, but sure enough, she recognized the deep blue eyes in the glistening, tanned face. Adrenaline helped her straighten up. "Guerrieri!" she gasped.

"Lisa Martin," he said, a silly frat-boy grin on his face. "It is Lisa Martin, right? Not Lisa Livingston, or Haley Martin, or . . ."

She glared at him. This was the same mess she used to hear from the kids at elementary school. But he was a grown man who should've known better. "So, Dr. Guerrieri's a funnyman," she panted.

Pointedly, she brushed past him and back onto the track. Unfortunately, he followed. "I said we should keep things teacher-student," he called after her, "but the 'Dr. Guerrieri' is a bit extreme, don't you think? You're the only student of mine who calls me that."

She thought about Carlette and all the other horny girl sycophants from the class. "That's 'cause I'm one of the few who don't want to fuck you," she murmured, then wondered if that was really true.

He was right next to her. "What?"

She blushed under the sweat. "Nothing," she said.

"Would it kill you to call me 'Marc'?"

She was hot, sweaty, and sore all over. Wit seemingly had taken a vacation. "Everything kills you these days," she remarked. "Coffee . . . too much sun . . . even sex."

"But what a way to go!" he laughed.

She stared at him with unvarnished disgust. "Excuse me."

She walked faster away from him. He caught up to her. "Hey, am I missing something?" he gently asked. "Are you mad at me?"

She realized she was being a bitch and softened somewhat. "I don't like being made fun of," she said.

"I'm sorry," he said. "It wasn't my intention."

Lisa looked him up and down. She knew he was genuine. "All right. Apology accepted."

With that, she ran faster away from him, but again Marc caught up to her. "You shouldn't wear sweats when you run."

She started, thrown off her rhythm. *Persistent white boy.* "Can a sistah get some peace and solitude?!" she cried, her breathing ragged.

"You should invest in a good spandex suit," he advised, his breath coming clean and even. "Spandex insulates the body better but at the same time, keeps you cooler than sweats."

Lisa hated admitting he was right, but she was broiling, even though the night was a mild one for early September. Her crotch tingled from an oversaturation of moisture . . . a yeast infection waiting to happen. And having him nearby didn't help matters any. She imagined that he, studly maven of the literary world, must've left a trail of damp crotches in his wake. "Thanks for the tip," she said.

He smiled brilliantly. "You're quite welcome."

Very respectfully, he went away, and she watched, horribly intrigued, staring at how his shimmering black spandex molded to every taut muscle and sinew of his lower body like a second skin, at muscles that were prominent even in his baggy white T-shirt. Her nipples rose to attention inside her running bra, crotch tingling stepped up. "I must be out of my mind!" she mumbled.

An hour later, Lisa abandoned her workout. Inspiration

for her assignment still eluded her, and her delusions of being Flo Jo would have to wait. She tried an effortless, gazelle-like spring across the grassy knoll to the asphalt where her car was parked under bright park lights. Somehow, it came out like a clumsy, graceless series of quick steps.

With a sigh, Lisa approached her shiny blue VW Jetta and pressed the remote on her key chain to deactivate the alarm. After she heard the reassuring chirp, she got in, put the key in the ignition, and turned it. Instead of the roar of the engine, though, all she heard was a feeble click. Lisa's heart thumped in her chest. "Oh, no fucking way!" she shouted.

Think, girl, think! She took a flashlight and the Jetta car manual from the glove compartment, got out of the car, and started pacing in front of it, thinking what could affect her beautiful car. Then she looked down. "God!" she whimpered incredulously. "I left the lights on!"

Lisa grabbed her jumper cables out of the trunk and looked around at the nearly empty park. Right then, she was every stereotype she hated about women . . . vulnerable, helpless, scared. Just as she was going to give in to the despair she'd been fighting for the past year and a half, she turned. As if on cue, Marc appeared, scrutinizing her with those all-knowing blue eyes behind his wire-rimmed specs. The blood drained from her face. *Of all the people to look like an ass in front of . . .*

"You okay?" he asked.

She wanted to tie the perfect slipknot with her cables and put her neck inside it. "Can you jump me, please?" she asked. "I left my lights on by accident."

The frat-boy grin returned, like he was enjoying a private joke. Which made her even more pissed. "Look," she said, testier than she had intended, "can you help me, or should I find someone else?"

Letting her mouth write checks her situation couldn't cash. The park was damned near empty.

"Look, just chill," Marc said. "My Jeep's just back there a ways. Give me a minute. I'll be right back."

"And I'll be here . . . chilling," she said sarcastically.

Marc disappeared into the shadows, and Lisa watched him . . . dissecting him, from his dark, curly head to his impressive, broad shoulders. She stared at his taut ass, the cheeks clenching under the spandex, his long legs with delicious calves. *This is what lack of companionship can reduce a woman to.*

About a minute later, Marc zoomed around before her in his black Jeep Wrangler and pulled up in front of the Jetta. Marc got out, leaving the motor running, and opened the hood. Looking determined, he approached Lisa, taking her jumper cables and flashlight. "Pop your hood!" he yelled over the noise.

Obediently, she got into the car and pulled the lever by her left leg. She then got out and watched as he lifted the hood and searched for her battery with a flashlight. "There it is," she said, pointing to the black box nestled behind all the other funny-shaped automotive things.

He leaned in closer. "Yes, but there are no positive or negative signs," he said. "Just a red wire and a black wire."

Hurriedly, Lisa flipped through the manual in her hand. Unable to hide the desperation in her voice, she cried, "It's not here. Does it really matter, Marc?"

"Doing this wrong could totally fry your electrical system—and me in the process."

Suddenly, Bryan's holier-than-thou, know-it-all voice came to her from her subconscious. "My soon-to-be-ex-husband says black is usually positive." She laughed. "No pun intended."

Chuckling, Marc went to his car and hooked his end of the cables to his battery terminals, then returned to do the same with the Jetta. "Well, if it doesn't work, you can send him the bill," he said.

Just imagining the look on Bryan's face after open-

ing a bill for a total electrical system overhaul made Lisa
smile. "Nothing would give me greater pleasure," she
laughed.

"Try it now," he instructed.

Lisa got into the car, put the key in the ignition, and
turned it. *Fuck!* "Nothing!" she called out the open window.

Marc leaned his head in. "Again," he said, his fresh
breath warm on her cheeks.

Nervously, she looked away and turned the key again.
The engine roared to life. Jubilantly, she leapt from the
car and listened to the engine purr. She turned to Marc,
who was rolling the jumper cables in a neat cylinder
over and under his arm. She was ashamed of how unpleasant she'd been. "Marc," she sighed, her smile con-
ciliatory. "Thanks. I owe you one."

He laughed, shaking his head as if to say, *women.* "So,
I'm 'Marc' again, huh?" he said. "That's progress."

"Look, I admit I don't know what to do here," she
said. "This is new for me."

"Me, too. But it's not like we went to bed, Lisa. We
talked, I massaged your feet, and we kissed each other
good night."

She shrugged. "Still, it's weird. The dynamic's changed.
I don't know what the etiquette is for this kind of thing,
and I'm sure Emily Post didn't write a book about it."

"Does that mean we can't speak to each other? Yes, I
dug how you wore that black dress at the party." He
smiled appreciatively, seeming to enjoy his little flash-
back. "But I also like how your mind works. You asked
solid, thought-provoking questions in class on Tuesday."

She beamed. "Thank you."

"It's true. Why thank me?"

Previously, men commented on her long brown hair,
her brown eyes, and her perfect C cups. *The softest titties
in the world,* Michael, her high school boyfriend, would

moan as he buried his head. "It's been a long time since anyone's valued my mind," she laughed.

"As long as you value it, screw the world," he said simply.

There was a tense silence between them. "Well," she said. "Better be getting home."

Marc handed her the jumper cables. "These are yours," he said. "You've got to leave the engine running so the alternator can recharge itself."

She felt like a moron. "Is there some special guy school where you men learn these things?" she mumbled.

Marc laughed. "Where do you live?"

"The Crescent, by the library. Why?"

Deep in thought, as if calculating the mileage, Marc stroked his chin. "That's too close. You've got to drive it longer."

The sweat in her clothes had begun to chill her, and she was at DEFCON Four in the humiliation department. "Well, I've got to go home sometime," she stated testily. "What do you suggest?"

"Let's go to The Primrose for coffee," he said.

Was that allowed? What were the rules here? "Coffee?" she questioned. "Us?"

"Yeah. Counting lights, it's about twenty minutes away. That'll do it."

"Didn't we just agree that fraternizing wasn't the swiftest thing to do?"

He threw his head back and laughed, and her face flamed. "Lisa, we're going for coffee, not a quickie at a Motel 6!" he hooted.

If she had a knife, she would've delighted in slitting him across his vibrating Adam's apple. "And you know what?" she snapped. "We're not even going for coffee."

Lisa brushed past him and to her car. He followed, grabbing her arm and turning her around. "Hey, hey, hey!" he laughed.

"What?!"

"Okay. Relax," he said in that tone of voice Lisa imagined they used with hysterical people just before slapping them. "I thought we could talk about what you want to accomplish in the class over a friendly cup of coffee. I don't think that constitutes the dreaded 'fraternizing,' do you?"

What could it hurt? She'd be in a crowded diner. The very second he became an asshole, she could get in her car and drive away. She was in control of the situation. That was what mattered. "I'll follow you there," she said, getting into her car.

The Primrose Diner, the SCNJ hangout, was hopping. Loud chatter nearly drowned out the tinny music coming from invisible speakers. There were mini jukeboxes at every table, including the one where a hostess sat Lisa and Marc. A busboy gave them glasses of water and left. Lisa pinched her damp clothing away from her body and dabbed at her face with a napkin. Yes, she had anticipated a crowd, but around so many people, she began to question her deodorant's effectiveness.

Marc studied her from behind his menu. He leaned in. "What's wrong?"

"I wish I could've had a shower."

"You're fine. I get a whiff of *Chloe* every time you move."

She stared incredulously at him. "How'd you know?"

He seemed wistful. "My ex-wife swore by it."

"Michele Aulisio," she said gently.

His eyes steeled, and she felt like a stalker, intruding into his personal life. "I see you've done your homework," he commented from behind the menu.

There was another awkward silence, and she searched her brain for something to say. "I'm almost finished with *Goombah,*" she said tentatively. "Not to blow smoke up your ass, but you're good."

He smiled. "Much better than smoke up the ass. Thanks."

"Everybody loves MarcAntonio Guerrieri."

Then the best-selling author, sexual fantasy of every Jersey white girl, did something she didn't expect: he blushed. "Yeah," he laughed awkwardly. "Today."

Lisa sipped her water, though she wasn't really thirsty, even after the run, if that was what one would dare to call it. The alarm signaling the start of meaningless conversation dinged in her head. "What's 'Guerrieri' mean?" she asked.

"It's the plural of 'guerriero.' Italian for 'warrior.' "

"Are you anything like that—warlike?"

"Me?!" he laughed. "Hardly. Are you anything like a martin? How's your singing voice?"

"Sorry," she said. "Guess that wasn't one of my solid, thought-provoking questions."

"Okay," he said. "Let's both stipulate that that conversation was the worst attempt at cultivating a friendship!"

They both laughed, and the tension abated slightly.

"Nina never told me what you did for a living," he said.

"I'm a graphic artist in the advertising department at Fidelity Data Processing."

"FDP, the paycheck people?"

"Affectionately called 'Fuckups Doing Payroll.' "

Marc laughed heartily, his Adam's apple vibrating. Tentatively, she followed suit. "It's okay working there, though," she said. "Hey, I have an art degree from Fordham. I'm just happy to have a job. And FDP's got decent tuition remission. That's why I'm here."

"You're on the rolls as 'Haley Melissa Martin.' How does that translate into 'Lisa'?"

Barbara mentally intruded on the moment. She would throw an embolism if she knew that Lisa was with this white man, even conflicted about her feelings for him. "My mom's maiden name is 'Haley,' " she said. Then she thought of her dad, and immediately, she brightened. "My dad wanted to name me 'Melisma.' "

He seemed intrigued. "Like from the Gregorian chant."

Well, what do you know? He was smart. Very few people kept that information in their mental Rolodex. "Yeah. But Mom said no way, so they settled on 'Melissa.' Daddy called me 'Lisa.' He said he didn't want his kid teased about some damned comet."

"That's 'Halley.' "

She rolled her eyes. "What five-year-old cares about semantics? And 'Melissa Martin' sounded like one of those perky, popular girls you love to hate."

"You didn't take Bryan's last name."

"Lisa Livingston?! Way too perky!"

Like a flash flood, the mood shifted at the table from light to somber. Gloria Estefan's "Don't Wanna Lose You Now" played on the tinny jukebox. Marc closed his menu. He looked sad. "Well, since you did your homework, you obviously saw that Michele didn't take my last name, either," he declared. "Said she was her own woman."

"When a woman gets married, she gives up so much of herself to her man. She should at least be able to keep her own name."

"Men give of themselves, too, Lisa."

"Men have the option of giving, Marc. For us, it's expected. We're expected to take his name, to define ourselves by his accomplishments."

"It's true. That happens sometimes. But I can't measure all women by my experiences with Michele. You shouldn't use yours with Bryan to do the same thing. It's not fair."

"You judge using what you know, Marc."

"Your marriage failed. That doesn't mean the whole institution sucks. Look at Nina and Tim."

Lisa scoffed. "Oh, the perfect couple. Who could measure up?"

"Joke all you want," he laughed. "I'm going to have that one day. You can, too."

A waitress with a careworn face, dressed in a pink uniform, appeared. She was straight out of central casting, right down to popping her chewing gum. "You two lovebirds ready to order?" she asked, her voice raspy.

Lisa saw unconcealed disdain in her steely grey eyes. This nigger and the white boy, not staying with their own kind. Unacceptable.

Marc looked over at Lisa. "Two coffees?" he asked.

Lisa's aversion to coffee began when she smelled that chocolate hazelnut on Bryan's breath as he violated her in her living room. "One coffee," she said. "For you."

"One coffee it is, then," Marc said to the waitress.

He smiled at her. Lisa's mouth trembled into a smile.

Instead of going straight home, Lisa took the Valley Road exit while pressing the preprogrammed button on her radio. She flipped to 98.7 KISS in time to hear her jam, Queen Latifah's "Ladies First," with Monie Love. She sang loudly, happily. *Thank God for music.* Particularly pro-sistah rap music.

She drove to North Mountain Avenue, stopping at the three-story house with the breathtaking view of Anderson Park. She chuckled. What a sense of humor Nina and Tim had, the interracial couple buying a black-and-white house. She parked and locked the car, then sprinted up the concrete steps to the black front door and rang the bell. "Is that you, Auntie Lisa?" called a small voice behind the wood.

Lisa smiled. "Yes, it's me, sweetie! You can finally reach the peephole."

The door opened, and Courtney Simon, all of six,

flew into Lisa's arms. Lisa picked her up and kissed her smooth cheek. May God forgive her for coveting some-one else's child, but every time Lisa looked at Courtney, she wondered if her baby would've been as beautiful if it hadn't died, undernourished, in her womb. "Where's your mommy?" she asked.

Courtney played with Lisa's long ponytail. "In the basement," she said. "Throwing pots."

Nina only broke out the wheel when she wanted to bust some ass. "Uh-oh. We'd better go save her."

Lisa and Courtney descended the narrow wooden staircase that led to the cool, damp basement. Nina, in a Rutgers sweatshirt and smudged overalls, sat at a pot-ter's wheel, shaping a pot out of wet red clay. Courtney led Lisa by the hand. "Mommy, Auntie Lisa's here!" she announced.

Nina didn't look up. "Well, hallo, Auntie Lisa," she said.

Lisa stared at the wet lump that Nina was working with. It looked like a flowerpot that had mated with an elephant. "What are you making?!" she laughed.

"I don't know," said Nina. "They usually make sense after I've fired them in the kiln."

"Where's your other kid?" Lisa asked.

"Tim took Craig out for ice cream after hockey prac-tice."

Courtney jumped up and down frenetically, like she had to pee. "Mommy, can Auntie Lisa and I watch TV?" she asked.

Nina patted Courtney on the bottom with the back of her hand, taking care not to stain her dress with the clay. "Sweetie, let me visit with Auntie Lisa first—then you can torture her with all the children's telly she can stand, all right-ee?"

Courtney turned on the heels of her little Mary Janes and ran up the wooden stairs. "Okay," she called. "I'll go finish my homework."

"Careful!" Nina loudly cautioned.

Courtney continued to run, slamming the door behind her.

Nina shook her head. "No one listens to me at work. No one listens to me at home."

Lisa pulled up the nearest chair, a stressed-out wooden confusion of folding slats. "You only do this pottery mess when you're pissed."

"If only you could teach without having to deal with the bloody administration," she remarked.

Immediately Lisa knew who the culprit was. "What did Grantham do now?"

The flower-pot-elephant suddenly crumpled into a wet red lump, and Nina sucked her teeth. "Because SCNJ's going to be a university, they have to put Ph.D. programs into place," she explained. "That's one of the caveats."

Lisa played with a stray lump of clay. "Okay."

Nina began fiercely working with the clay again. "The English Department will offer the first Ph.D. programs. So, they've got Marc to bolster the writing side. But we have some students who want to study literature from feminists and other marginalized people. So, I came up with a doctoral plan that I could implement as the Chair of the Radical Pedagogies and Literature Department."

"You're gonna be a department chair? You go, girl!"

"I'm not going anywhere, Lisa. Grantham and the Chancellor loved the plan, but may not make me the Chair, because I'm not tenured."

"But you've been there—December'll make it five years. It's September, for Christ's sake. They'll come around."

Nina seemed pleasantly surprised. "Bloody hell, you're cheering me up? I thought *I* was the optimist in this relationship."

"I flipped the script," she said simply.

Nina stopped and looked down at her work. She sighed hopelessly. "Let's talk about you. How's Marc treating you?"

Lisa's stomach clenched. Marc and his tight ass cheeks in those spandex pants appeared in her mind like an erotic movie clip. "You're so bad. He's my professor."

Nina winked deviously. "As long as it's consensual, you two can have a little slap and tickle."

Lisa remembered Michele, the NYU scholar and whitest white woman in America. That's who Marc was attracted to; Lisa had too much melanin for him. But she couldn't tell Nina that. Nina thought everyone was in the right headspace to date cross-culturally, like she and Tim had. "Girl, please!" she said. "Old boy's probably kicking chicks out of bed."

Nina's gaze was far away. "I never met Michele, the ex-wife. I heard when she left, he retreated into that book. That's why *Goombah's* so good. He put all his pain on those pages."

Lisa searched her mind for the right words. She thought of how Bryan degraded her, making her distrust her feelings and fear the intentions of all men. She knew that Nina wouldn't understand the race thing, so she attempted to break it down for her, woman to woman. She met Nina's clear grey gaze directly. "Nina, Marc's a good guy," she said softly. "And Helen Keller could see that the boy is fine. But every time I think of getting close to a man, I remember that rape kit in the emergency room at Mountainside Hospital." Nina's face blurred and Lisa blinked away the flow of tears, then laughed bitterly. "And magically, I'm cured!"

Marc entered the condo and tossed his keys in a sterling silver dish on the wooden credenza in the foyer. He took a second to appreciate the familiar, clattering sound.

That sound was the only thing that made this place a home for him.

He flipped on the track lighting, illuminating the open, ranch-style area. He crossed the carpeted foyer into the sunken living room, sparsely decorated with minimalist furniture that his decorator picked out. He made a beeline for the all-Sony mammoth TV and wall stereo system, tossed in a CD, and pressed a button. Instantly, the tinkly piano and husky sounds of Nina Simone's "My Baby Just Cares For Me" filled the room.

He entered the kitchen with its shiny appliances and butcher-block island and grabbed an ice cold Heineken from the fridge. He bounded up the hanging wooden staircase, the pounding of his size-elevens shaking the wood and metal. On the second floor, he passed a study, where he seldom worked, two guestrooms, and a bathroom to get to the master bedroom. Again, it was his gay decorator, not he, who left his mark in the master bedroom with blues and grays. He stripped off his workout gear and looked around. *Yeah, that's me. The master.*

In the stark black-and-white adjoining bathroom, Marc turned on the shower as hot as he could stand it and got under the streaming jets. He leaned against the black-and-white tiles and sipped his beer. His mind ground into action. Lisa Martin. Michele. The mysterious and forbidden versus the familiar but elusive. Why did either woman seem attractive to him? Was he horny or lonely? Was it because he couldn't stand another night in this condo that, for a year, was only a place to lay his head and nothing more? This was a nonissue, he knew. Lisa was his black student in a time and context when it was not smart to be fucking your black female student. And over a year ago, Michele had packed her bags and headed back home to California. *So, why did you apply for that consultancy at UCSD, then? You think Michele's going to fall back into your arms?*

Marc soaped up, washed his hair, and then quickly rinsed. He guzzled his beer, feeling sad and empty.

Toweling himself dry, Marc padded across the bedroom. He took a white T-shirt and navy blue sweat pants from his solid wooden chest of drawers. As he put the clothes on, he saw the message light flash on his answering machine on the nightstand next to the king-sized bed. He pressed the PLAY button, heard a beep, then, "Hi, Marc, it's me."

Marc would've known that voice anywhere . . . warm, endearing, honey-smooth. His heart fluttered. His legs gave way, and he sat on the edge of the bed. How did she know he was thinking of her?

"Oh, well, I guess you're out running," she continued, sounding excited. "Guess what! I'm getting married!" She giggled like a schoolgirl. "In June, I'm going to be Mrs. Kieran McManus!"

Jealousy devoured him. He certainly didn't begrudge her happiness, even if her idea of happiness was marrying a sixties relic of a Lit. professor who was twenty years older than she was. But still . . . *Oh, so you'd take that Irish dick's name but not mine!* "What a fucking difference a year makes," he spat childishly.

The rest of the message was the aural equivalent of a car crash he couldn't turn away from. "So, the big day's June 24," she continued, her voice dripping joy. "I'm giving you enough notice so you can scare up a date." She paused, as if letting it all sink in. "Anyway, I gotta go. Call me when you get this."

The tape clicked off, and it was official. MarcAntonio Guerrieri, the best-selling author who had the whole world at his feet, was now phenomenally depressed.

Lisa entered her studio apartment, just as the nearby cathedral clock struck eleven. Wisteria meowed loudly, rubbing her calico body against Lisa's pants leg. "Hey, baby!"

Lisa laughed as she picked the cat up and held her close. She scratched Wis between the ears, and the cat purred like a little engine was running in her tiny body. Yes, it was Friday night, and Lisa was alone, but this was all she needed in her life.

She turned on the halogen lamps, adjusting the light to fill the tiny living room that doubled as a bedroom when she unfolded the futon. She saw the answering machine light on the nearby desk blink three times. She looked down into Wisteria's green eyes, narrowed in contentment. "Should we check our messages?" she cooed lovingly.

Wisteria purred even louder.

"Let's go check our messages," she laughed.

She crossed over to the desk and pressed the PLAY button. After the beep, she immediately recognized the very crisp and subtly threatening male voice. "Mrs. Livingston, this is C. Richard Monaghan, your husband's lawyer." Tight-assed, strong-arming, as expected. "Bryan and I want to meet with you and your attorney to factor the recent sale of the house into the settlement. You have my number."

The house she'd bought with her father's money. Lisa sucked her teeth and slammed down on the ERASE button. "Yeah, I've got your number," she hissed. "Right here."

The machine beeped again.

"Haley Melissa, this is your mother, whom you do not call," said Barbara Martin in her exceedingly posh British drawl.

Lisa didn't know any white Brits who talked like that anymore. Guilt, English style. "Shit!"

"Are you coming down to the Bahamas for Christmas?" Barbara asked, like it was more of a done deal than something still left to decide. "All right, dear. You're right, I'm wrong. I shouldn't have said that you carelessly tossed Bryan away. Come help me with the new Billy Beaver book. Nothing like rum drinks and stiff willies to cheer you up. Call me. You know how I abhor talking into this contraption."

Lisa looked down at Wisteria and wished her relationship with Barbara was as simple as her relationship with the cat. "And she's a child psychologist, Wis," she said wryly. "I should sue her for malpractice."

Guilt prevented her from erasing the message. *I'll just leave it for now . . .*

The machine beeped again. "Oi!" came a cheery analog rendering of Nina's voice. "I almost forgot. Next Wednesday, NBC's news division's having a party at the Palladium. Tim and his cohorts are going to stroke their Emmys and do some nosh and expensive plonk. We want you to come with us, because we love you, Miss Graduate Student. Coo-cooca-chu!"

Definitely a keeper.

At that second she realized that even though her rapist soon-to-be ex was trying to fuck her over and her relationship with her mother was dysfunctional at its best, she had a home, friends who loved her, her faithful, adoring cat, and aching but healthy muscles. All the basic needs in Maslow's pyramid met. After all that huffing and puffing, the answer came to her in a moment of quiet reflection. This was the time to start burying ghosts. And she knew exactly how to do it.

4

Sunlight streamed through the windows in the apartment, illuminating a half-eaten bowl of oatmeal, a half-empty glass of orange juice, and balled-up papers tossed throughout the apartment. An ultra-brightly lit morning show played at a low volume on the color TV. In stark contrast to the tranquillity, Lisa hurriedly stuffed her typed assignment into her black leather case. She looked down at her gold Seiko. She was going to hit the hellish morning traffic on Route 280, and she was sleep-deprived from typing all night.

She turned suddenly and almost tripped over the cat, who rubbed against her black stockings, leaving a nice white trail of hairs. "Wis!" Lisa snapped impatiently. "Come on. I'm late!"

Wisteria meowed plaintively at Lisa's legs. After almost two years, Lisa knew what this behavior meant. She glanced over at the kitchen area. Sure enough, both food and water bowls were bone dry.

Lisa filled both bowls. Wisteria hit the solid food and

started wolfing it down. "That's why you leave those nasty puke balls all over the place," Lisa complained.

I'm talking to the cat!

Shaking her head at the insanity of it all, she grabbed her case and the TV remote from the coffee table. She had her finger on the POWER button when she stopped, transfixed, for some reason.

She recognized the bimbo ... Karin Anderson, stupidly young, blond, blow-dried, and made up to within an inch of her life. That bitch was the unattainable ideal. The thought made her sick. She was framed in a flattering close-up. "He is a professor at the State College of New Jersey at Montclair," she read from the TelePrompTer, all giddy. "His latest book, *Goombah*, just debuted at the top of *The New York Times* best-seller list. Good morning, MarcAntonio Guerrieri."

The camera cut to a close-up of Marc, bright-eyed, tanned, dressed in a black turtleneck. He gave off a vibe like he was accustomed to, and a little embarrassed by, all the fuss. "Good morning, Karin," he said, his tone professional but friendly. "Nice to be here."

The camera cut to a cover shot of Marc and Karin Anderson, seated facing each other in black stuffed chairs. They looked like two friends chatting in someone's living room, that staged informality that was a staple of morning talk shows. Karin turned right to Marc, her green eyes homing in for the interrogation. "Marc, tell us about this book. First of all, the title." She giggled. "What's a 'goombah'?"

The camera cut to a close-up of Marc, facing Karin with the requisite talk room at the left. The chyron flashed Marc's name at the bottom third of the screen. "It's Italian slang, Karin, for 'compadre,' " he said in the voice he used in the fiction class. "Later, it came to be associated with people connected to organized crime."

"Like the Mafia," prompted Karin. This was her idea of investigative journalism.

Marc laughed. "Well, Mario Cuomo says there is no such thing as a 'Mafia,' but yes. Like the Mafia."

Cover shot. "I read the whole book last night. It's a wonderful read."

Lisa rolled her eyes. *Yeah, right. You read.*

"Thank you," Marc said.

"Some would say it's a little heavy on the violence."

Close-up of Marc. "Well, the main character, Nick Scalia, is an enforcer. He leans on people who aren't compliant and has tortured and killed people. That's his life. Yes, it's violent, but it's very real, I assure you."

Close-up of Karin, green eyes narrowing, signaling her desire to probe further. "You were attacked while doing research at Rikers Island Prison here in New York, weren't you?"

Close-up of Marc. Obviously meant to be the money shot. He laughed again, but nervously. "Yes. Obviously writing checks my body couldn't cash."

I bet little Miss Prom Queen wants to wax that slammin' body. She was his type, blond with green eyes.

Close-up of Karin. "The button you're wearing says 'No Justice, No Peace.' Are you protesting the shooting of Yusuf Hawkins?" She looked directly into the camera. "Yusuf Hawkins was a teenager shot in Bensonhurst, which is a predominantly Italian section of Brooklyn."

The camera zoomed in on the button over Marc's heart. "That incident was tragic and senseless." Cut to cover shot. "We as a nation need to come to terms with our racist past and stop trying to solve our problems with guns."

Karin Anderson brightened. "Would you say that's *Goombah*'s message?" she asked.

"The message is that those who aren't righteous will eventually get theirs in the end unless they have an epiphany," Marc declared.

The newsy theme came up as bed music. "Like Nick Scalia," Karin concluded.

Marc chuckled. "I'm not telling," he said, cryptically.

The theme came up over a cover shot of Marc and Karin bantering mutely. The director slowly dissolved to a crane shot of Times Square, then cut to commercial.

So, A.J. was right. He was really hot shit.

After the most hellish commute across the Hudson River from the City, Marc, laden with papers and a heavy leather satchel, finally found his way to the fourth floor of the School of Humanities. He hadn't planned on taking so long, and now all the rest of his responsibilities, particularly the prep for his class that night, loomed large. He was close to his office when he stopped short. Perched strategically in front of his office door were the dean of the School of Humanities, Les Grantham, who embodied the mid-fifties, a pasty, lanky academic, and Chancellor Swift, who resembled George Hamilton so much that it was uncanny.

Grantham and Swift spotted their quarry and turned on the syrupy charm. "Marc!" Grantham said, something resembling euphoria coming through his uptight upbringing for a second. "Our telephones have been ringing off the hook. You've even gotten a few naughty marriage proposals from some strippers in West Orange."

Marc tried to be cordial, but his face just wouldn't cooperate. "It's nice to be loved," he said.

Chancellor Swift tag teamed the sucking up. "Marc, ever since you've come on board here, you've uplifted the image of this college immeasurably. When SCNJ becomes a university in three months . . . well, I hope I'm not talking out of school here . . ." He leaned in conspiratorially. "We're talking chair of the writing department."

Marc stared at the grinning fools before him who didn't understand a thing about education and inspiring students. *Oh, God, save me.*

Like a blond angel, Nina appeared as if answering that prayer. "Here's our telly star!" she exclaimed, embodying perky. "Such a big shot. I hope he hasn't forgotten our meeting."

Marc searched his mind. "Meeting? What time?"

She took his papers and satchel. "Now," she said, then turned to the unholy wonder twins. " 'Scuse us, gentlemen."

Swift and Grantham parted from in front of the door like the Red Sea. Marc fished the key out of his chinos pocket, unlocked the door, and ushered Nina in. He flicked on the lights and eased wearily down into his swivel chair. "I could kiss you on the mouth," he laughed.

She shut the door and tossed his things onto his compulsively neat desk. "God, this office is so bloody clean—you could make computer chips in here!" she teased, then bounced into the guest chair.

Marc smiled, relaxing even more. "What are we meeting about?"

She shrugged simply. "A ruse," she confessed. "To get you away from those insufferable bores."

"It was getting kind of hard to walk with their tongues up my ass."

"Speaking of tongues up your arse, how about that Karin Anderson, eh?"

He remembered Karin's piss-poor attempt to work him, both on and off camera. She did look like a low-budget Michele, but why would he go for aspartame when he'd had sugar? *Michele.* "Hey, I had a limo, the works. I was feeling great. 'Til we sat in fucking city traffic for almost an hour! I felt like opening the sunroof and yelling, 'I'm MarcAntonio Guerrieri! Who do I have to fuck to get traffic moving again?!' "

"You probably would've had lots of takers."

Marc rested his head in his hands. He wondered where his energy was going to come from for that night's class. "I don't regret moving back to Jersey for a second."

Nina leaned in, concern on his face. "Hey, are you okay?"

"I'm just tired," he sighed.

"What, like you can take a nap for fifteen minutes and feel refreshed, or . . . ?"

"No, like I'm burning out tired. I used to dream about this kind of success. My book is number one. Everyone wants to talk to me, and all I can do is resent the intrusion."

"Is there anything you can do to make you feel like yourself again?"

He searched her face. Shit, if he could explain to her how he felt about racial tensions, he could surely explain his feelings about less volatile aspects of his life and not be afraid she'd judge him. "Remember when you asked me if I was still in love with Michele?" he asked, and waited for the shit to fly.

"Yes, and you chewed my head off!" she declared.

He grimaced. "Well, I wasn't entirely truthful."

"My love, you've been divorced for over a year," she reminded him. "She's seeing someone else. How did that equal reconciliation in your mind?"

He laughed at the irony. "Oh, there's more. They're getting married. Next June."

Nina touched his knee. "Oh, Marc," she sighed.

"My craving for success destroyed our marriage," he said.

"Sweetie, I thought it was her having an abortion without telling you that drove a wedge through your marriage."

He had to admire Nina's flair for snapping him back to reality. Still, for whatever reason, he fought the trip with all he had. "I was horrible to her, Nina," he said. "Horrible and unforgiving. I thought with time apart, we could think our troubles through. That's why I applied for that consultancy at UCSD for next year. I thought I could go out to Cali and see if we were really through."

"So, she's marrying Kieran. Now what?" Nina asked. "Are you going to do something dumb and chivalrous like Dustin Hoffman in *The Graduate*? Or are you going to forget about her and live in the here and now?"

"Why did I even tell you this?" Marc snapped.

"Because I'm your friend," she declared, "and unlike the rest of these people here, I have no desire whatsoever to put my tongue in your arse."

He slouched in the chair. The only certainty in the moment was his confusion and her unconditional friendship. She smiled, touched his cheek. "What are you doing next Wednesday?"

The last thing he needed was another one of Nina's fix-ups, couched within a party.

"I'm up to my ass, Nina. I don't have time for fun."

He couldn't put his finger on what he saw in Nina's grey eyes. Whatever it was, he sensed it was a product of a mind working overtime. "Make time," Nina commanded. "NBC's news division's having a party. It'll be brilliant! Trust me."

He didn't have the strength to fight her. And what could a party hurt? "All right," he acquiesced.

"Jolly good!" she laughed, with a wink. "You'll see."

Barely able to see past a blinding headache, Lisa counted out twenty copies of her first-draft chapter. She cradled the telephone receiver between her neck and shoulder and cursed herself for having answered the phone. She focused on the radio in her cubicle, which she'd tuned to KISS-FM. Anything to distract herself from the pain and from her husband's selfish rhetoric on the other end of the receiver.

The male announcer described that day's primaries

like a sportscaster doing color commentary: "This primary day, voter turnout has been heavy. Rudolph Giuliani, the former prosecutor, is expected to sweep the Republican nomination. The battle to watch, however, is between the Democratic candidates. David Dinkins, the sole African-American in the race, is gaining momentum, following the shooting of Yusuf Hawkins in Bensonhurst last month. He directly challenges incumbent mayor Edward I. Koch, who is accused of contributing to the racial polarization of New York City during his twelve-year term as mayor. Polls close at 8:30—tune in to 98.7 KISS-FM for periodic Primary Day coverage and results throughout the day."

"Melissa, I'm merely trying to gain some information on the sale of the house," Bryan said, and she pictured him talking down to her from his opulent Madison Avenue office.

Lisa shook out tablets into her hand and downed them with a swig of water. "I don't have anything to say to you," she croaked over her thudding heart, and she hated that he still had the power to frighten her. "I'm busy."

"We're all busy, Lisa," he stated. "As soon as I hang up, I have to go vote. Monaghan called you on Friday. It's Tuesday. You haven't returned the call."

"I shouldn't be talking to your lawyer. I shouldn't even be talking to you. Isn't this conversation *ex parte* or something?"

He sniffed. "Someone's been watching too much *LA Law.*"

"Between my job, my school work, and this bottomless divorce, I don't have time for TV. What do you want?"

"The money from the sale of the house should be split fifty-fifty."

This greedy motherfucker! With each day, his unworthiness of her love continued to manifest itself in even more excessive ways. "Your memory is conveniently short, Bryan. The house is not community property. I bought that house before we were married. I used every penny my father left me as the down payment. I'll get it all back if I have to litigate your ass into the next century."

"Enter the drama queen" he scoffed.

"Christ, you're a fucking ingrate!" she cried. "Your ass should really be in jail, not in Manhattan, trying to shake me down for money."

"Enough with the emotional blackmail, bitch." Bryan spat, and venom dripped from the other end of the receiver. "No fifty-fifty, no spousal support."

She pressed a trembling hand to her forehead. *Why was this so hard?* "You asshole! Everything you are, you owe to me. You went from a Macintosh artist with no future to a summa cum laude Columbia graduate, selling people shit they don't need from Madison Avenue."

"Oh, bitch, please!"

The vein throbbed painfully in the middle of her forehead. She swallowed down the metallic taste of pain and fear. Her choices were flight or fight; she chose the latter. "Look, you whining motherfucker, have your lawyer call my lawyer, because as far as I'm concerned, this is our last conversation!"

With that, Lisa banged down the receiver. Almost immediately, her headache disappeared as if by magic. *Symbolism,* she thought as she pulled on the jacket to her navy blue business suit.

Lisa was late—horribly late. Like a gate-crasher, she peered through the glass part of the classroom door. She stared at the other students and A.J. listening attentively to Marc in denim that brought out his eyes and a caramel-colored cardigan that accentuated the tawny hues in his skin. Her instinct was to turn and run. Before she could, though, Marc looked up at her from behind his glasses. *Shit, he saw me!*

Lisa entered, and all eyes focused on her. Meekly,

she approached Marc, seated on the desk. "Sorry I'm late," she whispered.

His eyes were glacial, narrowed. "We'll discuss it after class," he whispered back.

Not good . . .

Resigned to her fate, Lisa handed over twenty copies of her chapter and took the desk next to A.J., who shook her head. "Are you trying to fail this class?" she whispered.

Marc got down off the desk and handed stacks of chapters to Carlette. "Everybody take one and pass 'em around."

Lisa watched her oeuvre make the rounds. All the things she'd said in those pages . . . Her life was reduced to so much fodder for her classmates' grubby hands and prying eyes. *What were you thinking, Melissa?*

Marc looked pointedly at Lisa, and she flushed. "Before we were interrupted, we were talking about technique and style," he began in his lecturer's voice, pacing before the class. "I presume everyone here thinks they're a damned good writer and raconteur. None of you, however, is the next Hemingway or Joyce, so check all attitudes and egos at the door. If you want to be an artiste and chance your work never seeing the light of day, then, to quote Bobby Brown, that's your prerogative. However, if you want to be a commercial success, you will, more often than not, have to rewrite."

The classroom was near empty, save for A.J., Lisa, and a couple of stragglers. "Why'd you even answer the phone?" A.J. asked.

"I was at work, A.J.," Lisa snapped. "I couldn't just let it ring."

A.J. made a beeline for the door. "Damn, the brothah's tired!"

Desperation was about to swallow her whole. She

needed a friend more than she needed recriminations. "Where you going?" she asked.

"Girl, I gotta go vote Ed Koch out of office!" she called over her shoulder. "Peace."

Only Lisa and Marc remained. She could feel his disapproval like a blanket around her. "Lisa, we need to talk," he announced.

The vein in her forehead began to throb. "What, your office again?" she asked.

Marc stood in front of her, looming large. "No, we can do it here," he said. "I want you to drop the class."

She felt like she'd been punched in the gut. "What?!"

Seemingly from thin air, Marc produced an Add/Drop slip. "It's not too late for someone to take your place," he said.

She blinked, trying to recover. "I don't understand!" she said. "What happened to my solid, thought-provoking questions?"

"You can't ask any if you're not here."

"I *was* here!"

"Forty-five minutes late. You're preoccupied with your divorce, your job, you name it. If you're not going to take full advantage of the class, then I'd rather have someone here who will."

"I don't believe this," she murmured.

"It's for the best, Lisa," he said, like he truly believed that he was doing her a favor by shit-canning her. "You can try this again when you get your life sorted out."

She thought a moment about Bryan, and now him, and all the men who thought they knew what was good for her when they didn't know shit. Suddenly, miraculously, she went from feeling victimized to positively irate in seconds flat. "So, let me get this straight," she said. "You want to kick me out of your class—without having read my work—because I deign to come late to hear the Oracle of Guerrieri speak?"

Now *he* blinked. "This is very counterproductive, Lisa," he lectured. "Not to mention childish."

"Well, you're being a presumptuous dick!"

Now *he* looked like he'd been punched. "Really, Lisa!"

"If you were a constellation, you'd be . . . *Assholus Majora* . . . lording your brightness over all the other stars."

Now *he* went from stunned to irate. "If you have a formal protest, put it in writing."

"No, I'll drop the class. Someone as intolerant and rigid as you has nothing to teach me."

Lisa snatched the Add/Drop Form, hurriedly signed it, and snatched up her stuff. She pressed the form into his hands. "You can fill in the necessary blanks," she said. "Just for the record, it's FDP's busiest time of year. A.J.'s never late, because she has flextime. I don't. So, if I have to choose between putting food in my fridge or making this class, food's gonna win every time."

He looked down at the Add/Drop form, obviously ashamed. He then sighed, looking up at her with sad eyes. "Look . . ." he began, the makings of an apology.

Lisa stormed from the room before she was tempted to forgive him.

Marc hopped up on the desk. No matter how brave she seemed, she was hurt and he was the cause. *Believing your own press.* "You fucking asshole," he said, shaking his head.

He flipped through the pile of assignments until he came to Lisa's. Centered on the whitest page he'd ever seen in neat, dark type were the words "Untitled, by H. Melissa Martin."

Marc absorbed every word. Lisa, in first-person narrative prose, frankly detailed the story of Vanessa Dean, a black woman originally from Westfield, the affluent

New Jersey town put on the map when John List snapped and killed his entire family, then eluded capture for almost eighteen years until the Fox TV show *America's Most Wanted* helped put him behind bars. When Vanessa was six, her biracial British child psychologist mother and American OB/GYN father moved to Montclair.

Vanessa met Kevin while she worked as a graphic artist in the advertising department of an international Fortune 500 payroll company. Instantly, she was attracted to him. He was the most handsome man she'd ever seen, kind of like her father. And his eyes . . . dark, intelligent eyes that seemed to see right through her. He was charming, with a riotous sense of humor. He was an excellent conversationalist, well versed on every topic. Unlike Vanessa, who tap-danced around the issues rather than confront them, he said exactly what was on his mind. She admired that.

After Vanessa had been with the company for three months, Kevin asked her out. She hadn't dated anyone seriously in two years, so thinking that it'd be a nice change, said yes. They made an adventure of it, driving to Secaucus to see *48 Hours,* with Eddie Murphy. Vanessa laughed so hard, tears came to her eyes. They also made out, something she'd never done, good Catholic girl that she was. Then they drove in Kevin's Corolla to a diner on Route 3, where they talked nonstop over chocolate shakes and piping-hot fries. Vanessa suspected it was love, but she wondered how wise it was to get involved with someone from work. "You don't shit where you eat," her mother used to say.

At the coffee station the next morning, while Vanessa was making her daily mug of Earl Grey tea, Kevin appeared. He matter-of-factly told her he loved her and that, before the year was out, he was going to marry her. He was right.

"The fundamental reason for the failure of the black man to communicate and interact healthily in society," Vanessa's father used to say to her after he and her mother got into it, "is that his woman doesn't believe in him and thwarts him every time."

Vanessa swore she wasn't going to be one of those black women. She supported Kevin at every turn. He wanted to get his MBA from Columbia, but he could only go full-time. Instead of complaining that they couldn't afford it, she scrimped and saved to make it work, because she believed he could be more than just a Mac artist. She supported him when he quit his job. She helped him study. She spent hours with him at every Essex County library, helping him to research papers that she surreptitiously typed at work. She gave until she was empty, and he still demanded more. By the time she'd realized she had spoiled him, it was too late.

To her utmost joy, Vanessa discovered she was pregnant. Instead of being happy, Kevin asked how she could let it happen. Because she swore she'd never be the shrewish woman her mother was, she bit back tears and kept working ten-, twelve-, and sixteen-hour days. Kevin needed the world on a silver platter.

In her fourth month, Vanessa miscarried—on the night of one of Kevin's midterms. The office-cleaning people had come at night to find her dazed, sitting in a pool of her own blood. An ambulance rushed her to Mountainside Hospital in Montclair. For hours, while her body rejected her own child, she cried out for Kevin. He'd gotten the news at Columbia but had chosen to finish his test. Instead of voicing her despair, Vanessa suffered in silence.

A year and a half later, Kevin graduated from Columbia. Two weeks after Vanessa watched the results of her labor come to fruition, Kevin took her to the same diner where they'd had their first date. They ordered chocolate shakes and piping-hot fries. Then he said, "Baby, I feel trapped."

The consummate caregiver, she asked, "What can I do?"

"I want out," he said.

Not wanting to cause a scene, Vanessa simply sobbed, "Okay."

They had come full circle.

Later that night, her Norwegian-Irish friend, Helga Paul, held her while she wailed as if she would disintegrate. "It'll be all right, luv," she said, soothingly.

So, Vanessa was trying to move on, but it was so hard. "Am I brave enough to pick up the pieces and start again?" Marc read aloud.

Sight unseen, Marc loathed Bryan Livingston. Any man who could do this shit to his wife should be capped between the eyes. Then he realized that his slate wasn't all that clean, either. He'd done some horrible things to Michele in the final months of their marriage. He wondered if Michele had similarly shared all the sordid details with Kieran McManus. Did Kieran want to beat the shit out of him, too?

It smacked him upside the head. Wasn't that the mark of an excellent writer, to draw characters and situations to which the reader could viscerally relate? Didn't learning, in fact, take place on reflection, on hitching new information to the old in long-term memory to create learning? Didn't he just learn something about himself from a first read of her first draft? He packed up his stuff. He had to find her.

Minutes later, he was driving his Jeep along Valley Road in the pouring rain. Wipers slapped water away from the windshield with a rhythmic, hypnotic sound. *What the fuck are you going to say?* What was the right approach? Go to The Crescent, kick the door in, and beg forgiveness? Pull over to the gas station and call her? *Where the fuck is that number?*

Marc saw some kind of logjam ahead of him at a light. *Shit!* He cut through the nearby gas station and then through a parking lot near the commuter railroad tracks. He was about to turn onto Bellevue Avenue when he saw a car reversing out from a spot. While the driver in the car was doing his three-point turn, though, something caught Marc's eye. Sandwiched between the now-empty space and another car was a blue Jetta. He read the plates. "HEI . . ." His heart lurched. *Lisa!*

The car in front of him drove off, and immediately Marc zipped into the spot. He grabbed his umbrella, locked the car, and stepped into the wet night. He rushed to the main street—Bellevue Avenue—then looked around. Between Bellevue Avenue and Valley Road, there were any number of upscale stores that she could be in. But logic hit; all the stores were closed. All that was lit up like a Christmas tree was the Bellevue movie theater. The red letters of the blinding-bright marquee spelled out *Do the Right Thing*, indicating that Spike Lee's latest flick was playing. Marc rushed across the street. Lisa was angry enough at him to want a fix of black anger aimed at an Italian—like him.

He stepped up to the small box office and saw a tall, lanky teen male with a full complement of acne pustules thriving in his T-zone. He regarded Marc with characteristic teen sullenness that came from being a member of an exploited work force, forced to wear a red vest over a Killing Joke T-shirt. "Yeah?" he asked, but his facial expression read *fuck off*.

Marc thought for a minute. How would he describe her? "Umm . . . did you see a black woman, pretty . . ." Marc put his hand to his shoulder, ". . . about this tall come in here?"

The teen squinted dark eyes. "Dude, it's Spike Lee," he said, like *duh*.

Duh, indeed! Marc looked down at his watch. Black

hands on a white face pointed out 8:10. "What time did the movie start?"

He squinted more. "What?" Sounded like white?

This kid's going to pay my social security when I get old. "Never mind," he murmured.

"Dude, maybe she went to eat," the kid piped up in a rare moment of helpfulness. "At Charlie Brown's. Behind this theater."

Couldn't hurt. "Thanks," Marc said.

Marc headed out, made a right, and headed down an alley to Charlie Brown's.

Inside Charlie Brown's, one of the town's favorite yuppie watering holes, the lounge was packed with the happy-hour crowd in suits and business attire. Peter Gabriel's "Sledgehammer" played on the massive CD jukebox in a corner. Both TVs above the packed bar showed news anchors making primary predictions with the volume down.

Marc ventured into the lounge, pointedly looking through the crowd. Through all the bodies, he saw Lisa. She sat, hunched over, at the bar, nursing her drink as if it gave her sustenance. *What do you know—that kid was right!*

Marc picked his way through the crowd, heading toward her. It must've been Providence, but the young urban professional sitting next to her got up. Marc shrugged off his raincoat, hung it over the back of the stool, and sat. He studied her soft profile. What was it about sad women in need of salvation that made them so sexy? He leaned in so she could hear him. "So, it *is* you," he said.

Lisa looked up from her drink. Once she saw who it was, naked distaste showed in her eyes. "Yes, it's me," he said with a laugh. *"Assholus Majora."*

"What?" she demanded. "You follow me here to humiliate me some more?"

She hated him. He could tell. *And you deserve it.* He

shook his head. "Saw your car in the parking lot as I was going home."

"The ubiquitous MarcAntonio Guerrieri," she commented.

A young white bartender, with dark, spiked hair and wearing the server's uniform of white shirt, olive green tie, and matching apron, sidled up. His name tag read *Joe*. He seemed poised to go into his server spiel when it hit him. His dark eyes lit up with recognition. "Oh, shit! MarcAntonio-Fuckin'- Guerrieri!" he exclaimed.

Lisa raised her glass, her red drink and crushed ice sloshing inside. "Fuckin' A!" she remarked, mocking.

Joe took Marc's hand, vigorously pumping it. "Man, Karin Anderson was all over you on TV!"

This was one of these times when celebrity was quite the ass pain. "She's a nice lady," Marc said.

"Man, I just read *Goombah*," Joe enthused. "You're a god among men."

"Thanks, man," Marc said sheepishly. "A thirsty god among men . . ." *Hint, hint.*

Joe smacked his temple, like he just realized he could've had a V-8. "Whoa! Where's my head at? What'll it be?"

He looked at Lisa's red drink. It looked like a chick drink, but it seemed fruity and refreshing. "Whatever the lady's having," he said.

"One Shirley Temple comin' up," Joe announced. "On me."

"Thanks."

Marc watched, fascinated, as Joe made the drink with the requisite impressive flourish, and then set it in front of Marc on a napkin. "Thanks again," Marc said.

Joe gushed. "You need something, just holler!"

He then went away.

Marc looked down at the drink, then at Lisa. "Shirley Temple?!" he hooted.

She shrugged, like it was the most natural thing in the world. "Yeah. I'm driving."

He laughed. "You're an enigma, you know that?"

She scoffed. "That's a switch. A little while ago, you had me all figured out."

If he had a cap, it would've been in hand, close to his chest right about now. "Look, you were right," he conceded. "I was an asshole. I'm sorry."

She seemed to soften some. Still, though, she wasn't ready to forgive him just yet. "Just don't prejudge my replacement," she said. "Maybe you'll get another Carlette."

The blonde in the tight sweater. "Carlette," he groaned.

She seemed to derive pleasure from his discomfort. She laughed. "It's so funny to watch her eyefuck you from her chair, staring into your baby blue eyes with puppy dog sincerity. How *Room 222!*"

He felt his face grow hot. He sipped his drink, looking away. "The shit women notice!" he murmured.

"Stevie Wonder would notice this woman!" she cried, then affected Carlette's breathy voice. "I bet for her next trick, her blouse'll fly open and her boobs'll fall out onto the desk!"

Marc chuckled. She was actually funny, insightful. Mostly, she was an awesome and promising writer. He looked down, suddenly seeing the Add/Drop form with her signature on it in his shirt pocket. He took it out, crumpled it up in his hands into a tight ball, and plunked it into the nearest ashtray on the bar's oak surface. "You've gotta see that, then," he stated.

She stared at him in disbelief. "You want me to stay now."

He nodded. "Give me a chance to show you I'm not as intolerant and rigid as you think."

Disbelief morphed into skepticism. He sensed what she was probably thinking . . . *who is this crazy white guy?* She seemed leery, but said, "Okay."

She turned away, her red lips puckered around the tip of her striped straw. He imagined those lips at work on a part of his anatomy, and he suppressed a sense memory shiver. He was right, the way he'd described her to the kid at the Bellevue. She was pretty, but in a different way from the party at Nina's. Pretty in the earthy, genuine sense. That night, she was pretty in a vampish way that made him want to rip her clothes off. The dichotomy intrigued him. There was also that palpable sadness that he saw in her eyes, and her chapter filled in the blanks. The fact that she was like everyone else, trying to keep it together in a veritable shit storm, made her approachable.

Lest she think he was unhinged, he looked away from her and up at the nearest TV. The channel broadcast the images of David and Joyce Dinkins from earlier in the day, standing in front of a voting booth, doing the expected thumbs up as bulbs flashed all around, and juxtaposed Ed Koch, picking his way through a crush of media to get into a long black stretch limo. "Koch is on his way out," Marc commented. "End of an era."

Lisa looked up at the TV, too. "Twelve years is a long time to do nothing," she said.

The TV broadcast visions of angry Italians on either side of a New York street shouting in vein-popping fury at marching blacks. Marc watched, riveted, filled with shame for his own people. "The Bensonhurst situation is ripping the City apart. Dinkins'll do a lot to stop the hate," he said.

"I like how he talks about the City as his beautiful mosaic, how all the colors make it beautiful. Not about that assimilationist, melting-pot shit."

"America can make you drunk. When you come down from the high and see things the way they are, it's a helluva reality check."

Lisa looked at him, and she seemed impressed. "You sound like those marginalized people that Nina talks about," she said.

"We used to be 'the niggers of Europe,' Lisa," he said, so hating that word. "Italians are just as marginalized as blacks. Howard Beach. Bensonhurst. If we'd just stop fighting each other, we'd realize just how much we have in common."

She shook her head, stabbing at the ice floats in her drink. "Noble sentiment, Marc. But no matter how well John Travolta can dance, and no matter how many black women Robert DeNiro marries, Italians can mark that 'white' box on their SATs and have all the privileges of that label. We can't."

He looked at her, well spoken, with her college education and her designer clothes. "How've you been denied any privileges?" he asked. "Nina told me your parents are respected black doctors."

Instantly, her hackles sprang up, like a reflex action to having been asked the question many times before. "Why can't they just be 'respected doctors?'" she asked, defensive.

Fucked up again, Marco. This was taking on the same tone as his conversation with Vito, before he'd gotten stabbed. He thought and thought, sipping his drink, trying to recover. There was a tense silence. "I get the point," he said. "I still say blacks and Italians have a lot of things in common."

"Oh, yeah?" she challenged. "Name three."

His brain screamed into action. "Like Hannibal."

She smiled. "Okay," she conceded. "One."

He took in her huge brown eyes, her dainty nose, her red lips parting to reveal a brilliant, even smile. Damn, she was pretty. He wanted to make her smile like that forever. "And Ethiopia," he said, tongue in cheek.

She giggled. "You went back to the archives! Did you have to dust that memory?"

The pressure was on to make her laugh some more. He thought and thought, then remembered the bright white marquee and the red lettering. "Oh!" he said, snapping his fingers. "Giancarlo Esposito."

She laughed incredulously. "What, the actor from the Spike Lee movies?!"

"He's half-black, half-Sicilian."

"Sicilian, not Italian."

"Oh! Same thing!" he insisted, even though he knew it wasn't. He remembered his grandfather, himself an immigrant, denigrating coarse Sicilian new Americans who would blow their noses in their hands. Grandpa Pasquale would probably spin like a rotisserie chicken in his grave if he'd heard the comparison. Then again, he'd probably spin in his grave if he knew his grandson wanted to take a long, lusty dip in this black woman's gene pool.

Lisa laughed, shaking her head. Then she sucked the last red remnants of her drink through the straw. "Listen, I gotta go. Nina and I are going shopping. She invited me to some NBC party tomorrow, and she thinks I need something new to wear."

At last, Nina's motives were revealed. "Really, now?" he asked.

She eyed him quizzically. "What's up with that face?"

Was he smirking? "What face?"

"That's the same face you had when I asked you to jump me in the park last Friday."

And was thinking about the same thing . . . jumping her. "I didn't realize," he said. *Liar!*

Lisa stood up and fished a fistful of bills out of her purse. The gentleman inside him instantly appeared. He took her hand and guided the money back into the purse's silky folds. Her hand . . . soft, warm. "No, no, no," he insisted. "I got this one."

She sized him up, as if weighing how much she'd owe him for buying her a drink. Apparently, one drink was acceptable quid pro quo. "As long as I can get you next time," she declared.

He took his hand away before he wouldn't be able to stand up for another hour. "You're going to be in class next week, right?" he asked.

She waved dismissively. "Yeah, yeah, yeah," she said. "God, throw in some melanin and a rack, and you'd be my mother!"

With that, she headed for the door, weaving her way through the yuppies before disappearing. *What are you doing?* She was his student. His ex-wife, with whom he thought he still had unfinished business, was marrying someone else. *Did life ever make sense?*

Right then, the jukebox shut off, and only the muted chatter of the patrons inside could be heard. Marc looked down at his watch. The hands pointed to 8:30. From behind the bar, Joe turned up one of the televisions, just as Channel 7's suited-down, bespectacled anchorman appeared onscreen. "It is 8:30 P.M.," he announced in his ultraprofessional television voice, "and polling stations across New York City have closed. Early returns are in, and David N. Dinkins is the projected winner of the Democratic Party's nomination for mayor. Let's go live to Dinkins headquarters for more."

The excited chatter from the patrons drowned out the report from Dinkins Central. Marc sighed. Maybe there was hope after all to end all the madness that threatened to end the City and the Jersey that he knew.

Joe materialized. "Refill?" he asked

"Make it champagne," Marc said. "Dinkins won."

"Yeah, that's a good thing," Joe offered.

"You think?"

The perky Joe turned so suddenly before his eyes, it left him breathless. "Yeah. Now the moolies should be happy and stay the hell outta Bensonhurst. I'll go get the bubbly."

Joe disappeared, leaving Marc stunned, and very little stunned him these days. So much for the hope of the tri-state area.

*   *   *

Lisa sank into the luxurious passenger seat of Nina's Saab. Nina zoomed along Route 23, blasting Living Colour, singing woefully off-key, along with Corey Glover. Lisa resisted the urge to cover her ears. Instead, she looked out the window just in time to see two Cedar Grove cops in the act of profiling a group of black men in a shiny black Beemer that they'd stopped at the side of the road. *New Jersey's fucking finest.*

Once they arrived at Willowbrook, the sprawling commercial jewel in Wayne township, near the murky Passaic River, Nina made a beeline for women's wear on the second floor. Immediately, Nina began channeling her inner Nazi. "Find a dressing room," she ordered. "I'll bring you the clothes."

Like a lost child, Lisa gazed at all the expensive clothes surrounding her, clothes fresh from the showrooms of the top designers—Liz Claiborne . . . Anne Klein . . . Evan-Picone . . . Perry Ellis. Thank God Marc spotted her on the drinks, leaving her with twenty dollars to her name. "Nina, did I happen to mention that I don't have any money?" she asked.

Nina aimed her in the direction of the dressing rooms and pushed her. "Did I happen to ask?" she said. "Now, shoo!"

Obediently, Lisa skulked away, her shoulders hunched. *Bossy bitch.*

In the dressing room, she stripped until she was standing in only her black bra and panties and thigh-highs in front of three mirrors—one in front and one each flanking her on the sides. Without mercy, she studied herself from all three angles. She squeezed her ass. It felt firm, thanks to running. Cursed with her mother's enormous boobs that she had literally had to talk into the C-cups every morning, she'd been the first girl in seventh grade at Montclair High to develop. By the time she was eleven, she was an A-cup. Sophomores, juniors, seniors, even college boys from SCNJ Montclair would chase her with a vengeance, and she'd retreat into her books, slouch, anything to camouflage her body that was warping through puberty. Whenever she'd walk into a room, the other girls would sing, *"Mammaries, like the corners of my mind . . ."*

"Those bitches are just jealous, sweetie," Barbara would say in one of those rare moments of maternal sympathy. "Jealous because you have naturally what they'll need to get from a plastic surgeon."

So Lisa stood straighter as she got older. As she became more confident, she sorted the boys with substance from the boys who just wanted a piece of ass. In eleventh grade, she met Michael Bross. He was quarterback on the football team, and he sat next to her in English. He was smart and fine—genes courtesy of a Puerto Rican mother and a black father. He told her he was going to Clemson on a football scholarship and that he spent most of his free time working at the record store in the mall. So, obviously, there was no way he could be serious about any one girl. Lisa took him at his word and kept sorting.

But wherever she was, Michael would suddenly show up, talking small talk. He'd honk his horn every time he'd pass by her house on Grove Street in his Mustang. Then, one day in class, he slipped her a piece of paper. She opened it and read:

A Haiku for Lisa

Not the Taj Mahal
Nor any world wonders can
Compare to Lisa

She was in love.

She adored everything about Michael . . . his smile, his silky hair, the cut body that came from hours beating the shit out of other teens on the field. They would lie on the carpeted floor in her room, play records, and kiss endlessly. She'd take off her blouse and bra and press him close. "I love you," he'd shudder.

"Why do you love me?" she'd tease.

" 'Cause you have the softest titties in the world."

One weekend, while her parents were away in the Poconos, Lisa and Michael went "all the way." They'd carelessly thrown off all their clothes, and although the room was nearly dark, she got to see what a man looked like naked. He held her close, towering over her, because he was so tall. He took her hand and put it against his crotch, and she gasped, in awe of the strength that seemed to be so separate from him. He kissed her, his breathing ragged. "It's okay," he whispered in her ear, then sucked on the lobe. "I won't hurt you."

"I know," she whispered back.

Michael put on a Miles Davis record that Lisa's dad had given her for her sixteenth birthday and led Lisa over to the bed. Instinctively, she got in, but he didn't join her. From the bed, she watched, intrigued, as he took his dick into his hands and massaged it possessively with one hand. *Doesn't that hurt?*

He reached down onto the floor and came up with a foil Trojan packet. He ripped open the packet and rolled it onto his dick. Her heart raced as Michael came to bed. He kissed her, parting her thighs with eager hands. "You ready for me?"

Even though she wasn't, she nodded.

It hurt like nothing she'd ever experienced. The first thrust felt like someone was trying to pry her open with a crowbar. The spermicide reeked, and it evaporated quickly, leaving her bone dry. Tears welled up, and she bit down on her lip to stop them. After what seemed like forever, he collapsed on top of her, his head buried between the softest titties in the world. "Lisa," he gasped. "I love you so much."

She kissed his sweaty head. "I love you, too."

Only then did she realize that Miles had blown the same riff for over a minute. The record was skipping.

As time passed, Lisa had the crib on Grove Street to herself, enough times for Michael to show her different positions, ointments, colored ribbed condoms. Lisa practically hummed like a fine-tuned machine when, after hours and hours, they were done. But he was still going to Clemson on that scholarship, and she was doomed to go to Fordham, her mother's alma mater. "I refuse to send my daughter to Jockstrap U, down south nonetheless, just so you can be with Michael Bross," Barbara declared.

No matter how much she and Barbara argued, no matter how she begged her father to intercede, in the fall, she and Michael went their separate ways. After a semester of passionate, romantic, and sometimes pornographic letters and phone calls, Michael came home for Christmas. Something about him had changed, though. Time apart had changed them both. At the start of the spring semester, the letters suddenly stopped. Lisa never heard from Michael again. She did find out, though, that other guys thought she had the softest titties in the world.

Just then, the curtains to the dressing room flew open, and Lisa screamed, covering her breasts with her arms. Then she saw the blond head. "Fuck, Nina, how about a warning next time, huh?!" she cried.

"Sorry," Nina laughed, then shoved three dresses of different colors in Lisa's midsection. "Try these. If you don't like them, I'll get you another set. God, this is fun, *ja?*"

"*Ja,*" Lisa said, pissed. "Now close the curtain before I have to charge a quarter a head."

Nina complied, and Lisa sighed. She gazed down at the dresses in her arms. They were all so egregiously ugly.

5

Wisteria sat on the marble bathroom sink, her tail sweeping rhythmically from side to side. With hypnotic green eyes, she watched as Lisa smoothed red lipstick on her full mouth, then inspected her killer black dress in the full-length mirror behind the bathroom door. The intercom buzzed right then. "That's Nina!" Lisa exclaimed.

Wisteria leaped down onto the tile floor and followed Lisa into the small hallway. Lisa pressed the TALK button on the intercom. "Nina, is that you?" she asked.

"Yes," came Nina's voice, metallic-sounding in the box, "and you'd better look stunning!"

Lisa bent, staring down into Wisteria's little kitty face. "No wild parties while I'm gone," she laughed, then shook her head. *I'm talking to the cat.*

Lisa grabbed her purse, spritzed on some *Red Door,* flung her wrap over her shoulders, and left the apartment.

As she locked the door, she looked up at the night sky through the skylight in the hall. She hoped the wrap was enough. The hallway was always deceptively warm; the glass from the skylight held in heat, creating a nice little greenhouse effect. Lisa hurried down the hall and the two flights of stairs to the first floor, then went through the first glass door that was always locked, the door that led to the carpeted anteroom. She then stepped out into the night and deeply breathed in the cool fall air.

Nina, rocking a revealing red velvet dress with a matching bolero and blood-red stiletto pumps, was standing on the sidewalk. Lisa secretly wondered if there was any truth to the theory that beautiful people hung out with plain people to accentuate their assets, and if so, was that why Nina hung with her? Nina spun like a seasoned runway model. "You like?" she asked gleefully, already knowing the answer to her question.

"That is the shit, girl," Lisa said.

Nina stood, arms akimbo. "Todd Oldham," she announced.

"And they say professors don't make any money?" Lisa teased.

Nina snaked her arm within the crook of Lisa's, and they made their way across the street to Tim's bronze Isuzu Trooper. "Guess what?" Nina prompted.

"What?"

"Tim got his hands on an extra ticket, so someone else'll be joining us."

She didn't even smell a rat. "Who?"

The back passenger door of the Trooper opened, and Lisa saw Marc sitting inside. "Hi," he said sheepishly.

Marc Guerrieri slipped under her fix-up radar. Lisa turned to Nina, glaring daggers. Far from afraid, Nina looked quite pleased with herself. "Get in, sweetie," she prodded, pushing her toward Marc. "We're running late."

Lisa looked longingly over her shoulder at the door to her brownstone. She had two choices: make a run for it, or get in the car like a nice girl and play along. Just as

she was deciding, Marc held her squarely under her
armpits and gently helped her inside the SUV. His
thumbs inadvertently grazed her nipples. Lisa gasped
from a combination of surprise and desire. "This leap
up can be a killer," he said.

Her head was still reeling when he leaned across her,
closed the door with a solid *thunk,* and proceeded to
buckle her seat belt.

Tim turned around in the driver's seat, and he
looked so uncomfortable—undoubtedly forced to go
along with his wife's plan. "Well, Miss Lisa," he said.
"Shall we go?"

"Yes, darling," Nina said, getting in front next to her
husband. "Let's."

Tim eased the car from the curb and turned onto
South Fullerton Avenue. Lisa stared at Nina. She'd pay
later.

Janet Jackson's *Rhythm Nation—The Remix* hit them as
they entered the dimly lit foyer inside the Palladium.
But Lisa couldn't care less about Jimmy Jam and Terry
Lewis's techno wizardry. On top of being pissed at Nina,
she was remembering the last time she'd gone dancing.
Bryan had taken her to a club in Paterson on their third
date, the type of black club where the music was slamming but they frisked you and ran that whooping metal
detector across you to make sure you weren't strapped.
She and Bryan had practically fucked on the dance
floor, slow-dragging to the upbeat grooves and to the
slow jams, until after a half-hour, they flew in Bryan's
Celica to his apartment in Bloomfield, where they fucked
for the first time . . . for hours and hours. He had her
head swinging so that in the morning, when he asked
her to marry him, her body screamed *yes* before her
mind could catch up.

Nina and Lisa stripped off their wraps and gave them

to Tim and Marc respectively. "Can you men please check these?" she asked.

"Yes, I'm going to powder Nina's nose . . . real hard," Lisa declared.

Tim leaned in toward Marc. "Uh-oh," he whispered. "This is the part where they troop to the ladies' room and dog us behind our backs."

Lisa grabbed Nina's hand, dragging Nina away. "We'll be back."

Lisa pulled Nina through red-carpeted halls under high-vaulted ceilings until she found the swinging doors of the ladies' room. Lisa shoved her into the room's opulence. A thin crowd of high-maintenance women in designer dresses milled around, fixed makeup and hair in the huge mirror, and chatted mindlessly. A uniformed, middle-aged attendant, looking like the Latina embodiment for Donna Summer's hit "She Works Hard for the Money," sat patiently in her chair, in front of a dish of tips.

"If you rip Todd, our friendship is over," Nina laughed.

Lisa manically paced, trying to find the words through her anger at being manipulated. "Okay, let's examine the evidence," she began. "The invite to this party. You spring for this serious fuck-me dress. The sudden appearance of the . . ." air quotes . . . " 'extra ticket.' Marc Guerrieri in the fucking car! This is a two-page Agatha Christie."

Nina shrugged simply. "All right. You've found me out."

A brunette in a beaded black gown leaned in. " 'Scuse me, I couldn't help overhearing," she said. "Did you say Marc Guerrieri's here?"

Lisa looked at her in disbelief. *Gold digger!* "Yes," she snapped.

"Like, the writer, Marc Guerrieri?" the brunette persisted.

"Yes!" Lisa shouted.

As if motivated by a current of pheromones on the wind, the high-maintenance women emptied the ladies' room, save for the attendant. Lisa stared incredulously.

"Uh-oh," Nina laughed. "Competition."

"You make me so mad when you do this shit, Nina."

"What shit?"

"This playing fast and loose with people's lives."

Just as suddenly as the ladies' room cleared, Nina turned serious. She trained her grey eyes on Lisa with chilling intensity. *This must be the last thing the mongoose sees.* "Call it what you like," Nina declared. "I want my friend back."

"What are you talking about?" Lisa demanded. "I'm here."

"You've become your mother!" Nina stated.

"Well, you might as well hit me!" Lisa gasped.

"It's true," she said. "You've become Barbara. We used to shop, and go to concerts, and swill ice cream and Red Stripe lager and talk about men. Now you cry non-stop, and talk about your bills, and how much you think your life rots. I want my friend back!"

Ah, the ugly truth. Lisa felt her eyes moisten. She fidgeted with the candies in a dish on the counter. "I wish you'd've told me," she croaked.

"Would you have come?" Nina challenged.

Lisa thought a minute. Her days of getting tarted up for a guy were over. It was never worth it. "Probably not," she confessed.

Nina smirked, quite pleased with herself. "I rest my case," she said, taking her hand. "Come on. We've got to find Marc before those women do."

Marc and Tim checked the wraps and took their position by the stand, just as a tall, Waspy, corn-fed, Kendoll type sidled over. Marc recognized him . . . Greg Hayhurst, the anchorman on the six o'clock news. He stared at Marc, his too-blue-to-be-real eyes lighting up. "MarcAntonio Guerrieri!" Hayhurst cried effusively. "Tim, you never told us you knew MarcAntonio Guerrieri."

Tim gave Marc that he's-so-full-of-shit look over the top of Hayhurst's blow-dried head. "You never asked me, Greg," Tim said.

Hayhurst took Marc's hand, pumping it furiously. "MarcAntonio Guerrieri," he repeated. "Greg Hayhurst. I interviewed you on the *Today* show when *Benny Blues* first came out."

Ah, *Benny Blues*. When he was happily married to Michele, living in the City, creating together. What a difference eleven years made. "Of course," he said.

The smarm effect from Hayhurst was palpable. "You've got to come on the show to promote *Goombah,*" he insisted. "You've got to."

He had an instant appreciation for Linley and all the opportunists she kept at bay. "Just call my agent," he said, forever pleasant.

"Excellent," Hayhurst said.

With that, he nodded at Tim, then disappeared.

Tim shook his head. "Man, I'm sorry," he said. "This was supposed to be fun."

Marc laughed, shaking his head. "How were you to know that all your colleagues would solicit me for interviews?"

"*Goombah*'s a kick-ass book. Everyone wants a piece of you now."

"I can't keep up."

"Enjoy the moment."

Marc looked around the foyer, at the people who made a poor attempt at glancing over surreptitiously. "When I started writing, I always dreamed of this, the adoration. Now I wonder. I can't even talk to a friend in peace." He thought back to a second ago and laughed. "And that parade of women just now! What was *that* about?"

Tim shrugged. "Money and power turn women on, man."

He thought back to the car ride across the Hudson, how Lisa, in another black dress that played havoc with his groin, practically ignored him, seemed pissed at him even. "Lisa doesn't seem fazed," he said.

Tim conspiratorially leaned in, like he was about to drop a bomb. "That's 'cause even though Lisa's broke, she comes from money and power," he declared. "You know who her mother is? Two words—Billy Beaver."

Marc's mouth practically fell to the floor. The penny dropped. Of course. Her first name was Haley, her mother's maiden name, she'd said. "Barbara Haley-Martin?! Newbery Medal winner? Caldecott Medal winner?"

"That's the one," Tim confirmed. "Lisa's got pedigree."

"No wonder she's such a good writer," Marc mused.

Tim suddenly looked disgusted. "And a good woman. The shit she put up with from Bryan Livingston. *She* deserves a medal."

Marc tempered his rage. "I gather he wasn't Husband of the Year."

"Not even close," he scoffed. "The fucking-around she knew about but could never prove, the way he used her to help him get his MBA. You know, she had a miscarriage."

He thought of the chapter. "She mentioned it in passing."

A frown appeared between Tim's thick brows. Marc sensed a protective, big-brother vibe from him. "She was in Mountainside ER, with the kid dying inside her. Nina called me at 30 Rock to get me to bring Bryan home from Columbia. Don't you know that tired bastard finished his Econ final before he would come see to his wife?"

He remembered how he felt when he'd found out what Michele had done to their child. What man, no matter how he felt, would be oblivious to the death of his own flesh and blood, especially a life he'd created? "Dick!" he hissed.

"That's all right. In three months, she's gonna cut that zero and roll with a hero."

Ah. Tim and Nina were working in tandem to engineer a love match. "And I'm supposed to be John Wayne?" he laughed.

"Hey, you got the requisite blue eyes. And we're both guys here. Those same blue eyes have been giving Lisa that look all night. I know what you want to do."

Marc blushed, thankful for the sparse lighting. "I didn't know I was that transparent."

Just then, the record blended into the merciless beat and twangy guitars of Depeche Mode's *Strangelove*. "I know what you're thinking," Tim said. "You're getting up there. You've got all this money and success and no one to share it with. You like Lisa, but the racial climate being what it is, you don't want to risk getting played."

Marc was impressed. "What are you, The Amazing Kreskin?"

Tim chuckled. "No, Nina takes good notes. Nine years ago, when I met Nina, I was having the same crisis of faith. You know, both black and white folks think that all a brothah wants to do is bag some blonde so he could have what Massa had."

"What made your mind up for you?"

Tim elbowed him in the ribs. They both turned to see Lisa and Nina approach. Marc felt the characteristic tightening in his gut. In this setting, he again saw Lisa in a carnal light. The last woman he'd been with was Veronique, an interpreter at the French consulate, six months ago. Something shifted in his brain, and he was back to that night when he met Lisa at the party. The classroom seemed to be an interlude between moments in which he wanted to fuck her. He wondered what it would be like to be with her. He wanted to touch her breasts that stood at attention in that killer dress. A vivid mental picture of him thrusting into her, her shapely legs wrapped around his waist, seemed all too real. He buttoned his jacket over the pesky erection pressing against his trousers.

Tim looked at him like the answer was a given. "Look at the woman!" he said. "She's brilliant, she's the best wife and mother, and she's fine! And she loves me. That's hard to come by. If you're lucky enough to get it, you don't question the color of the wrapping it comes in."

Marc controlled his envy as Nina embraced her husband and kissed him squarely on the mouth. "Were you good while I was gone?" she asked.

"Were *you* good while you were gone?" Tim asked. "Our ears were on fire."

Nina took his hand. "Let's go and dance."

Marc watched them go, then shifted his gaze to Lisa. If only she knew about his mental pornographic film she just starred in. He got a teasing whiff of some delicious perfume that blended wonderfully with her body chemistry. "You realize you're stuck with me, don't you?" she said shyly.

"Lucky me," he said. "Let's go."

The last time Marc had danced, he was with Michele. They used to hang out at Nell's and the Limelight, shoot the shit with Tama Janowitz, and Brett Easton Ellis, and Jay McInerney, and other young writers and creative types who'd claimed the City as their own in the early part of the eighties, who drank and drugged and sucked the marrow of life. He and Michele were beautiful, popular, and madly in love.

Marc flashed ahead to his present reality. He was standing on a huge black speaker, feeling the beat from the dance music travel up through his feet and disperse throughout his body. Next to him, under the flashing colored lights, Nina and Tim were tearing it up. Nina was the embodiment of the rhythmless white girl, while Tim moved like he'd just stepped out of Alvin Ailey's studio. In front of him, Lisa gyrated passionately, her eyes tightly shut, like she was feeling the music. Marc launched into a steady groove, shifting his weight from one leg to another, snapping his fingers to the beat, all the while watching Lisa with loitering-with-intent eyes. *Can you jump me, please?*

Right then, the deejay mixed the Madonna cut into a slow song, and Lisa opened her eyes. She came closer to him, and instinctively, he encircled his arms around her. Adrenaline kicked in, the metallic taste of it in his mouth. He looked down at the curls on her head. He felt his fingers trail the length of the metal zipper of her dress, stopping at the top, fighting the urge to pull it down. He couldn't hold her close; she'd feel the wicked chubby he was working on.

"Want a drink?!" he shouted over the music, even though he wasn't thirsty.

She cupped a hand to her ear. "What?!"

Marc made a drink motion with his hand, and she nodded appreciatively. With hand signals, he told Nina and Tim where they were going, then Marc jumped down from the speaker to the floor. Carefully, he grabbed her by the waist and lifted her down. She tiptoed and said in his ear, "Did you see where the bar was?"

He took her hand. "Yeah. It's this way."

Protectively, he led her through throngs of tanked NBC employees and their guests. Unable to resist, he let go of her hand and slipped an arm around her waist. He felt her muscles and flesh bounce back against his fingers. She looked up at him in surprise. He smiled down at her. "I don't want to lose you," he said in her ear, and he realized he meant every word.

He looked around at the young couple who knew all the words to the songs, couples sucking face in the corners. "I'm getting old," he said, and he didn't realize he'd said it out loud. "This isn't as much fun as it used to be."

They were within spitting distance of the bar when, seemingly out of nowhere, a hyperkinetic blonde, in her forties, popped up, complete with her very own photographer. "MarcAntonio Guerrieri!" she squealed.

With all the overpowering sensory stimuli present, it took a second or two to register. Susan Simon, practically a New York institution, contributor to *The New York Times'* New York section called *Simon Says*. She'd always been very good to him, allowing him to plug his work. Nina always joked that Susan Simon was Tim's long-lost Jewish sister.

Marc smiled graciously. "Susan Simon!" he said. "At an NBC party nonetheless."

"I go where the gossip is," Simon said in her characteristic, raspy Long Island cadence. "I hear your book is flying off the shelves."

He felt his face go red. This part always made him feel uncomfortable, at a loss for words. He finally settled on, "People are very kind."

"Stop with the false modesty, Marc," Simon said. "Everyone's got high praise . . . your old friends Brett Easton Ellis, Jay McInerney, Tama Janowitz. They're saying this one is your best yet."

He was still trying to pick up the pieces from the hell that book put him through. "I promise you, high praise and the *Times* bestseller list were the last things on my mind when I was writing *Goombah*."

A revolving red light swept across Susan Simon's

face, showing a flicker of recognition in her green eyes. "That's right!" she declared. "Your wife had gone back to California without you, and that awful inmate almost killed you."

Memories were everywhere. He couldn't escape. Marc turned to Lisa. "She's thorough, isn't she?" he laughed uncomfortably.

Susan Simon trained her green eyes on Lisa. The red light swept across Simon's face again, and she looked like the Devil. "And who is this shy creature letting you do all the talking?" she asked, as if she'd caught on to some serious piece of gossip.

Marc brought her forward. "This is my friend, Lisa," he announced.

He had to hand it to Lisa. Faced with a New York institution, she handled herself like a cool customer. Then again, with Barbara Haley-Martin for a mother, she'd probably had venerable New York institutions over at her house all the time. "Nice to meet you," Lisa said, extending her hand.

Simon shook her hand graciously. "What's your opinion of him?" she asked.

Lisa looked at Marc. He tried to put his finger on what he saw in her eyes. "I think he's the greatest," she said simply.

He nailed it: naked admiration. She thought he was special. He smiled brilliantly at her. She winked at him. A blinding flash cut through the darkness right then, and Marc realized that the photographer accompanying Simon had snapped their picture.

Gradually, the blinding whiteness subsided, and they were back in the disco, in the previous moment. "Thanks, Marc," Susan Simon said. "Good luck to you, you hear?"

The bright spots playing before his eyes made her and her crony look like a Seurat painting. "Thanks, Susan," he said.

Just as suddenly as they'd appeared, Susan Simon and the photographer disappeared, swallowed up in a sea of partygoers.

Everyone wanted a piece of him. Everyone except Lisa. "I have an idea," Marc said.

"What?" Lisa asked.

"Let's get out of here," he suggested.

She thought for a second. "Okay."

An hour and one cab ride across the Brooklyn Bridge later, they were sitting on a green bench, staring at the Statue of Liberty in the blackness of New York Harbor. Roller skaters whipped past them on the cobblestones. Couples strolled leisurely. A couple of feet away, a patrol car did a cautious drive-by. Compared to the disco, this was tranquility central. Lisa sighed, at peace for the first time in a long time. "Brooklyn Heights. This is a nice slice of heaven," she said, turning to Marc. "So, tell me, Marc. Does this constitute the dreaded 'fraternizing'?"

Marc laughed. "Come into the English office tomorrow. I'll have Merilee write up the paperwork. We'll call it a mini-independent study."

Smart-ass. "You're full of shit."

There was a contemplative silence, like his thoughts were heavy. "Tim told me about your mom," he finally said. "She's brilliant."

So much for the peace and quiet. "It's not easy being the mediocre daughter of such a brilliant woman, Marc," she commented. "When my mother steps into a room, she sucks all the air out. And all the people in the room, giddy from oxygen debt, bow before her. You should see my mother work a book party. All those agents and readers killing each other for her acknowledgment. She's in her element."

"You two don't get along."

Understatement of the century. "I'm the swan's only baby . . . an ugly duckling at that."

"Stop that," he said gently. "You're a full 180 degrees from ugly and mediocre."

Yeah, right. She'd come to accept the fact that she was a poor facsimile of a great woman, and nothing she could've ever done would've changed that. "Barbara nurtured me in her own perverse way and taught me what she thought I needed to know," she said matter- of-factly. "When it was time to hit the lake, I went the other way, and she's been pecking at me ever since."

A look flickered across his face, as if he had a sense of what she was talking about. "You know how mothers are."

The only champion Lisa ever had in her household was her dad. Gabriel Martin treated her like a princess. He guided her, and when she made her youthful mistakes, he did not judge her. When Lisa's mother acted like a fucking lunatic, he treated her with humor, which pissed her mother off all the more. Gabriel Martin spoiled Lisa for any other man who would come into her life. She smiled at the thought of him. "I was more like my father," she said.

He looked surprised. "Was?"

She'd come to think of this moment as if she was having a dissociative episode, floating safely over her pain. "He died when I was twenty," she declared. "He was giving this woman a routine pelvic in his office and just slumped right over her."

"Oh my God," Marc whispered.

She laughed bitterly. "She thought he was getting fresh with her. He was only having a fatal heart attack."

A crisp breeze blew a stray wisp of hair into her face. Before she could, he raised a hand and gently caressed it away. She looked over at him, and she saw compassion in those dark blue eyes. She laughed, shaking her head. The last time she let a man get close, she ended up in divorce court. "Let's talk about you," she suggested.

"Me?" he laughed. "Nah, I'm boring."

"Yeah, all boring people have Susan Simon jocking them for interviews."

"Okay," he said, mentally girding his loins. "I'm Italian. Both parents are still alive. I'm from Fairfield. Third and last child. B.A., M.A., Princeton. Ph.D., NYU."

She'd learned this in the library. "You're right. Boring!"

"What do you want to know?!" he laughed.

"The juicy stuff!" she giggled. "Tell me how you met Michele."

He shook his head, looking down. He was savoring the memory. "I was an English major on scholarship at Princeton, thinking I was going to have to get a real job at Pabst Blue Ribbon in Newark like my old man when I graduated," he began. "My advisor, Dr. Branch, this crazy English bastard, had other ideas. He filled out the paperwork. Next thing I know, I'm at Oxford for my second year of grad school."

What were the odds? "I did my junior year in London," she said. "Even though my mother grew up there, I ran up against the worst culture shock!"

"So did I, but nothing like a woman to make a homesick Jersey boy forget he couldn't get Ray's Pizza in England."

Men. Hounds, all of them. Although the running joke was that you couldn't call men dogs, because dogs were loyal. "Michele?" she asked.

He seemed sad suddenly. "No, Christian," he said. "From Belfast." He stared out at the Statue of Liberty and sighed. "You know, Italian boys and Irish girls. I fell for her, like POW! I was thinking marriage, kids, and a life in occupied Northern Ireland."

"You break up?" she asked, her tone meant to soothe.

He looked at her, and she saw unadulterated pain and loss. "No, she was killed," he said quietly.

On instinct, she took his hand and squeezed it. "Oh, Marc," she said. "I'm so sorry."

He laced his fingers between hers. "It happened before the term ended. She was visiting a friend who was suspected IRA. Guilt by association. That's what the British soldiers who murdered her said."

"Is that when you wrote *When Irish Eyes Are Crying?*"

Marc shook his head. "No, later." A smile trembled across his mouth. "I channeled my grief in less healthy ways. After the term ended, I spent a month in Italy chugging Chianti, eating shitty pizza, and making condom stockholders very happy."

She nudged him. "So like men to fuck their way through their problems."

"Hey, I was twenty-two!" he laughed. "Allow for maturational reform here!"

"What happened when you got back to school?"

"Enter Michele. She was like Malibu Barbie come to life."

I know. I've seen her picture.

"I thought I could get any woman into bed with me," he said. "What twenty-two-year-old doesn't?"

"What thirty-nine-year-old doesn't?" she teased.

He snickered like a devious frat boy. "I approached Miss Aulisio, stated my intentions in the crudest way I could think of. To which she said, 'If your dick is as enormous as your ego, I may just take you seriously.' "

So, she's not the typical vapid blonde. "Go, Michele!" Lisa giggled.

"She took me seriously," he said, then winked.

She was still trying to figure out why her marriage went south. What made couplings with so much promise end up in the mushroom cloud of divorce? Michele and Marc looked so happy in their photo, so immersed in love for each other. With all they brought to the table, why weren't they immune? "What happened?" Lisa asked.

He looked like even he didn't know. His brow furrowed, and he looked away, as if he was wondering, too. "It's complicated," he said. "The right people fucked by circumstance."

A b-boy with a boom box sat on the bench next to theirs. Soul II Soul's "Keep on Movin' " played at discreet volume, blending into the background sounds of the City. Caron Wheeler sang sweetly over Jazzie B's slow beats. Goosebumps crept across Lisa's skin. She closed her eyes, moving to the beat. Jazzie was the man. "I love this song!" she moaned.

Marc got up from the bench and guided her to her feet. She looked at him in surprise. As if to answer, he slowly took her into his arms, holding her close. He led, and she followed, swaying to the rhythm. She laughed tentatively at first. After all, she'd never been one for public displays of affection, of dancing in public. But then, as the song progressed, she relaxed her body into the natural hollows of his. They fit perfectly together like two tectonic plates. His spicy cologne danced in her nostrils, invaded her brain, set up shop. She searched his face with her eyes. He looked at her like he'd known her all his life, like he treasured her. How the hell was she supposed to respond to that? *What is this? What am I feeling here?* "I think teacher-student's down for the count," she said, near-whispered.

"Like it's in the ring with Mike Tyson," he laughed softly in her ear.

They swayed to the rhythm, and she soaked in how hard his body felt against her, how deliciously masculine he smelled, how soft the hair at the nape of his neck felt sifting through her fingers. Finally, a man's touch didn't feel dirty anymore. She stayed in his arms even after the song faded out.

6

It came in grey hazes, morphing in fuzzy images and shadows. She was in the living room in the old house, the back of the couch pressed against her stomach, crushing the air out of her chest. Bryan had her bent over the back of the couch. His butt cheeks clenched and unclenched as he thrust violently into her. The pain seared straight up her spine. She screamed on the air she could force out of her bruised rib cage. He laughed maniacally and he covered her mouth. "Ooh, baby . . . I missed you," he moaned.

She sobbed loudly through the fingers clamped over her mouth. Snot flew from her nose and ran down her face. Bryan thrust without mercy. "Aw, baby!" he gasped. "Your ass is so fucking tight . . ."

The sensation overwhelmed him. He pulled his hand away as he came, lurching against her back. She straightened up, and with all she had, she let out a blood-curdling scream . . .

Lisa started into consciousness in her futon, her breathing labored. Sweat drenched her to the bone. Tears she'd shed in her sleep left her face hot and wet. Wisteria bolted off the mattress into the semidark apartment. Her heart boomed so loudly in her chest that she could practically taste it. Maniacally, her eyes darted around her, and slowly she realized that she was surrounded by her familiar reality. "Shit," she whispered.

Belatedly, she realized the telephone on the side table was ringing like an invader in the quiet early morning. She snatched up the receiver. "Hello," she breathed.

"Lisa, it's Jaye Barraclough."

Lisa had had Jaye on retainer for almost a year and a half, and Jaye still announced herself like they were meeting for the first time. Lisa pictured her, six feet tall, a dark, thin black woman with a short Afro, wearing a smart linen suit, perched behind her polished wooden desk in her opulent office.

Lisa looked over at the clock. Glowing black hands on a white face pointed out the time. "Jaye?!" she cried. "It's 6:45!"

"I hope you truly know what time it is, my sistah," Jaye declared. "I just got a letter from Bryan's shark. They want half the money from the sale of the house and no spousal support for you."

The familiar headache seared through her left temple. "What?!"

"Monaghan's also set a date to depose you. October 6."

Lisa tried to wrap her groggy mind around this new development. "He was saying that shit on the phone on Tuesday," she mumbled. "I didn't think he meant it."

"Lisa, this is a divorce," Jaye reminded her, and Lisa could actually see her roll her eyes at Lisa's naiveté. "He means everything he says and does. And why were you talking to him? That's my job."

First A.J., now Jaye. "He called me at work, Jaye," Lisa snapped. "I had to answer my phone."

Silence. Lisa could hear her thinking. "This smells

like some last-ditch attempt to hold up these proceedings," Jaye finally theorized.

Not the way Bryan broke camp barely two weeks after graduation. "He was the one who wanted the divorce," Lisa reminded her.

"Are you sleeping with him, Lisa?" Jaye demanded, her tone accusatory. "Because if you are, everything we've worked for's gone to hell."

The very thought made Lisa want to puke up her entrails. "After what he did to me?" she sobbed. "For hours and hours? How could you ask me that?"

"Lisa . . . about the rape kit," Jaye said gently. "I have it."

Her stomach roiled. Everything flooded through her psyche . . . the rape kit, the cops and their well-meaning questions, the Essex County DA looking at her like the whole thing was some misunderstanding between husband and wife, being raped again when, despite there being no marital rape exemption in the state of New Jersey, the DA decided he wasn't going to prosecute. Bryan walked away scot free, smirking at her as he left the Essex County courthouse. "How'd you get that?" Lisa asked, her voice trembling. "Why'd the Montclair police keep it?"

"Our dumb luck, I guess," Jaye said. "I have everything. The reports. The pictures . . ."

"Oh my God, the pictures, too?!"

"Lisa, we can nail Bryan if you'd let me use the kit."

The ugly reality slowly sank in, and all she could do was cry. This was the shit that sent her to The Couch, revealed that to her very core, she was weak. "Jaye, I can't do this again," she wept.

Jaye, of course, was the antithesis of weak. "You realize you're sending me to a gunfight with a can of mace."

"This is private!"

"This is a divorce. Get real! 'No fault' doesn't necessarily mean 'no acrimony,' Lisa. Women historically get screwed financially in divorce. We've got to use every advantage to win."

She squeezed her eyes shut and sighed. She'd just gotten up, and already she was tired. "Well, we're going to have to do it without entering pictures of my private parts into evidence," she stated, then hung up.

She barely made it to the bathroom. She slapped up the toilet seat and surrendered as hot, acidic vomit cascaded up her throat and splashed into the bowl.

Marc sipped his coffee and stared across the misty, early-morning quarry. He actually would've enjoyed the view, if the familiar dull ache in his abdomen had not risen up to accompany this particular phone message. "MarcAntonio Pasquale Fiore, are you avoiding me?" came a digital imprint of Michele's voice through the earpiece, eerily, as if she were in the room with him. "Please call me. I have a favor to ask you, and I don't want to do it over the phone. 'Bye, sweetie."

He played it repeatedly, curiosity eating him alive. *What other fucking favor can I do for you, Michele? I let you go, didn't I?*

The very first favor he'd done for her played in his head like a video of happier times. She wanted someone to go down to London with her for an Henri-Georges Clouzot film festival, and she asked him. He was surprised, considering she'd given him a hard time since Day One. She'd made it clear that he would be nothing more to her than a friend. He'd accepted that, even though he knew he was falling for her. Hard.

The night before, though, she'd broken a contact lens and had to wear her thick dark glasses. He knew she felt self-conscious. All he could think of was how cute, and smart, and funny she was. Miss Rabid Feminist had a shy, soft side.

They only barely made it through *Diabolique*. After the movie, they silently left the theater, found the closest bed and breakfast, and made love until the sun rose. "It *is* bigger than your ego," she laughed afterward, basking in the glow.

The teacher function in the voice mail system said that, to erase the message, he should press seven. Marc pressed down on seven like he was trying to purge her from his mind. *I'm going to be that writer who eats his gun!*

With his hand pressed to his throbbing gut, Marc dialed the seven numbers for his internist's direct line. Marcus Davidson was the last stop on the train that had begun with delicate microsurgery to repair his torn flesh, countless hours of painful physical therapy, and powerful analgesics. All the while, Michele had been at his side through his agony. Which was why it hurt worse than his injuries when she dropped her news on him and abandoned him just as he was getting better.

"Dr. Davidson," Marcus said.

"Hey, Marcus, it's me," Marc announced.

"It's the Fake Doctor!" Marcus laughed. "What's up?"

Only Marcus could get away with that. After all, they were inseparable throughout high school in Fairfield. "Look, Wise Ass, it's happening again."

"Your stomach," Marcus knowingly concluded.

"Can you phone in the Tylenol 3 prescription for me?"

There was silence on the other end, and Marc heard papers rustling from the other end. "Okay," Marcus finally said from the other end. "I'll call it in to your drugstore. One month's supply, with one refill. I also want to see you in here at the end of next month, okay? The nurse will call you to schedule the appointment."

"Thanks," Marc said gratefully.

Marcus laughed. "*No mench,*" he said. "Remember. Next month."

"Next month," Marc sighed.

He hung up, relieved. *Next month.* He wondered when they were going to stop poking and prodding him.

He diverted his attentions to the *Times* in front of him. Instinctively, he opened the paper to the New York section. Susan Simon's column drew his attention. More importantly, he saw the photo that her companion had snapped. There he was with Lisa, looking like they belonged together despite the obvious difference. "Guerrieri and friend attend NBC soiree," the caption read. Instantly, his mood brightened. She was the obvious cure for his ambivalence.

But in a day shaping up to be a testament to harmonic convergence, Nina stormed in and angrily tossed *The Star Ledger* down on his desk. Marc looked up. He'd never seen her so pissed. "Well, good morning to you, too!" he laughed.

She pointed to the paper. "Look at this shit!" she prompted.

Obediently, Marc examined the paper. Above the fold of the newspaper, a staff reporter detailed the latest developments of the Yusuf Hawkins case across the river. "The boys talked?" he asked, somewhat surprised. Those kids were the type who reveled in the Mafia mystique, that *Omertà* shit.

"Not there," Nina said impatiently. She pressed her index finger on the paper, on the story next to that of Yusuf Hawkins. "Here!"

Obediently, Marc read, " 'Rutgers-Newark. An Italian-American male was beaten by a group of African-American males last night on University Avenue. The student, identified as Americo Chirieleison, was rushed to University Hospital following the attack. His condition is stable but critical. Five members of the Sigma Nu Pi fraternity have been arrested in connection with the attack'."

Right then, he felt how he imagined the legions of

black people felt across the tri-state area, the growing legion of students demonstrating in the quad downstairs. Furious. Frustrated. Helpless. "Great," he spat. "We've got ourselves a nice little race war going on here."

"Has everyone lost their bloody minds?!" Nina cried.

Rick's door had been closed all morning. At first, Lisa assumed he was working feverishly on the year-end report. Then she realized that no writers or designers had gone in or out of the office all morning. She found Genie in an unflattering knit dress with a woolen dog splayed across her bullish chest. Genie was hunched over a filing cabinet, her facial expression clearly speaking to the lack of meaning in her life. "Hey, Genie, is Rick okay?" Lisa asked.

Without even turning around, Genie grumbled, "How should I know?"

You could check, bitch.

Lisa tentatively approached Rick's office and stared at him through the strip of glass in the wall. He sat at his desk in the dark, gloomy day, watching a flock of long-necked Canada geese drop green turds onto the asphalt of the industrial complex. She knocked on the door. Rick continued to stare at the geese. She knocked again. No answer. Finally, she opened the door and stuck her head in. "Rick, I'm going to grab some lunch," she said. "You want anything?"

Rick started, staring at her with wild, wet grey eyes. "Lisa!" he laughed sheepishly. "I didn't hear you come in."

Lisa closed the door and moved in closer. "Rick, are you okay?"

He made a weak attempt at pulling his supervisor demeanor together. "The report?"

Fuck the report. "The report's fine," she assured him.

"We're all working like good little drones. I'm going to grab some lunch from the caf. Can I get you anything?"

He sighed. "I don't feel much like eating."

Lisa sat on a corner of the desk. "Rick, I've known you for five years, and you know all of my business," she said, gearing up for a painful trip down memory lane. "That day after Bryan left me, I sat at my desk outside and cried my eyes out. And there was this guy who brought me tea, and held my hand, and let me blow my nose on his clean white hanky. And he took that snotty, eyeliner-stained hanky back, too."

A smile tugged at the corners of Rick's mouth. "I remember that day," he said, nodding.

She leaned in closer. "Rick. What's wrong?"

He gazed at her, his head cocked to one side, then turned again to stare at the geese. "My father's dying," he announced, as matter-of-factly as he'd asked about the year-end report.

As if Scottie had beamed her there, Lisa was back in her dorm room at Fordham after her last final when a tearful Barbara had come to her room, unannounced, to tell her that Gabriel had had a fatal heart attack while examining a patient in his office. Lisa remembered hearing screaming and seeing faces stretched out for miles before her. It was only later that she realized the screams were hers. She sobbed and screamed her way through every conscious moment, until Barbara had her hospitalized for acute depression.

At the institution in Frenchtown, a picturesque enclave just across the Delaware River from Pennsylvania, Lisa took her lithium like a good girl, rode and groomed horses, picked vegetables from the garden, and dutifully attended every session until finally, her pain was manageable enough that she could return to school. But she felt that loss in some way every day she breathed.

Lisa took his hand, looked down at it, with each nail painstakingly manicured, the left wrist accentuated with a gold Rolex. *Pull it together, Lisa.* "Rick," she croaked, her throat closing up before she could say more.

"Prostate cancer," Rick said. "Apparently they caught it too late. The doctors think he has less than a month left."

"Why aren't you home in Pennsylvania?"

"Because I've got to stay here. Ever since Mom called yesterday, I've had to be this fucking superman. For her and my sisters. And Pat and the kids."

He looked up at Lisa, and her heart squeezed painfully in her chest. "I spoke to him on the phone, Lisa. He taught me how to be a man. Now he's dying, and I can't do anything about it."

Fathers were special. Lisa remembered Gabriel, how much he reminded her of James Earl Jones, his laugh, hanging with him at the movies, his killer record collection. Her sixteenth birthday, Barbara wanted to make it this annoying affair replete with party favors, but Gabriel overruled her, took Lisa to the City, and snuck her into the Village Gate to hear Nina Simone sing. They drank champagne and sang along, and when the photographer took a picture of "Sir and his date," Lisa had actually forgotten she was an awkward kid with acne and baby fat.

"You're right, Rick," Lisa said. "You can't stop your dad from dying. But the beauty part is all the things he taught you that you can share with Sean and Megan. That's the way your dad'll still be alive."

Rick blinked, and tears spilled down his lashes and reddening face. "Lisa," he said, but it came out like a garbled mess. He threw his arms around Lisa's waist, buried his head in her lap, and sobbed like a baby. "What am I gonna do?!" he cried.

Lisa held him close, rocking him gently. She wished Barbara had done the same for her, instead of paying strangers to hug her and medicate her when she'd grieved for her dad. She looked down at Rick's bald spot. "Everything's gonna be all right," she whispered. "I promise."

Marc buttoned his tweed woolen coat against the windy black night and approached Adam's rambling white country house, perched high on a hill in Little Falls. On a clear day, you could see the SCNJ quarry from Adam's living room. Marc's classic ambivalence reared its ugly head whenever he came to visit Adam, which was often. Marc made more money than his brother, even though Adam was four years older and had his own thriving architectural firm. But Adam was richer in ways Marc only dreamed of. Adam had the home, Diane, the aggressively devoted wife, Lily, the adorable child. Adam had the life that Marc wanted. Adam's life both sustained Marc and saddened him all at once. *Sick fuck, jealous of your own brother . . .*

Seconds after Marc rang the doorbell, Adam threw open the door. Marc saw a taller, heavier version of himself, only with friendly brown eyes. Adam's eyes brightened behind his trendy specs—picked out by Diane, no doubt. All the fashion sense in the family went to Marc.

The Brothers Guerrieri warmly embraced. "You fucking *faccia di mort'!*" Adam laughed. "You actually have time for your big brother, huh?"

Marc grabbed his crotch. "I got your *faccia di mort'.* Right here!"

"What did Diane say to get you over here?" Adam asked.

Marc recalled Diane's surreptitious phone call. "She said, 'Chicken *Francese.* Dress nice.' "

Adam took the bottle of white wine that Marc was carrying and let him into the soothing ivory foyer. Scratching his salt-and-pepper head, he examined the label. The look in his eyes said he approved. "You could always pick good wine," he said.

Affirmation from Adam meant more than praise from his legion of fans. He beamed proudly. "One of my many talents," he chuckled.

Adam elbowed him in the ribs. "Help you get laid?" he teased.

When had he last been laid? "No comment," he said.

Lily, Adam's five-year-old daughter, came bounding down the stairs, and Marc's world stopped. He looked at her and all he could see was Diane pushing her into the world, this little squealing, scowling, writhing creature. And he had looked over at his brother. The guy he'd shared the same room with when they were kids was now this creature's father. Emotion had crushed his chest, and he'd sobbed loudly.

He looked at Lily now, and he instantly missed the child he'd almost had. "Uncle Marc!" she cried happily, her green eyes wide.

Marc scooped her up and kissed her in the crown of her brown curls. She smelled like baby lotion and shampoo. "Hi, Lillabelle!" he laughed. "How are you?"

"Fine," she said, all excited. "Guess what?"

He stroked her pink cheeks. "What?"

"Daddy's getting me a puppy for Christmas," she announced.

"Only if Mommy says yes," said Adam in that parental tone that Marc knew only too well.

Diane came down the stairs just then. Despite the responsibilities of having just made partner, running her home, and raising her child, she epitomized blond cool. She wasn't particularly stunning; historical novelists would've called her handsome. "And Mommy says no," she pointedly declared. She kissed Marc's cheek. "Hello, Marco."

Marc glared at her with mock animosity. "Mommy's mean, huh?"

Diane's smile was sly, devious. "Now, would a mean

person ask one of her lawyer friends over to keep you company?"

The meal, the request to dress nicely . . . the trap snapped shut. *Shit!* He turned to his brother. "Adam, you let her do this to me again!" he said.

Adam threw up his hands. "Hey, I'm Switzerland with this matchmaking thing. Jimmy's here, too."

Marc had the perfect solution. "So, give her to Jimmy."

Adam shook his head. "She's Sarah Lawrence. Jimmy's Joe Construction Worker. He wouldn't know what to do with her."

Diane stared at them disapprovingly. "I like how you two Neanderthals are discussing passing my friend around like a . . ." she leaned in, covering Lily's ears, "J-O-I-N-T."

Lily wriggled free. "Mommy, what's a J-O- . . . ?"

Diane playfully pinched her cheek. "Never mind, you," she laughed.

He was there, he was dressed, and he'd brought wine. What could he do? Turn around like a pussy and walk out? He sighed, resigned to his fate. "What's her name?"

"Eastley," Diane replied.

Eastley. "Nice Italian girl," Marc sarcastically commented.

Diane laughed. "I'll get everyone for dinner."

Diane stepped down into the sunken living room. They watched her go. Then Marc whacked Adam in the arm. "Ow!" Adam laughed.

Clearly, no one was feeling Marc's pain. "I could kill you," he whined.

Lily held Marc's face. "Uncle Marc, what's a fach . . . um . . . fachie?" she tried to ask.

"Faccia di mort"? It means 'face of death,' sweetie," Marc answered.

She looked like she was wrestling with the concept. "Death has a face, Uncle Marc?"

Marc peered into the living room and saw Eastley's flaming frizz of red hair and her thin form in black crushed velvet. It was going to be a long night. "We'll see, sweetie," he said, filled with dread.

For someone who was only Italian by Injection, Diane cooked like she was raised at some nonna's thick-stockinged knee in Bay Ridge, or Bensonhurst, or even Bloomfield. In fact, Adam's ambivalence over whether he wanted to marry Diane disappeared when he tasted her sauce. He'd raved that it was better than Rosalie Guerrieri's, and Marc guiltily agreed. Diane's lemony, garlicky Chicken *Francese* over linguine, deliciously served with fresh antipasto, melted in Marc's mouth. And her tiramisu, with the ladyfingers soaked in espresso, and the mascarpone, and chocolate . . . he was already planning for that extra lap around the track at Brookdale. So focused on his palate, he purposely ignored Eastley, perpetually smiling, her features thin and pinched, strategically placed next to him at the table.

Adam, Eastley, and Jimmy LaFrat, Marc and Adam's cousin, sat around the table nursing espressos, Diane, green tea, and Lily, a glass of milk. "I bought your book today, Marc," Eastley announced in a voice that sounded as if she'd been sucking on a helium balloon. "I wanted to see what you were all about."

Nonetheless, Marc was the gentleman Adam had raised him to be. "Hand to God, I've never been an enforcer for the mob," he laughed.

Adam leaned over and wiped his daughter's crusty mouth. "That we know of," he interjected, teasing.

Eastley laughed, this horrid sound, like a nails-rustling-on-tin sound that Marc remembered from working construction during his summers in college. He stared incredulously at her, and he realized he wasn't alone at the table. As an attorney, she must've had an incredible case clearance rate; what judge would want to listen to her talk for any length of time?

For the love of God, Marco, change the subject! "So, Jimmy, *cugeen*, what's up with you, man?" Marc asked his cousin across the table. "I haven't seen you since last Christmas."

Jimmy, the son of Rosalie's older sister Terri, could've been out of a Martin Scorsese flick: short, thick-necked, unenlightened, fiercely Italian. In short, he was the guy who popped anyone in the mouth who threatened Marc when they were kids, playing in Brooklyn. He shook his head on that bullish stump of a neck. "I almost didn't get here, Marco," he complained. "Between Dinkins winnin' the primary and Al Sharpton leading marches through Brooklyn, traffic's been a bitch."

Adam glared at him disapprovingly, pointing at Lily. "Yo, Jimmy, language?" he cautioned.

Jimmy got that "I-fucked-up" expression on his craggy face. "A bitch is a female dog," he explained, looking like he knew full well his attempt to dig himself out was piss-poor.

Diane shot him that yeah-right look. "In a perfect world," she said.

Eastley piped up in that annoying voice. "I voted for Koch."

"Ay yo. Giuliani!" came Jimmy's ringing endorsement.

As far as Marc was concerned, neither of them knew what they were talking about. "Koch didn't do squat in twelve years, and Giuliani's answer to everything is to throw people in prison," he stated.

"That's a good answer, no matter what the question," Jimmy countered.

"What prisons, Jimmy?" Adam asked. "There's hardly any room for the people they got there."

Jimmy leaned in toward Eastley, obviously in search

of an ally. "This is Home of the Bleeding Heart Liberal, honey," he scoffed.

Diane looked lovingly over at her husband, and he looked the same way at her. Two people together so long they even had the same opinions on the important things. The green-eyed monster popped up again in Marc's face like toast. "Adam's right," Diane said. "If we spent half as much on rehabilitating criminals as we did on warehousing them, the world would be a better place."

Lily's eyes darted back and forth between the combatants, like she was watching a tennis match. "Mommy," Lily said, "what's . . . ?"

Diane looked down at her. "Just a second, honey—grownups are talking."

"We've tried nothing, and we've tried prisons," Marc said. "Dinkins is the only one with a humanist agenda."

"Sharpton's got him in his pocket," Jimmy declared, ill-informed as usual.

Jimmy sounded to Marc like those assholes screaming at black folks and holding watermelons on the TV. A part of him imagined that Jimmy was just fine with what happened in Bensonhurst that night. But it was Adam who broached the subject. "Why, 'cause he's black?" Adam asked.

"They all stick together," Jimmy stated confidently, like he was the expert on black people.

Lily again tried to enter the conversation. "Mommy, what does . . ."

Diane looked down at her again, this time less patiently. "One minute, Lily," she said firmly, then focused her intense grey stare on Jimmy. "What a narrow-minded thing to say."

Jimmy drained his wineglass, then dropped the bomb. "I never thought I'd see the day they'd let a moolie get this close to Gracie Mansion."

Nobody could believe it. Marc knew people who thought that way. The whole Yusuf Hawkins situation alerted him to the fact that some of his people felt that way. He just didn't want to believe that shit could come from someone in his own family. But then again, why was he even surprised? That desire to protect your own from the enemy that had made his cousin so tough had become irrational, affecting the ability to discern who the enemy was.

Adam put down his napkin and looked Jimmy unflinchingly in the face. "I'm not having that in my house, Jimmy," he said, his voice stern, grave. "One more, cousin or not, and you won't be back."

Jimmy looked away in shame, and Eastley followed suit. Marc looked over at his brother and he couldn't have been more proud of him.

Then a little voice broke the silence again. "Mommy?" Lily said.

Diane sighed. "Yes, sweetie?"

Lily looked up at her mother with serious green eyes. "What does 'get laid' mean?" she asked innocently.

Marc was stunned for a second, then he remembered his little exchange with Adam in the foyer, when they were talking about the wine. Adam grimaced. Diane looked away, laughing despite her embarrassment. Eastley did her horrendous nails-on-tin thing, and Jimmy roared, his social gaffe seemingly forgotten. "I've gotta keep her away from you boys," Diane said.

Adam and Marc, the enlightened Italian males, cleaned up while Diane entertained Jimmy and Eastley. Marc marveled at how the old-world attitudes toward women knowing their place didn't seem to stick with them for some reason. After all, the first time he'd brought Michele home to meet the family, he saw nothing wrong with Michele watching the Knicks game with the fellas while he and the women cleaned up.

However, Rosalie and Suzanne, Marc's older sister, lost it. They glared barbs from the kitchen at Michele in the living room as she drank beer Marc's dad made at work and yelled when the Knicks' point guard shot for three points. "Just 'cause your prissy Northern Italian book bitch got some college don't mean that she can't help out, Marco," Suzanne had declared. "You'd better train her right."

Marc had been dumbstruck. "She's not a dog I have to train, Sue," he'd protested in defense of his woman. "If she wants to watch the game, that's her prerogative."

" 'Prerogative,' " Suzanne had repeated mockingly. "Already he's a p-whipped snob."

Marc, for the life of him, couldn't figure out why they were so angry. He did know that his famous temper was on a slow boil. "Fuck you, Suzanne!" he'd hissed.

"Ma!" Suzanne had whined.

"Language, MarcAntonio," Rosalie had said. "You get a little culture, and you act like a *gavone* with your family. It's that blonde, and she's going to hurt you, son."

After the final divorce decree, they didn't say "I told you so." They helped him move his belongings from the City to his condo in Clifton. Doug, Suzanne's husband, even helped him paint. Marc hated that they were right.

Flash ahead fifteen years to Adam's kitchen. The dishwasher ran quietly. Marc and Adam were at the sink, Marc washing and Adam rinsing the last of the pots, just like they used to do when they were kids. But what happened at the table still resonated, particularly since he had a totally different take on blacks. Hell, he had one black woman in particular in his sights. "That fucking Jimmy," he said angrily. "I could've popped him right in the mouth."

Adam nodded in agreement. "Jimmy's not the most liberal of Italian souls."

"Where'd he get that fucked-up belief system?"

Adam nudged him. "Shh! Some of us are racists," he said sarcastically.

Adam stacked the last copper-bottomed pot in the drain. While Marc dried his hands, Adam opened the fridge, pulled out a couple of Michelobs, and popped off the tops. He passed one to Marc. "So, what do you think of Eastley?" he chuckled.

Marc rolled his eyes, that laugh playing itself over in his head. God, that was what was waiting out there for a single guy. "Don't even."

They sat at the kitchen table. "You know she and Diane are in the living room, debriefing," Adam teased.

"You need to talk to your wife."

"She's doing it 'cause she loves you, and she's got a vested interest in getting your knob polished."

"Eastley ain't the answer, bro. That voice would make a dildo go limp!"

They laughed uproariously. Tears came to Adam's eyes. "Oh shit!" he hollered.

"What's with those Sarah Lawrence girls?"

"Must be something in the air that makes them freaks. My wife knows the combination to my safe, my friend. The only challenge is keeping it down so we don't wake the kid."

It must've been something about blondes. Michele was like that. He still couldn't figure out how she could be the ultimate Phi Beta Kappa one minute, and in the next, could give exquisite head that left him quivering like gelatin. *Michele.* "Speaking of wives," he said tentatively, "guess who's getting married. Michele."

Adam's mouth dropped. "Get the fuck out!" he cried. "To that Kieran guy—the low-budget Timothy Leary?"

Marc scratched at the paper label on his beer bottle. "Yup."

Adam studied him. "And you're feeling . . ."

Marc thought for a minute, trying to find the words. "Torn," he finally confessed. "I'm trying to figure out what I really feel for her. And I'm ... well, there's this other woman ..."

"Your friend from the New York section," Adam concluded knowingly.

Marc nodded. "Lisa."

"Who's black."

"I think I'm falling in love with her."

There. He'd said it. Put it out there in the universe. He pondered what he'd done.

"You gonna tell me more, or am I supposed to guess?" Adam asked.

He hadn't realized the silence was that long. He laughed quietly, let his mind enjoy his memories of her. "I met her through Nina. Then funniest thing, she wound up in my class." He sipped his beer. "What else can I say? She's twenty-nine. She's divorcing this major dickhead ..."

Adam held up a hand, and Marc steeled himself. "Okay, stop," Adam said. "Just running this through my left brain here. You think you're in love with one of your married black students who is ten years younger than you."

Should've kept your fucking mouth shut. "I'm a professor," he declared, taciturn. "I know the scent of an impending lecture."

"Have you thought this through?"

"Repeatedly."

"The age thing may not be such a big deal, but the race thing? You heard that venom that came from your own cousin's mouth."

Marc shrugged. Who said it was supposed to make sense? "Hey, I know."

"Dude, the minute you sleep with her, you're committing adultery."

This from Adam, the two of them lapsed Catholics. "There's no logic below the navel."

But Adam persisted. "And suppose this thing with her crashes and burns? I read about women suing professors for abusing their power positions over this shit and winning. It was even on *Oprah.*"

Great. The Oprahfication of America manifesting itself in his life. Marc rolled his eyes. "Well, if it was on *Oprah,* then it must be a massive social problem!" he commented sarcastically.

"Okay, settle down," Adam said gently, like he was talking to Lily. "You're my baby brother. I'm just looking out for you."

Marc sorted through his long-term memory, finding something there to describe just what he was feeling about Lisa, what the attraction was. "Remember when you came down to Princeton to visit me that time . . . you know, when Yoko Ono was there?" he asked.

Adam had this faraway look behind his eyes, then he looked like *Aha!* He snapped his fingers. "You were trying to impress that girl who wouldn't shave her pits," he said, then hit the table repeatedly as the memory flooded back bit by bit. "Adriane. She was the hairiest woman I'd ever seen! She ended up giving you crabs."

That's the shit you'd remember. "Oh, like you'd turn down primo weed and pussy without strings," Marc said.

"This isn't about me," Adam laughed.

"Anyway," Marc purposefully segued, "I'm talking about Yoko. Remember she did that performance piece, where someone would cut her clothes off, piece by piece, until she was sitting there naked on the stage?"

"Yeah," Adam recalled. "She called it *Cut Piece.*"

"Every morning I get up, I feel just like that."

"What, like you want to break up the Beatles?"

"No, *stunad.* Everybody's cutting away at me, wanting a piece of me. Very few people in my life don't do that. Lisa's one of them. Get it?"

Adam was quiet, letting it sink in. "You're taking a hard road, Marco," he finally said. "She feels the same way about you, though."

Marc beamed. "Yeah? How do you know?"

Adam sipped his beer. "The way she looked at you in that picture? Man, she's digging you in the worst way."

7

Dean Tom Stefanowski looked around the chancellor's office, trying not to be impressed but failing miserably. He wondered what cherrywood forest had laid down its life to provide Chancellor Swift with the dark furniture, polished to a burnished richness. Stefanowski looked around at the naked opulence in the office, at the oil paintings, at Swift's numerous diplomas and accolades vulgarly displayed in frames on the wood-paneled walls.

Stefanowski had seen other faculty members experience the heady intoxication of being allowed into Swift's inner sanctum. All the times he'd been in this office, all he could think about was retreating to his office in the Shaw Field House. From his childhood in Syracuse, to being a starting cornerback on the Syracuse University football team . . . experiences which led him to his gig as dean of the athletics department at SCNJ, a third division school but a great program nonetheless. He'd only embraced the prissy trappings of academe so that he could live his two passions that had sustained him during the sixties at SU—athletics and activism. As both dean and the faculty advisor of the Student Government Association, he was able to do just that.

Swift looked down at his desk calendar, which had entries in ink at every hour line. "Hi, Tom, how is everything?" Swift asked with that practiced, faux-sincere smile that Stefanowski knew all too well.

Stefanowski dispensed with the niceties. "Thank you for seeing me, Donald," he said, then showed Swift the memo in his hands.

Swift's brows crinkled in his extra-tanned face. "What's this?"

"I was about to ask the same thing," Stefanowski said. "You denied the Black Student Union's request to represent SCNJ at Sharpton's march through Bensonhurst two weeks before Thanksgiving?"

The fake sincerity was gone in a second, replaced by a palpable air of authority. "Yes, I did, Tom."

"They want to know why."

Swift laughed disdainfully. "Because I'm the chancellor, Tom," he said.

Stefanowski persisted. "They want to know how you can have a say in what goes on in student government. SGA fees fund trips like these, not college money."

"SGA fees are college money," Swift declared.

Idiot. "You're on shaky ground here, Donald," Stefanowski countered. "All these kids want is to join other school organizations—black and white—at this march to protest the shooting of Yusuf Hawkins."

Swift was unmoved. "Next, the kids from the Italian Club will want to use our funds to go to Rutgers Newark to protest the beating of Americo Chirieleison."

"And, as faculty advisor for the SGA, I'm telling you that you're overstepping your bounds by intervening this way in student government."

"We're not going to have a pissing contest about this, Tom. SCNJ's about to become a university. I don't want this place connected to militants like the Reverend Al Sharpton or anybody else. They won't go, and that's final."

Stefanowski knew if they took this to the field, he would be able to use Swift like a tackle dummy to get his way. Pity that life didn't take place on the gridiron. He'd have to make his point in more articulate ways. "You'll have my strong protest of this decision on your desk by end of business today, Donald," he stated.

"Whatever," Swift said, obviously not threatened. "And if the niggers or the wops do anything to jeopardize SCNJ's university bid, I will personally yank their charters myself."

Stefanowski looked at this racist bigot in his nicely pressed suit, in his opulent office. Sometimes life was such an unfortunate paradox.

Oh, God, why today?

As usual, Lisa was running late for work. What made the day not like any other was that she was going to have to leave early for Bryan's fucking deposition. And to cap the day, she was cradling the phone between her ear and neck, listening to Barbara's British-accented mother guilt coming through loud and clear. "Melissa, you weren't raised to be a failure at anything," Barbara declared. "Especially marriage."

Lisa could picture her, languishing on her own private beach in Eleuthera. What the fuck did she know about her problems? "Ma, I worked with what I was given," she said. "Not everyone's lucky enough to marry a man like Gabriel Martin."

"You think he came that way?" Barbara asked. "I worked with your father, darling. Women your age don't have the same patience with men."

Lisa looked down at her watch: 7:30. She should've been on the road a half-hour ago. Her pulse thumped its way up her neck. "Mom, my lack of patience didn't make Bryan cheat on me and take everything I had. If anything, I patiently invested in him, and he turned into one big junk bond."

"You thought you were investing. Supporting him, earning the paycheck. You forgot to be the girl, Melissa. Of course, Bryan saw it as you usurping his role as the male in the family. He couldn't help but assert his manhood."

Lisa laughed bitterly, shaking her head. So much for motherly support. "All roads lead to you analyzing me. Okay, Ma, you're right. I'm wrong. As usual."

Barbara huffed. "You want me to tell you what you want to hear."

"Even if you believe all that stuff, would it kill you to defend me just once? I'm your daughter, for Christ's sake. Lionesses defend their cubs in the wild without intellectualizing everything!"

"That's what separates us from the animals, Melissa."

Why am I surprised? All of Lisa's memories of her mother were as a cold intellectual, unforgiving in her desire to build the perfect daughter. And Lisa came up short. Every time. "I got to go, Ma," she sighed, dejected. "I'm running late."

"I love you, Melissa," Barbara said, and it sounded perfunctory, like her psych books had told her that it was acceptable to define what she felt for her offspring as love.

Lisa looked down at her watch again: 7:35. "I'm sure you do, Ma," she said. *In your own way . . .*

As Lisa rode with Jaye in the elevator to C. Richard Monaghan's office, she was glad she hadn't had lunch. Her stomach churned like a washing machine. Jaye, on the other hand, exuded power. Her natural hair was closely cropped to her well-shaped head. Except for her trademark coffee-colored lipstick, Jaye didn't wear makeup and didn't need to. She had flawless mocha-brown skin. Her black trench coat and the cut of her navy pinstripe suit made her look even taller and more imposing. Lisa opened her own brown trench and looked down at her frilly white collar peeking out from her kelp-green cardigan, black calf-length woolen skirt, and black suede boots. She felt like the bourgie rich girl that Bryan accused her of being.

Jaye leaned in. "How are you feeling?" she asked.

Lisa pressed a hand to her tortured belly. "Like shit," she replied.

Jaye reached into her purse and pulled out a roll of lemon-flavored antacid. "Here," she said. "Keep it."

Obediently, Lisa unrolled one and popped it in her mouth. It tasted like lemony chalk. She looked up to see Jaye looking at her, apparently sizing her up. Lisa wasn't naive enough to think that every lesbian would find her attractive. "Let me do all the talking," Jaye advised. "That's what you pay me for. You just sit there and look confident and in the right, because you are. This is the last stop on this ride. Once this is through, we're home free."

Lisa wished she could be as optimistic. "Okay," she said weakly.

The elevator doors opened to the sixth floor, and for the first time in a year and a half, Jaye smiled at Lisa like she was mentally lacing up the gloves. "Show time," she said gleefully.

They stepped through double glass doors into the tony offices of Monaghan, Matthew, and Smythe. Immediately, a well-put-together secretary breezed past the leather sofas, oak tables, and crystal chandeliers toward them. Reflexively, she took their coats. "Ms. Barraclough, Mrs. Livingston, I'm Margaret," she announced, practiced, efficient. "Mr. Monaghan is running a tad late. He asked me to show you to the conference room. He and Mr. Livingston will be down shortly."

Lisa followed Margaret and Jaye down a long, blue-carpeted hallway to a room enclosed in glass. Was this really the end? This was what five years of marriage came down to? Standing in this fishbowl of a conference room in front of a polished oak table that seemed to stretch forever? It all seemed anticlimactic somehow.

Margaret shook the coats in her arms. "I'll just hang these up for you," she said. With a flick of her red head, she indicated the veritable spread on the credenza by the picture window. "There's coffee, tea, and biscuits—help yourself. The gentlemen will be down shortly."

"Thank you," Jaye said.

Margaret turned on the heels of her sensible pumps and disappeared.

Lisa paced, popping another antacid. "God, I want this to be over," she murmured.

Jaye opened her briefcase and began taking out files. "We'll be fine," she said. "Of course, the rape kit would solidify things . . ."

Lisa shot her a withering look. Jaye obviously got the message. She shrugged. "You're the client."

Suddenly, Jaye stopped. "Shit."

Lisa's heart lurched. "What?"

"I forgot my daytime planner in the car. Without that, I'm fucked." Jaye loaded her files back into her case and snapped it shut. "I'm going to the garage, okay?"

"But what if they come and you're not here?!"

Jaye headed toward the glass doors, covering the distance in three leggy strides. "Don't panic," she said casually. "Just take deep breaths, and don't say anything until I get back. Okay?"

Obediently, Lisa took deep breaths. "Okay."

Jaye left, and the deafening silence in the conference room enveloped her. Lisa moved to the window and stared at the flags flapping in the breeze in front of the United Nations building. *What now?*

She could smell Bryan's signature Tuscany cologne before he even said a word. She turned to see him . . . tall, suave, gray double-breasted Italian suit, wire-rimmed glasses. The last time she'd seen him, he was descending the courthouse stairs in Newark, laughing at her as he stepped into a waiting cab. Free as a bird. He eyed her covetously even now. "Hello, Lisa," he said.

Just to have something to do with her hands, Lisa moved to the credenza, got herself a plate, and proceeded to plunder the Lorna Doones. "Where's your attorney?" she asked.

"Still on his conference call," he answered. "Yours?"

"She'll be right back any minute now," she said pointedly.

She then started to make herself some tea, keeping her back to him. She could hear the cup clatter in the saucer that trembled in her hand, punctuated by the awful silence in the room. *Come on, girl. Keep it together.*

"So, you're not going to talk to me," he finally said.

You really don't want me to say what I want to you. Lisa finally turned around and took her food over to the conference room table. "That's what our lawyers are for," she reminded him.

He chuckled, low in the throat. "Well, I'll talk to you, then," he said. "You look good."

Despite you. She looked at him and quietly bit into a cookie. Inside, she wondered what the fuck was keeping Jaye.

He tried again. "Seeing anyone?"

Like I would want anything to do with a man after you. Silently, she finished off her cookie, refusing to avert her eyes.

He slipped his hands into his pockets and shook his head, laughing. "Well, I'm seeing a wonderful woman," he announced. "Her name's Mia. She's got a ten-year-old daughter, Andi."

So you can raise some other man's seed when you didn't give a shit about your own? She took a swallow of tea to drown the furious words in her throat.

Bryan kept pushing the buttons. "We're getting married," he announced, smiling brilliantly.

It was like he'd slapped her across the face. Right then, she felt even more used, even more expendable. She couldn't drown her feelings in tea and cookies any longer. "How nice for you all," she stated.

Bryan's eyes danced. He'd pushed the right button. "Well, thank you," he said. "We haven't set a date yet. We've found a house, though. Mount Kisco."

"Westchester County," she remarked. "Too rich for my blood."

"Westchester's quieter," he said. "Plus we'd be able to get Andi into a nice school. They live in the Bronx now, and the public school there is seriously lacking."

Where was this kindness when we were married? Her anger showed up again in its familiar form . . . the steely pain gripping her chest. "You're all heart, Bryan," she remarked sarcastically.

"So you understand why we must split the money from the house fifty-fifty, don't you?" he concluded, more of a statement than a question.

Bryan looked at her, quite pleased with the argument he'd made, and Lisa resisted the urge to lunge for him and scratch the haughty expression from his face. Instead, she took Jaye's advice, took deep breaths, and forced a smile. "I think it was The Stones who said, 'You can't always get what you want.' Sorry."

In a heartbeat, Charming Dapper Bryan became Threatening Potentially Violent Bryan. "I always get what I want," he declared, his voice low. "You of all people know that."

Fuck the tea and cookies. "I'm sure you, and Mia, and

Andi will get to the country eventually. You're just not going to do it with Daddy's money!"

Bryan rolled his eyes. "Here we go again!"

"He didn't die of a heart attack so you could live in Westchester-fucking-County!"

"You've got a bee up your ass, because I've found someone, and you're alone and bitter."

"I've seen your sweet little Mia's future. It's me. In a few years, she'll be in the shower, trying to wash the stench of you off her. She'll be giving blood for two AIDS tests!"

His narrowed eyes were like black ice. "Regardless of this separation, you are my wife," he declared. "I had every right to have sex with you."

Lisa stared at him in utter dismay. "You really and truly believe that?!" she gasped. "You're not even the slightest bit sorry for what you did to me!"

His eyes melted then blazed. "Sorry?! I only stayed with you as long as I did for the pussy. And even then, it wasn't worth the aggravation! You were jocking me from the first minute we got married, Lisa. The first minute! 'Did you study, Bryan?' 'We can't go out, Bryan, there's no money.' 'Did you do this, Bryan?' 'Did you do that, Bryan?'" He clasped his hands to his head. "If I had to listen to your voice one more minute, I would've snapped your fucking neck and put your ass at the corner in a Hefty bag. So, Melissa, I asked for a divorce. You're not worth life without parole in East Rahway!"

Lisa stood there, numb, her face hot, the realization that she'd shared her body and bed with a psychopath slowly sinking in. He was officially beyond redemption. Mentally, the gloves came off, and she realized that all the humiliation she'd suffered being married to him had to have a purpose. She knew what it was.

Jaye entered the conference room with Monaghan, a smartly dressed older man who looked like a leprechaun. "Such a touching soliloquy," Jaye commented.

"And me without the stenographer." She opened the door a touch wider and let in a mousy young girl. "Come in, everybody. Mr. Livingston's particularly talkative today."

C. Richard Monaghan glowered at his client like he'd been a naughty boy. "Jaye," he said. "Mrs. Livingston."

Monaghan and Bryan took a seat on one side of the table, Lisa and Jaye on the other side. The stenographer sat behind her machine. Lisa leaned in toward Jaye. "Use the kit," she whispered.

Jaye practically beamed. "Really?"

"Do whatever you have to do to get this motherfucker out of my life."

"You're the client," she whispered, ecstatic.

"Okay," C. Richard Monaghan began, "we're here to work out an equitable settlement regarding the property, the house at 88 Gates Avenue, Montclair, New Jersey."

"My wife is aware that half of the money from the sale of that house is mine," Bryan declared.

Monaghan gripped Bryan's forearm to silence him.

Jaye sprang into action. "My client disagrees. As we've said countless times, Mrs. Livingston bought the house before the marriage. She used her inheritance for the down payment and closing costs of said property. Only Mrs. Livingston continues to pay the mortgage. The house is hers."

"Then Mrs. Livingston forfeits any spousal support Mr. Livingston may have paid," Monaghan said, the same old threat.

"Gentlemen," Jaye sighed, "we've been down this road before. Mr. Livingston is a creative director at a top advertising agency on Madison Ave. He earns a six-figure salary. Because of his wife. She helped educate him. She's entitled to a percentage of his income. This is a dead issue."

"Well, I'm giving it mouth-to-mouth," Bryan piped

up, despite a second cautionary forearm squeeze from Monaghan. "She didn't pay for everything. I owe fifty grand in student loans. I'm not giving this greedy bitch any more than I have to."

Monaghan leaned in and whispered frenetically. That seemed to calm Bryan down for a second.

"Let's examine who's greedy here," Jaye said. "Melissa Livingston provided you with a home. She cooked your meals."

"Ooh, Hamburger Helper," Bryan mumbled.

"She cooked your meals," Jaye repeated. "She washed your crusty BVDs. She paid for most of that MBA from Columbia that you're so quick to wave under our noses. You, on the other hand, are a consummate user who defecated on her since Day One. Any other woman would've killed you in your sleep."

Bryan was so angry, he looked like he would levitate from his chair. Lisa quite enjoyed seeing him riled. "I don't have to take this from my wife, and I especially don't have to take this from this dyke," he snapped to Monaghan.

Like a parent separating two children, Monaghan intervened. "That's enough, Jaye," he declared.

He should've rethought the condescending tone. "I agree, Richard. We've had quite enough," Jaye stated, then turned to Bryan. "Mr. Livingston, where were you on May 20, 1988?"

Instantly Bryan went pale, and Lisa knew this was the moment she'd have to relive that horrible night. "Umm . . ." he stuttered, ". . . I was at 88 Gates Avenue, getting the rest of my stuff. Why?"

There was a rhythm to Jaye's building argument . . . slow . . . methodical. "What did you do there?"

Bryan shot a glance at Lisa, as if he were stunned that she would actually defy him like this. She saw the same anger in his eyes when he'd forced her to her knees in front of him. *Oh, God.* "I got my things and left," he lied confidently.

"How long did it take you to get your things and leave?"

His fingers pried open her lips; he thrust his erection into her mouth. Bryan shrugged. "A few hours."

"You arrived at the house at three in the afternoon and left after seven, didn't you?"

He bent her over the couch, forcing himself into her ass. "I guess," he said, a thin film of sweat popping up above his top lip. "I didn't look at my watch."

"You went somewhere for four hours, and you didn't look at your watch even once?" Jaye asked, disbelieving. "Why was that?"

His semen stung in her torn flesh. "I don't usually look at my watch when I'm having sex with my wife," Bryan declared.

The pain crushed against Lisa's sternum, as if it had no other way to come out than in tears. They spilled nonstop in rivulets down her face, suffocating any semblance of dignity she had left. *Oh, God! Make it stop!*

The stenographer had even stopped clicking away at her machine. She looked up at Lisa with moist eyes. Monaghan looked like the only person in the klatch who didn't get it. "Jaye, where are you going with this?" he demanded, and the stenographer began clicking again.

Jaye ignored him. "Consensual sex?" she persisted.

"Of course, consensual sex," Bryan declared. "Even the Essex County DA says so."

"Bryan, not another word!" Monaghan angrily cautioned.

Smart attorney that she was, Jaye knew that threatening someone on the record could, at the very least, get her disbarred. She turned to the stenographer. "Stop for a second, please," she said.

Obediently, the stenographer ceased clicking. Jaye then opened her briefcase and laid a stack of police photographs out like solitaire cards on the conference room table. Lisa couldn't look. Her body still bore the scars from those very same wounds.

"Let's look at some of your handiwork, Mr. Livingston," Jaye suggested, pointing at each of the gruesome displays of a perversion of sex, of reddened, bruised flesh. "Here's one of Melissa Livingston's torn anus. She needed 20 stitches to close that wound." Again, she pointed. "Here's one of bruises on her throat. I do believe that happened when you forced her to . . ." she did air quotes . . . " 'Suck your dick, just the way you like it.' " She pointed to another. "Here's one of her bruised vagina." Pointed to another. "Bruised inside of her thighs. Is this your idea of consensual sex, Mr. Livingston?"

Bryan sank into his chair, deflated, all that bravado dissipated. Even Monaghan looked repulsed at the photographic spectacle that lay before him. "This is a deposition, not a rape trial, Jaye," he said quietly.

Bryan focused on Lisa that wounded little-boy gaze that used to get him so far with her. "What do you want, Lisa?" he asked.

Jaye locked her gaze on him like a torpedo. "You talk to *me,* not her!" she demanded. "There's no conservative Essex County DA who thinks that marital rape is a myth here to save you. Stop messing around with us, or we will take this to court and make it 'Yo-Fault Divorce!' "

Bryan and Monaghan began their frenetic whispering yet again. Jaye sat down and watched the wreckage of Bryan's case before her. Then she turned to Lisa and handed her a hanky. "It's done," Jaye whispered.

Lisa looked up at her and dabbed her swollen eyes. "Thank you," she mouthed.

Uncharacteristically tender, Jaye squeezed her hand. "You done good, girl," she whispered, shooting her a soothing smile.

It was over, and *she* was the one left standing. What an encouraging switch . . .

While cradling the phone between his ear and shoulder, Marc stared out at the demonstrators, led by a young man in African cloth, from his office window. Under the black night sky, their candles created a vast, peaceful sea of flames. Even through the hermetically sealed plate glass window, he could faintly hear the strains of "We Shall Overcome." All of this for a boy that Marc's own people had so savagely murdered, shot down as if he'd been an afterthought. The last thing that seemed important was his sister-in-law and her machinations.

"Adam, I told you I wasn't coming to Diane's dinners until she stopped with the Sarah Lawrence friends," Marc declared to his brother on the other end.

He could picture his brother, seated at his drafting table with blueprints unfurled on the surface. "This week, it was Dagney, frizzy blond hair and all. She looked like she wet her hand and plugged in a toaster!" he laughed.

Marc rolled his eyes. " 'Dagney.' 'Eastley.' Is Diane the only one with a normal name?"

Adam chuckled. "Listen, I'm supposed to pump you to find out what you want for the big four-oh."

Oh, God! "I can tell you what I *don't* want," he snapped. "Some huge, overblown affair that's supposed to be a big surprise."

The awkward silence spoke volumes. "Well, I guess I'll warn you now, then," Adam finally said.

Marc turned away from the window. "Whose stupid fucking idea is this?"

"Suzanne."

Suzanne went from not paying attention to him to loving him like a pillow over the face. "God, she's such a middle child!"

"Hey, she's your sister, and she wants to do something nice for you," Adam said gently, forever the peacemaker. "Come on, we'll have it at my house. Not a Dagney or Eastley in sight, I swear."

He was feeling weird, and turning forty next month was only part of it. The whole world seemed fucked that day. Firstly, the jaded New York press had gotten wind of a certain idiot chancellor who'd denied a student government group permission to march in the City, and they came across the bridges and tunnels in droves to seize upon a new angle to the story still gripping the tri-state area. Then six o'clock came and went, and Lisa didn't show up in class. Both he and the rest of the class were in a strange funk where nothing clicked. After only an hour and a half, he dismissed everyone, with instructions to work on their next assignments. And then *Rolling Stone* canceled a phone interview that he was looking forward to. Just a day in the life of a man who supposedly had everything going for him.

"Hey, you still there?" Adam asked.

"Yeah. Just thinking," he said.

" 'Bout what?"

"About entering another decade. Never dreamed it would be like this."

Adam sighed. "The only being whose life is like He wants it to be is God. And even then, I look around at this Yusuf Hawkins mess, and I wonder."

Marc quietly let the words sink in.

Just then, he heard a knock on the door and turned. As if he'd conjured her up himself, Lisa, clutching her tote bag, stood there in the doorway, smiling that same wobbly smile that he found so sexy. His gut constricted. "Hi," she said, then her eyes darted to the receiver between his shoulder and ear. "I'm sorry," she mouthed. "I'll come back."

No fucking way! Furiously, he waved her inside to the

guest chair and held up an index finger. "One sec," he whispered.

"Hello?" said Adam. "Are you thinking about what I said, or is this your creative way of telling me to go fuck myself?"

Marc watched Lisa sit. "I'm thinking about it," he said.

"Promise me you'll think about the party, too, while you're at it."

Again, he rolled his eyes. "Yes, Big Brother!" he laughed. "Now I got to go." He looked at Lisa and winked. "I've got a student here who's about to throw herself on my mercy for missing class."

Again with the wobbly smile. Again with the fluttering stomach.

"Okay," Adam said. "See you."

"Later," Marc said.

He hung up the phone and sighed. Shamelessly, he stared at Lisa, especially at the teasing glimpse of cleavage in the frilly white blouse. She looked like a naughty Catholic schoolgirl. Then he looked at her face. She looked like hell. *Don't pry.* "My brother Adam," he announced.

She nodded in acknowledgment, then wearily sighed. "Look, before you get a wedgie, I have a good excuse for missing class today," she said. "I was being deposed."

That explained it. *Try humor.* "What, like the Shah of Iran?"

The wobbly smile became a weary laugh, but a laugh nonetheless. "I wish. He was only deposed once."

"No wedgies today. This is the new flexible Marc. I dismissed the class early anyway."

Innocently, he touched her left knee and was stunned when she nearly jumped out of her skin. "What?" he asked. "I hurt you?"

Lisa held out her left leg and raised her skirt. A bloody wound gaped through a hole in her black tights. Instinctively, he recoiled. "Let me guess," he said, disgusted. "Bryan Livingston threw you down a flight of stairs."

She laughed. "As much as I'm sure he wanted to, no. I fell over some demonstrators in the quad on my way here. There are, like, fifty million of them now."

The protective Italian sexist popped up from deep in his psyche. He patted his lap. "Let me have a look."

"Marc, after the day I've had, this is nothing. I'll be okay."

Again, he patted his lap. When she saw he wasn't taking no for an answer, she tentatively rested her leg across his thighs. He opened the top desk drawer and produced a first-aid kit. He held it up to her. *"Semper paratus,"* he laughed.

"I feel like such a big baby," she moaned. "A big, clumsy baby."

He opened the kit and pulled out a tiny can of antibacterial spray. "You'd feel more adult if the cut got infected and your leg fell off, then."

"They say unearned suffering is redemptive," she said.

He concentrated, taking a pair of scissors and gently cutting flaps in her tights. "Hope these weren't expensive," he said.

She waved her hand dismissively. "I'll live."

There, splayed open, was the result of concrete meeting creamy brown skin. Flesh and blood gleamed in the light. The shit really looked like it hurt. Quickly, he sprayed the wound and felt her leg tense. He hated that he was causing her even a nanosecond of pain. He hurried, taking out a bandage and taping it to her leg. He looked up at her and tried to soften the look of terror on her face with a smile. "See?" he said, hands up, wiggling his fingers. "All done."

Unabashed relief washed over her face. "Thanks."

He looked at the tote, on whose handle she had a death grip, her knuckles near white. "What's in the bag?"

"My assignment. You have time to discuss it?"

"All the time in the world."

She dug into the bag for her assignment. He didn't notice the bag sliding from her lap until it was too late. It crashed to the floor, spewing papers every which way. Reflexively, they both bent to pick it up, and he felt his head connecting with a painful *thunk* against hers. They both wound up on the floor. "Ow!" she cried, laughing.

Marc massaged the knot that was forming fast in the center of his forehead. "Office hours with you are a contact sport," he grinned.

"I heard of a meeting of the minds, but this is ridiculous!" she giggled.

He leaned in closer, so close her floral perfume teased his nose. *Fuck, you smell so good!* He gazed at her face. It was like all her trials and sorrow made her even more beautiful, gave her layers, and he wanted to peel away each one. "You okay?"

She laughed breathlessly. "Uh-huh. You?"

"Where did I get you?"

She pointed to the middle of her forehead. He leaned in closer, trying to concentrate on the spot. But that perfume . . . Knowing full well he was taking all kinds of license, he touched her face, and he shuddered, marveling at how soft she felt. He traced the outline of her cheeks, her nose, her full mouth. All the while, he stared at her, as if the harder he stared, the more of her he could commit to memory. His rational mind screamed to be heard over his ache for her. The open door . . . the demonstrators outside protesting this very thing . . . teacher-student. He could give a shit.

He bent his head, brushed his mouth against hers. She moaned, and a shock thundered through him like he'd been tasered. She tasted like mint, and lipstick, and Lisa. He closed his eyes and kissed her again, deeper, and this time, she opened her mouth eagerly to him. He held her face in his hands as he tasted her, sucked her flesh. All too predictably, his cock thumped demandingly in his briefs.

"Doc, Dean Grantham wants . . . oh my!" Merilee cried.

He cruelly dropped to earth. They flew apart. Deprivation kicked him squarely in the stones. Lisa began stuffing all her things into her tote bag. "I was just leaving!" she squealed.

They scrambled to their feet. He could still taste the kiss in his mouth. "Lisa, wait!" he begged.

She hobbled at top speed from the office. Marc stared longingly after her. "Isn't she in your class?" Merilee asked.

Bereft, he watched her disappear into the stairwell like the rabbit in *Alice in Wonderland.* "Yes," he murmured.

"Well, someone's going all out for that A, huh?" Merilee laughed.

Marc glared at her, and the freckles on Merilee's nose trembled. She turned on the heels of her Birkenstocks. "I better go," she said quietly.

For numerous reasons, that hadn't gone well. Marc held his head in his hands.

On automatic pilot, Lisa meandered into her apartment. Wisteria did her usual slalom course with Lisa's legs, happily meowing. Lisa barely registered that the cat was even there. She shut the door and leaned against it. She touched her mouth, and her heart thudded in her chest. She remembered the feel of Marc's mouth on hers . . . moist but firm, with just the right teasing presence of his tongue. She became aware of the familiar thumping moisture between her legs. She'd wanted to fuck him right there on the cold concrete floor. Her! After reliving the horror of her last sexual experience only hours ago, nonetheless. She saw her flushed reflection in the mirror on the wall. *What the hell am I doing?*

She sat down on the couch, opened her bag, and took out her assignment. Her eyes scanned the pages, particularly his margin notes in his masculine script in strong black ink. *Lyrical,* he wrote, at key paragraphs. *Beautiful. Excellently crafted . . .* She looked down at her left leg, at the bandage peering through the hole in her tights. Why would he come into her life now, like this, in these times? "See, God?" she said, looking up. "See how you are?"

Mercifully, the phone rang right then, giving her a reprieve from waiting for Him to intervene. She moved over to her cluttered desk to answer it. "Hello," she said.

"Lisa, it's Marc," he said from the other end.

She went hot and cold, a combination of pure joy and unadulterated lust. *Down, girl!* "Hey."

"I didn't disturb you, did I?"

If only he knew how much. "No."

"Well, I'll come straight to the point. I don't make a habit of putting my female students in a lip lock in my office."

He sounded so coldly professional. Her glow instantly vanished. "I didn't think you did," she said.

"We need to make a concerted effort to keep this relationship strictly professional."

The joyous heart-thumping morphed into something that felt more like acid reflux. She didn't even try to hide her disappointment. "Teacher-student," she sighed.

"Yes," he confirmed. "I take full blame for everything that's happened so far. After all, I'm the one in the position of authority. I should exercise more restraint."

She numbed, like this was happening to someone else. "No, no. It's a two-way street."

"This is the best way to save both our reputations and to stay beyond reproach. Agreed?"

Is he trying to convince himself or me? "Agreed."

He sighed wearily, as if answering Lisa's question. "See you in class next week."

" 'Bye."

He hung up, and she listened to the dial tone in her ear for a very long time. If sadness had a sound, that was it.

8

There he was again, in a shapeless cloth gown, in the same stark room, lying on the examining table under fluorescent lights that made him look washed out. He closed his eyes and drifted into a reverie while Marcus Davidson, his ultra-blond internist friend, poked and prodded his scarred abdomen.

It had been three weeks since he'd sent her away and suggested that they remain teacher-student. It was one of the harder things he'd done in his almost forty years on the planet. Class days were the hardest. He would practically burst with anticipation at the thought of seeing her. Then she would appear—invariably late—and anticipation would morph into extreme depression. He'd go running to clear his head and she'd be at the park, gamboling around the track. He'd be doing publicity for the book, and she'd pop into his mind, derailing his train of thought. He'd lie awake at night, staring out at his impressive view of the City, and could only imagine what it would be like to have her there with him. *What the fuck am I doing?* Wanting someone he couldn't have. Times two. He was better off indiscriminately fucking a cavalcade of women, like before. Anything to avoid the emotional investment that sucked him in and killed him every time.

Suddenly, Marcus pressed way too hard against a bundle of raw nerves, and Marc's eyes flew open. Marcus hovered over him, concern in his deep blue eyes. "Did that hurt?" he asked. "I'm sorry."

Marc glared at him, and his first instinct was to grab a fistful of Marcus's nuts and ask if *that* hurt. Instead, he merely nodded. Marcus patted Marc's knee. "Okay, you can sit up now."

Obediently, Marc sat up and self-consciously reached back to make sure that the opening of the gown covered his ass. "So, what's the verdict?" he asked.

Marcus sat on the metal stool in front of his patient. "Marc, you took seven inches of metal in your gut."

As if on cue, residual agony seared through his abdomen. He bit down hard on his bottom lip. "I was there, Marcus. Remember?"

Marcus sighed, eyeing him like he was the ultimate hypochondriac. "Every six months, we do this dance, Marc. There doesn't seem to be anything out of the ordinary. All the tests and x-rays are normal. It's probably just your nerve endings going haywire."

Doctors! Marc understood why his Grandpa Pasquale distrusted them. Those old Italians believed that anyone who went into the hospital never left alive. How ironic that that was exactly where his grandfather met his fate. Self-fulfilling prophecy. "Twelve years of medical school," Marc said sarcastically. "And you had the nerve to tell me the other day that I'm not a real doctor."

Marcus hooted. "All you can do, buddy, is tell me to read two chapters and call you in the morning."

"You're a regular fucking laugh riot, Marcus," Marc declared. "When can I get dressed? I'm catching a draft up my ass."

"Marc, you're a normal, red-blooded, healthy American male," Marcus assured him. "I felt that dull ache, too, years after I had my appendix out. It's phantom pain."

He hated feeling so helpless. "What can I do about it?"

Marcus shrugged, then walked over to the stainless steel sink. "Just keep taking the Tylenol with Codeine when you feel the pain," he instructed over the running water as he washed his hands. "I have to ask you, though. Do you think this pain may be psychosomatic? Is there some unresolved issue that could be manifesting itself in your gut?"

Are you kidding? His whole life was a mess of unresolved issues. "You're suggesting I'm a head case," Marc concluded.

Drying his hands, Marcus moved over to the side table and then began to prepare the familiar apparatus. "Just something to think about," he said.

He came toward Marc, sporting a covered 16-gauge needle and a purple-topped sample tube. Marc suppressed a shudder. "Now for the infamous blood sample," he murmured.

Marc held out his left arm and let Marcus run an alcohol-saturated gauze square over the inside of his elbow. "Anyone who's had twenty units transfused through the body should have an HIV test, Sunshine," Marcus laughed. "Look on the bright side. Twice, you've been negative."

Twice he'd avoided a deadly fate. He was past the first four of the five phases of dealing with the prospect of death. He was the trophy of acceptance now. "Third time's a charm," he mumbled.

There was Marcus again, with the you-hypochondriac face. "Shut up and make a fist," he ordered.

Obediently, Marc made a fist and lay back down. He felt the needle pierce his skin and winced. He closed his eyes, zoning out. Lisa's face appeared in his mind's eye, and he smiled.

* * *

Lisa knocked on the door to Rick's office. Just as she was starting to worry, he called weakly, "Come in."

Lisa turned on the lights in the office to find Rick in a disheveled heap on the floor, amidst a pile of old year-end reports. He looked up at her with lost grey eyes, and her heart squeezed her chest like a metal band. He looked so pitiful. "Rick," she said gently. "What on earth are you doing?"

He looked slowly away, at the reams of paper around him. "You know, I was looking for something," he mumbled. "Now I can't remember what."

Lisa helped him into his chair. "Come on. Sit down."

Rick sighed. "I'm such a bad manager. I'm probably the worst manager you've ever worked for."

Usually, Rick was so on the ball, so different from all the other managers who embodied the Peter Principle. "Hey," she said tentatively. "How's your dad doing?"

Lost grey eyes misted. "No change," he said. "They've got him so doped up to stop the pain that he doesn't know who he is sometimes. When he is lucid, he says he wants to be taken off the medication."

"He probably doesn't want to be in a fog," she offered, trying to be helpful.

"Some study recently found that older men with prostate cancer are better off with no treatment, as opposed to surgery or radiating the shit out of them. Either way, the outcome's the same."

Death. Lisa blinked back tears. "Are you preparing yourself for that eventuality?"

Rick laughed wildly, desperately. "Lisa, my father's got one foot in the grave, and my project's hotter than July. I'm just trying to function!"

The phone on Rick's desk rang. Rick sighed. "Case in point," he said.

Lisa snatched up the receiver. "Rick Farrelly's office," she said, then listened as Genie droned her question into her ear. She put her hand over the mouthpiece and turned to Rick. "It's Genie. She wants to know if we're doing a table of contents for every section of the year-end, like last year."

He carelessly waved his hand. Without thinking, he replied, "Tell her yes."

This was no on-the-fly decision; this was the year-end report, the most important publication to come out of FDP every year. "Are you sure, Rick?" she asked.

"Yes, I'm sure," he snapped.

Some arcane survival instinct told her that this decision was going to come back to bite them both on the ass. Nonetheless, she said, "Okay . . ."

Déjà vu all over again, as Yogi Berra would say. He had the ritual down by now. Marc sat on the examining table in the amorphous gown and sucked nervously on a lollipop. As he enjoyed its strong cherry taste, he got up, padded across the room to the window, opened the blinds, and stared out at the parking lot.

He'd always liked autumn days, and this was one of the more beautiful he'd seen. Soft winds blew yellow and brown leaves from the trees, so it looked like leaves were raining from the sky. In one of the few deep, meaningful moments they'd had, his mother told him that the temperature had dipped below freezing on the day he was born. She was food shopping at the A&P the afternoon of November 7 when her water broke. She stood there in her own amniotic fluid, crying for help and clutching a box of Cheerios until it dawned on someone to call an ambulance.

By the time they'd arrived at the hospital, the sky had turned dark, and huge snowflakes fell on Brooklyn, snarling up traffic. Just as Daniel and his mother Alessandra arrived at the hospital, the doctor had delivered Marc by cesarean section. Which was a good thing, the doctor said, because the umbilical cord had been wrapped around Marc's tiny neck. One push, and he would've been strangled to death before he'd taken his first breath.

Nonna Alessandra had said that a baby born the day of a freak autumn snowstorm was a blessing, a sign of good luck for the Guerrieri family. But still, moments after Marc had supposedly brought good luck to his family, Rosalie had her tubes tied.

Even more depressed now, Marc shut the blinds. His last birthday with Michele, they had a party at their East 80's apartment to celebrate his recovery from the stabbing. What was supposed to be a celebration looked more like organized camps—Michele's friends, who gave him dirty looks all night, and Marc's family, who returned the favor. Then Michele proceeded to get drunk off her ass on champagne and explain to Marc in a very loud voice why she couldn't come to her husband's side, that she was coming down from the local her doctor had given her to numb the pain of sucking their child from her womb. His first inclination was to slam his fist into her beautiful, tearful face. Instead, he locked himself in their bedroom with a bottle of Jack Daniel's.

Marc heard the door open and turned to see Marcus come in with his chart. "Hey, your ass is showing, birthday boy," he laughed.

Marc fruitlessly tried to pull the two ends of the gown together over his ass. He grimaced. "It's tomorrow. November 7."

"Ah, Election Day," Marcus said. "I see the nurse gave you a lollipop."

He pulled it out of his mouth and showed it to Marcus. "Cherry."

Marcus opened the chart in his hands, and Marc's heart lurched. "Well, I've got good news," he announced. "You're not gonna die—not from AIDS, anyway. You're negative."

The taste of relief mixed with the cherry flavor in Marc's mouth. "Thanks," he croaked, then cleared his throat. "It would've been such a drag to find out I was going to die the day before my birthday."

"Speaking of which, you got anything special planned?"

He actually asked the question with a straight face. He should've considered acting. "Don't even pretend you don't know about the party at Adam's."

The straight face yielded to the oh-shit face. "If Suzanne knew you knew, she'd be so pissed!" Marcus laughed.

"She'll get over it," he said.

Marcus shut the chart with an air of finality. "Well, hey, I've gotta run," he said. "Got sick people to look after." He swatted Marc on the ass with the chart. "See you tomorrow."

Marcus left Marc alone in the solitude of the room. This was one of those good news-bad news moments. He was going to live, but now he had to sit through a party when all he wanted to do, again, was lock himself in the bedroom. He doubted that God was listening to him, lapsed Catholic that he was. Nonetheless, he looked up. "About tomorrow," he said. "Can we skip it?"

Silence.

A strong contingent of demonstrators huddled in the cold quad with banners that read "No Justice, No Peace." The sheer crush of them dwarfed the mighty Student Center. Marc stared down at them and turned up the radio, listening acutely to the announcer. "Today, November 7, marks a new day in New York City's political history. For the first time in twelve years, the incumbent is no longer a candidate in the race for mayor. Today, New Yorkers will choose one of the two challengers—David N. Dinkins, the Democrat, and Rudolph Giuliani, the Republican candidate—to be mayor of their city. It is the hope of many New Yorkers that the victor at the end of this day will heal the racial divide that has polarized the City and has spread across bridges and tunnels to profoundly affect her neighbors."

Marc switched off the radio, turning his attentions to the growing stack of pink message sheets on his desk. Everyone wanting a piece of him. *Cut Piece.*

"So, you are alive," came the honey-warm voice from the doorway behind him.

It felt like every molecule in his body had suddenly burst out of alignment. *No, it can't be!*

Marc whipped around in his chair to see Michele, dressed in a white pants suit, coiffured and manicured to the nines. This fucking birthday was shaping up to be a winner. "Michele?!" he exclaimed in disbelief.

Her brilliant, perfect smile seemed even whiter in her beautiful, tanned face. "Happy birthday, Marc," she laughed.

Say something, Marco. "Umm . . . thanks."

She looked disappointed. "What, no hug?"

God help him, he hesitated. He hadn't held her since he'd seen her last year. That trip down memory lane was too much for him to bear. But he saw the hurt in her striking green eyes and relented. "Of course," he said. "Come here."

She moved into his arms, and he held her close. *Chloe* mixed in with the scent of her shampoo lingered in his nostrils. The full range of emotions tugged at him . . . guilt . . . love . . . fear . . . confusion . . . plus others he felt but couldn't name. Finally, he pried himself free and moved away to a safe distance. She looked like she had to justify wanting a hug. "I haven't seen you since Dad's funeral," she reminded him. "Last year."

He remembered it well. He'd jetted out there to comfort her and save the day, only to see that Kieran had beat him to the punch. "What are you doing here?" he asked.

"Writer's conference in the City," she said. "My publisher flew me out here. I'm staying at The Royalton, on West 44th."

He knew the swanky hotel well. "Sweet," he remarked.

"Listen," she said, upbeat, "I've got *Les Miz* tickets. Let me treat you to the show tonight for your birthday."

Thank God for the best-laid plans of Suzanne Gliatto. He tried hard to look disappointed. "As much as I'd love to, tonight's bad. Suzanne's having a surprise birthday party for me at Adam's house."

She looked puzzled. "But you know about it."

He laughed. "Yeah, the surprise is on her."

"I called your parents' house to find out where you'd be today. They didn't mention a thing about a party." She shook her blond head. "Can't say I'm surprised. They never did like me."

Their misguided way of showing what they considered love for him. "They hate everybody."

"That's comforting," she said sarcastically. With arms akimbo, she looked around his office. "Nice. This is the first time I've seen your office. Of course, you saw mine at NYU."

Yes, he had, when, to celebrate her new job, he brought over sandwiches and wine. They had a makeshift picnic in her office, after which they made love like horny teenagers on top of her desk. He still marveled at the passion she hid behind an academic's facade. "Some kid's probably still got my butt print on one of his papers!" he laughed.

Michele laughed, too, and for a split second, the wall fell between them. She was the same Michele he'd spent all those years with. He wanted her more than he had the first time he'd seen her. He probably would've acted on it, too, had he not glimpsed the impressive engagement ring on her left hand. Suddenly, there were light years between them again. "I'm sorry," he said, as he would say to any guest. "Would you like something to drink? A soda? Tea?"

She shook her head. "I'm fine, thanks."

"If you'd called, I would've been better prepared."

"I *have* been calling you, Marc. For two months now."

Oh, shit. "I've been so busy, with teaching, and the book . . ."

Her eyes were an accusatory green. "Funny, this flurry of activity coincided with my wedding announcement."

"Michele, these past few months have been insane." Which was entirely true.

He knew that face. She looked like she was about to cry. "Too insane for you to pick up a phone? I was your wife. We've even deluded ourselves into saying we're friends."

There he was, hurting her again. "We *are* friends."

"You could've called to say congratulations. Or that I was making the biggest mistake of my life. Anything would've been better than your hurtful, selfish silence!"

MarcAntonio Guerrieri, King of the Dickheads. He couldn't even look her in the face. "I had no idea my opinion still mattered to you."

To his ultimate surprise, Michele laughed. "For a Ph.D., you're not the sharpest knife in the drawer, are you? I love you. Of course I care what you think."

As always, she was forgiving his dumb-man behavior. "If you're guilting me, Michele, it's working," he declared.

She came closer, and this time, he didn't move away. She beamed proudly, taking his hands into the softness of hers. "Marc, I want you to give me away at my wedding," she announced.

The molecules shot back into alignment, and the sensation was still the same. "What?!" he croaked.

"I want you to give me away," she repeated.

He was surprised he could still talk. "But . . . why me?!"

Her eyes misted. "Because I've only loved three men

in my life. Dad's gone, and I'm marrying Kieran. That leaves you."

Lucky fucking me. He snatched his hands away. "Michele, this is too fucking weird!"

"What's so weird about it?"

Because I think I may still have feelings for you! I applied for a consultancy at a university to be closer to you! But he was hurt, and lashing out at her was the only way he knew to lessen the pain. "No," he stated. "Find an uncle or something. Me giving you away ain't gonna happen!"

Her eyes flashed. Marc had seen that many times before. He knew he was in for a knock-down, drag-out fight.

Her heart drummed with every step she took toward Marc's office. She clutched a small, wrapped present. Even then, she wondered if she was over the top. *It's a fucking CD, Melissa, not a violation of teacher-student.*

As she got closer to the office, though, she heard heated arguing coming from behind the door—Marc and another woman. Morbid curiosity propelled her closer. Through the glass in the door, she saw him with Malibu Barbie, making hand motions that were larger than life. *Oh, shit! Michele!*

"God, you're so selfish!" she said, a sob in her voice.

"You were my wife, Michele," he angrily reminded her. "Now you're asking me to give you away to another man? I only just got over you walking out on me!"

"You believe I came all this way to hurt you?"

"I wonder."

"If that's the case, then the fourteen years we were together meant nothing . . ."

She'd eavesdropped enough. They were getting into some heavy shit, shit that she didn't want or need to hear. She walked away from the door as quietly as possible, colliding with Merilee, who regarded her suspiciously. "It's Election Day," she announced. "There's no class."

She smelled like mustiness and patchouli. "I know," Lisa said.

"Isn't he down there?"

"Yeah, but I don't think he wants to be disturbed." She gave Merilee the present. "When he's done, could you give this to him, please?"

Merilee took the package and stared down at it, like she wanted to know what was inside. *Nosy bitch.* "Sure," she finally said.

Lisa headed for the stairwell, feeling like a big fool.

Adam's darkened foyer was the last place Marc wanted to be, the last thing he wanted . . . people, cake, mock sincerity. He wanted to spend his fortieth birthday at home, on his couch, with ESPN and a six-pack. Nonetheless, there he stood, smartly dressed, in the open doorway, facing his brother. Adam leaned in. "You're on," he whispered, smirking. "And make it look real."

Marc winked. Louder, so that everyone hiding in the dark could hear, he said, "Yo, Ad, why's it so dark in here? You pay your PSE&G bill?"

Adam, also louder, replied, "We've blown a fuse. Diane's checking the box in the basement."

Marc stumbled into the darkness with Adam. *God, get me through this.* Suddenly, the lights came on in the living room; a crowd of familiar heads, wearing party hats, screamed out, "Surprise!"

Now for the Oscar-winning performance. "You guys!" he laughed. "I'm shocked and stunned!" He surveyed the crowd. "There's Mom and Dad. And Nina and Tim. And Marcus and Amber." He squinted, as if he couldn't believe what he saw. "And Jimmy and Eastley?!"

Adam leaned in. "Don't ask. We're still trying to figure that one out."

Suzanne came forward, and Marc realized that his sister embodied the myth that all women eventually turned into their mothers. Even though she'd only recently turned forty-two, she'd decided to dye her once-luxurious dark hair a brassy blond, and start wearing elastic clothes to camouflage middle-age spread. She kissed Marc on the cheek. "Happy birthday, baby brother," she said with begrudging happiness.

Even though he knew the answer, he gave her the much-needed ego stroke. "Who did all this?" he asked.

Adam and Marc exchanged glances. After years of growing up with her, they knew Suzanne's M.O. by heart. She desperately needed the affirmation, but would never snatch at it herself. "Sue did," Adam announced. "All by herself."

Sated, Suzanne beamed. For a second, she was their pretty sister. "Thanks, Adam, for throwing me a bone," she said.

Adam opened his mouth, thought for a moment, then closed it. "Nah. Too easy."

Marc saw his parents, his mother with bleached blond hair and severe makeup, and his father, average height with a pot belly, and stoic, with the look of a worn-down, blue-collar man. They might as well have been strangers. Rosalie kissed Marc's cheek, which was the usual extent of her affection for him. "Forty years ago, my water broke in the A&P while I was clutching your father's box of Cheerios!" she squealed.

"I never did get my Cheerios," Daniel laughed awkwardly, then patted Marc on the shoulder. "Happy birthday, son."

His lack of a relationship with them grieved him. "Thanks, Mom . . . Dad," he said.

Suzanne grabbed Diane's arm as she attempted to come kiss Marc and stuck her 35mm camera in her hand. "Take a picture, Diane," she implored, then commanded her brothers, "Birth order, please."

Field Marshal Sue. Nonetheless, Adam and Marc obediently lined up, Suzanne popped between them, and Diane snapped the picture. Marc squinted against the black dot that the flash produced on his retina and tried to pay attention to his mother. "MarcAntonio, you wouldn't guess who called us today," Rosalie said.

Daniel's face turned up like a squall of rain. "That girl who refused to take your name," he angrily declared.

Should've stayed home. "Her name's Michele, Dad," he corrected him, irritated.

Daniel pouted. "She didn't want my name—I don't want to know hers."

Suzanne rolled her eyes. "I hope you told her to burn in hell," she said, disgusted. "Nicely, of course."

Adam seemed surprised. "Michele's in town?"

"She wanted to know where to find Marc," Rosalie said. "She's marrying some Irishman."

"His name's Kieran, Mom, and I know," Marc said. "She told me."

"Hah!" Suzanne scoffed. "That *disgraziata would* go lower on the food chain. There you go, Marco. Getting her out of your life for good is better than any birthday gift I could've given you."

Marc stared at his disapproving sister, at the evil side of familial protection. *What the fuck do you know?* "You start any shit tonight, and I'm outta here," he declared, knowing he was minutes away from that beer and ESPN. "And I mean it."

He stormed away, into the safety of the crowd of friends and family in the living room. He could feel his parents' and his sister's disapproval following him through their stares. And for once, he didn't give a fuck.

* * *

Lisa entered A.J.'s Brooklyn loft, peeling off her coat. As usual, all of the fifteen guests that A.J. had invited were there before her. She looked up at the decorations . . . the streamers and the Mylar balloons that read GO DAVE hanging from the rafters. Some of the guests were helping themselves to smorgasbord from a designated food table in A.J.'s eat-in kitchen. Babyface crooning "Tender Lover" played at low volume from massive stereo speakers. Sound from the huge 35-inch color TV that oversaw the expansive living area competed with the music on the stereo. A.J., the hostess with the mostest toting a bottle of Moët and glasses, turned to see Lisa. "Am I too late?" Lisa asked.

A.J. sucked her teeth and poured her a glass of champagne. "No, it's 8:28," she said. "You know how to cut it close, girl!"

Lisa hung up her coat on the hand-carved Ghanaian coat rack by the door, and she and A.J. rushed over to the TV.

"Someone kill Babyface!" A.J. yelled. "Here it comes."

Some obedient soul turned off the music, and everyone formed a semicircle round the TV. A heady mixture of hope and anxiety filled Lisa. She was gripping the glass in her hand so tightly, she was surprised it didn't shatter. "Dave's got this," she said.

"If he doesn't, there'll be some angry brothahs and sistahs up in here," A.J. said.

Official-looking Election Watch '89 graphics moved across the TV screen, along with important-sounding music. The image dissolved to a white male anchor and a bubbly African-American female anchor, at the news desk. Chyron flashed their names under their images. The male anchor stared into the camera lens with a practiced serious expression. "It is 8:30, and the polls are closed across New York City," he announced. "With 75 percent of the precincts counted, Democrat David

Dinkins is the projected winner of this mayoral race, making him the first African-American mayor of New York City."

The party erupted joyously. *Finally!* Maybe all this madness that had gripped everyone's lives recently was going to end. Impulsively, Lisa hugged A.J. "He did it!" she laughed.

A.J. kissed her cheek. *"We* did it, girl!"

Hours later, Marc had had enough. So, like any mature male faced with acting overjoyed at turning forty, he hid downstairs in Adam's basement. Not like it was a punishment. The basement was more like a leisure room, complete with a pool table, stereo, weight set, and a 25-inch TV. He sought the company of one of the few beautiful, nonjudgmental females in his life—Lily. He sat on the couch in front of the TV, with Lily in his lap, looking up at him with unconditional love in her sleepy green eyes. Usually so used to expressing himself with a complex network of words, he couldn't even begin to describe what he felt for her right down to his soul. The only interruption to the moment was Rudolph Giuliani, larger than life on screen, giving his hypersibilant concession speech. "Uncle Marc?" she said, her little voice thick with fatigue.

He ran his fingers through her baby-soft hair. "Yes, sweetie?" he near-whispered.

She seemed to be struggling with a concept beyond her five years. "What's consesh . . . ?"

" 'Concession?' It means 'to give up.' "

"Why did he concession?"

She was so cute. He smiled. "Because another man won, honey."

"The one Jimmy called a moolie?"

Marc bristled. *Fucking Jimmy.* "He's not a moolie,

Lillabelle. He's a black man. 'Moolie' is a bad word for 'black person.' You should never use that word."

She looked confused. "But Jimmy did."

Marc sighed. "Lily, adults don't know everything."

"You know everything," Lily insisted. "You answer all my questions."

If only he did know everything. He'd know why a mob of his people thought they were justified in gunning down a kid just because he was black and in their neighborhood. He'd know why he couldn't seem to bridge the gap with his parents and his sister. He'd know why and what he still felt for Michele. And he'd know why he was so afraid to reach out to Lisa when she obviously made him happy. "I don't know everything, Lillabelle," he said. "I just know more than you, because I'm older than you."

"How much older?"

"Well, you're five."

"Yeah."

"You'd have to live your life eight times to be as old as me."

Her dark brows crinkled. "You're old!"

Marc laughed deep from the gut. "There goes my ego!"

"What's an ego?" she asked.

Marc searched his brain, wondering how he'd explain Freud to a five-year-old. Mercifully, he heard footsteps on the wooden steps and looked up to see Diane and Nina descending the staircase. "I knew immediately where to find her," Diane laughed. "Just follow the questions."

"She's fading fast," he said quietly.

Diane took Lily into her thin but sturdy arms and kissed her forehead. "Say good night to Uncle Marc, Lil," she said.

"'Night, Uncle Marc," Lily obediently said, mid-yawn.

"'Night, sweetie," Marc said. "We're gonna work on Mommy 'til she says you can have that puppy."

Diane looked over at Nina. "He's evil."

Nina giggled. "I know this."

Diane turned and headed for the steps. "I'll see you guys later."

Marc stared after Lily and Diane. "'Bye," Nina and Marc chorused.

Once Diane left, Nina eased down next to Marc on the couch. "Thou shalt not covet thy brother's child," she singsonged.

"I want one," he said.

"Well, you know how to get one."

Nina, Forever Yenta. "You put the most hardened Times Square pimp to shame, you know that?"

"We're leaving in a few moments. I just wanted to give you your birthday kiss."

With that, she kissed him on his smooth cheek. He stared at her, this blond vision in blood-red. Again he envied Tim, not because he had her, but because for him, the search was over. He had someone to share his life with. "Thanks," he mumbled.

"Don't take this the wrong way, but I think your sister's a toss artist. She was trashing your ex-wife with a gaggle of cackling women upstairs."

Classic Sue. "Thank God you can pick your friends."

Nina leaned in, her grey eyes probing, coaxing. "Speaking of Michele," she began, picking nonexistent lint off his wool tweed pants, "if she's in town, this'd be a good time to get unconflicted, don't you think?"

I need a drink. "I'm all thought out, Nina," he declared.

"Which is why I'm here to help," she announced, then handed him a card. "Here."

"What's this?" he asked.

She elbowed him. "Open it."

Nestled between the red lips on the envelope was his name, written in blue ink in Nina's feminine penmanship. He opened the envelope and revealed a matching card. "The card has red lips on it."

"Look inside."

Laughing, he scanned the card. " 'Smooches gracias for being my friend. Happy Birthday.' Cute," he chuckled, then looked at the very bottom, under Nina's signature. "What's this . . . 718-555-7645?"

"That's where Lisa'll be for the next few hours," she simply replied. "Just in case."

His heart thumped. "Too cheap to buy me a birthday gift, huh?"

Nina laughed. *"Gratulerar med dagen,"* she said. "That's 'Happy Birthday' in Swedish, you Ugly American. I'll say this in English and only once. If life supposedly begins at forty, you'd better get cracking!"

The lobby of The Royalton looked like something out of the movie *Caligula*. The lobby was dark, with swaths of white cloth draped all around. The main floor, replete with white stuffed chairs, gave way to a sunken dining room, with tables covered in cloths and sparsely populated fish tanks built into grey stone walls. This used to be his world—expensive hotels, people catering to his every whim. Now he felt so out of place, his stomach throbbing, sweating in his suit, carrying a hunk of foil in his hands.

The blonde at the front desk greeted him with a rehearsed smile that reeked of efficiency. She looked more like a runway model than a desk clerk and probably was. Everyone in New York City was something other than what they appeared to be. "I'm here to see Dr. Michele Aulisio," he announced. *Because I'm insane.*

The desk clerk gave him her room number—413—

and told him to call her on the courtesy phone in the lobby. Apprehensively, he dialed. After a couple of rings, he heard her voice. "Hello?"

He closed his eyes, letting the voice invade his brain. Finally, he said, "It's me. I'm in the lobby."

"Come on up," she said.

Minutes later, the elevator stopped on the fourth floor so smoothly that he jumped when the doors opened. He stepped into the hallway with its indigo walls and dark carpeting. He turned a corner and found room 413. He thought his heart would explode in his chest. *Here goes nothing.* He knocked four times.

Instantly, the door opened, and Marc swallowed hard. Before him stood his ex-wife in a white terry bathrobe, her hair wet, her glowing face scrubbed clean. She smiled at him, and his groin started to rumble. "Come in," she said.

How smart is this? He did as he was told. As she shut the door, he looked around the room. The room was small with minimalist Bauhaus decor, as reflected in the desk, the chairs, the bed. Strategically placed mirrors added dimensions. A bathroom with a round tub and steamy mirrors abounding adjoined the room. "I didn't think you'd come," she said.

"Neither did I," he said.

"I'm glad you did," she said.

The jury's still out here. He handed her the foil. "Here." She took it. "What's this?"

"Birthday cake," he said. "Your favorite. Chocolate."

"Thanks."

Michele put the foil package on the desk and sat on the bed. Purposely, Marc sat in one of the stuffed blue guest chairs in the corner by the windows . . . miles away from her. He glanced around the room again and saw his face in one of the mirrors. He knew that expression on his face all too well. It was fear. He cleared his throat. "Ad says mirrors add depth to small spaces," he commented—anything to avoid confronting this situation unfolding before him.

"How are Adam and Diane?"

"Good. Lily's five now. She's growing like a weed."

"That's great. They were always wonderful to me."

Another cursory glance around the room revealed the absence of any male presence, other than his. "So, where's Kieran?" He almost choked on the fucker's name.

"Back home," she announced. "Kieran hates New York."

Well, fuck him! Aloud, though, he said, "Oh."

She looked hurt. She patted a spot next to her on the bed. "Marc, come closer," she urged. "I won't bite you."

He laughed nervously. "You used to bite me, and I liked it. That's why I shouldn't sit there."

She looked at him like he was being silly, which he was. She patted the spot again. "Sit," she ordered, sounding like Barbara Woodhouse scolding a naughty hound.

His heartbeats drummed in his ears, his willpower tank officially on empty. Silently, he got up, crossed the seemingly endless distance in three steps, and sat beside Michele on the bed. She smelled like shampoo, and soap, and her own scent. As she turned to face him, her robe shifted, and Marc got a glimpse of her cleavage, dusted with freckles and startlingly white against her deep tan. Instantly, he remembered how good she felt when he held her naked, the mind-blowing sensation of being inside her, her body gripping him and relaxing, gripping and relaxing. All of his senses were on alert, resurrecting memories of how she tasted, smelled, looked without a stitch of clothing, how her skin felt hot and sweaty against him, that sound she made at the moment of maximum joy. The rumble became a full-on erection.

"Have you changed your mind?" she asked.

Marc looked away and found himself staring into yet another mirror. He looked deathly pale. "Why do you really want me to give you away, Michele?"

"For the same reason I told you in your office," she said. "After that breast cancer ate up my mother when I was fifteen, my dad was everything to me. Until I met you, I thought I would be hanging with him until one of us died. Then you came into my life . . . You were just like him."

He didn't see it. Mike Aulisio was like a huge, blond Norseman of a man, and he acted like one—in and out of the courtroom. And Marc was the antithesis of that. "Me and the judge alike?!" he hooted. "I don't intimidate people. That time he came out here to visit us? It was your brilliant idea to tell him we were living together. In the Village, of all places, with the great unwashed masses. And I damn near cleaned out my bank account so I could take him to Mama Leone's to ask him if I could marry you. And then, just as I was about to shit myself from fright, he says . . ." Marc affected Mike's deep-timbered voice, ". . . 'Well, obviously, you're fucking her.' "

"He was only playing!" Michele giggled.

Marc pouted. "He was being a dick."

"He loved you and respected you. You were like the son he didn't have."

And Mike was cool. He hadn't let the end of Michele's marriage tarnish the relationship he had with Marc. Mike appreciated Marc's talents in a way that Daniel Guerrieri never had.

Marc returned to the present to find Michele staring at him intensely, her green eyes like an emotional tractor beam. "What?" he asked curiously.

"I was thinking about Oxford."

Marc groaned, slapping his hands to his forehead. "What? In the dining hall, when I asked you if you'd like a slow, comfortable screw up against the wall?"

"No," Michele laughed. "Although that was one of your smoother moments. That day we went down to London together to see what the big deal was."

"God! I did everything but slit my throat to get your attention."

"I can't remember what tube station that was. With that annoying recording of the guy saying 'Mind the Gap' so you wouldn't get your leg caught between the platform and the train."

It was like he was standing on that same platform right now. "It was Maida Vale Station, and you weren't paying attention."

"So you jumped on the train, lifted me in your arms, deposited me on the train, and said right in my face . . ."

". . . Mind the gap!" they howled in each other's faces.

Marc looked down at her face. She was glowing then, just as she had for the split second she was in his arms that day. "I wanted to fuck you right there on that train," she laughed. "In front of all those stodgy Brits."

"Now you come clean!" Marc exclaimed. "The way I remember it, when I put you down, you declared that you'd never marry an Italian man, because we're all sexists."

"Too much Gloria Steinem, not enough Erica Jong."

"I got ya anyway."

There they were, laughing like people who shared over a decade of history. It seemed almost natural that she'd move and her robe would open. He felt almost entitled to that long glimpse of her cleavage. "That was the exact moment I fell in love with you," she said quietly.

Marc stared at her eyes, at her bare pink mouth. All he knew was he wanted to kiss her. He bent his head and pressed his mouth against hers and waited for her to push him away. When she didn't, he parted her lips with his, met her tongue with his. Instinctively, he slipped his hand inside her robe. He cupped her breast, teased the hardening nipple with his fingers. His groin was throbbing mercilessly. But the same tingling senses told him that something wasn't right.

He broke away from Michele as if she were on fire and shot to his feet. The farther away he was from her, the safer he felt. "What the fuck am I doing?" he asked breathlessly, more of himself than of her.

"Marc," she said softly. "Kieran and I talked about this. If you need for us to . . . you know, to have closure, then that's okay."

He stared at her with both anger and disgust. "What, Kieran give you permission to mercy-fuck me?!" he roared. "So I can have . . ." air quotes, ". . . 'closure?!' "

Her eyes widened. "That's not what I meant!" she cried.

He started pacing—anything to keep his reptilian brain where it was supposed to be. "You remember exactly when you fell out of love with me, Michele? Huh?"

She buried her blond head in her hands. "Why are we going there, Marc?" she groaned.

"Because this is shit we should've said three years ago instead of hiding behind lawyers," he spat.

"People fall out of love all the time. It just happened."

"All that good shit that came flooding back just now? Well, it brought some of the ugly moments of our marriage back with it."

Tears welled up in her eyes. "Marc. Don't do this," she pleaded.

Marc turned to her, and all the poisonous anger he'd felt toward her in their marriage flooded his brain, making his head swim. "Like why no one could find you when I got stabbed. You were scraping our child out of your womb. I fucking hated you for that."

She wiped tears from her face with her fingers. "Which you let me know every night when I came to bed. I was afraid of you! You actually enjoyed what you did."

"I wanted to kill you. I wanted to wrap my hands around your neck and snap it like a twig!"

"So, it was either fuck me to death or strangle me to death, Marc. How ever did you decide?!"

She looked smaller. Her fear of him had shrunk her into a soft ball on the bed. He turned and caught a glimpse of himself in still yet another mirror. He hated what he'd become. *You repulsive fuck!* Tears blurred his mirror image. He blinked, and they rained down his flushed cheeks. "No matter how much you hurt me, I still loved you so much."

"Our marriage was over long before I got pregnant, Marc."

"I thought you were happy."

"I was going crazy!" she sobbed. "The depressing weather. Your family hated me. Nobody gave a damn about my work at NYU. All people wanted to know was what it was like being married to you!"

Was he that blind? So vain that his happiness was all that mattered? He thought he and Adam were the only sensitive Italian men on the planet. "Why didn't you tell me?" he asked.

She smiled at him, that beautiful smile that lingered at the corners of her mouth. "Because you were happy. And productive. But the bigger you got, the smaller I got. Like *Alice in Wonderland.*"

"I should've tried harder to make you happy, Michele."

"I had to do that myself. That's why I left. For a while, it was wonderful. Special. And it was ours. I wouldn't trade that for anything."

Tentatively, Marc sat next to her on the bed. He stroked her beautiful hair, her soft, tanned face. *God, you're so pretty!* Right then, he realized he had to let go. Coveting her through their memories was hurting them both. "Kieran's good to you?" he asked.

The same glow she had on their wedding day returned.

Only, this time, it was for another man. "Good to me and good for me," she said.

His heart squeezed painfully. " 'Cause it's nothing for me, and Jimmy LaFrat, and some of my boys from Rikers to get on a plane to Cali and kick his narrow Irish ass," he laughed wistfully.

She rolled her reddened eyes. "Oh yeah, gangster with a Ph.D.," she laughed. "I'll be sure to warn him."

Do I even want to know the answer? "You love him?"

"Very, very much."

"You gonna wear white?" he teased.

She leaned against him, giggling. "Not after being married to you!"

It was definitely time for him to go. He stood up, and she followed suit. "I'll give you away, Michele," he announced. "If that's what you want."

She hugged him tightly, like she was saying good-bye, too. "I love you."

Almost instantly, his gut that had troubled him for nearly a year and a half stopped roiling. "I love you, too," he whispered. *Always.*

She pressed her cheek against his heart. "It's time we got on with our lives," she sighed.

Three die-hard, after-party stragglers hung out at A.J.'s, sitting on the floor around a round coffee table with A.J. and Lisa. The bass from Janet's "Miss You Much" thumped from the speakers in the background. Lisa looked around at the crew: Ione and two young black guys, Vance and Phil, Ione and A.J.'s coworkers in I.S. Lisa had had lunch with them once or twice in the FDP cafeteria—she, the artist, at the same table with the tech-heads.

Vance dug into the peanuts and sprinkled the fistful into his mouth. "So, I hear the chancellor at SCNJ Montclair is buggin'!" he said between chews.

Lisa shook her head. "That asshole personally denied the BSU's request to march with Sharpton," she said. "Talk about micromanagement."

Ione sipped her staple, cold chardonnay. "Sounds like a racialist arsehole."

Phil took the peanuts from Vance. "I went to SCNJ Montclair," Phil announced. "I graduated the year Swift came in with all his grand ideas and plans. He's the whitest white man around."

Lisa had seen his picture on all the brochures and catalogues. "What's up with the George Hamilton thing he's got going on?" she giggled.

Everyone laughed. She felt validated. Everyone except A.J. She was the picture of seriousness. "I hear the BSU's going anyway," she announced.

Fucking fake activists. "That's a nice slice of stupidity," Lisa commented. "Swift'll yank their charter."

A.J. went on, like she didn't even hear her. "Kwame, the president of the BSU, says they're gonna do it. They're trying to get two Decamp buses together right now."

"Kwame. That's the brothah that's always demonstrating? With the kente cloth hat?"

"That's the one."

"He needs to sit his ass down in a class or two and realize the sixties are over."

"If they do get their shit together, I'm going."

Lisa stared at her in disbelief, A.J. the wannabe buppie activist. "I don't believe you!" Lisa exclaimed. "Swift may be a big joke, but he won't play."

Phil piped up. "I agree with Lisa. That white man don't care about a bunch of niggahs. He's probably thinking, 'One less place for them to congregate and plan the revolution, the better.' "

A.J. was unwavering. Lisa knew only too well that look of unbridled determination in her eyes. "We have to show folks like Swift that we aren't going to roll over."

"Maintaining the BSU's authority to do and legitimize the work it does is not rolling over," Lisa said.

"We shouldn't even have to legitimize our work," Vance declared.

I'm surrounded by reactionaries! "And one day," Lisa reasoned, "we won't have to, but now we do. Kwame's done a lot to raise consciousness, but this is so not a good idea."

Ione drained her glass. "But Lisa, Kwame, and the BSU have worked within the system. They applied for the permit, and played by the rules, and Swift still said no."

"Then he's gotta work the system some more," Lisa insisted. "I've heard Stefanowski thinks Swift's out to lunch on this. He should talk to him."

A.J. sucked her teeth. "Talk, talk, talk."

Lisa wanted to scream sense into her head. "When talking doesn't work, then you go to the other extreme. But, this fake the-revolution-will-not-be-televised-two-fists-up shit is tired. Huey Newton's dead. Bobby Seale's writing a cookbook! And where the hell is Eldridge Cleaver?"

The look of unbridled determination in A.J.'s eyes morphed into one of volcanic anger. Anger directed at Lisa like a laser beam. "If you spent more time with your peeps and less over in your Montclair ivory tower, you'd see that those folks you're dissing are alive and well in the community," she spat.

Here we go again. Only this time, Lisa wasn't having it. "Don't fuck around, Aretha Janet," she said, pissed. "Say what's on your mind."

And she did. "Moms is a psychologist. Pops was an OB/GYN. How did you suffer? A black-and-white TV in your room?!"

"I'm so sick of this shit, A.J.," Lisa snapped. "Your crib's twice the size of mine."

"You know the very second you're in trouble, Mommy writes a check. I don't have that luxury."

"When last did Mommy write a check, A.J.? Wasn't it you who lent me the money to retain Jaye?"

"You never had to suffer like I did."

"So, because my folks have some cash, you're blacker than me."

Lisa looked around at the audience, which looked embarrassed to be watching this drama unfold before them. "Excuse me, has anyone ever heard about a correlation between money and the amount of melanin in the skin?"

Vance looked away. "Yo, my name's Paul, and that's between y'all," he mumbled.

"All right, all right," said Phil, the peacemaker. "All of us have at least one Massa up in our family tree."

"Yeah," said A.J. venomously, "but Massa's closer in Miss Quadroon's family tree."

Ione looked at A.J. in a pitying sort of way, like she knew A.J. was capable of better than this. "A.J., you need to stop before you say something you'll never be able to take back," she begged.

"What the fuck brought this on anyway?" Phil asked.

Lisa stared at A.J. *Five years of this shit . . . why am I your friend?* "Aretha Janet has some issues," she declared.

A.J. looked mad enough to kill. "Fuck you, Lisa," she hissed.

The phone rang just then. A.J. made no move to answer it. She sat there on the floor, glaring daggers at Lisa, daggers that Lisa returned. Finally, after three rings, Ione got up. "I guess I'll get it, then," she said.

Lisa had this overwhelming urge to get out; she just didn't know how to engineer her exit. She listened to Ione on the kitchen phone. "Hallo . . . sure, she's right here. Just a second." Ione called from the openness of the kitchen. "Lisa, phone!"

Lisa got up and stormed into the kitchen. "What's wrong with her?" she whispered.

Ione covered the phone mouthpiece with her hand. "I don't know," she said, shrugging her broad shoulders. "You know A.J."

Lisa sighed, taking the receiver from Ione. "Hello," she said.

The first thing she heard through the earpiece was Aerosmith's Steven Tyler wailing to the tune of "Love in an Elevator." It sounded like Janov's primal scream therapy with guitars. "Lisa, it's Marc!" she heard over the noise.

Her heart leapt. *Oh, fuck, here come the goose bumps.* She pictured him huddled over a payphone in a bar. Then she remembered that he'd sent her away. She adopted her best teacher-student tone. "Yes."

"Look," he shouted, "I'll understand if you say no, but can you meet me?"

"Where?" she shouted.

"I'm at a bar called Donahue's," he shouted. "On Forty-deuce and Second, by the U.N. You know it?"

Lisa peered over the kitchen counter into the living room, at what was waiting for her . . . scowling, militant A.J. and a divided camp. A bar on Forty-second Street sounded like heaven. "I'll find it," she shouted.

Lisa hung up, crossed the open, expansive room in five long strides, and got her belongings off the coat rack, under the watchful, confused eye of the I.S. crew. "I'm outta here," she declared, shrugging into her coat.

She turned and left, slamming the door behind her.

By the time Lisa had walked from Flatbush Avenue to Lincoln Road, caught the lurching D train to Port Authority in Manhattan, then walked out onto Forty-second and Eighth, and then taken the M-104 bus up to Second Avenue, anticipation was on overkill. Anticipation warring with her inner pragmatist. *What the hell are you doing, girl? Have you lost your mind? You swore off men. Why are you here?*

Shivering against the cool November wind, Lisa looked through the picture window into Donahue's, which was packed. TVs over the packed bar relayed election results. Drunk yuppies danced to music. She then saw Marc, sitting on a stool at a high, round table. As if he sensed her, he looked up from his beer and straight at her. He smiled brilliantly, like every ounce of him was glad to see her. She laughed and waved. Instantly, she knew she'd made the right decision.

Minutes later, she was sitting with him at the table, nursing a pint of Killian's Red. She had never seen him so happy. "What else can we toast to?" he asked. "We've already toasted the new Dinkins administration."

Lisa clinked his half-full glass. "We toasted you ... Old Man River," she laughed.

Marc ran his fingers through his hair. "Don't even," he said. "There's not even snow on the roof." He sipped his drink. "Being forty has many advantages."

Lisa saw a young couple over by the bar. They were kissing so deeply that they looked like they were trying to probe each other. "Well, it's not the sexual peak thing," Lisa mused wistfully. "That's for us."

"Hey, the equipment works just fine," he declared in adamant defense of his package. "At least it did six months ago."

Lisa sighed. For the first time since May of 1988, she wanted it and wanted it badly. "God," she said, running her finger around the rim of her glass. "The last time I had any kind of sex, Reagan was president."

He literally perked up. "First or second term?"

She slapped his arm. "Second—God! What, you think I'm a Quaker?" she laughed.

Marc raised his glass. "To Lisa, reaching her sexual peak in five years," he declared.

They clinked glasses and sipped. She saw him looking over the rim of his glass at her, and she blushed. She knew that look. That look spoke volumes of what was going on in his BVDs. "I got one," he said. "To the closure I finally experienced a few hours ago with my ex-wife."

That explained it—his demeanor, that wide, ear-to-ear smile. "Wow," she said. "Come to think of it, you seemed . . . *peaceful* when I came in here."

He grinned, his gaze implacable. "Knowledge brings peace," he said.

Oh, shit. More goose bumps. "What do you know?" she asked. *Do I want to know?*

"That Michele's not the one I want to be with."

"And who do you want to be with?"

He winked a gleaming blue eye at her over the rim of that glass. "You know her," he said. "Intimately."

Oh, shit. Lisa nervously drained her glass in gulps. "Well, I'm done," she announced, just to have something to say.

"There's beer at my place," he said, his voice husky.

She looked away at that couple at the bar. Her head, heart, and libido were engaged in full-on, three-way combat. "What kind of beer?" she asked.

"Any kind you want," he said.

She pictured heart and libido—those evil twins—standing over a bloody, mortally wounded head on an imaginary canvas. She met his lusty gaze head-on. "Let's go, then," she said.

Unbelievable. She was there with him, drinking wine while staring out at the much-touted impressive view of the City that had been foreplay for so many of his sexual conquests. He loved how she looked in the moonlight streaming in through the French windows. "This is beautiful!" she whispered, awestruck.

You're beautiful. Unable to resist, he raised a hand and stroked her cheek. "It is, isn't it?" he said.

She turned to look at him and smiled shyly. "Does this work with all the chicks?" she teased.

Clearly, it wasn't working with her. He laughed guiltily, tapping her glass with his fingernail. *Change the subject.* "More wine?" he asked.

"No, I'm good, thanks."

He took her hand, leading her down the wooden, suspended staircase to the living room. He'd built a fire, which crackled with life in the stone fireplace. "Wait here," he said.

He left her standing there. "What are you doing?!" she giggled.

He moved over to the sound system, then popped in a CD. Almost immediately, Nina Simone's "I Loves You, Porgy" came flowing from the speakers, like audible cream. Her face brightened. "The CD I gave you for your birthday!" she squealed happily.

He approached her, took her wineglass, and set it on an end table. He slowly pulled her into his arms, dancing her toward the fireplace. The same thing he felt in the room with Michele returned, only this time, minus the guilt. She was supposed to be right there, pressed against him, in the warmth of the fire. "How'd you know I love Nina Simone?" he asked.

"Nina told me," she said.

He searched her face, stroked her cheeks. She was so beautiful, it hurt to look at her. "I'm sorry I sent you away before," he whispered. "Emotional CYA . . . you know . . . 'covering your ass.' "

"It's okay," she said.

She looked like she was so open to every emotion of the moment, so open to him. *Who are you trying to fool?* He couldn't resist her, and she didn't look like she wanted him to. He bent his head and kissed her slowly. He'd been dying to kiss her for two weeks, and the fantasy of it paled in comparison to the reality. The heat of it overtook them both. She responded to him, kissing him passionately, tongues dueling, tasting, sucking. "Lisa," he moaned. He knew that, with her pressed so close to him, she could feel every inch of him against her. And he didn't care.

Suddenly, she moved away, gasping for air. *Fuck!* He was so stunned, he was still puckered. She looked like she was fighting to stay in control. "I'll have that wine now," she panted, running her thumb across her glistening mouth.

He laughed, shaking his head. Such sweet torture.

Shannon Amadeo strapped on his backpack and hunkered down against the cold and the crushing weight of being the first black male in his family to strive for a college education. Through the darkness of the night, he could see the welcoming lights of the SCNJ off-campus student apartments. So focused was he on getting home that he didn't see the red vintage Mustang until it pulled in front of him. Three Aryan-looking white boys in Delta Kappa Pi jackets jumped out of the car . . . Delta Kappa Pi, known on campus as the fraternity for jocks and shit-kickers dying to start some stuff. Shannon Amadeo knew instinctively that this was not going to be good.

He puffed out his broad chest and tried to look imposing. "You guys lost or something?" he asked, hating that he'd heard a catch in his voice.

The most menacing of the three stepped forward, thin lips curled up in a sinister smile. "No, I think we've found exactly what we're looking for, nigger," he said calmly, his flint-grey eyes glistening in the darkness.

As if he were channeling the ghosts of all the black men who found themselves swinging from a noose,

Shannon Amadeo took off and ran with everything he had toward those lights.

She didn't know if it was the wine, or if it was his mouth on hers, but her head was spinning. He'd kissed her, and just as she'd try to catch her breath, he'd kiss her again and again. He held her hands, stroked her face. She felt the roughness of his hands against her cheeks. She felt those hands on her body, contrasting against the softness of the leather couch under them. Her very clothing seemed confining. *What the fuck are you doing to me?* "Shit," she whispered.

He linked and relaxed his fingers with hers. "Lisa," he laughed. "You feel so good."

"I aim to please," she giggled against his mouth.

"I like your aim," he grinned.

He moved to roll on top of her, and she turned on her back to accept him. Unfortunately, she overshot the end of the couch and landed smack on the carpeted floor. She giggled and giggled, even when she saw his face hovering over her, even when he lay on top of her, muscles and sinews pressing against her. But he wasn't laughing. He had that familiar look she'd seen many times. He kissed her, and she felt his hands against her belly, fingers reaching below the elastic of her tights. And there was that enormous, myth-defying erection pressing against her thigh. Sense memory from that horrible night intruded just then. *I can't do this.*

She pushed him away. "Wait, wait, wait," she gasped. "Wait!"

She sat up, trying to clear the fog in her head. The CD had stopped, the fire burning down. She held her head in her hands. *Fucking Bryan.* She doubted memories of her interfered with his nights with his fiancée, the lovely Mia. She lifted her head to see him looking at her, smiling. Far from pissed, he seemed okay. He took her hands, linking her fingers between his. "Why are you staring at me?" she asked.

He laughed. "Because you're pretty."

She looked away. *Speak up, girl; you have an English tongue in your head!* "Look, I . . ." she quietly began. "He hurt me. Bad. I really like you, but I need to take this real slow."

He leaned in and pressed his forehead against hers. "Sweetie, it's your ride," he said softly. "We'll take this as fast or as slow as you want."

There he was, more concerned about her than his rock-hard dick. *You're wonderful.* She held his face in her hands and kissed him.

"I better take you home," he laughed. "Now."

9

Dean Stefanowski had been summoned to Swift's cherrywood inner sanctum yet again. Only the usually icy-calm Swift clearly looked strained in his grey Italian suit. He and Stefanowski stared down at the hungry throng of journalists and TV news reporters with cameras congregating in the cold on the lawn outside. "Look at them," Swift said with unveiled contempt. "They want their pound of flesh."

Stefanowski looked over at Swift. Swift's aura of self-pity disgusted him. "That kid Shannon Amadeo already gave, Donald," he declared.

Swift whirled away from the window, glaring hatefully at Stefanowski. A smaller man would have withered. "Not his. Mine!" Swift exploded. "The phone's been ringing off the hook."

"I'm not surprised," Stefanowski said. "This campus used to be peaceful. Now we've got hate crimes. We've got a kid in the hospital half beaten to death."

"Governor Florio called me this morning, demanding to know what I'm doing about this," Swift said, a cry in his voice. "And Dr. Smith from the Commission on Higher Education. Apparently, a hate crime goes against our proposed mission for a culturally pluralistic university. They may pull our application, Tom. We'd have to reapply in two years!"

If only the students could see their chancellor, two minutes from simpering idiocy in the face of a crisis. Nonetheless, Thomas Stefanowski was a team player. "How can I help, Donald?" he asked

The old Swift returned, if but for a second. "I want this thing contained, Tom," he declared, with authority.

Even team players had their limits. "I'm afraid I can't do that, Donald."

An angry vein pulsed in the middle of Swift's tanned forehead. Any vestige of the cool, Waspy facade was all but a memory. "You can't do that?!" he roared.

"I'm the faculty advisor," Stefanowski calmly explained. "I advised. You didn't listen."

"Well, you can just wind-sprint down to the field house and clean out your Ben-Gay and jock straps, Tom," Swift said. "I have no use for anyone who's not committed to my vision for this institution."

Stefanowski would've laughed in his face if the situation weren't so dire. "Donald," he said carefully, "you've been in academe for a good number of years, so I'm positive I don't have to explain the concept of tenure to you."

Swift's face had the oh-shit look. That satisfied Stefanowski that he'd made his point. He looked out the window at the madding crowd. "Well, Donald, I'll leave you to fielding all your important calls," he said. "Good luck with the Fourth Estate."

With that, Stefanowski left. He had some calls of his own to make.

Rick Farrelly sobbed as if he would break in half. He rocked himself in his swivel chair, keening like a mourner at a wake. Lisa stared out through the picture window into the darkened parking lot. The lights in the lot flickered on, and Lisa looked for any sign of Pat Farrelly's white BMW. Lisa gripped Rick's arm in order to get him up. He snatched it away, sobbing inconsolably. "Rick, I've called Pat," she said loudly over the crying. "She's coming to get you out of here before Joe Siegrist sees you like this."

"She can't leave the kids alone!" Rick wailed. "Their grandfather just died."

She offered him coffee in an FDP mug. "Your neighbors are watching them, okay?" she said. "Here, have some coffee."

Rick slapped the mug away. It *thunked* onto the floor, the black coffee seeping into the beige carpet. "Leave me alone!" he pleaded.

"Oh, Rick," she sighed helplessly.

Over the sobs, she heard a noise and looked up. Genie, stoic as usual, entered the office and shut the door. "Genie," Lisa said, relieved.

Genie looked at Rick with the haughty scorn that only someone unfamiliar with deep loss could. "He's drunk," she said.

No shit! "Of course he's drunk," Lisa snapped. "His father just died."

"And you're enabling him," she stated.

Genie just didn't get it. "Look, have you seen Joe Siegrist?" Lisa asked.

"Frank Lane's had him in a meeting on the third floor. It's about to end now."

That bought them some time. Lisa looked out the window again for the white BMW. "Good. Where's the printing requisition for the report?"

Genie produced a thick carbon form seemingly from midair and gave it to Lisa. "He's in no condition to sign that form, much less verify the specs," Genie declared.

"We used last year's specs," Lisa said. "As for him signing it . . ."

Lisa snatched up a pen and forged Rick's signature. Genie's eyes widened. "No, you didn't just do that!" she cried.

They both looked down at Rick, who was still a teary mess, huddled in his chair. "Look at him!" Lisa commanded. "He just lost his father. You want him to lose his job, too?"

"I don't want to lose mine. I guess you're not as concerned about yours."

Lisa handed Genie the form. "I'm going to stall Siegrist. You make sure Pat Farrelly gets her husband out of here."

Lisa ran from the office in an attempt to head Joe Siegrist, Rick's boss, off at the pass. She rushed through the maze of grey cubicles, looking frantically for him. *Damn, damn, damn!*

She breezed by the well-cared-for flora and ficus trees in the expansive FDP atrium under the glass ceiling, so focused on the quarry that she didn't realize that she'd just bumped into Joe Siegrist, the mid-fifties division vice president. Although to look at him, with his baggy, rumpled brown suit, greasy hair, and pinched features, one could not imagine the amount of money he made heralding FDP's good fortune through the annual report. Everyone did know, though, that the man was insane. He'd once pulled an Australian hunting knife on an underling with an attitude. When he did come down from the fourth floor of Mt. Olympus, he felt the need to regale Lisa with stories of all the black people he knew as a boy in Minnesota, as if she knew them, too. Of course, all black folks knew each other.

Lisa trembled like she'd just had a double espresso. Even her smile shook uncontrollably. *God, please let Pat be here.* She tried to be casual. " 'Night, Joe," she said.

Joe Siegrist glanced down at his brown-band Rolex. Even from her vantage point, she could see the hand pointing out a quarter to eight. "You're still here," he said, amazed.

Lisa shrugged, again in an attempt to be casual. "Report's gotta go out to the stockholders," she said.

Siegrist eyed her with admiration. "You're conscientious. Rick has high praise for you."

She glanced over her shoulder. *Rick.* "He's a good guy."

"Speaking of Rick, let me stick my head in and see what he's up to."

He must've seen the terror that masked Lisa's face. "You okay?" he asked.

Lisa laughed nervously. "Why wouldn't I be?"

They walked together, the only sound between them their heels on the brick floor of the atrium, and then the shuffling of their shoes on the beige carpet. Joe wasn't much for small talk. Which was just as well. Lisa was seconds away from a full-blown myocardial infarction by the time they arrived at Rick's office.

The office was empty, with the lights off. Relief suffused Lisa. Genie hovered at a safe distance. "Where's Farrelly?" Siegrist asked.

Genie shot Lisa a quick look. "You just missed him," she announced. "You know his father died."

"Shame," was the extent of Siegrist's outpouring of sympathy. "The report's ready to go to print tonight, though, right?"

So much for priorities. Lisa waved the forged requisition. "All done," she assured him.

Genie looked away. "Good," Siegrist said. "Well, good night, ladies. Don't stay much longer."

Siegrist turned and disappeared through the grey maze of cubicles. Genie looked at Lisa, a look that said, *You're fucked.*

* * *

Adam and Marc sat on the floor of Adam's garage, amidst the cars and power tools. Marc held the squealing golden retriever puppy in his arms. She looked up at him with unconditional love in her big brown eyes, and immediately, Marc understood how Adam could defy his wife. Who wouldn't want to give their daughter a pure gift like that look? Marc held her up to his face. Instantly, her warm tongue darted out, and she repeatedly slurped his nose.

"Man, I don't want to see Diane's Irish temper," he laughed.

Adam clipped on her little pink collar and ran a hand over her fuzzy head. "You invited Lisa to have Thanksgiving dinner with us," he said. "We're both 0 and 1 for smart decisions."

Easy for you. You're the model son. Marc cradled the puppy protectively in his arms. "I want them to see that I'm a big, happy boy who can choose whom he wants to spend time with," he stated.

"The point of being a big, happy boy is not caring if they're unhappy with your choices."

"All right. They're family. I want them to like her as much as I do."

"And evidently, you like her a lot."

He knew he was beaming. "Yes, I do," he confessed. "A lot."

Adam looked at him and laughed, like he was a hopeless case. "Well, this is the acid test, Marco," he sighed, shaking his head. "Before the turkey's finished, she'll know if this is the family for her."

It was like a car crash they couldn't look away from. Nina, Tim, and Lisa sat on the white sectional in the Simons' living room, staring, transfixed, at the images flashing across the 50-inch TV screen. Students of all colors had been peacefully marching, flanked on each end by New York's Finest, dressed warmly from head to toe in blue. On the sidewalks in front of closed businesses, Italian-American males and their women with mile-high hair screamed expletives and racial epithets at the marchers.

Then one of the agitators leapt from the sidewalk through the wall of police and popped a young black guy in the chin, knocking him to the ground. A sea of black demonstrators dropped onto the agitator as if they were the wrath of God Himself. Demonstrators and agitators began violently mixing it up, with police trying in vain to restore order.

The male TV announcer did the color commentating like a poor man's Al Michaels. "What started out as a peaceful student demonstration through the streets of Bensonhurst ended when a fight broke out, resulting in over fifty arrests," he said clinically over the images of screams, tears, and bloodied flesh that disturbed right down to the very pixels.

Lisa felt sick with dread. "A.J. and the BSU were out there," she said.

Tim reached over and gave her shoulder a reassuring squeeze. "We were out there shooting that footage," he said. "No one was seriously hurt, just banged up and a little pissed."

Nina shook her head, looking like someone mercifully foreign enough not to understand the reasons for the events unfolding before her. "They're going to lose their charter, and I doubt this hardly even made a difference," she declared.

Tim switched off the TV. "Only time'll tell," he said cryptically.

10

Lisa rushed for the lobby of her apartment, in her haste reflecting on how she, in her best pink cashmere suit, came to be waiting for Marc to pick her up for Thanksgiving dinner.

After Election Night, they saw each other almost every day. Her mother had sent her some grouper and guava from Eleuthera, so she decided to make him dinner. In his gleaming condo kitchen Lisa guessed he'd rarely used, she cooked him the only Bahamian foods she could make: peas and rice and grouper almondine, complemented by crisp asparagus tips and a lush green salad. Dessert was guava duff with a sweet butter rum sauce. She'd forbidden him to help, so he watched her appreciatively in his gray turtleneck, looking nearly as delicious as the food. She was a sucker for a man in a quality woolen turtleneck.

They put out the entrees in the middle of the kitchen table, which he'd set. "Damn, girl!" he laughed, eyeing the spread. "I'm impressed."

That was the point. She beamed with pride. "Go on," she prompted, urging him toward his place setting.

"You go first—you did all the work," he said. "If I wanted some servile babe, I'd be with an Italian girl."

Laughing, she hopped up onto her chair. They held hands, and he initiated grace. She opened one eye to look at him. *Okay, now I'm impressed.*

He filled her glass with white wine. "You were telling me about work," he said.

She started serving the food. "You know, it used to sustain me, but I think I need a new gig," she declared. "Rick's falling apart, and because of that, everything's suffering."

"Well, what do you want to do?"

It took a second for the question to register. "What do you mean?"

"What's your passion?" he asked.

She had to go way back into the mental Rolodex for that one, the reason how she got from there to here. "Honestly?" she said. "When I was younger, I loved to draw. I used to sketch everything, anything. But when I went to Fordham, drawing was like boot camp. 'Six still lifes before this day, one nude sketch at the end of this period of time.' It was like going to Mass. I wanted to rediscover it again, but . . ."

He looked like he'd seized upon something serious. "So, why don't you?"

"Because sketches don't pay the bills," she declared.

"You've got to do what sustains you, Lisa," he said simply.

She looked around the understated opulence of the condo. *Easy for you to say.* "You can say that, because you're . . ." she faked a bow, ". . . 'The Voice of Italian America,' " she teased, but she meant it.

He playfully pushed her, and, as if he'd read her mind, said, "Don't let all this fool you. I wasn't always

'The Voice of Italian America.' I'm from Fairfield. My old man makes beer for a living, and I thought I was going to be right next to him on the factory floor. But I knew that I was going to have a pen in my hand."

She saw the determination in his eyes and wondered if drawing could inspire such passion in her again. Lately, all of her passion was drenched in trying to survive her divorce with her sanity intact. Now that that was winding down . . . "You really know how to ask the tough questions," she said.

She watched as he took a forkful of grouper and held her breath in anticipation as he put it in his mouth. An angelic smile spread across his face. "Oh, that's so good!" he moaned.

She blushed, even though she heard the voice of her die-hard feminist in the back of her head. *This is what you've come to, Melissa. Knocking yourself out to please another man. Don't you know how this story ends?*

He nudged her. "Hey," he said, nodding in the direction of the couch. "Your purse is ringing."

She leapt up. "Oh!" she exclaimed. "My new toy. The only person I gave the number to was Nina."

She rushed over to the couch, opened her leather purse, and switched on the phone. "Hello?"

"Luvie, it's me!" Nina effused over the tubular-sounding cell phone. "Where are you?"

Lisa looked over at Marc and nodded. "Nina. I'm . . ." *What do I say?* "I'm away from the house." It wasn't entirely a lie.

"Well, I shan't keep you," she said. "Tim and I are inviting you to dinner this Saturday. We want to invite Marc."

Poor Nina, trying to engineer something that was jumping off all on its own. Lisa knew better than to put up a fight. "Okay," she said.

"Okay?" she asked, surprised.

"Nina, it's your dinner party. You can invite whoever you want."

"All right then. I will ring him. Be here on Saturday at eight."

"Yes, ma'am."

Nina clicked off, and Lisa put the phone away. "Dinner party?" Marc asked.

"Yeah, that was Nina. She's trying to fix us up on Saturday."

Lisa joined him at the table. He put down his fork. "That doesn't seem to sit well with you," he said gently.

Lisa sighed, trying to find the words. "Marc," she began, "I'm trying to figure if this is live or if it's Memorex. Plus my unfinished business . . . the divorce . . . the class."

Marc took her hand, pressed it against his cheek. She felt the bony line of his jaw and the roughness of stubble against the back of her hand. "You're right," he said. "We should see where we're heading. But I want it clear that I'm not trying to keep you in the closet because you're black."

Where the fuck did you come from? She kissed his mouth, tasted the grouper on his lips. "Well, I'm keeping you in the closet strictly because you're white," she teased. "Bring you out in front of the brothahs and sistahs? They'd cut my Black Girl Card up. Right in my face."

He nudged her. "Fuck you," he laughed.

"What's that, Italian foreplay?"

He winked at her. "Is it working?"

You devil! She was thinking of an answer when the high-tech phone on the kitchen wall bleated. He grinned, shaking his head. "Guess who," he said, getting up to answer it.

Nina Interruptus. She watched him go. "She's quick," she laughed.

That Saturday, they met up at the Simons' house, in separate cars, feigning disinterest but secretly itching for each other over Nina's Swedish meatballs and lingon-berry sauce. Under the excuse of washing her hands, Lisa ducked into the downstairs half-bath. Marc slipped in as she was drying them. He eagerly reached for her. "I wanted to kiss you all night," he laughed.

"Shh!" she whispered, giggling.

Marc kissed her again and again, hungrily, his hands cupping her ass. "You're wearing the shit out of that red sweater!" he gasped.

He was all muscle against her; it was like being embraced by a warm, tensile wall. His kisses left her drunk, strung out, foggy. Her crotch wooshed and throbbed. "Marc," she whispered his name.

"What," he moaned against her mouth.

So much for restraint. She was two seconds from clearing off the marble sink top and dropping her panties when a knock at the door saved her from a rookie mistake. "Melissa, are you in there?" Nina called.

She and Marc stifled a giggle. She cleared her throat. "Umm . . . yeah!" she called back.

"Have you seen Marc?" she asked.

Lisa stared at his handsome, flushed face. She looked into his eyes and saw so deeply that her heart squeezed. She caressed his cheeks. He stared at her quizzically. "What?" he mouthed.

She passed her thumb across his wide mouth, smearing off the red lipstick the kiss had imprinted. "I'll see if I can find him," she called to Nina through the door.

Together they counted to twenty, then ducked out of the bathroom, laughing conspiratorially. Until they got to the TV room, where they first met. David Rasche was mugging on the TV screen as the title character in the sitcom *Sledge Hammer!* "Who's in here?" Lisa wondered out loud.

She and Marc ventured in . . . and saw Courtney and Craig, sleeping the peaceful Sleep of the Ages on the couch. Beautiful brown angels basking in the Technicolor glow from the TV. As if he was feeling the same thing she was, he snaked gentle arms around her waist and pressed her close against him. "Hey," he whispered against her cheek.

"What?" she whispered back.

"Kids or no kids?" he asked.

She stared down at them, instantly missing what she'd almost had, feeling the loss as if she could touch it. She sensed he was doing the exact same thing. "No question," she said. "Kids."

Later that week, they went running together, though Lisa wondered if she was crazy, freezing her ass off. But her ass, her stomach, her thighs . . . everything was much tighter, leaner. She felt beautiful, confident, strong, healthy. The fact that she was falling hard for him merely added the extra glow. He eyed her appreciatively, nudged her. "All right, Flo Jo," he breathed evenly.

She laughed breathlessly. "You're just jealous, 'cause I can keep up with you now!"

"Hey," he said.

She glanced over at him. "What?"

"Marc or Bryan?" he asked.

"No question," she said.

He beamed happily, his expression like, *I thought so.* She nudged him. "Bryan," she teased.

Playfully, Marc grabbed her, pulling her down onto the grassy circle in the middle of the track. He tickled her mercilessly, and she laughed so hard she thought she'd wet her Spandex pants. She was lying on the cold, damp, dirty ground, and she'd never been happier. And he was the cause of that.

So, that was how she came to be waiting on the curb as Marc's black Jeep rounded the corner. Her heart practically leapt out of her chest. *Shit, girl, what are you, sixteen?!*

He stopped the car—just barely—and she got in. She turned to him. He looked so handsome in his cream cowl-neck sweater over a denim shirt, blue corduroys, and a black pea coat. "Look at you," she laughed. "You clean up nice."

Marc helped strap her into her seat. Even from behind his aviator sunglasses, his gaze was lusty, appreciative. "Pretty in pink," he said, a husky catch to his voice.

He leaned in and kissed her. She held his face, stroked his cheeks, as his tongue found hers. *Lord, help me to keep my head!*

Marc moved away. "Happy Thanksgiving," he grinned deviously.

Boy knows how to push my button. She stared at his mouth, now stained with her pink lipstick. "Same to you," she said shyly, rummaging in her purse for a hanky. "Wipe your mouth. You look like a Kabuki."

He let her draw the white cotton hanky across his mouth, then shifted the car into first gear. They were off. Only then did it occur to Lisa that she was about to meet his family. The nervous feeling in the pit of her stomach that she'd first felt when he'd asked returned. She watched as Marc drove along Bloomfield Avenue, staring at the trees with orange, red, and brown leaves swaying in the wind. She felt safe and warm inside the car, listening to U2's moody, bass-heavy cut "With or Without You" coming from the Blaupunkt speakers. "Who's going to be there?" she asked.

She saw a strange expression set in his face. What was that? Was he nervous, too? "My mom and dad. Rosalie and Dan," he said. "My brother, Adam. You're going to love him."

"I'm sure. He's your brother."

He drove on, and she stared out the window at the businesses and car dealerships that whipped past. "Let's see, who else?" he continued. "Adam's wife, Diane, and their daughter, Lily. My sister Suzanne, her husband Doug, and their twins D.J. and Claire. I think that's it."

She was starting to rethink this whole thing. Being

black amongst a crowd of Italians was hazardous to the health as of late. Plus she didn't do the family thing all too well. Bryan's parents only barely tolerated her. His father was a downright unpleasant chauvinist who would refer to Lisa as "that girl," in front of his son. Bryan's mother was sweet, but she made it clear that the man's needs in a marriage came first. She applauded Lisa for putting Bryan through school. After all, a woman's job was supporting her husband at all costs, catering to his every unrealistic whim. When she had Bryan arrested for raping her, that sweet old sistah would call her house at all hours of the day and night and call her a whore who was trying to ruin her son's life. As if Lisa had somehow asked Bryan to force his dick into every orifice in her body. And the state of New Jersey, through not prosecuting, validated Dorothy Livingston's very assumption.

She came back to earth to find Marc cruising along on Route 23. "Hey, are you okay?" he asked.

She smiled weakly. He didn't need to know the details of that particular piece of history that was her marriage to Bryan. "Yeah," she assured him with a blasé shrug.

He must've taken her silence for nerves. "Relax. They're gonna like you," he assured her. "At least half as much as I do."

She laughed, basking in the glow that assertion provided . . . until she looked out the window and saw two fat Cedar Grove cops pulling over a group of suit-and-tie Puerto Rican men in a cream-colored Benz. Bigotry, it seemed, never took a holiday.

Sometime later, Marc pulled up in a circular gravel driveway in front of a small, brown, two-story A-frame house. "This is it," he announced, killing the engine.

They got out of the car. Lisa's heart thumped in her chest. She surveyed her surroundings. A wooden fence separated the Guerrieri property from the other expansive piece of land at her left. The road emptied almost immediately out onto the main thoroughfare. She saw a tiny brook next to the wooden fence. This must have been a nice place to have been a child. "Adam and I used to catch frogs in there when we were kids," Marc said, coming up behind her.

"From modest beginnings to *The New York Times* best-seller list," she said. "I love it."

He took her cold, sweaty hand and led her toward the house. She looked around. *Can't run now. What do I know from Fairfield?*

They walked up the concrete steps, and immediately, the door opened. The guy standing in the doorway looked almost exactly like Marc, only he had smoldering, dark eyes and graying temples. He was a couple of inches taller, wore his khakis and olive turtleneck like a male model. *This must be Adam Guerrieri.*

"It's about time!" he said. "We're starving!"

"Yeah, Happy Thanksgiving to you, too, *chooch*," Marc laughed.

He enthusiastically hugged his brother. Lisa felt a little shard of envy. Sometimes it sucked being the only child of only children.

Marc's brother then turned to her. "You must be Lisa," he said. "I'm Adam."

Lisa put out a hand for him to shake, but he slapped it away, locked her in a hug, and dropped kisses on both her cheeks. Caught off guard, all she could do was let him. "Nice to meet you!" she cried.

Adam pointed at Marc. "This guy talks about you nonstop," he said.

Lisa flushed. "You'd think he'd have better things to do."

Adam screwed up his handsome face and exhaled air through pursed lips, the classic Italian scoff. "Who, 'The Voice of Italian America?'" he teased. "Nah. Come inside. It's freezing!"

Lisa grasped for Marc's hand and held on for dear life as she set foot into what looked like the set of an Italian *Leave It to Beaver*. The house was modestly decorated with pictures of the children and grandchildren. A modest stereo and rack of records, big-screen color television, an organ, and stuffed furniture—covered in the requisite plastic—occupied the room. People turned and Lisa could see them trying valiantly not to let their jaws drop. She'd seen that struggle for civility before, from the parents of her blissfully ignorant playmates when they'd invited her over to their houses to play. Fortunately, Marc was just as blissfully ignorant. "Everyone, this is Lisa," he announced. "Lisa, everyone."

He pointed to the older, squat, bleached blonde and the worn-down man with a pursed mouth next to her. "My mom, Rosalie, and my dad, Daniel," he said.

Rosalie nodded. "Hello," she murmured; Daniel said nothing.

Lisa guessed that Daniel must have been a stunner in his day. His two sons looked just like him. The other man in the group with friendly brown eyes came forward. He nodded his dirty-blond head toward the younger bleached-blond woman, who clutched her small son and daughter against her girth as if she were protecting them from mortal harm. "Hey, I'm Doug Gliatto," he said, smiling warmly. "The brother-in-law. That's my wife, Suzanne, and our twins, D.J. and Claire."

He seemed for real; his wife was another story. She seemed tensed, like a bitch in waiting. "Hi," Lisa said.

Just then, a tall, attractive blonde rolled into the room like a whirling dervish, with an adorable little brown-haired girl in tow. "You're here!" she laughed, her grey eyes sparkling. She came forward and embraced her warmly. She smelled like shampoo and expensive perfume. *Damn, you folks like to hug!* "I'm Diane, Adam's wife, and this is Lily." She pushed her daughter forward. "Say hi to Uncle Marc's girlfriend, sweetie."

"Hi," Lily said obediently, with a wave of her tiny hand.

Lisa's heart clenched. She and Marc exchanged glances. *So . . . I'm the girlfriend. Definitely not Memorex.*

They sat at a round cherrywood table in the living room, surrounding a full, orgiastic spread consisting of a massive turkey and other traditional Thanksgiving fare, as well as meat lasagna and ziti. Lisa sat next to Marc, Diane, Adam, and Lily. Save for the sound of the pre-game show coming from the living room TV, the room was tense and quiet.

"Should I play some music?" Adam asked.

Daniel sucked down the last of his double Scotch. "No music," he barked. "I want to hear myself think."

"Audible cognitive processes, Dad," Diane commented. "That's a new one."

"Diane's a lawyer, Lisa," Suzanne said, and her name sounded like poison in Suzanne's mouth. "She likes to use big words."

Marc glared at his sister, and Lisa could tell immediately that she was the attention-seeking troublemaker of the family. Every family had one. "Not today, Sue," Marc said wearily, as if he was tired of a lifetime of shit from her.

Rosalie ran a trembling hand over her peroxide-blond hair. "Why don't we go around the table and have everybody say what they're thankful for?" she suggested, looking over at her baby son. "Why don't you start, son? Since we hardly see you."

Marc sighed. "Okay," he said. "I'm thankful for this year's successes."

Adam raised his Chianti glass. "Here here, Dr. Best-seller!"

Marc raised his sapphire-blue eyes to the ceiling, as if thinking hard. "I'm thankful that I'm alive, because a couple of years ago, it was touch and go there." Then those eyes drifted down from the ceiling and onto Lisa. "Most of all, I'm thankful that I met Lisa."

She had that sensation similar to when she daydreamed in class, only to hear the teacher call her name, catching her with absolutely nothing to say. He took her hand under the table. *Oh my God!* "You inspire me every day," he said, smiling brilliantly.

Mercifully, her English tongue returned, but it was like they were the only two people in the room . . . on the planet. "That's so sweet!" she said, her voice catching in her throat. "Thank you."

Suzanne looked away. "I feel a gag reflex coming on," she mumbled.

"Don't hurl yet, Sue," Adam said. "Tell us what evil you're thankful for doing this year."

Suzanne and Adam were miles away. That's how Lisa had heard them. They were inconsequential to the gaze of someone who thought she was special. Then it hit her. *Oh, shit. I'm in love with this man.*

It was a Guerrieri family tradition. Near-comatose on a combination of carbo loads and tryptophan from the turkey, the only exercise they got was scraping all Rosalie's blue Currier and Ives dinner plates and stacking them at the end of the table nearest the door. Diane leaned in toward Lisa. "Lisa, wanna help me take the dishes to the kitchen?" she asked with a wink.

Women. They had to separate from the men and debrief. They had done the same thing at Michele's first Guerrieri Thanksgiving dinner.

Lisa giggled deviously, like she knew it was time to dish the dirt about him. "Sure, Diane."

He relaxed his grip on her hand under the table. "Don't believe a word she tells you about me," he laughed.

Lily tugged at the sleeve of Diane's blinding-white blouse. "Mommy, can I help?" she asked.

Good. Take her with you. That way, the conversation about him would at least be rated PG.

"Of course you can," Diane said, then cast her gaze over to the seemingly shell-shocked twins. "D.J. and Claire, you wanna help, too?"

Claire looked up at Suzanne. "Is it okay, Mommy?" she pleaded.

Suzanne looked at Diane, then Lisa, then back at Diane. In the back of Marc's mind, he wondered what the fuck that was about. Finally, she said, quite pointedly, "Yes, it's okay, sweetie. You and your brother go help *Aunt Diane.*"

Lisa and Diane trooped out of the dining room with dishes; the children followed carefully behind with the silver cutlery. Marc stared after them. He wondered what it would be like to have his own family, maybe with her. He gazed at how that pink wool dress flattered her body, caressed her ass as she moved. She was the whole package—beautiful, smart, talented—and with a body that he could barely manage to keep his hands off. *Go slow, Marc.*

"*Madonn'!* Bringing eggplant into this house. What are you, *stunad?!*" Suzanne cried.

Stunned beyond belief, Marc turned to the shrieking shrew he'd grown up with. She was many things, but this? "What?!"

Even Doug looked ashamed of her and embarrassed at the outburst. "Honey, that's enough," he declared.

"Shut up, Doug!" she barked. "He's *my* brother." She whirled to Adam. "You're no better. You knew she was black, and you didn't say anything!"

Adam shook his head. "You sound suspiciously like a racist, Sue."

Not to be outdone in the drama queen department, Rosalie clutched her breast, trying her hardest to look frail and appropriately wronged. "MarcAntonio, how could you?!" she gasped.

"How could I what, Ma?!" Marc asked.

"The same people who beat your father almost to death when you were just a baby," she cried. "The same people who your cousin Jimmy's trying to keep out of his neighborhood. You bring one right here to our table. To eat with us!"

He looked at his dad for a modicum of support. True to form, Daniel just sat stooped in his chair, shaking his head. It was Adam who came to his brother's aid. "I don't believe you people!" he declared, obviously disgusted. "You're probably collecting money for the Bensonhurst Legal Defense Fund."

Marc looked unflinchingly at his parents, his sister. So much more concerned with maintaining social order than with the happiness of their own flesh and blood. Was he that romantic to think that, even though they were largely indifferent toward him, they would appreciate where he'd been almost two years ago, and how far he'd come to be happy? "I was wondering why Jimmy thinks the way he does," he said. "I didn't check my own immediate family!"

Daniel was still shaking his head. *"Tu hai introdotto una negra nella nostra casa?"* he asked in disbelief.

That upset Marc even more. He and Rosalie used to purposely speak Italian so they could talk around their children without them knowing what they were saying. "English, Dad!" he exploded. "I want to hear you insult that wonderful woman in English. That way, it doesn't lose anything in the translation."

Suzanne sucked her teeth. "If she's the alternative, then bring Michele back."

Marc shot to his feet, knocking his chair over. His fury made his skull thump mercilessly. It took amazing control not to beat her ass. "You need to stay out of shit you don't know anything about!" he roared.

"I do know I don't want any nigger babies calling me 'auntie,' " she huffed. "That's the God's honest truth."

"You could actually use God's name in that sentence and not see the irony!" he scoffed.

Rosalie banged the table, her fleshy upper arms quavering like a bird's wings. "I don't want to hear any more," she ordered. "MarcAntonio, I forbid you to see her."

She looked like a mother who was fighting like hell to maintain control over her children . . . by hook or by crook. And his instinct to rebel against her control was stronger than ever. "You *forbid* me, Ma?!" he laughed incredulously. "What, you're going to send me to bed without supper? I'm forty years old!"

Daniel pointed a bony, arthritic index finger at his son. His eyes were hard, like dark stones. "You see this woman, you are not part of this family, MarcAntonio," he declared, dangerously calm. "That's the last word on this."

"I'm with Dad," Suzanne declared.

Adam laughed bitterly. "What a shock, Suzanne. Have you ever had an original opinion in your life?"

Doug scratched furiously at his dirty-blond mullet. "For Christ's sake, people," he pleaded. "He's family!"

"Shut up, Doug!" Suzanne spat, and immediately Doug, a man who worked back-breaking construction for a living, was emasculated.

A clearing of a throat broke the only silence in the heated arguing. Heads whipped to see Diane and Lisa standing in the doorway. Marc saw Lisa's face—stunned, pained, aggrieved. He hated that he even subjected her to that. His protective instinct rose up strong. He stormed across the dining room in three strides and snatched her hand. "Come on, we're outta here," he said.

"Fuck!" Adam spat behind him.

* * *

Marc raced the Jeep down Route 23 like it was the track at Indy. Lisa clutched onto the armrest for dear life, feeling her nails dig into the leather. She glanced at the odometer; the red needle tapped at 70. No U2 this time. The deathly quiet in the car was its own music. After that horrid display of race theater at the Guerrieri home, the last thing she needed was to tangle with overzealous cops. "Marc," she said gently.

His knuckles were white, the steering wheel in a death grip. "What!" he snapped.

"You're going really fast," she said.

"May I drive the fucking car please, Lisa?"

"By all means drive the fucking car, Marc, but at this speed, we're going to get . . ."

As if cued by some evil director, sirens wailed behind them, lights flashing in the rear window. Marc punched the steering wheel, and Lisa jumped. "Shit!" he swore.

"I don't believe this shit!" she laughed at the sheer incredulity of the situation.

Marc slowed to a stop and shut off the engine. "Yet another thing to be thankful for," he said, sarcasm dripping from his voice.

Minutes later, a Cedar Grove cop, wearing a uniform two sizes too small for his bulk, sidled over. His name tag read *DeVos*. He looked like an extra from Smokey and the Bandit movies. He shined a high-powered flashlight into the car, then tapped on the driver's side window. Lisa immediately recognized him as half of the racial profiling team from earlier that day. "Slowly roll down your window, sir," he said in a voice that sounded like moving gravel.

Marc reluctantly complied. DeVos sized up the situation in the car and smirked, like he was about to have some fun at their expense. "License and registration, cowboy," he ordered.

Marc slowly reached in his pants pocket for his wallet, took out the laminated license and registration, and handed it to the cop. DeVos read the documents by flashlight. "You know you were going way over the posted speed limit, which, by the way, is forty miles per hour," he said.

"Yes, I know," he snapped.

Lisa gripped his forearm tightly. Black folks knew not to mouth off at cops. A lethal combination of impatience, poor diet, racism, and bad coffee all too often resulted in a cap in some unfortunate soul's ass. Clearly, this wasn't the time to flex.

DeVos chuckled. "Ain't too repentant, are you, Mr. Guerrieri?"

"Look, I said I was wrong, and I'll take the ticket," Marc said.

Again, Lisa gripped his forearm. "Marc, chill," she whispered.

DeVos shined the light right in Lisa's eyes, and she held up a hand to shield the glare. "Yeah, Marc," he said, his icy grey gaze fixed on her. "Chill."

Marc erupted. "Excuse me?!"

"I want you and your little lady friend to step outside," DeVos declared.

"Why?" Marc demanded.

"Because I'm the cop, and I said so. Both of youse step slowly out of the car."

Lisa's heart fluttered wildly as she fumbled for the door catch, her hands quaking. "This was probably the last thing Schwerner, Goodman, and Chaney saw," she whispered.

Lisa and Marc got out of the car and moved to the back of the Jeep. Smirking DeVos was joined by his doppelganger right down to the clothes. His name tag read *DiBiase*. He jotted down the plate number of the Jeep, walked to the green-and-white squad car, and got in. "My partner's gonna run your plates," DeVos explained.

"Why?" Marc demanded.

"Car could be stolen."

"I gave you the registration."

"Could be fake."

DeVos apparently saw that Marc wasn't impressed by his authority, so he turned his attentions toward Lisa. He shined the flashlight on Lisa's purse. "Ma'am, the shape of your purse looks irregular," he said, affecting the air of a casual observer. "You wouldn't happen to be carrying a concealed weapon, would you?"

Make yourself as small as possible. Don't mouth off. "No, Officer, I'm not," she said quietly.

He became charming all of a sudden. "Could I just have a tiny peek in your purse? It'll only take a minute."

Marc raised a hand in front of her, the way someone would shield a rider from crashing through a windshield. "No way!" he shouted. "There's a little thing called illegal search and seizure. Or didn't they teach you that in Pig 101?"

"I still have probable cause to frisk the little lady here."

"No, you do not!"

It was like watching Testosterone Wimbledon, lobs and volleys back and forth. Marc fired for the match point. "I don't know what you're trying to pull, but I'm on the phone with my lawyer tonight!" he roared.

Clearly cop-citizen relations favored white folks. No black man could talk to this asshole like Marc was, strafing him with attitude. DiBiase returned right then, waddling the distance between them and the squad car. "Clean," he breathed heavily.

Marc seemed sufficiently triumphant. "I hope this is a lesson to you," he declared.

DeVos revealed his true colors just then, throwing Marc's license and registration on the cold asphalt. "I know who you are, Mr. Voice of Italian America," he sneered, looking like evil incarnate, "and no matter how special you may think you are, I will not hesitate to put a bullet in your nigger-loving ass if you ever set foot into Cedar Grove again. *Capice?*"

And this time, Italian America lost its voice. All he could do was watch, in shock, as DeVos and DiBiase sped off in the green-and-white cruiser.

Lisa shook uncontrollably, fighting the overwhelming urge to projectile-vomit all of Rosalie Guerrieri's cooking on the nearby shrubs and grass. She hated that these white folks, this poor white trash, would make *her* feel inferior. "Jesus!" she sobbed.

Marc stared after the car peeling off into traffic. "Fucking pricks!" he yelled furiously after them.

She leaned over, hyperventilating, staring at the asphalt. "I can't breathe!" she gasped.

Marc gently rubbed his hand against her back. "Shit," he sighed. "Lisa."

Don't cry! Don't you fucking cry! "Oh, God!" she panted. "Oh, God."

He helped her up, made her face him. The anger was gone. He looked genuinely afraid. He held her, and she clutched onto him for dear life, lest she'd faint right there on the highway. "What's wrong with the world?" she cried.

He pressed her close, rocking her to the sound of the traffic whizzing by. "Let's get out of here," he said.

Where could the freaky mixed couple go? "To where?!"

11

She woke up to gentle shaking. It took her a second or two to realize where she was ... in the Jeep, in front of a stone cabin. She rubbed her eyes, and Marc's face floated before her. Now she remembered how they'd gotten there. Yes, they'd decided to run away with only the clothes on their backs. She was still reeling from the twin hideous encounters with both his family and the cops. Why else would she voluntarily take her black ass to camp out in the Poconos? With not a black face for miles.

He'd been upset that the Kings megastore in Verona was closed for the holiday. It figured he'd shop at Kings ... very high-tone. She was a loyal Pathmark customer herself. Which was just as well, because it was the only food store they could find open so late on the holiday. He filled the cart with all the staples and luxury items. Just as she wondered how she was going to kick in with her half at the checkout, he handed over a platinum Amex. The check girl swiped it. There. Problem solved. She remembered when she had money.

He filled up the car with gas, then they hit Route 80, each of them digesting the events of the night. Her eyelids were getting heavy. At the blazing lights of the Delaware Water Gap, where New Jersey met Pennsylvania, she turned away and drifted off to sleep. Next thing she remembered, he was shaking her awake. In the Pennsylvania wilderness.

On autopilot, Lisa and Marc silently took their belongings out of the car. She put the food away in the small kitchen with all the amenities, while Marc did the manly things, like turn on the water and the heat. He came into the kitchen just as she emptied the last bag into the refrigerator.

Lisa watched him as he took off his coat and hung it over a chair at the round kitchen table. She rubbed her hands together and blew on them. *What are we doing here?* "That's all of the stuff," she announced.

Marc looked her over. "You're shivering," he said.

She was feeling the heat from the vents already. "I'm fine." She looked around the kitchen, the solid wood beamed ceiling, the breakfast nook nestled cozily in the bay window. Definitely not the rustic camping trip she'd imagined. "This is a nice cabin."

He came closer, following her gaze around the room. "It's Adam's. He lets me use it when I need to get away."

Tentatively, he approached her and peeled off her coat. She watched as he lovingly folded it and placed it on the counter. He took her hands and rubbed them vigorously, generating heat. "Hey," he said softly. "I'm sorry about my family. I blew it. I should've prepared them before. I guess I wasn't thinking. I would never hurt you on purpose. You do know that, don't you?"

The sincerity in those blue eyes was so present, it was as if she could touch it. She knew from the way he'd so selflessly protected her from his family and those cops.

Could God have actually made a man that she could trust? "I know," she said.

He looked at her face. She knew that look, and she was so tired of fighting. He bent his head to kiss her, and she closed her eyes and let him. She moaned as he sucked her mouth, darted his tongue into her mouth. He stroked her face, her hair. Every nerve ending in her skin stood at attention. She could literally feel her nipples grazing the silk inside her bra. He pressed her against him, and all she wanted to do was unzip him, reach in, and help him inside her. But then maybe that was his plan, get her up here and out of her panties. "Shit," she gasped, pushing him away.

He looked confused. "What?" he moaned.

She pressed her hand to her mouth to stop it from throbbing. "Did you bring me up here just to have sex with me?" she panted.

He seemed hurt. "No!" he exclaimed.

At first she was relieved. Then, she took offense. "So, what, you don't want to have sex with me?"

He laughed, shaking his head. "Honestly? More than I want to breathe." He took her hands and meshed his fingers between hers. "But that's not why I brought you here. I brought you up here so we could talk and try to make sense of this shit. Try to figure this out. I just want to be with you, Lisa. We can play Scrabble, or watch movies. Whatever you want."

Whatever you want. What do I want? Damn, he looked so good, and he felt so good. When he touched her . . . *shit!* God, she was so horny! But for some reason, this was different. It wasn't like she was selling her heart and soul for some dick. This felt real . . . *live.* "Well," she finally said over her pounding heart, "maybe we could play Scrabble or watch movies later."

His eyes sparkled, like those of a man supremely confident that he was going to get some. He ran a pointed tongue across his wide mouth. "What do you want to do now, then?" he asked, his smile brilliant.

Marc turned down the bed by the light of the lamp on the nightstand. *How do I play this?* He could strip down and wait for her under the covers. *Nah, too eager.* He could hide behind the door and rush her when she came in. *Way too eager!*

Just as he was strategizing, the door eased open, and she stepped inside. She laughed nervously. "Had to pee," she said. "Although that was probably more information than you needed."

Her gaze drifted from him to the bed. Her eyes widened. "Wow," she whispered.

He saw the bed in a whole new light, with its majestic four posts and bed boards, on a platform with drawers on its sides . . . all carved painstakingly out of hard, dark wood. He ran a hand along one of the posts. "Yeah," he said appreciatively. "It's a Javanese wedding bed. Diane's got a great eye."

She moved in closer. He watched her intensely as she lovingly touched the post. "It's beautiful," she said.

His gaze on her never wavered. "Yes. Beautiful."

She sat down on the mattress and looked around the room. He sat next to her and studied her profile. With her hair pulled back, she looked almost regal. Kind of like Sade, minus the massive forehead. He reached up and ran a hand lovingly over her head. Unable to help himself, he pulled off her pink ponytail holder, letting her hair fall loose around her shoulders. It felt soft . . . not as fine as his, but soft and silky nonetheless. She turned to him, and her gaze was so striking that his breath caught in his throat. "I've been thinking," she said.

Uh-oh. "Thinking and peeing," he chuckled. "Boy, can you multitask."

She nervously scratched her dainty nose, grimacing. "I don't have any birth control."

He remembered he had at least six condoms in his wallet from six months ago, the last time he was in this same situation with Veronique, the freaky, uninhibited, Catherine Deneuve-lookalike interpreter from the U.N. "I got it covered," he assured her.

"And we haven't had . . ." air quotes . . . " 'the talk.' "

"Ah." Air quotes. " 'The talk.' "

She blushed. "No STDs. Had two AIDS tests. Negative." She shook her head, laughing bitterly. "My dear husband wasn't exactly the fidelity poster boy."

Bryan-fucking-Livingston. If he was the benchmark, Marc had no worries about outachieving him in her eyes. He vividly remembered his last, ultraintrusive visit with Marcus. "Same on the STD front," he announced. "Three AIDS tests. All negative." He saw the questions on her face. "The transfusions. After I got stabbed."

The questions disappeared. "We're going to do this, aren't we?"

"Only if you want to." *Oh, God, please want to!*

Lisa quietly pulled off her black suede boots.

Thank you, God. He kicked off his nuskin bucks and watched as she stood up. Eagerly, he stared as she pulled off her pink suit jacket to unveil her sleeveless dress. The pinkness of the dress and the darkness of her hair contrasted with her creamy brown shoulders. She turned to face him, revealing a zipper a mile long. She held up her hair, exposing the nape of her neck. "Can you help me with this?" she asked.

He practically leaped up to do so. He clutched the clasp of the zipper and gently eased it down, resisting the compulsion to ram it down and rip the dress from her body. He pushed it from her shoulders, and she did the rest, pulling it down. At her waist, she pulled her black tights under her fingers, and pushed them to the wooden floor. She turned to face him. She was the color of a milky latte, highlighted by her white, lacy strapless bra and matching bikini undies. She was a beautiful combination of soft curves and subtle musculature, long arms, shapely legs with defined calves, a thin gold anklet around one of her fine ankles, and those wonderful feet with red toenails that he remembered from the first night they met. Crotch and heart both pounded like a Keith Moon drum solo.

"Okay," she laughed, waving a finger at him. "Not another stitch comes off until you show me the goods."

He was so enthralled with her that he didn't realize that he was still dressed. *Stunad!* Grinning, he pulled his sweater over his head and dropped it in the pile of her clothing. Next, he yanked his denim shirt out of his cords, unbuttoned it, and slowly peeled it off. He tossed that in the pile too. She stared appreciatively at his chest. She touched his stomach, and his gut tensed. "Impressive six-pack, Dr. G.," she giggled.

There was something so naughty and so sexy about her calling him that, with them both standing there in various states of undress. "You're not too bad yourself, Haley Melissa," he laughed.

Those same hands drifted to his belt buckle. He looked down as she separated the metal and leather, then worked the button and zipper of his cords. She helped him push his pants down in a heap at his feet. He stepped out of them, then pulled off his wool socks. "I knew it," she said. "Tighty whiteys."

So she fantasized about him, too. Only in his fantasy, she went beyond the undies. "You next," he near-whispered.

She unhooked the bra and let it hit the pile. He gazed at the wonderment . . . two full breasts with nipples that looked like tiny brown pencil erasers. Saliva collected in his mouth at the anticipation of tasting them against his tongue. "Wow," he breathed.

"So, you're a breast man," she said.

"I'm digging the whole package," he said.

Next, she pulled down those infernal undies, revealing what lured every straight man throughout history. Hers was shaved into a dark, curly Mohawk between her thighs. "Damn, girl!" he laughed. "You look like you've got Mr. T. in a scissors lock."

She hooted. "And what do you have in a scissors lock?"

He chuckled nervously. She'd seen her share of naked black guys. *How am I going to measure up?* Nonetheless, he held his breath, pulled down his shorts, feeling that familiar *doing,* and waited for her approval. She stared at the package, her eyes wide as saucers. "Whoa!" she gasped. "Mr. Ed!"

Fuck being a gentleman. He gave in to what he wanted to do all night. He took her hand and pulled her close. His cock nestled comfortably in the Mohawk. "Lisa," he whispered dizzily against her mouth. "You feel so soft."

She stroked his face. "You feel so hard," she gasped.

He'd waited so long to be with her, just like this. He wanted to enjoy every second. He stroked her soft skin, and touched her, and kissed her slowly. He bent his head and kissed a trail, from her mouth, down the curve of her throat, to her torso, then down to the breasts he'd cupped in his hands. He put one of those nipples into his mouth and sucked her flesh. "Marc," she moaned wildly, scratching the scruff of his neck with her fingernails.

He sucked the other nipple, while he gently ran his hands down the length of her back. He grabbed handfuls of her ass, grinding her closer to him. She locked a leg around one of his, and the tip of his cock brushed against the soft, moist velvet between her thighs. A film of hot perspiration covered his skin. *Shit, you feel good!* "Baby, I'm going to explode," he whispered.

In response, she sat on the bed. He frantically rummaged around the floor. *Where the fuck are my pants?* He found them and fished his wallet out of the back pocket. The condoms were right in the fold behind his license and credit cards. He tore one from the sheaf and dropped the wallet back on the floor as if it were inconsequential. He stood in front of her, and she looked up longingly at him. She slowly stroked his thighs in deliberate circles, her nails leaving flaming trails on his skin. *Shit, you're so hot!* "I'm going to need your help," he said.

Instinctively, she took the foil packet from him and tore it open. Giggling, she tossed the foil, blew on the condom to expose the reservoir tip, and took him in her hands. He gasped as she massaged him, with just the right amount of pressure against her soft skin to make him reach maximum hardness. Then she rolled the latex condom onto his cock. It felt cold and slimy. *I hate these things!*

She leaned back across the bed with her legs parted, and he eased himself on top of her. She laughed, wrapping her arms around him. He stared down at her and felt his heart constrict. She looked happily disheveled. He wanted to look at her like that forever. "What?" she whispered.

"You're so beautiful," he said.

She closed her eyes and kissed him. "You're sweet."

Marc reached between his legs, aimed for the end of that Mohawk, and thrust into her, his gaze locked on hers. She moaned, arching her back to meet him. *Damn!* She felt soft and warm inside, closing around him like a glove. "Lisa," he whispered.

She opened her legs wider, and he thrust deeper and out, deeper and out. She moved her hips in a circle, working him inside her. He squeezed his eyes shut, savoring the feel of her, of her sweaty skin against his, of rock-hard nipples against his tongue. She ran her fingernails back and forth along his back, and he cried out, gritting his teeth. All the while, he thrust into her as deep and as hard as he could, as if he could become a part of her until they melded together as one person. He thrust, every neuron in his body on fire, begging for release. He stared at her face, contorted in ecstasy, listened as the low, distinctive sound deep in her throat evolved into an all-out cry. "Marc!" she gasped. "Oh God, yes! Yes! Yes!"

He stared at her face as she came, going limp under him. Then the flood gates opened inside him. In sensory overload, he rammed madly into her, his muscles out of control, his raw nerves firing electronic signals throughout his body. In the sex haze, he heard moaning in a vibrating throat, and realized that it was him. After what seemed like forever, his constricted groin relaxed suddenly, and everything was quiet.

With the glow in full effect, Marc raised up on his forearms to look at her. Then he realized that her breathing was shallow and labored not because of the stress of sex, but because she was crying. In the lamplight, he saw tears streaming down her face, mixing with the sweat on her skin. He'd never had that reaction before, and he'd been with his share of women. He took her face in his hands, staring quizzically at her. "What, honey?" he asked, concerned. "I hurt you?"

She buried her face in his shoulder and clung to him for dear life. He made her look at him. Again, he held her face in his hands and brushed the tears away with his thumbs. She sobbed like a little girl, her breath catching repeatedly in her throat. "What's wrong?" he asked.

"Nothing," she sobbed. "You're wonderful."

What did he do to you? "Oh, sweetie," he sighed. "It's okay."

He rolled onto his side, wrapped his arms around her, and held her tightly. He kissed her forehead, rocked her gently as she cried on his shoulder, and whispered assurances in her ear. *Bryan-fucking-Livingston!* Marc made up his mind that, from that moment on, no other man would ever hurt her again.

Lisa stirred into consciousness. She felt Marc sleeping behind her, his arms wrapped protectively around her. She surveyed her surroundings and remembered . . . making love with him . . . beautifully, repeatedly. She was a healthy, sexual being again.

She eased out from his grasp and sat up. She turned to look at him, sleeping there so peacefully. She could've sworn she saw a smile on his mouth. That wonderful mouth. She ran a hand along bruises on her neck, her nipples where he had kissed and sucked her flesh.

She got up off the wedding bed, went over to the pile of clothes, and picked up his denim shirt. She inhaled his scent, then put it on. She had to find a phone. Someone needed to know that she hadn't just disappeared off the face of the earth. Although Pennsylvania was damned close.

She padded silently across the wooden floors and left the bedroom. In the dark, she got her bearings, studied the layout of the cabin. In addition to the bathroom adjoining the bedroom, there was a half-bath in the hall. The wide, expansive living area was a mix of different furniture styles, electronics, and seats with throw pillows nestled in the windows.

Lisa tiptoed toward the kitchen. This seemed familiar territory. She spotted the phone on the wall, next to the fridge, picked up the receiver. The numbers glowed in the dark. Reflexively, she dialed the 201 number. It rang three times before someone knocked the receiver on the other end off the hook. Seconds later, she heard a sleepy, "Hallo."

Lisa looked over her shoulder. "Nina," she whispered. "It's Lisa."

"It's after midnight—where are you?" she demanded, now wide awake. "You were supposed to come over after dinner with Marc."

"I'm still with Marc."

"How was the family?"

That was going to take longer than she had. "Later," she said. "I'm at Marc's brother's cabin in the Poconos."

Lisa could literally hear her put two and two together. "Ah," Nina said. "And is there snogging?"

Lisa snickered. This Ph.D. mother of two was talking in code like a naughty teenager. A naughty, self-satisfied teenager who'd gotten what she wanted. Obviously, she and Marc were not up in this romantic hideaway playing backgammon. "Yes," Lisa conceded. "There is much snogging."

"And is there shagging?" Nina persisted.

God, you're impossible! "Yes," Lisa giggled. "World-class shagging."

"Excellent!" Nina cried, then covered the mouthpiece with her hand. "Nothing, sweetie. Go back to sleep." She uncovered the mouthpiece; Lisa guessed she must've awakened Tim for a second. "I'm so chuffed for you, sweetie. Marc is a wonderful man. He'll make you very happy."

Lisa felt hands caressing her ass, just as Marc came from behind to kiss her neck. She giggled. *What are you, psychic?* "Yes, he does," she said.

As Nina enthused about Marc's numerous positive qualities into the phone, Lisa watched intently as Marc walked over to the fridge, opened it, and pulled out a bottle of Evian. In the light from the fridge, she studied the sleek lines of his naked body, the dents on the sides of his ass cheeks. She felt the heat rise from her toes to her face. "I should be home soon," Lisa assured her. "Can you go to my place and take care of the kitty?"

"Like Marc's taking care of your kitty?" Nina teased.

She was starting to sound like a sistah now. "Nina!" Lisa exclaimed.

"Don't worry about the cat," Nina said. "Enjoy yourself. See you when you get back."

"If you need me, you have the cell number."

Lisa hung up and watched as Marc came closer. Her heart pounded. He dropped a kiss on her mouth, then handed her the water. There he was again, anticipating her needs. She sipped, and it went down cold and satisfying. "I woke up, and you weren't there," he said. "That's not good."

"I'll try not to let it happen again," she said.

He held her hands and studied her. "You look good in my shirt," he said.

She pirouetted like a model, and he whirled her around by her waist. "Thank you," she giggled.

He slowly unbuttoned the shirt and laid it open. She could feel his blue eyes on her breasts, her stomach, between her thighs. "Even better with it off," he whispered.

They made it back to bed in record time. He laid her down on the wedding bed, and much to her extreme delight, began to kiss and lick a trail down her throat, to her sweetly aching breasts, down to her navel. *Oh my God! Is he . . . going to . . . oh yeah!*

He buried his head between her legs, the stubble of his cheeks creating friction against the insides of her thighs. His tongue licked, tasted, sucked, fucked. She cried out, clutching handfuls of his hair. She shook, trembled, goose bumps dotting her skin. *Shit!*

She was seconds away from completely losing it when she felt him inside her, hard, persistent, gloved. This was more than her body could stand. She screamed his name as her senses exploded, leaving her limp, wrecked, twitching under him. Nanoseconds later, he moaned loudly, collapsing on top of her. "Marc," she whispered. *I love you.*

He trembled as he raised himself off her. Their bellies parting made a kissing sound from the sweat collected between them. He rolled off to her side and groaned, laughing. She laughed breathlessly, too. *Damn, can you fuck!* "I sure love how you serve up lunch at the Y, Dr. G.," she panted.

He buried his nose in her hair. "Let me know if you want all three squares."

That was, after all, the myth, that white boys loved to munch carpet. She would have to beg Bryan to even consider it, and even then, he did it begrudgingly, as if there was a gun to his head.

She ran a hand down his chest to his stomach. Her fingers found a lengthy horizontal scar, raised welts of flesh as a memory of a vicious, painful moment in his life. She stroked it lovingly. "This is where he hurt you," she whispered.

"Uh-huh," he said.

Lisa turned over on her stomach and looked up at him. He looked serene, blue eyes hooded. She'd seen the pictures of him being airlifted from Rikers after the stabbing. She'd survived the panic of waiting for the results from AIDS tests. She'd known what it was like to throw dirt on the corpse of a marriage. His reaction puzzled her. "How could you not be angry?" she asked.

Marc stared up at the wooden ceiling, as if trying to find the right words. "I *was* angry," he finally said. "For a very long time, I was mad at the world. I almost let that anger eat me alive. But then when I stopped feeling sorry for myself, I realized that was the best thing that could've happened to me. I saw that my marriage was over. I wrote the best work I ever had. And all that led me right here. Right now. With you. Not a bad deal."

She thought about all the shit she'd gone through with her mother, with Bryan, her money woes . . . everything. But suddenly, she saw them in a new light, as the pain that ultimately led her on a road to happiness. Right there in his arms. *Not a bad deal at all.*

* * *

They spent all Friday in bed, eating, talking, laughing . . . making love. Sharing each other's intimate secrets and dreams and generally getting to know each other. She marveled at how open he was with her, so trusting with his feelings. No head games, no power plays, no withholding of his affections. A man could be that open without sacrificing his masculinity. He single-handedly renewed her faith in men.

Finally, they decided that it was in their best interest to wash off the sex funk with a shower. He lovingly washed her, soaping her up and rubbing against her. She giggled as he ran his soapy hands along her skin. She kissed him over and over. *Damn, you feel good!*

He was toweling dry and came up behind her as she rummaged through the stuff they brought. "What?" he asked.

"I don't have any hair grease," she sighed, frustrated. "You know, the pink lotion?"

He looked blank. "No."

She looked in the bathroom mirror at her freshly blow-dried hair, sticking up in every direction. "Black folks grease their hair to keep it from drying out," she explained. *Great. One of these wacky cultural quirks that rears its head.*

"Your hair's beautiful, baby," he said casually, toweling his crotch as he walked away.

Yeah, right! She nurtured her hair. It was her treasure. Now she looked like Eddie Murphy doing Buckwheat. She raked a brush through and sighed. How could she explain black women and their hair to him?

Exhausted from their seemingly nonstop exertions, they climbed into bed and talked themselves into a sound sleep. She loved being in his arms. It made her feel safe . . . so safe that she drifted off in seconds.

* * *

Marc half-awoke to the early dawn light streaming into the bedroom. She lay, spooned, in his arms. The smell of her filled his nostrils. Her skin brushed softly against his. He was rock-hard, literally throbbing for her. She moved against him, reaching around to stroke the sensitive nape of his neck, and he tangled his legs with hers. He was one thrust away from heaven. "Mmm, baby," he moaned.

"Condom," she gasped.

Impatiently, he turned over and reached for his wallet, now on the side table. He frantically fumbled between the folds, through the bills and credit cards. "Fuck!" he hissed.

"What?" she said.

"We're out."

She snuggled against him. "Well, let's get up and get some," she suggested simply.

After breakfast, they got dressed—him in workout clothes and her in a hodgepodge of her boots, his drawstring pajama pants, sweater, and a baseball cap—and drove along the grey darkness of the Pennsylvania side of Route 80 for what seemed like forever. Finally, they came across a gas station with a convenience store and went inside. The market was chock full of racks of chips and candy, brightly lit coolers of ice, soft drinks, and beer. A white woman with a beehive 'do stood behind a wall of bulletproof glass. She looked at them and smiled. She looked like his grandmother. He prayed he didn't have to ask her. How could he explain to her that he wanted condoms so he could fuck his girlfriend's lights out? "I'll go look," he said in Lisa's ear, and she nodded.

He found them almost immediately, hanging from the rack with the travel-size antacids and pain relievers. *Jesus!* Sheepskin. Latex. Ribbed. Smooth. Ultra-sensitive. Magnum. Durex. Ramses. Trojan . . . He remembered being married, not having to worry about all of this shit, having the supreme ecstasy of feeling his partner without a rubber barrier.

Speaking of his partner, he looked up and scanned the store for her. Then he saw her near the magazines. His manly propensity to be territorial rose up like smoke. *What do we have here?*

A young black man in hip-hop gear was talking to her with pure sex in his eyes. Was it because he was another man or because he was black that set his radar off? He kept watching as they laughed, as the man was bold enough to reach out and touch her arm. *Okay, Marco. Don't be an ass . . .*

He took down two of the boxes of condoms and meandered over to the magazines with practiced cool. *Steady . . .* He snaked a possessive arm around her waist. "Hey, sweetie," he said.

"Marc!" she squealed. "Hey."

He revealed the two boxes in his hands. "Well, I've found these," he said. "Ultra-sensitive or ribbed. For your pleasure. What do you think?"

The milky latte face flushed red. "Umm . . . ribbed, I guess," she stuttered.

"Cool," he said, then turned to her friend. "Marc."

He looked shocked, thrown off guard. "Umm . . . Dante," he said.

Marc knew he'd made his point . . . subtly. He extended his hand, and Dante took it and shook it, soul-style. "Nice to meet you," he said.

Dante's dark eyes darted from him to her, to him again. He looked quite disapproving. And Marc could give a shit. "Yeah," Dante said with an air of finality. "Well, you two enjoy those condoms."

Marc winked deviously at her friend. "We intend to," he laughed.

Dante walked away in that cool, baggy-jeans strut Marc had seen fellas on *Yo MTV Raps* co-opt. Marc looked down at Lisa. "He seemed nice enough," he commented.

Lisa looked up at him and smiled weakly. For a fleeting second, an expression passed across her face. Only as they were headed to the Jeep did the meaning of that expression register. It was guilt.

They entered the cabin. Marc locked the door and threw his keys onto the table by the door. "You're so bad," she chided him. "Baiting that brothah like that."

"I was just having a little fun," he laughed boyishly.

She looked at him, standing there all sheepish in front of her. *Am I mad at him or with myself?* Dante's look said it all . . . she was a race traitor . . . sleeping with the enemy. In condoms ribbed for her pleasure. "He didn't need to know about us getting busy," she murmured.

She peeled off her coat, hung it up, and meandered over to one of the windowseats. She looked around the living area in the light of day. *What am I doing here?*

He sat next to her and nudged her. "Hey," he said. "You're cool with us, right? Being together?"

Am I? "Can I ask *you* a question? Did you do that because he was black or because he was a man?"

He laughed, shaking his head at some irony she wasn't aware of. "Lisa, I'm never going to be comfortable with other guys looking at you like he did, wanting to do things with you that you do with me," he confessed. "They could be fucking green for all I care."

He kissed her, and every bit of opposition melted from her mind. He moved away, then reached into the crinkly bag with the condoms. "I have something for you," he said.

Boy's mind on his crotch 24-7. "I know that," she laughed.

He pulled out a jar of petroleum jelly. "For your hair," he said.

She slowly took it from him, and her heart fluttered. *Where did you come from?* "You remembered," she murmured.

He beamed proudly, obviously happy he'd pleased her. "I always do."

She got up and headed toward the bedroom. "Bring your bag," she said over her shoulder.

He practically rocketed up and ran behind her, laughing.

God, can I trust this? She sat in the windowseat in the bedroom and watched him sleep. Her heart squeezed. He was unreal. This was unreal . . . the awesome sex, the heat, the unbridled affection. But what happened when they left the wedding bed, this cabin? Trying to make something work facing bigots like his family, accusatory stares from men like Dante, in a world where innocent young black men got shot for going into neighborhoods that restricted them in a supposedly free country.

But then, she *had* done the right thing. She'd married the so-called correct match and tried to make a life with him and still got slammed. And then Marc Guerrieri . . . secure, nurturing, peaceful. He rested his dark head on his hands like one of Raphael's angels, his mouth curled up like a bow, long lashes fanning dark, stubbled cheeks. The flannel sheets were pushed back, exposing the muscles, and lines, and planes of his long body.

She suddenly had the urge to capture him, serene like that, for eternity. Pushing the tears from her eyes, she got up in search of a pencil and some paper . . .

Marc sat up in the dark bedroom and shook the fog from his head. Right then, he smelled the delicious aroma of broiling meat, along with redolent herbs and spices. She was cooking. It reminded him of life in the bonds of matrimony, the comfort of a life in a classic six in Manhattan, insulated by love in a hostile, unforgiving world. Someone watching his back. Him watching hers. It came to him as an epiphany. *That's what's missing.*

He took a hot shower to clear his head and slipped on a T-shirt and sweats. He ambled into the living room and made his way over to the stereo system. He flipped through the old records. Elvis. Mario Lanza. Tony Bennett. He shuddered to think what Diane and Adam did to that music. Then he came across a Van Morrison album. *Oh my God!* He'd seen this very concert in San Francisco. He looked at the back of the album. "1970," he said out loud. When he was younger and free, dancing with pretty California girls and getting laid.

He put the record on the turntable and put the needle to his favorite cut. Instantly, Van sang softly, his voice floating among the acoustic and bass guitars to form the haunting strains of "Crazy Love."

By the time he made his way to the kitchen, he felt like his old self again . . . lucid and in love, enveloped by the scents of a busy kitchen. He stared at her, in his baggy plaid drawstring pajama pants and one of Diane's T-shirts. She was vigorously scrubbing the sink, and he watched, mesmerized, as her ass and bra-less breasts shook deliciously with her exertions.

He came up behind her and wrapped his arms around her waist. She gasped, then laughed. He nuzzled her neck, inhaling the smell of soap on her skin. "Hey," he said.

She turned in his arms and planted a kiss on his mouth. "You're up!" she exclaimed happily.

"Umm-hmm," he said, looking over at the tiny oven. "What ya making?"

"Steak and potatoes," she said. "And a salad. In the fridge."

My little gourmet chef. He patted her on the ass, then

meandered over to the stools to watch her. "I'm making some tea—you want some?" she asked over her shoulder.

All he wanted to do was watch her move. "Sure," he said.

She got two mugs and did her thing, and he stared. Madness seized him. The thought of them going their separate ways tomorrow when they returned to Jersey filled him with a blackness similar to death. He imagined her with him 24-7, ordinary days, birthdays, holidays. *Holidays*... "You have plans for Christmas?" he asked.

Blissfully unsuspecting, Lisa stirred sugar and lemon into the two teas. "I usually go to my mother's in the Bahamas," she said, sucking the spoon. "We could always make room for one more person."

She brought his mug of tea over and set it down in front of him at the counter. He reached out for her, raised the end of the T-shirt, and ran eager fingers over her belly. Heat began brewing in his groin. "Mmm," he moaned. "The Bahamas. Lying on the beach. Rubbing each other with warm coconut oil. Skinny-dipping in the moonlight..."

He could see from her eyes that she was thinking the same naughty things. "Yeah, right," she laughed. "And where does Barbara fit into all this?"

Then his subconscious spoke. "She's giving me her blessing to marry you," he said simply.

Lisa literally stopped. He could feel her stomach clench under his fingertips. "What?" she croaked.

Why not? Now that the words were out in the atmosphere, it suddenly seemed like an excellent idea. "I want to marry you," he repeated.

She looked confused. She moved away from him, and he could sense that this wasn't going to go well. "Aren't we warping through this?" she asked.

"Does it take all night to recognize the moon and

stars?" he asked, sounding a little too desperate for his own comfort. "I love you. You love me."

Her absence of an instant response smarted deeply. "You love me," he repeated, a little louder. "Right?"

Finally, she said, "Yes. I do love you. But I'm still married. Or have you forgotten?"

He raked her with his gaze. He couldn't see past his hurt. And as hard as he tried, he couldn't resist the impulse to lash out at the object of his affection. Her. "No, damn it, I can't forget, Lisa," he snapped, and she jumped back. "He fucks you over, and I end up paying for it. I'm so busy not being Bryan that I wonder if I'm being Marc anymore!"

She looked like she'd been punched in the gut. "That's enough of that shit," she stated, then turned to flee.

Fuck, what is *it with women?* "You come back here, Lisa!" he commanded. "We're gonna talk about this!"

Lisa rushed from the kitchen. Seconds later, he heard the eye-popping sound of a phonographic needle being dragged across vinyl, and Van Morrison was a memory. The silence in the kitchen was deafening. Furiously, Marc swatted the mug of tea off the counter and onto the tile floor. It shattered into a million pieces, leaving a puddle of brown liquid and ceramic shards in its wake. He didn't feel any better. "Shit," he rasped through gritted teeth.

Lisa sat perched on the covered toilet in the half-bath . . . where she'd been sitting for a good half-hour. *Great, Lisa, you're hiding in the toilet. This is what you've come to.*

The first fifteen minutes, she tried to calm down. Here was yet another fucking man trying to strong-arm her into something she didn't want to do. Then she got less pissed, began to think things through. *Why don't I want to be with him?* Damn, he treated her like she was a prize to be earned. He defended her in front of his racist family. He was a wonderful lover, patient and gentle when she needed that, forceful and freaky when she needed that.

But there was the specter of Bryan, of all the mistakes she'd made trusting him. She didn't trust fast, hot, and heavy. Why couldn't Marc understand that? She'd asked Nina the same thing, why men didn't understand women and their needs. "Because women don't ask for what they want, sweetie," Nina had said simply. "Men can't intuit. You have to tell them."

You have to tell them . . .

Lisa entered the bedroom. She saw him lying on his side, his hands cupped in his armpits. She could tell from his breathing that he was awake and still angry, like a wasp just ousted from its nest. She took a deep, galvanizing breath and carefully got next to him in the bed. She touched his shoulder, and he pointedly moved away. *Okay, I deserved that.* "I'm sorry," she said.

He scoffed, and the bed shook. "I thought love meant never having to say you were sorry," he said sarcastically.

Great. Quotes from Love Story *as a weapon.* Lisa sat on the side of the bed and held her head in her hands. Her inability to find the words frustrated her to no end. "I love you, Marc Guerrieri," she said, garbled; belatedly, she realized she was crying. "Besides that temper—which you need to work on, by the way—you've treated me like a queen. Who couldn't love you for that?"

They remained with their backs to one another. "And for some reason, that doesn't translate into you wanting to be with me," he concluded.

"I do want to be with you," she insisted. "You caught me by surprise. I mean . . . we've only known each other three months. God, Bryan and I were together a year before we got married. You and Michele? Six years."

He laughed bitterly. "Both resounding successes."

You have to tell them . . . "It's just . . . I haven't had the best luck with men. Bryan left me ass-out. If we really want to go back to the archives, my dad died and left me with practically no knowledge on how to handle men." The tears rained down between her fingers. "I'm scared! I'm scared this is going to crash and burn, and I'm going to end up grieving for you. For this. I don't think I'm brave enough to go through that again!"

He came up behind her, sitting with his arms wrapped tightly around her. He felt so hard against her, rocking her in those big, strong arms. "Oh, baby," he said softly. "It's okay."

"I'm sorry!" was all she could say.

He pressed his stubbled cheek against hers. "Hey," he whispered. "You're one of the bravest women I know. I love you, and I want to make a life with you. Because you are brave, and smart, and you have the biggest heart in the world. For purely selfish reasons, I want you with me for the rest of my life.

"But I can't promise that I won't hurt you. There are going to be times when I won't know what you need, or how to give it to you. But I swear I'll try as hard as I can to make you not regret wanting to be with me, Lisa. I can promise you that."

She covered his hands with hers, around her waist. *I love you so much.* He rocked her gently, and ever so slowly, her sobs hiccupped to a halt. "Let's just live together," she said.

His soft laughter reverberated from his chest through to hers. "Jesus. I thought that was my line."

"Seriously. Let's try it for a week."

"What, like Grape Nuts?"

She giggled, remembering the cereal's commercial slogan. "Yeah, like Grape Nuts. We live together for a week. If it feels good, we can talk marriage vows and ugly taffeta dresses."

He squeezed her tighter, like he didn't want to let

go. "I'll take you any way I can have you," he whispered in her ear. "For now."

Marc sensed something different about her, an irrational apprehension. All that Sunday, she procrastinated, cleaning and packing with uncharacteristic slowness. The only time she moved fast was when they caught a delicious post-shower quickie in a soft pile of towels on the wooden bathroom floor. She deliberately stroked his now smooth-shaven cheeks. "Let's stay right here," she whispered.

They'd fallen asleep. It was early evening when he stirred awake and realized they had to hurry if they were going to return to Jersey at a reasonable hour. They hurriedly dressed and packed, then hit the road.

The skies opened up, releasing a pelting, ice-cold November rain. Route 80 East was bumper-to-bumper due to construction. Marc had to constantly shift and downshift to accommodate sluggish traffic flow. Remotely, he heard her sigh. "Let's go back to the cabin," she suggested.

His concentration on the road was unwavering. "If only we could, but we both have to work tomorrow," he said absentmindedly.

The usual hour-long trip took twice that, because of the horrible weather. By the time they made it to Montclair, it was way after nine. Marc was starving. He took her to Spolini's, his favorite Italian restaurant, on North Fullerton Avenue. It was very fancy, very Italian, reminding him of those lavish restaurants in Coppola films where mobsters did business and ordered hits. The waitstaff did the usual fawning over him. After all, he was The Voice of Italian America. He ordered his favorite, the fettuccine alfredo, with the sauce so thick and creamy that he could feel his arteries hardening with every bite he wolfed down.

Unfortunately, she was not having the same good time. She hadn't said a word since they had arrived in Montclair. She stared at her veal piccata, then looked around at the restaurant patrons. "What's wrong, baby?" he asked, concerned. "You not eating?"

She looked down at her veal balefully. "I'm not very hungry," he said.

That stung a little. He loved this place; this was a part of his life that he wanted to share with her. A novice waiter popped up suddenly to replace their carafe of Chianti. He topped off Marc's glass, and Marc thanked him. As the waiter refreshed Lisa's glass, another waiter jostled him. Chianti spilled like blood on Lisa's shoulder. She gasped, like she'd been doused with ice water. "Ah, *signora*, I so sorry!" the young waiter cried.

Marc leapt up, protectively dabbing at the wine, which was fast setting into the pink cashmere. The other waiter, an older man in the requisite black and white, pushed the younger waiter away and surveyed the stain. "Naturally, we will pay for the cleaning," the older waiter promised.

She looked meek, small in her chair. "It's ruined," she sighed.

Marc sensed she was not talking about just the sweater.

Finally, after it seemed like dinner would never end, Marc parked the Jeep in front of Lisa's building. He switched off the engine and turned in his seat to look at her. He'd never seen her look so unhappy. And, of course, it was his job to make her otherwise. He crooked his index finger under her chin and made her face him. "Baby, tell me what's wrong," he implored. "You haven't been yourself all night."

She sucked her teeth. "Those people were rude," she said. "You didn't see them staring at us . . . the freaky mixed couple?"

So that's it. He'd been so focused on his alfredo that

an alien ship could've landed in front of him. "No," he confessed. "And even if they were, fuck 'em."

"You're used to people staring at you. I hate it."

He sighed. "This is all new. I never had to worry about this stuff before . . . the cops, the stares because of whom I'm with. I guess I'll have to get a clue. I want to be with you, and I want you with me. And I don't want you to ever be uncomfortable being with me. I love you."

She smiled weakly. "I love you, too."

He nuzzled her cheek. "Come on. Let's get the cat."

Marc got out of the Jeep, then went over to the passenger side and helped her down. He pressed her close, and she giggled. He couldn't wait to get her home. He had visions of them having breakfast in his massive king bed and staring at the impressive view together.

Marc held her hand, and they turned toward the building. Suddenly, Lisa stopped in her tracks, clutching his hand in a death grip. It was then that Marc saw him, sized him up. He was a pretty boy—tall, lean, and only a couple minutes shy of wiry. And cocky. He stood on the sidewalk in his winter gear, arms akimbo, smirking like he was extremely self-satisfied. *I could take you.* "So, it's true," he declared. "You *are* doing 'the white thing.' "

So this is Bryan-fucking-Livingston.

Lisa's grip on his hand tightened even more. "What, Jaye too much man for you to handle?"

Bryan turned to Marc with a sickening, greasy smile. "I haven't had the pleasure," he said, offering a hand like they were having a business meeting.

This miserable excuse for a man was the main reason why Lisa was so scared and freaked out about men, about being with him. Marc didn't even acknowledge that hand. "That's painfully evident," he declared.

It was eerie, like his pupils were replaced by unadulterated anger. "Look . . . dude," Bryan said, affecting a surfer's voice, "go eat a cannoli or something. I want to talk to my wife."

"Don't you have a final to take or something?" Marc shot back.

Bryan tried to shrug it off, but his pupils seemed to get darker and darker. "Let's not turn this into 'My dick's bigger than your dick,'" he said with a fake laugh, "because you'll lose."

"Secure men measure manhood in more substantive ways," Marc declared.

"What do you want?" Lisa demanded.

"Talk to your lawyer," he ordered, like he was talking to an underling, not his wife. "Stop her from squeezing me. You've made your point."

She let go of Marc's hand and moved toward Bryan. "No, you get Monaghan to talk to her," she commanded. "I'm so sick of this shit. Why do you even have a lawyer? You're always calling me at my job. Now you show up at my home?"

"Yeah, remember what happened the last time I showed up at your home," he said, his tone eerily menacing.

She literally began to tremble. Marc could see her fighting to maintain control. He suddenly put it all together. That's when Bryan "hurt her," as she'd put it. Something told him it had been something brutal, sexual. Anger burned at his midsection.

Lisa laughed wildly, her eyes shining. "Is that how you get off, Bryan, trying to threaten me?" she asked. "You small, pathetic brothah. The days when you could get your way by bending me over the couch are gone. You don't scare me anymore. So go the fuck home and leave me alone!"

Bryan Livingston looked stunned, like he was wondering how dare she stand up to him. "Looks like you're done here," Marc declared, cool as ever.

Bryan tried to out-cool him. "It's not over 'til I say it's over," he declared.

"Well, Bryan, there's a new sheriff in town."

Bryan snapped. He practically got up in Marc's face, and Marc felt very little satisfaction at having won that particular testosterone slap fight. "Oh, so you've had some black pussy now, so you da man?" Bryan roared.

The anger rose up Marc's esophagus, and he didn't even try to swallow it. "You're dismissed," he declared. "Take the hint."

Bryan didn't, unfortunately. "You enjoy fucking my wife?" he asked, sounding desperate. "Goofy white boy. I sleep like a baby at night, knowing I had her first."

The anger flooded Marc's brain. Some sensory impulse made him make a fist and effortlessly cold-cock Bryan in the face. The release felt like an orgasm, as he watched Bryan-fucking-Livingston go down like a ton of bricks onto the hard, wet sidewalk. Bryan slapped his hands to his astonished face. Blood streamed from between his fingers. "You broke my nose!" he cried, his voice muffled.

Marc felt potent, protective, in defense of his woman. He stared down at Bryan like a god from Mt. Olympus. "You come near her again, I will kick your bony ass up and down this street," he declared. "That's a promise."

"Jesus!" Lisa exclaimed.

Marc only realized just then that she was still there. He reached for her, expecting her to be happy that he'd come to her rescue. He was puzzled when he reached for her, and she slapped his hand away. "He just won, Marc," she said.

What is this shit? "You're mad at me?!"

"Who are you, Mighty Mouse, come to save the day? I had this covered!"

"Yeah, right, you had it covered."

Right after he said it, he wished he could take it back. The expression on her face said it all . . . hurt, her confidence shot. He reached for her hand again. "Lisa . . ."

She pushed him away. "He did the same thing those cops did. He provoked you, and you lost it!"

"I defend you both times, and you're mad at me?!"

"What is it, open season on brothahs with you fucking Italians?!"

That felt like a blow right to the solar plexus. After being physically and emotionally bare with him that weekend, she could think he was like those homicidal maniacs on Bay Ridge Avenue in Bensonhurst, like his cousin Jimmy. All because of a skirmish with two racist cops and her husband. "This is hardly the same thing as Bensonhurst!" he exclaimed.

"It's exactly the same thing," she insisted. "Striking out at somebody in anger!"

"I hope you have a good lawyer!" Bryan moaned from the sidewalk.

Marc surveyed his surroundings, caught between Lisa, who was angrier than he'd ever seen her, and her husband, lying on the sidewalk, with blood cascading down the front of his white sweater. *Get her out of there . . .* "We're not having this conversation here," he declared. "We're going upstairs, we're getting your shit, and you're coming home with me."

Unfortunately, she wasn't down with the plan. "I'm not going anywhere with you, Marc Guerrieri," she said, hurt. "Ever again!"

Marc watched, helplessly stupefied, as she fled into the building, the glass security door slamming behind her.

12

Alone, Marc lay in his king-sized bed, under the covers, staring at the view of the City. When Michele left, he was mercifully drunk. This second time at heartache, he was extra-sensorily sober. His body seemed to ache from missing her. It didn't help that his memory of their last time together was as vivid as if it were happening right then. He could smell her on him from that last time, and he was torn between inhaling deeply or giving himself a Silkwood shower. *What happened?*

He still didn't know. One minute he was kissing her, the next minute, he was walking through the door to his condo. Alone. Listening to the sound of his keys clattering into the sterling silver dish on the wooden credenza in the foyer. Dazed, he dragged himself and his bag up the stairs to the master bedroom, where he saw the red answering machine message light glowing in the darkness on the nightstand next to the bed.

On autopilot, Marc crossed the room, switched on the lamp, and sat on the end of the bed. He pressed the play button, heard a beep, then, "Marc, it's Ad. Listen . . . I don't know what to say. I'm as stunned as you are. Just give me and Diane a call when you get in . . . Nobody spoke for us at that table . . . Please just give us a call, okay?"

Not even Adam's unconditional love could suck him out of his sinking depression. Another beep. Marc expected another message from Adam. He certainly didn't expect to hear the next voice, that of a perky Valley girl emanating from the machine. "Dr. Guerrieri, this is Allison Esteban, the Dean's assistant from the English Department at UCSD. We'd like to offer you the consultancy here, if you're still interested. We've faxed your letter of acceptance to the English Department at SCNJ with all the details. Please call me when you get the letter. We're so happy that you're going to be joining us for the next year!"

The ultimate irony. He was getting the consultancy, after he'd come to terms with Michele, after he'd met someone else in Jersey.

He lay wide awake in bed, running the events of the night over in his mind. More than once, he picked up the phone in an attempt to call her, only to put the receiver slowly back into the rest. She didn't want anything to do with him. In her eyes, he was one of those people on TV who screamed expletives at blacks, people he was ashamed of. He couldn't reconcile it, even in his very logical brain. How could she have touched him, kissed him, let him inside of her if she thought he was like that?

He was dog tired, his eyes sticky and red, as he watched the sun peek up from behind the skyscrapers in the City. He slowly got up and pulled the blinds closed in an attempt to shut out a world selfishly going on when he was so brimming with sorrow. Unfortunately, the outside world entered . . . through the phone. It jangled once . . . twice . . . three times while he waited for the machine to pick it up. Then, for a split second, he thought it might be her calling. He snatched up the receiver. "Hello," he said eagerly.

There was a charged pause from the other end. *Please let it be her!*

"MarcAntonio, it's your mother," Rosalie said.

She sounded like she'd been crying. The bigot who'd let him gestate in her body for nine months. *What do you want?* "Hello, Ma," he said warily.

Another pause. The first time in forty years that she was ever at a loss for words with him. "How are you?" she asked.

"I've been better, Ma," he confessed.

"Umm . . . well, I'm making some prime rib for dinner tonight," she said. "Your favorite. Roast beast, you used to call it."

When he was twelve. A reluctant smile nipped at the corners of his mouth. "Yeah."

"I . . . well, your father and I want you to come over for dinner tonight."

Like Thursday never even happened. He admired her ability to dissociate. "Is it just me you're inviting for dinner?" he asked.

Longer pause. "Yes," she said.

She ripped open the wound again. "Then you and Dad enjoy that prime rib, Ma," he said.

"MarcAntonio," she sighed. "You're going to throw away your family for that little black girl?"

Little black girl. Like she was talking about Butterfly McQueen. He could literally taste his revulsion. "Since when did you start hating black people, Ma?" he questioned. "I remember you used to hang out with that lady, Mrs. Samuels, when we lived in Brooklyn. That lady you used to work with at the phone company. Dad would leave the light on for you, you'd come home so late from cocktails with her."

"That's different," she insisted, working that mother logic. "There's nothing wrong with being friends with them."

"Oh, you just can't date them."

"They are not like us, MarcAntonio."

"Well, Ma, I can personally vouch for the fact that anatomically speaking, Lisa's no different from one of those nice Italian girls you want me to be with."

"Don't be crude. You know exactly what I mean. She's not our kind. Like the Italian proverb says, 'Your cattle and your wives should be from your home town.' "

He didn't have the strength to try to bring his mother around. She was the product of her own environment. "You know, Ma, you're right," he said. "She's not our kind."

Her tone brightened. "You agree with me, then?"

"I agree, Ma. Lisa's mother is a child psychologist. She writes those Billy Beaver books that Lily and Claire read. Her dad was a gynecologist. She's smart as a whip. She's cultured. She's got a heart as big as the ocean, and she goes through life perpetually concerned for other people's feelings, sometimes at her own expense." *And I miss her.* "So, yeah, Ma, clearly, she's not our kind."

Another pause, this one connoting blatant disapproval. "Well, that's that, then," she finally said.

"That's that, then," he repeated. "Good-bye, Ma."

"Good-bye, son," she said.

He listened as she hung up. That was going to be the last thing his own mother said to him.

Or was it? He'd barely hung up the phone when it rang again. Again, he peeked up from under his covers like a turtle and stared at the instrument. *Ma . . . ? Lisa . . . ?* He picked up the receiver. "Yes," he said.

"Where are you?" Nina asked from the other end.

"I'm not coming in today."

"Well," she said, her voice dropping to a near whisper, "some nosy fuckers heard through the grapevine you got the UCSD consultancy. You've got to be here promptly at five and be very surprised. All right-ee?"

Oh, great. Another fucking surprise party. The last one had gone so well. He sighed. "You know me. When duty fucking calls . . ."

"Good," Nina said. "See you at five."

She crashed down the receiver, practically deafening him.

The clock on the nightstand glowed out 10:05 A.M. He guessed he should get up and face the day. He sat up, almost kicking the duffel bag at his feet. A reminder of the happiest weekend he'd spent in a long time. He unzipped it and dumped its contents onto the carpeted floor. He saw the grey flannel sheets they'd made love on, his denim shirt he'd peeled off her, cute Hanes cotton bikini underwear he'd bought for her at the Pathmark. They were going to do laundry together once he'd brought her home. God help him, his eyes welled up. He blinked, and hot tears plopped down his cheeks dusted with five o'clock shadow. *How the fuck do I make this right?*

Just then, though, he saw something peeking out from under the sheets. He prodded the soft pile with his big toe. The sheets fell away, revealing a piece of white paper. Curiously, he fished the paper out from under the flannel. He opened it, and his heart squeezed agonizingly. He stared down at his sleeping image on the paper, lovingly immortalized in pencil, faithful in its detail. He felt like he was staring into a mirror. She'd done this for him. With the hand that still smarted from punching Bryan-fucking-Livingston, he ran his index finger over the lines, feeling the grain of the paper under his fingertip. His eyes welled up again. He blinked, and a tear dropped onto the painstakingly sketched image in his hands. His heart was so heavy it hurt.

* * *

Her period came down like a red torrent, as if her body were trying to erase any evidence of Marc's presence. Lisa sat at her desk, practically doubled over . . . a combination of hellish cramps and profound grief. She knew she'd overreacted. She saw the look on his face when she said those horrible things to him. He looked like she'd kicked him in the nuts. She wished she could suck the words back down into her lungs, push them back into the deep recesses of her brain where they belonged.

When she'd gone upstairs, she fumed, rightfully so. Those two assholes on the sidewalk, both asserting dominion over her—Bryan wanting her to do his bidding, Marc pushing her to move in with him, neither of them caring what she wanted.

What do I want?

She thought about it as she lay in bed, unable to sleep and resenting Wisteria for snoring loudly in a calico lump at her feet. She didn't want it to end, that weekend at the cabin. She felt so wrapped in a cocoon of joy and love. She'd never felt that way before . . . treasured, sated, rested. It was obscene how reality would so easily intrude on the dream.

What the fuck do I want?

Finally, she gave up fighting to sleep. She sat up and switched on the nearby lamp. Wisteria stirred irritably and stared at her with pissed green kitty eyes. Lisa met the stare. *I pay the rent, bitch!*

Lisa pulled on her robe and slippers. Like she used to roam the house at 88 Gates when she couldn't sleep, she found herself in the hallway, making her way down to the basement, clutching keys in her hand. She opened the white metal fire door to reveal a vast gray brick room with tons of locked barbed wire cages, stuffed with other tenants' belongings that couldn't fit into their apartments. She located her cage, worked the combination lock, and stepped inside . . . into the remnants of her former life, her furniture, appliances she'd gotten as wedding gifts, clothes . . . boxes and boxes of stuff.

She eased up onto the cherrywood dresser and picked up the first box her hands touched. She opened the flaps and peered inside. There were tons of photos, which didn't surprise her. She didn't have her mother's discipline for placing photos neatly into albums and cataloguing experiences. The photos in the box were jumbled in the same way all of her experiences rubbed up against one another, influencing one another. She saw pictures of her and Bryan, when he used to look at her the way Marc looked at her now . . . like she was the only thing that sustained him. Someone had snapped them together at a party. Looking handsome and dapper, he was kissing her cheek, and she was laughing so hard she'd nearly spilled her wine. Dispassionately, she ripped it in two and tossed it on the floor.

She saw pictures of her parents, together, sending her off to Fordham . . . then pictures where her father was conspicuously absent. Then, suddenly, her hands lit on an old black-and-white photograph of her grandparents.

The caption on the bottom once-white trim read *Drs. Gareth and Patsy Haley, Wedding Day, June 17, 1925.* Patsy was brown, with smooth, high cheekbones, huge brown eyes, and a brilliant white smile that looked like she'd been raised eating Eleuthera sugar cane straight from the yard. Lisa could see herself in her young grandmother. Barbara, on the other hand, looked like her father's blond head had opened and she'd popped out, like Zeus had given birth to Athena. Barbara had her father's square, strong features and narrowed light eyes. Patsy had given her just a taste of the melanin.

The Haleys had met and fallen deeply in love when Patsy left the Bahamas to study in the United Kingdom, as was the custom until fairly recently. They looked so happy, despite the fact that they couldn't emigrate to

America to practice medicine as they'd planned. Their union was illegal and unnatural in certain states in the so-called Land of the Free. That illegal, unnatural union lasted fifty years. Lisa's legal, supposedly natural union lasted five. The law was definitely an ass.

Lisa kept the picture and closed up the box. She'd seen enough. She picked up another box, marked Fordham, and opened that. She flipped through . . . grade reports, old papers from freshman year. Suddenly, though, she came across folders and folders of sketches, still lifes that led to pencil drawings of children and adults together . . . then drawings and text. She remembered that . . . her first attempt at a children's book. She'd hidden it away, totally horrified of becoming her mother.

She eyed them critically, remembering the rush of creativity that had occupied her for hours upon hours. How to teach children about romantic love, about how to love someone that others don't approve of. The idea had come out of her own experiences with Michael. To make a point, she'd made him white. It was way too prophetic. She felt a chill, straight from freshman year, 1977. This was what she was meant to do, not some roman à clef about Vanessa Dean. She remembered Marc's advice, dispensed over a plateful of grouper. *You've got to do what sustains you, Lisa.*

Rejuvenated, she took the box upstairs and worked on into the night. As the sun rose, though, she felt spent and weak. Raw. Ultrareceptive to her feelings, memories of what happened on the sidewalk, the horrible things she'd said to him. She started to sob, and unlike at the cabin, Marc wasn't there to hold her and tell her that everything would be okay. She formulated a plan in her head to make this right. *Clearly, you overreacted and said some shit you shouldn't have. You have to apologize.*

The formulation of a plan brought her peace, a peace that netted her a grand total of two hours of sleep. A hot shower and three cups of coffee later, she was at work, at her desk, near blind with fatigue, with the sensation of a metal fist squeezing her uterus down to the size of a grape in her pelvis. *Why the fuck isn't this Tylenol working?* Self-consciously, she rolled the neck of her red turtleneck sweater up to camouflage the numerous hickeys Marc had left on her throat and chest. The sweater that he'd appreciated so deeply at Nina's that night she'd had them over for dinner. *You're wearing the shit out of that sweater!*

She hadn't realized she'd fallen asleep, with her hand cradling her left cheek, until she felt a hand on her shoulder. She started awake, massaging the crinkles out of her cheek. She became aware of a faint trail of drool on her skin and brushed it away. She looked up and focused. The fluorescent ceiling light gave way to Vance, hovering over her. "Are you okay?" he asked, concerned.

Everything around her was fuzzy, dream-like. And she just felt bad . . . twitchy and nervous, the way she did in college when she used to take caffeine pills so she could pull all-nighters. "Vance!" she cried. "Yeah, I'm fine. Everything's fine."

"Aren't you coming?" he asked.

"Coming where?"

"To the atrium. The kickoff for the year-end report."

All of their hard work realized. She felt nothing but bad . . . "Yes, the kickoff," she said. "Sure. Let's go."

They made their way along the carpeted halls and cubicles to the elevators. "God, the last time I saw you, I was watching the back of your head out of A.J.'s door," he said.

She shook her head, remembering that night. "That A.J. knows how to test a friendship."

They got into the elevators, and the doors shut. They were all alone in the brightly lit metal box. "Listen," he said tentatively, "I was wondering. You like to dance?"

"Yeah, I like to dance," she said, disconnected.

"Well, there's this club in Brooklyn. They play reggae, rap, dance mixes. I was wondering if you'd want to go. With me."

The seven-second delay caught up, and Lisa realized that Vance was asking her out. *Oh, shit.* She looked at him, so hopeful, and sweet, and young. If he was twenty-one, he was a day. She had albums older than him. It buoyed her spirits that looking and feeling like shit, she could be the fantasy of a kid almost ten years younger. "Vance," she sighed, smiling as she touched his arm. "There are so many reasons why we shouldn't do this. The biggest one is that even my cat knows you don't shit where you eat."

He looked like he had a light bulb moment. "The work thing."

That'll work. "Yeah, the work thing."

"We won't always work together, you know," he said hopefully.

The elevator eased to a halt, and the doors opened onto an atrium streaming with light and crowded with people and plants. "That's true," she acknowledged. *And when you grow up, give me a call.*

From the sea of faces, Lisa saw Ione and A.J. Ione, looking stunning in a cream sweater suit, beckoned to them. "Lisa! Vance!" she called over the din of conversation. "Over here!"

A.J., rocking a black pantsuit, looked at her like a squall of rain. Leery, Lisa made her way over to where they stood. A.J. looked her up and down. "What's up with your hair?" A.J. asked.

Self-consciously, Lisa ran a hand over her head. All the pink lotion in the world could not style Lisa's hair into her signature chignon. Parts of it stuck up in frizzed, reddened ends. Ione elbowed her. "A.J.!" she said. "That's enough of that."

Suddenly, John Philip Sousa music filled the air from strategically-placed speakers in the atrium. The bombastic music seemed incongruous, in the midst of the lush green plants and the sunlight streaming through the skylight. "Here we go!" A.J. shouted over the din.

Very P.T. Barnum-esque, Richard Underwood, FDP's exuberant CEO, ran from the shadows and into the light in the middle of the atrium, to a round dais complete with a cordless microphone on a stand. He was attractive, in shirtsleeves, a thick head of salt-and-pepper hair moussed into place. He looked more like a TV star than CEO of a data processing company. This was business near the dawn of the decade. CEOs were now like Oprah, trying to pump up the cogs so they'd produce and keep FDP maintaining annual double-digit growth.

"Yeah!" a pumped Underwood bellowed into the mike, and the cogs applauded wildly.

"All right!" he said; again cog applause. "Can you believe it's December already? You know what that means, right?"

"Year-end report!" the cogs yelled.

Lisa stared, in awe, at the circus around her.

With hand-over-the heart sincerity, Underwood began. "Before we start, I just have to thank you all for your hard work over the past year. Each and every one of you, in your own way, has kept FDP the leader in payroll processing throughout the United States and Canada!"

Driven by the upward inflection in Underwood's voice, the cogs applauded again like toy windup monkeys. "I also have to thank Joe Siegrist's Marketing and Advertising group," Underwood said once the applause died down. "This year, as usual, they worked tirelessly to put out the year-end report on time and under budget, which is just what we like." He looked over his shoulder. "Joe, come up here. Bring Rick Farrelly, too!"

Obediently and appropriately sycophantic, greasy-haired Joe Siegrist and a shell-shocked Rick made their way up to the dais, amidst thunderous cog applause.

Lisa felt for Rick. He still hadn't recovered from his dad's death. This seemed to be too much stimuli for him to take. "Okay, okay, okay," Underwood said. "Well, enough of the fanfare, ladies and gentlemen, I give you . . . The year-end report!"

From the rafters, a system of lifts and pulleys slowly began to lower a massive replica of the cover of the year-end report. Cogs clapped, confetti swirled, and Sousa blared. Until the massive cover lurched to a stop on its strings. Lisa looked up at the cover she'd designed. Her eyes stared at the FDP logo, which was an outline of the headquarters building on a blood-red field. She stared at the letters in gold against the red field and read them. Then, suddenly, she wondered if she'd just become dyslexic, or if Marketing and Advertising had made the most gigantic fuckup of the year. Those letters in gold leaf spelled out FIDELITY DATA PROCESSING YEAR-END REPROT. *Year-End Reprot!* She was mortified.

As if everyone else had caught on, the applause stopped. The confetti swirled to a stop on the atrium's brick floor. Sousa became silent. Murmurs became the music that bounced off the walls, circulated around the plants. Underwood, Siegrist, and Rick huddled on the dais like Bill Parcells and his coaching staff on the sidelines at Giants Stadium just before two-minute warning. "Oh, snap!" A.J. laughed incredulously behind her hands. "Rick Farrelly is fucked!"

Lisa surreptitiously navigated the halls in SCNJ's School of Humanities. Noisy commotion echoed through the halls. People wearing party hats and carrying plate-fuls of chocolate cake trooped through the halls. *Good. Maybe he's distracted somewhere else.*

Her resolve to apologize to Marc had waned since early that morning. After the day she'd had, her humiliation tank runneth over. She didn't need to add rejection to the mix.

After the kickoff that became the kick in the teeth, Underwood demanded that each department at FDP proof the galleys of the year-end report for errors. He ordered that four months' work be corrected in exactly four days, so that the report could be delivered to stockholders on Monday, on time, as planned. She'd hardly had time for lunch. Even coming here meant slipping away into the night.

Lisa found her way to Marc's mailbox. *Just put the shit in and get out.* She stuffed in her envelope with her assignment and was almost in the safety of the stairwell when Nina caught up to her. "Hey!" Nina cried happily. "Look at you!"

Lisa laughed awkwardly. "Look at me!" she said.

Nina pulled her aside. "So are you going with him?" she asked.

She blinked. Was it just me, or had the whole world turned upside down that day? "What?"

It was Nina's turn to look puzzled. "Marc. He got the consultancy," she announced. "He's going to UCSD for a year."

So much for her apology. The point was moot now. Lisa sighed, ambivalent . . . dejected, and pleased for him at the same time. "San Diego," she said. "That's great for him."

Nina stared at her. "For two people who spent the weekend together, you're both miserable!"

Lisa stared longingly at the orange doors to the stairwell. "One of those dumb, impulsive things that you regret in the long run."

The happy expression on Nina's face evaporated. Lisa knew that look. It was as if she could read Lisa's mind. "You believe it's the black-white thing, don't you?" Nina concluded. "You of all people."

Shit, why lie? Nina must've sensed in all the years she'd known her and Tim that, on some level, the interracial thing made her uncomfortable. "Yes," she finally confessed. "Fundamentally, we're human beings, but culturally, we couldn't be further apart."

Nina's grey eyes hardened. Lisa had seen that look; she'd just never been on the receiving end. That look said that Nina had shut her out of her heart. "Then A.J. Wood, the Minister of Propaganda, got to you, too," she concluded. Her eyes melted, welling up. "You break my heart, Lisa."

Nina spun on her sensible Marks and Spencer heels and stormed in the direction of her office. Lisa watched helplessly after her. *Who else can I alienate today?!*

Marc shut the door to his office, slumped down into his swivel chair, and leaned over with his head in his hands. *Thank God that's over.*

Adam sat down in the guest chair and sighed. "So, those are the people you work with," he laughed.

Marc looked up at his brother. *A friendly face.* "I'm glad you came," he said.

"Nina," Adam said. "She thought you could use one other person there who didn't want to—and I quote— 'put their tongue up your arse.' "

Marc laughed, in spite of his fucked-up mood. "The way I feel right now, a tongue in the ass wouldn't be the worst thing in the world."

"Hey, I heard that Grantham dude's homoerotic speech . . . about how you were loved, how you were going to be missed. If anyone here was going to try to put his tongue up your ass, my money's on him."

Marc held up a hand. Just the thought of staring at Les Grantham's pale, Waspy ass was enough to make him puke up his entrails. "Stop. Please!"

"So," Adam sighed. "You're going to California."

It just began to sink in. "I'm going to California," he said.

"What does this mean for you and Lisa?"

His heart constricted. Could he have had at least one second in the day where he didn't think about her? He scoffed through pursed lips. "The last place Lisa Martin wants to be is with me," he declared.

Surprised, Adam asked. "What happened?"

Marc told him, spat out the events of the past four days in a hail of emotion, as if it wasn't real until he told it all to Adam . . . those wonderful days and nights at the cabin, the dinner at Spolini's, that poisonous argument on the sidewalk. Adam sat and listened quietly, like he always did, his dark eyes thoughtful. When Marc was done, he sat back and waited for the sage wisdom to come forth. "Well," Adam sighed.

That's all I get? "Well?!" Marc echoed.

"Marc, after that display at Ma and Dad's, and especially with all the shit that's going on around us, you can't blame her for thinking all Italians are assholes," Adam said.

"How many times do I have to insist that I'm not like that?" Marc asked, frustrated. "I have to wear the mantle of those Y-Os holding watermelons and screaming at people to get out of Bensonhurst?"

"Just like she has to wear the mantle of the gold-tooth, ghetto, welfare mother, rapper stereotype," Adam said gently. "She loves you, Marc. I can tell. You've just got to give it time. She'll cool off, you guys'll kiss and make up, and that fight'll be old news."

"There's no such thing as old news, Adam," Marc declared. "Speaking of which, what was that shit Ma mentioned? About Dad getting beat up by some black guys when I was a baby?"

Adam's eyes darted around the room, like he was remembering really far back. "Yeah," he said. "God, I was seven, Shithead was five, and you were just about to turn three. Dad was fixing cars down in Bed-Stuy then. He was finishing up one night, heading out to his truck when these three black guys mugged the shit out of him. The only thing that saved him was crawling under his truck and hiding there 'til the cops came."

Shit. That was heavy. He couldn't imagine it, his stoic, hardened father, being menaced by some black guys, trembling under his truck. He couldn't imagine his father being afraid of anything. It suddenly made sense. Their baby son, whom they'd tried to protect, had brought the enemy right to their table. "That's why we left the City, isn't it?" Marc concluded.

"Ma was scared to death of losing him," Adam said. "She couldn't get to Jersey fast enough. Before that, she used to be nurturing . . . maternal. And Dad used to be more demonstrative, engaging. It's a shame you didn't get that side of them."

So, that's why. Just as he missed the child he could've had, he'd wished for a relationship with his parents. Worse still was not knowing where the love and attention had gone, why his own parents felt indifference toward him. He'd spent most of his life knocking himself out to build a bridge to them, only to find out now that the absence of one wasn't his fault after all. "And I find out about this thirty-seven years later?" he asked, anguished.

Adam shrugged. "Our family's dysfunctional, Marc. Or haven't you noticed?"

And in the aftermath of the week's events, there never would be a relationship. "It's just as well," Marc sighed. "Ma called me today. Apparently, I'm still disowned."

Adam rolled his eyes. "Please! They both know Lisa has nothing to do with something that went down on a corner before she was even born."

His mother made a science out of holding a grudge. "You're assuming they're rational."

"Well, I haven't disowned you," Adam said, grinning deviously. "You're the only uncle my new baby's going to have. Of course, there's Doug, but it's just not the same, is it?"

Did he really hear his brother right, or was he just tired? "What?"

Adam beamed proudly, like a man whose seed had found the mark yet again. "Diane's twelve weeks pregnant," he announced happily.

For the second time in five years, his explosive happiness for his brother was intermingled in almost equal measure with envy. Nonetheless, he stood up and embraced his big brother and held tightly, patting him forcefully on the back. His brother smelled like Polo cologne and wool tweed. "You horny bastard!" he laughed. "You knocked up your wife listening to Mario Lanza records?"

"Never underestimate the power of an Italian crooner to separate a girl from her panties," Adam chuckled.

They separated, and Marc saw unvarnished joy on Adam's face. He couldn't lie to his big brother. "I'm so jealous," he admitted.

Adam gently slapped Marc's cheek. "Your time'll come," he warned. "Before you know it, you'll be ass-deep in shitty diapers, formula, and vomit. You'll be crazy from no sleep, and you'll have absolutely no disposable income."

Bring it on . . .

There was a knock at the door. Marc and Adam ended their embrace and turned to see Chancellor Swift and Dean Les Grantham enter. The moment was officially destroyed. Chancellor Swift looked characteristically tight-assed in his grey double-breasted suit; Grantham, pale and tweedy, with patches on his brown corduroy jacket. "Marc," said Swift, greasy smile on overkill. His steely grey eyes darted for a second to Adam. "I do hope we're not interrupting anything."

Said like he couldn't care less whether he was. Marc indicated Adam with a wave of the hand. "Of course not," he lied. "This is Adam Guerrieri, my brother. Adam, you remember the Chancellor and Dean Grantham from the party."

"Hello," Adam said politely.

"To what do I owe this visit, gentlemen?" Marc asked.

"Perhaps we should come back later," Grantham suggested.

"No," Marc insisted. "Come on in."

Swift and Grantham came in and shut the door. Grantham looked sheepish. *What the fuck's wrong with you?*

"Marc . . ." said Grantham, ". . . well, how do we put this delicately?"

"We don't," Swift declared, turning to Marc. "Marc, it's come to my attention that you've been having an affair with one of your students."

Marc stared incredulously at the unholy alliance. Here were the chancellor and the dean of a state college about to become a university, wanting confirmation of whom he was making love with. He would've laughed in their faces if they didn't look so intent on corroborating their suspicions. "You're serious," he said.

Grantham looked away; Swift persisted. "Deadly serious, Marc," Swift declared. "Ordinarily, this kind of thing is usually overlooked, as long as it's consensual. But we're about to become a university, and with us under such close scrutiny from the state . . ."

Marc's incredulous stare morphed into one that was angry, focused on the two buffoons before him. "Okay, let me stop you here," he said. "We're not going to have this conversation. In your professional capacities, your sole concern should be what goes on in my classes, not what occurs between my sheets." Pointedly, he walked to the door and opened it. "Thank you, gentlemen. Have a good evening."

Swift glared at Marc, as though he were a petulant child. Marc returned the favor, meeting Swift's gaze full-on, until finally, Swift averted his eyes. "Well, then, Marc, I wish you luck in San Diego," he said, fake greasy smile back in place like a mask.

"And I wish you luck in diffusing the issues on your plate here," Marc pointedly shot back.

Swift looked at Adam and nodded, then he and Grantham begrudgingly left the office, leaving the door wide open. Marc stared after them in disbelief. "You believe that shit?" he asked.

Adam shook his head. "You're out of here—be thankful."

"Him even mentioning it is blasphemy," Marc declared.

Adam put a friendly hand on his arm. "Look, let's go to Charlie Brown's," he suggested. "Get you drunk."

Before he could express how attractive it was to crawl into a bottle, there was a knock at the door again. Angrily, they looked up, Marc preparing for Round Two. This time, though, it was Tom Stefanowski, clutching a hardcover book to his chest, standing in the doorway. Big and imposing, Stefanowski defied the stereotype of the dumb athlete. His record of crushing the competition as a cornerback next to Jim Brown at Syracuse belied the friendliness in his twinkling blue eyes. He actually cared about the students. Marc's demeanor softened slightly. "Tom," he said, relieved.

Stefanowski tentatively came forward. "Marc, thank you for having me at your send-off," he said, patting his taut midsection. "That chocolate cake was delicious. Trying to make me fat?"

Yeah, right. Stefanowski was all lean muscle. He could probably snap Marc's ass in two like a dry twig. "Thanks for coming," Marc said. "This is my brother, Adam."

Adam looked at Stefanowski, then picked up a recent copy of *The Clarion* on Marc's desk. He looked up from the paper at Stefanowski. "This is you," Adam said.

Adam held up the paper. There was a photo of Stefanowski, serving cups of cocoa to the demonstrators in the quad in front of the Student Center. The headline read, "Dean Warms Quad Demonstrators." Marc looked from the paper to Stefanowski. *He should be chancellor.*

Stefanowski shrugged. "They were cold," he said simply, then proffered his book, a well-worn copy of *Goombah.* "Can I ask a favor, Marc? Before you go, could you autograph this for me?"

"Sure," Marc said.

"You have to come back when you're done at UCSD," Stefanowski said while Marc signed. "The college needs you."

The unpleasant scene with Swift and Grantham replayed in Marc's mind. "We'll see," he said.

"Your department has so much talent," Stefanowski mused. "You . . . Nina Johanssen-Simon. I read her dissertation. *Sexism and Racism in Shakespearean Theatre.* If there's a person who needs to get tenure, like, yesterday, it's Nina."

"The old leadership doesn't seem to think so," Marc commented, disgusted.

"You know," Stefanowski said, as if he was about to share a big secret, "I've been going 'round the campus and talking to people. Just talking. The prevailing sentiment is that the old leadership is no leadership."

Tired sapphire blue eyes met twinkling blue, and the penny dropped. *You're about to make a move!* Again, Marc thought about those two clowns that left his office. "Well, Tom, any proposed new leadership would have my full support," he promised, handing him his book.

Stefanowski grinned from ear to ear. He patted Marc on the shoulder. "Well, Marc, I'm not going to keep you and your brother," he said. He embraced the book in the crook of his massive arm. "Thanks for this. You've got to come down to the field house for a workout sometime."

"I'd like that," Marc said.

With a quick nod to Marc and Adam, Stefanowski disappeared through the door. Marc looked over at his brother. "Let's go before someone else comes," he pleaded.

Silently, Adam tossed him his coat.

On the way out, Marc checked his mailbox. He sifted through the messages and assignments until he came to a plain brown envelope with his name on the front. He recognized the handwriting. She'd been there, and he'd missed her. His heart sank. "What's wrong?" Adam asked, concerned.

Marc squashed the pile of papers into his satchel. "Nothing," he mumbled. "Let's go get hammered."

Lisa sat in the comfortable stuffed chair in front of Jaye's expansive, Nigerian wooden, hand-carved desk, polished to blindingly bright. Jaye, working the long lines of her black power suit, strutted back and forth, then stood behind the desk. She looked down at the speakerphone, waiting for a response from the other end. Finally, she said, "There should be no surprises, Richard. We went over these papers already. Your client should be satisfied."

"How satisfied should someone being fleeced be?" Bryan whined from across the lines.

"How's the nose, Mr. Livingston?" Jaye asked, then looked at Lisa and winked.

Lisa giggled from behind her hand. Payback for Bryan trying to drag out the inevitable until the final hour. She glanced down at her watch. It was 4:30. She'd hoped to be out of here and on her way to class. The anticipation of seeing Marc, the hope that he'd hear and accept her apology, filled her.

"My client is signing the papers now," C. Richard Monaghan announced. "We'll have them messengered over. You should have them within the hour."

The sound of the dial tone filled the air. Lisa glanced down at her watch. *An hour!* She was going to be late. Marc hated it when she was late.

At 5:30, a harried, road-weary bicycle messenger produced blue-covered divorce papers. Lisa sat at Jaye's desk, Jaye hovering behind her, pointing at specific paragraphs that read like Latin to Lisa. "See?" Jaye said, proud of her work. "You get the money from the house, spousal support pro-rated to Bryan's projected lifetime income, half of his FDP stock, should he sell. You won, girl!"

So, this was what five years of marriage came to—her signing on the dotted line under Bryan's masculine, angry scrawl. Years of nurturing him, sharing her life, her body, everything she had. A rush of emotion swallowed her, and she was overcome. Her signature on the papers blurred through the tears. "Yeah, I won," she laughed at the irony. "I'm the winner."

She was horribly late. In the Jetta, she'd flown like a bat out of hell along Valley Road in rush-hour traffic. In a snake-bitten series of events, she parked in the quarry and leapt onto a shuttle bus, only to have it break down halfway back to the main campus. She got off and ran in the dark as fast as she could, weaving through slow-moving traffic and slower-moving demonstrators in the quad. It was after seven when she breathlessly barged into the classroom.

The students, working in dyads, turned and looked at her in surprise. Even A.J. shook her head, as if to say, *You're pitiful.* Marc, looking gaunt and haggard, stopped mid-lecture. He focused poisonous blue eyes squarely on her. Panting, she met the gaze, her pulse thumping deep in her throat. *He's pissed.* "I'm sorry I'm late," she gasped. "The shuttle bus broke down in the quarry, and . . ."

Eyes he'd once trained on her lovingly now looked like blue ice. "At the break," he stated. "My office."

She gulped. *This can't be good.* "Okay."

She felt his gaze on her as she peeled off her coat and looked to see if anyone would make room in their dyad for her. Her fellow students looked at her with disdain, like they were channeling Marc's rage at her, too. Finally, A.J., sitting with busty Carlette, begrudgingly pulled up the nearest desk chair. "It's supposed to be a dyad," Carlette whispered in protest.

"Fuck it, now it's a triad," A.J. angrily whispered back.

Lisa draped her coat over the top of the desk and eased wearily into the chair. "Dag!" A.J. whispered. "What did you do?"

She looked at Marc, who was still glaring daggers. *You don't want to know.*

They were alone together in the elevator going up to the fourth floor. The adrenaline coursing through him literally made him sick to his stomach. He resisted the urge to look at her. He didn't need to. The way she wore that black skirt, the white shirt through which hardened nipples peeked, and her black beret were burned into his brain from the moment she burst into the class. Her perfume filled the charged air in the metal box. Much to his horror, he began to get hard just standing next to her, smelling her scent. He hated his body for responding in such a primal fashion. And, of course, he had to hate her for having that effect on him.

The doors opened, and he walked out onto the fourth floor. The clicking of her boot heels on the linoleum told him that she was following quickly behind him.

Finally, after what seemed like they were walking the long mile, he ushered her into his office and slammed the door behind them both. She jumped, turning to face him. The scarf around her milky latte throat shifted slightly, and he caught sight of hickeys near her carotid artery. Hickeys he'd put there. A torrent of mental images flooded his brain . . . grinding his pelvis into hers . . . sucking those pointed nipples . . . listening to her screams as she came . . . holding her close. He got harder still.

A laugh trembled from her mouth. "Marc," she said softly. "I'm sorry."

Part of him wanted to kiss that mouth; part of him wanted to smash her face in. Did she mean she was sorry for being late, or for overreacting on the sidewalk two days ago? Whatever. He didn't want to hear it. He picked up her assignment and tossed it at her. "What is this?" he demanded.

She bent to pick it up, leafing through the sketches and the typed pages. "My assignment," she murmured.

"How can that be?" he asked with faux ignorance. "In the previous assignment you handed in, Vanessa Dean was about to meet the parents of her white boyfriend, the vet whose parents lived in the Ironbound. The Ironbound was about to erupt, because a white cop shot a young black kid. How does that become . . ." he pointed to the papers she cradled in her arms, " . . . this?"

She blinked, looking like she was trying to find the words. "Umm . . . I thought this was better," she explained.

"It's not," he spat. "You were supposed to hand in 100 pages of fiction. You can't change horses midstream."

"Not to split hairs, but you didn't say that it had to be a hundred pages of the *same* fiction," she reminded him. "I can show you in the syllabus."

The nerve! So what if he hadn't said it; it was implied.

"I know what's in the syllabus—I wrote the fucking syllabus!" he snapped. "I say this submission is unacceptable."

He sensed right then that he'd crossed the line, that she'd reached her tolerance limit. Her eyes hardened, nostrils flared. "Pardon me," she said, "but I was the most promising writer you'd seen until I started giving up the box."

"That amazes me, too, Lisa," he declared. "Perhaps you thought, since I was fucking you, that I'd let you slide."

Hurt filled her face. "God, we never should've done this," she near-whispered, like she was talking to herself.

For a brief second, he felt remorse, but his temper . . . his infernal temper. "Why cry over spilt milk this late in the game?" he said.

"Is this shit necessary?"

"Isn't this what you've painted me as . . . the cruel white man? Bobo? Mr. Charlie? Some homicidal *guido*?!"

"Look, what if I rewrite the assignment?"

"It's your funeral."

She looked worn down to a nub suddenly, and this time, he was the cause of it. *So much for your promise to protect her from other men. Who's going to protect her from me?*

She sighed deeply. "This isn't going to work," she said. "I'm skipping the last class. I'll have A.J. tape it for me."

First you come late; now you don't take this seriously? Me seriously?! Unadulterated fury filled his head, staining his vision red. "You do that, and I will flunk your sweet ass as sure as the day is long!" he bellowed.

"Look, you inflexible fuck, do what you have to do!" she spat back. "You're not the only game in town . . . in or out of bed!"

She stormed out of the office. On impulse, he tore off after her. "I hate you!" he yelled.

"Get over it!" she shot back.

Lisa ran for her life down the halls, seconds later disappearing into the nearest stairwell. It was at that very moment that he realized where he was. Students and his colleagues stared at him like he was insane. He felt emotionally exposed. Like any normal person naked in public, his first impulse was to retreat. So he did . . . to his office, slamming the door behind himself.

Lisa ran from the School of Humanities building and out into the night. She stared as traffic whizzed by on Main Avenue. It was official. She'd lost him. None of this made any sense. How could things have gone from sublime to ridiculously insane in the space of forty-eight hours? *Get it together, girl! This isn't the end of the world.*

"Lisa, wait up!" she heard through the haze, and turned to see A.J., flaming Marlboro Light between her fingers, sprinting to catch up to her.

More shit I don't need. Still, Lisa stopped, properly putting on her coat. After all, A.J. stood up for her with Carlette. That meant something. "What," she said.

Tentatively, A.J. approached. "Listen," she began with a nervous laugh. "I'm sorry for what I said Election Night. I was a bitch."

I'm not going to make this shit easy for you. "Yes, you were," Lisa said.

A.J. nodded, as though she knew she deserved that jab. Then her plucked eyebrows knitted. "What's up with you and Guerrieri, man?" she asked. "He looked mad enough to kill! He was doing that white-boy-throbby-vein-in-the-forehead thing they do. I know he hates you being late, but damn!"

Lisa turned away. "Leave it alone, A.J.," she begged.

A.J. grabbed her shoulder. "No, I want to know," she insisted.

Lisa looked at her curious face . . . the calm before

the storm. She drew in a deep breath and let it rip. "Marc and I have been seeing each other."

The curious face morphed into the scornful, angry face. "You fucked the blue-eyed devil," she concluded, nodding. "Why am I not surprised?"

This was the limit. "You know, I'm black enough for his family to yell eggplant-this and nigger-that at me," she said. "I'm black enough to have cops pull me over in Cedar Grove and threaten to smoke my ass. But for some reason, A.J., I'm not black enough for you."

"I had such hopes for you, Lisa. I thought you'd cast off that Jersey rich-white-girl persona and realize what you are."

For the third time that day, she was witnessing another little death. This time, she let go of a toxic, conditional friend who had masqueraded as the real thing. "And A.J., I hoped that eventually you'd accept me as I am and just be my friend," she sighed. "Guess we're both disappointed, huh?"

With that, she clutched her coat close to her and walked away into the night that was as dark as her mood.

13

It took upper management at FDP exactly one week of closed-door meetings to find a scapegoat. Lisa sensed that heads would roll once the nonstop flurry of activity resulted in the year-end report being mailed out to shareholders. She had not imagined they would drop the hammer so soon.

Lisa saw her summons to Joe Siegrist's office late that Monday afternoon as fact-finding, informational. When she entered, though, and saw Rick seated dejectedly in front of Joe's desk, she sensed an inquisition. *Poor Rick.*

Never one for formalities, Joe Siegrist waved her to the other guest chair in front of his desk. "Sit down, Lisa," he commanded.

Lisa's legs gave way, and she collapsed into the chair. "Genie says you wanted to see me," she said over a dry throat.

"Yes, Lisa," Joe announced. "I'll get to the point. Rick maintains that the report is flawed because you acted alone, and you didn't consult him. You made major decisions without consulting him. You even forged his signature on the requisition."

It took a second to register. The hammer was being dropped . . . *on her.* Lisa turned to Rick. She knew Joe was an asshole, but she needed to see in Rick's face that he was toeing the party line. Rick looked away from her and down at the hands in his lap. *Wimp.*

Lisa took her bitter pill. "Yes, Joe, I did all those things," she said simply.

The usually unflappable Joe raised his bushy, salt-and-pepper eyebrows in unvarnished surprise. "You're not even denying it?" he asked.

Lisa again looked to Rick. Desperately, she wanted to give him a chance to be the Rick she knew and fought for. "You have nothing to say," she concluded.

Rick looked up from his lap, through her, and out the picture window at the rapid snow flurries. "I have nothing to say," he repeated.

Lisa's heart sank with her crushing disappointment. Death Number Four. She turned to Joe. "Then, Joe, I'll save you the trouble of firing me," she declared. "I quit."

Joe's imperious air returned. "I hope you've learned your lesson."

Lisa laughed bitterly, shaking her head. She met Joe's gaze head-on. "Believe me, Joe, I have," she declared. "I've learned that the next time my boss is paralyzed with grief and incapable of doing his job, I should just mind my own business like everyone else and let him twist in the wind. After half a decade, I of all people should've known that's how fuck-ups do payroll."

With her dignity shredded but still present, Lisa got up on shaky legs and calmly walked out of the office.

Under a grey sky swirling with tiny snowflakes, two burly black security guards escorted Lisa to the vast employee parking lot, sparsely populated with cars of every make and model. In her hands, she clutched a file box, which they had searched, containing the remnants of six years of her life at FDP. She imagined she could feel all the eyes of the FDP employees staring at her as she opened the trunk of her Jetta and tossed the box inside. "Thank you," she said, smiling sweetly. "I've got it from here."

The security guards gave her the once-over again, and, judging her benign, turned and walked ramrod-straight toward the western entrance of the complex. Lisa disabled the alarm, which sounded a sharp chirp, and she got in, slamming the car door with a *thunk*. She sat in the silence for what seemed like forever, listening to her breathing. *What are you going to do now, Billy Bad Ass?*

Lisa finally started the car and headed for home. Thoughts raced through her head. How much longer was she going to have a home? She had no money. The divorce had taken every penny she had. Any liquid part of her settlement—money from the sale of the house, for example—would be a long time coming. Now she had no job, because she decided to cover Rick Farrelly's ass. She'd alienated Nina and A.J., so she had no friends. Mostly, she'd lost Marc. She was completely and utterly alone for the first time in a long time, a crippling loneliness she felt right down to her soul.

By the time she made it to winding Upper Mountain Avenue in Montclair, she was sobbing as if she could never stop. Her windshield wipers furiously swatted away tenacious, now enormous, snowflakes from her windshield. Between her tears and the snow, visibility was practically zero. Then she felt the Jetta slip and slide against the icy road below it. The speed, the treacherous nature of the roads, and inertia combined to send the Jetta into a furious, rapid spin-out. Lisa's sobs gave way to screams as the car jumped the divider. As if in slow motion, the steering wheel came closer and closer. She felt an agonizing thump against her forehead. Suddenly, everything went black.

Sad and unshaven, Marc packed the last of his precious belongings into a box, then looked around his office. He remembered his first day here, how this office embraced one mangy, sickly, divorced man almost a year and a half ago. He remembered wondering how he'd become a teacher, how he was going to dispense wisdom when he himself felt so unwise. He was going out the same way he'd come in.

She didn't come to class, just as she'd promised. Last week, after that fire-and-brimstone argument, he'd gone home and ripped her sketch of him into a million pieces. Later, he hated himself. He spent the rest of the night with a roll of cellophane tape, piecing it back together. One week later, he missed her more than he did in the aftermath of the events on the sidewalk in front of her building. He wanted to apologize, but he sensed it was over. He was off to California to dispense wisdom and watch Michele and Kieran play the hopelessly-in-love couple.

Just as he slapped the lid on the last box, he turned and saw Nina through the glass in the door. She looked teary-eyed, seemingly out of her mind with grief. He beckoned her in. "Nina," he said, concerned. "What's up?"

Nina pressed tears out of her swollen gray eyes. "It's Lisa," she announced. "She was . . ." she hiccupped, ". . . she was in a car crash last night. She's at Mountainside."

He blinked as it sank in. Whatever it was, it was not good. "I'll drive," he croaked.

Marc raced the Jeep from Valley Road to Bloomfield Avenue, arriving at Mountainside Hospital in record time. Minutes later, Nina and Marc rushed from the elevators and into the frenetic, sterile Intensive Care Unit.

They arrived at the main section of the floor, a rotunda with nurses in scrubs, ringing phones, computers, and charts. A horseshoe slip of blue-carpeted hallway separated the rotunda from single rooms with closed doors. Tim, Bryan-fucking-Livingston, and another woman— light-skinned black, bereaved, dressed in black—waited in front of one of the doors. Marc had seen her photo thousands of times on dust jackets, in *Publishers Weekly*. *Barbara Haley-Martin!*

Bryan's and Marc's eyes locked and flamed, like the equivalent of two rams meeting on a snowy mountaintop just before running headlong into each other. *I'll beat your ass again!* Then Bryan blinked. "What's *he* doing here?!" he roared.

Barbara looked confused. "Who is *he?*" she asked.

"The white boy Lisa's fucking," Bryan replied, smirking.

Nina rushed him, pushing him in the midsection. "You need to do this now?" she sobbed.

Bryan pouted. "He shouldn't be here," he decreed. "He's not family."

"Neither are you!" Nina reminded him. "Jaye filed the papers, remember?"

It took a minute to sink in. *So, she's finally free of this motherfucker.*

Finally, Tim intervened. He took Bryan by the elbow. "Bryan, we're not having this," he said softly, calmly. "You're going to come with me, and you're going to chill. Understand?"

Tim escorted a belligerent Bryan to the elevators. *Good fucking riddance.*

Marc turned to Barbara. Even in grief, she exuded a palpable aura of strength and supreme confidence. He could understand why Lisa feared her. "I'm Marc Guerrieri," he announced, offering his hand. "I wish we didn't have to meet like this."

Barbara grasped his hand; hers was ice cold. "It's

been a very shocking couple of hours all around," she said, her throaty, British-accented voice hoarse, Marc assumed, from crying.

"How is she?" he asked.

Barbara sighed. " 'Serious head trauma,' " she scoffed. "That's the diagnosis. What a euphemism. Looks like a coma to me."

Not good. "What's the prognosis?" he desperately asked.

"Just wait and see," Nina said.

"May I see her?" he asked.

Barbara trained those light eyes on him, as if she was marveling at his very cheek. Marc gulped, the gaze chilling his blood. "My former son-in-law is an idiot," she declared. "But I agree with him on this. Only family. I'm sure you understand."

Marc's heart sank. He guessed Bryan was right. All things considered, Nina, and Tim, and Bryan were like family; he was just the one who'd spent one idyllic weekend fucking Lisa. He didn't rate. "Of course," he said quietly.

With that, Barbara entered the room. Marc tried to peer past her, but all he could see was an industrial brown curtain around the wheels of a hospital bed. Nina took his hand. "We'll try to persuade her," she promised.

He nodded. But he decided not to hold his breath.

Marc prowled the halls of the ICU, watching Lisa's room from a respectable distance. He watched as Bryan-fucking-Livingston left an hour after their initial confrontation. *Probably needs to get his beauty sleep.* He watched with envy as Tim, then Nina, then Barbara alternated trips into the room. Finally, he watched as Barbara shooed away Tim and Nina, who protested mightily, around 11:30. Barbara sat in one of two chairs in front of Lisa's room. She looked so alone, slight, her protective, imposing aura gone. Marc sensed this was the time to move in.

Toting two coffees, Marc wended his way through

the usual ICU traffic and tentatively approached Barbara. "May I?" he asked.

Barbara looked up at him with reddened eyes. Wordlessly, she waved him to the other chair. He eased himself down. "Any news?" he asked.

She shook her head. Her curly hair brushed against her broad shoulders. "No change."

Marc handed her one of the coffees. "I thought you could use this," he said. "Cream and sugar."

She took it warily. "Thank you," she said.

Making progress . . . "No problem," he said.

She sipped her coffee, leaving a waxy brown lipstick half-moon on the white lid. "So, you're The Voice of Italian America," she said.

He laughed. Next to her and all her accomplishments, he was just a baby. "And you're the face of children's literature," he volleyed back.

A smile softened the laugh lines around her mouth. "Heavy burdens, aren't they?" she said. "Given Bryan's nasty little outburst, I should ask you what your intentions are toward my daughter."

"I want to marry her," he declared.

Silence. He didn't envision her leaping up and down with joy, but he'd expected some kind of reaction. Finally, Barbara said, "My father was white. Did Lisa tell you?"

Oh, shit. That explained a lot . . . her coloring, perhaps her hostility toward him. "No," he confessed.

Barbara grimaced. "He and my mother lived in England, because they didn't want to raise me in an environment that was so intolerant of their marriage," she announced. "I was their little racial harmony experiment. Unfortunately, the world saw me as a freak. Ignored by whites, grudgingly accepted by blacks. I wouldn't wish that on anyone, especially any grandchild of mine."

And not any child of his. He would fiercely protect his child from the assholes of the world. "I'm sorry about your experience," he said, "but times have changed."

Barbara practically laughed in his face. "Have they?" she asked. "Read *The New York Times.* Yusuf Hawkins was shot because those boys thought he was dating a white girl in their neighborhood. What was your family's reaction?"

His mind touched on that horrific scene around his parents' Thanksgiving dinner table. He looked down in shame at his coffee cup. "Not favorable," he murmured.

Barbara looked self-satisfied. "I rest my case."

"I love Lisa!" he protested.

"And she was so excited about that love, she ran her car off the road!" she cried.

"That's unfair! How could you know that?!"

A nurse at the nearby station looked over at them disapprovingly, pressing an index finger to her luscious red lips. *Calm down, Marco.*

Barbara calmly handed the coffee back to him. "Go home," she said. "There's nothing for you here."

With that, she got up and entered Lisa's room, pointedly closing the door in his face. He stared down at the half-moon on the coffee cup. He could taste his frustrations.

Marc watched the events from a safe distance behind the wall . . . close enough to hear and to see without being seen. His life for the past two days was stalking the hospital room, going home to shower and cry until he fell into an exhausted, fitful sleep, then returning to the hospital. To see without being seen. By Thursday, he was emboldened by his fatigue, by his singular determination to care about nothing but being with her.

He watched as Tim and Nina comforted Barbara. She looked a mess. Her curls were limp and oily. Fatigue settled in the lines in her face, making her seem older. Her creamy skin looked pale and washed out under the fluorescent lights in the hall. He supposed she was just like his mother . . . well-meaning and protective, even though their ways of protecting their children were suspect. Her grief seemingly reached out and tore at his heart, and his eyes misted.

"How's girlfriend doing?" Tim asked.

Barbara's stooped back convulsed with a sob. "She won't wake up," she said. "What have I done? God took Gaby from me, and now He's going to snatch away my one and only child?"

Nina lovingly massaged Barbara's shoulder. "Barbara, you need a break," she said. "You've been here for three straight days."

"I can't leave her," Barbara insisted.

"Barbara, you need to eat something," Nina said. "We'll be just downstairs in the cafeteria. We can tell the nurses to find us if there's any change. All right?"

"All right," Barbara relented.

Obscured behind the wall, Marc watched as Tim and Nina escorted Barbara to the elevators. Marc watched them get on, watched the big metal doors shut behind them. *Go . . . go for it!*

Looking as casual as he could, given that his heart was racing wildly in his chest, Marc strolled boldly toward the door to Lisa's room. Anticipation about to eat him whole, he pushed the door to the starkly lit private room open as if he belonged there. Suddenly, though, he stopped short. *Lisa.*

She lay in the hospital bed amidst beeping machines with flashing lights, signaling life. A swaddle of white bandages wrapped her head. Tubes protruded from her mouth and nose. An IV dripped saline and medication intermittently into her arm. Only a week ago, they were together, professing love for each other. She was vital, happy, pulsating with life. Now, she looked slight against the bedsheets, machines keeping her alive.

His eyes moistened. He approached her slowly, closer and closer. Taking care, he sat on the edge of the bed.

He ran a gentle hand over her beautiful face, now cut, bruised, and swollen. "God!" he whispered.

The machines beeped; the lights flashed. He sat there, watching her for what seemed like hours, cherishing his memories of her. He held the hand that didn't have the device for measuring the oxygen levels in her blood. Finally, he sighed. "Haley Melissa," he said. "Well, I met your mother. You're right. She is a piece of work."

He looked over his shoulder at the door, as if it would open at any second and Barbara would come shrieking in. "Jesus, I'm sneaking in here, praying she doesn't find out." He stroked her battered cheek. "How'd this shit get so complicated, huh?"

The machines beeped; the lights flashed. Again, he just sat and watched her, as the ventilator breathed for her. "For once, you're quiet," he laughed. "I can say what I want to you, without you interrupting."

Marc glanced over his shoulder again. Still no Barbara. "Ever since I met you, all I wanted was to be with you," he said. "But what with the shit you went through with Bryan, and your mother's baggage about her father, I understand now why you're conflicted about being with me."

He longed to hear her voice. Instead, all he got was the beeping and flashing. His eyes filled, and her face blurred. His face felt hot and sweaty. Veins bulged in his neck with emotion begging for release. "God, if you could just talk to me again!" he sobbed. "I love you, Lisa. But as much as I love you, I'll go away, if it gives you a moment's peace. All I want you to do is wake up!"

He didn't know what was worse, losing her in death, or opting to give her up to end her confusion so she could have a life of peace. Either way, the loss crushed his chest like a 100-pound weight. Grief opened up like a tidal wave. He clutched her hand in his as he cried. He knew that either way, this was the last time he was going to see her again.

After what felt like forever, Marc shot a quick glance at the closed door. He was officially pushing his luck; it was a miracle he hadn't been caught already. He closed his eyes and held her scraped hand to his reddened, wet face. Then he trailed her hand down his cheek, slowly weaning himself off the feeling of her skin against his. He kissed the point where lines intersected in the middle of her open palm. A sigh trembled from his chest. Slowly . . . finally, he rested her hand on the gleaming white bedsheets and covered it lovingly with her blanket. *I'm never gonna touch you again . . .*

Then he looked up, and his heart seismically lurched. Lisa was staring at him from the depths of gauzy bandages and bruised, swollen flesh. Her eyes were hooded and glazed, but nonetheless open. He gasped in disbelief. "Lisa?" he questioned, tentatively.

She sluggishly blinked, seemingly with all the energy she had. He laughed, orgasmic relief rushing through him. "Lisa," he sighed. "Baby . . ."

He stroked her cheek, meeting her gaze. Even though the tubes invading her body, as well as her weakness and confusion, prevented her from speaking, he connected with her on a level more profound than he had on those nights they'd made love. *Thank you, God!*

Then he remembered. He was saying good-bye. It cut him to the core, having to leave her. She'd be fine, though. Knowing that took the edge off the pain, if for just a little while . . .

She didn't know whether she was wobbly and fuzzy because of the aftereffects of all the medicines in her system, or because her muscles were weakened by days of inactivity. Nonetheless, Lisa clutched onto Nina's arm as if it were a life preserver. Barbara gently tucked Lisa's white terry cloth robe around her. "Please be careful, you two," she cautioned.

Nina playfully slapped Barbara's hand away. "Don't be such a Nervous Nellie, Barbara," she laughed. "We're just going to walk."

Lisa laughed wearily, enjoying the attention. "It's all right, Ma," she assured her.

Barbara let them go down the hall, arm in arm. Lisa trembled with every step, at one point leaning half her weight onto Nina, who shifted her own weight to accommodate Lisa. "Don't let me go now," Lisa laughed.

"Never," Nina giggled.

They wobbled in silence. Lisa slowly shifted to look over at Nina, at the freckles dusting her nose. The last time she'd seen her, those freckles were practically vibrating in anger. *You break my heart, Lisa!* "It comes back to me in little fuzzy pictures," Lisa began, "but I remember we had a fight."

She waited for Nina to step aside and let her drop to the hard linoleum floor. Instead, Nina shrugged. "Water under the proverbial bridge."

Other fuzzy little pictures began to come back to Lisa like little blurred jigsaw puzzle pieces. Signing her divorce papers . . . that horrendous fight with Marc in the School of Humanities . . . Rick and Joe Siegrist . . . "God, I hope I still have insurance," she sighed. "I quit my job, you know."

Nina got a look on her face, as if she'd just tasted concentrated lemon juice. "A.J. Wood told me," she announced. "Something about Rick Farrelly 'punking out,' she said."

The fuzzy jigsaw piece with A.J. on the street with her snapped into place in her mental tableau. "With friends like those two," she scoffed.

Nina's supporting arm evolved into a loving embrace around her waist. "Well, everything came to a head while you were Sleeping Beauty," she said, practically incandescent. "The SCNJ Board of Trustees ousted Swift!"

"Get the fuck out! George Hamilton's out of a job?"

Nina nodded. "Stefanowski's the Acting Chancellor of the State *University* of New Jersey."

Another fuzzy jigsaw piece snapped into place. She remembered who Dean Stefanowski was. "That's great. He's a good guy."

"So good that he gave me tenure!" Nina laughed.

"See?" Lisa said. "I told you."

So, Nina had kept a full accounting of the happenings of A.J., Rick Farrelly, and SCNJ. Only one person remained unmentioned. Myriad fuzzy jigsaw pieces with his smile, his eyes, his face, the sound of his voice . . . all snapped quickly into place. "And Marc?" she quietly asked. "I know you're just itching to tell me."

Nina sighed as she brushed a stray lock of hair from Lisa's still-bruised face. "He's getting ready to leave for UCSD," she announced. "He's got a lovely home in La Jolla Cove, I'm told."

So, it was final, the last chapter of their dalliance written. No amount of Percocet could dampen the pain cutting her heart. "La Jolla Cove," she repeated. "Well, I hope he's happy."

Sympathetically, Nina pulled her closer still. "He was with you when you woke up," she said in Lisa's ear.

Lisa wasn't surprised. In the recesses of her mind, she remembered his presence, hearing his voice, feeling wrapped in his love. But it was one of those things that was not meant to be. *The right people fucked by circumstance.* She and Nina walked the corridors in silence.

As challenging as her relationship was with Barbara, Lisa loved having her mommy with her. Barbara cooked her meals in the tiny efficiency kitchen. She helped Lisa to the bathroom whenever she needed her. She made sure Lisa took her medicine on time. She gave Lisa warm sponge baths. Having Lisa nearly as helpless as a baby again seemed to appeal to Barbara's nurturing side.

Mostly, Lisa enjoyed the company. They talked, ate ice cream, and watched movies on HBO. Barbara took Lisa to Immaculate for nine o'clock Mass, something Lisa hadn't done since she'd been under her mother's roof. Listening to the solemn hymns, smelling the incense, and taking the body of Christ, she remembered a time when she was innocent, from her first Holy Communion, to trooping up the street in her white dress and knee socks, clutching her collection money in a tissue in her tiny hands. Now she was battered, her heart and body aching. She looked up at the light streaming through the stained glass windows. Tears filled her eyes. *Can you hear me, God?*

Early the next morning, Barbara gave Lisa her medicine and propped her up in the arms of her headless husband on the sofa. She looked quizzically at Lisa's red tartan woolen blanket, running her hands over it. "Bloody hell, you still have this?" she laughed.

"You gave it to me when I went off to Fordham," Lisa reminded her.

Barbara eased down next to her. "My goodness, my mother gave me that blanket when she put me on the BOAC flight, from Heathrow to Idlewild Airport . . . JFK, to you," she sighed, shaking her head. "I was just a baby then. I'd never been on a plane before. Boy, was I scared!"

Lisa's eyes widened. *The Iron Maiden, scared? "You?"* she echoed.

"Yes, me!" she said. "I was twenty-five, leaving my home for the very first time to practice medicine. But there was this old black businessman. He talked to me, and watched out for me for the whole ten hours to New York."

Lisa found it hard to imagine her mother as a naive, insecure twenty-five-year-old, much less needing anyone to watch out for her. "You were brave," she said. "I pitched a fit about going across the Hudson to the Bronx for college."

Barbara touched Lisa's slightly bruised cheek. "Lisa, you're brave, too," she said.

Yeah, right! Sobbing her way through all of her problems as of late. "Right," she murmured. "I belong in the Pantheon of strong black women."

"Haley Melissa," Barbara said, "life has been beating you up relentlessly. Bryan, the divorce, your job . . ." her voice quavered, ". . . that horrific crash. Never once did you back down. You fought like a tigress. That's bravery. I've never been more proud of you."

She'd waited almost thirty years to hear that. "Really?" she asked.

"Really," Barbara returned.

And just like that, their warm-and-fuzzy mother-daughter moment was over. Barbara began straightening the magazines on the coffee table. "God, Melissa, how do you let all this stuff pile up?" Barbara asked testily. "This tiny place. Honestly, you live like a graduate student!"

Lisa realized Barbara couldn't help herself. "I *am* a graduate student, Ma," she teased.

Barbara came across the envelope with Lisa's name on the front. Instantly, Lisa remembered that night in the School of Humanities hallway when Marc exploded with his scathing criticism. She tried to snatch the envelope from her mother, but she couldn't reach without hurting herself. "Ma, give it to me," she begged.

Too late. Barbara opened the envelope and pulled out the sketches and typed pages. Lisa closed her eyes, preparing herself for the ultimate in judgmental. "You did these?" Barbara asked, not even looking up.

"Yes," Lisa sighed.

Finally, Barbara looked up at her. *That can't be pride in her face!* "Melissa, these are excellent!" she said.

That's two in one day. "Honestly?" Lisa asked, incredulous.

Before she could reply, the intercom buzzed. Barbara with the work in her hands, rushed to get it. "We'll talk about this later," she declared.

Meanwhile, Marc stood on the same sidewalk that was the scene of his breakup with Lisa. He couldn't leave without saying good-bye, and seeing if she was well. The indecent haste with which the team of nurses hustled him from the room when Lisa had opened her eyes still gnawed at him. *I just want to see her, and then I'll go away.*

It was Barbara's voice, sounding metallic, that came through the speaker next to the first of two glass doors, the ones that locked. "Hallo?" she singsonged.

Oh, shit. Well, no one said this was going to be easy. He cleared his throat and screwed up his confidence. "It's Marc Guerrieri," he announced.

Lisa heard his voice through the speakers. Immediately, her nerve endings jangled and her stomach churned, as if she'd just had three double espressos at the coffee bar down the street. She felt her mouth stretch into a brilliant smile. Barbara, on the other hand, looked over at her disapprovingly, her mouth looking like she'd been sucking a bushelful of lemons.

The silence was intolerable. Just as Marc wondered if he was destined to freeze his ass off on the sidewalk, the intercom buzzed, and he heard the lock snap open. Eagerly, he snatched open the first glass door and entered the building. He took the carpeted stairs in the hall two at a time, practically running through the warmth under the skylight to get to her door. *Number 8.* Then he realized he was breathing heavily. *Easy, Marco.*

Lisa's heart thumped inside her bruised ribs as she listened to the knock on the white metal fire door. Instantly, Barbara pulled the door open, and he appeared. Her breath encountered a logjam in her throat.

He looked fine as ever, in a black coat, thick grey woolen turtleneck, jeans, and black hiking boots with red laces. She remembered what he looked like totally in the raw, lean and muscular. She then realized that her dear, sainted mother was in the same room with them, wearing her aura of disapproval like a heady perfume on the tense air. Marc's blue gaze centered on Barbara. "Dr. Martin," he greeted Barbara, as if he was meeting the high school principal.

"Hello," Barbara reciprocated, her tone the epitome of curt.

Then the gaze drifted to Lisa. He flashed her a tremulous smile. "Lisa," he said.

Lisa struggled to her feet. She looked infinitely better than she had in that hospital bed. Nonetheless, she still seemed shaky, fragile. His first instinct was to slip his arm around her waist to prop her up. Then he remembered . . . it wasn't his place to do that anymore. He shoved his hands into the pockets of his coat.

She smiled at him. His gut clenched. "Hi," she said. "How are you?"

So like her, forever selfless. She was, after all, the one who'd been in the car accident only a week ago. "Fine," he said. "You look great!"

She gave him, all agonizingly fine six feet of him, the once-over. *He thinks I look great!* She waved a dismissive hand. "It's the Percocet," she giggled.

He fondly remembered the excellent pain management he'd had when he'd gotten stabbed. "Oh, yeah," he chuckled. "Better living through chemistry."

They laughed, the nervous laughter of two people who'd once been emotionally naked, now trying to come to terms with that in a different context.

In her peripheral vision, Lisa saw Barbara snatch a

ring of keys from the wooden rack near the door. "I'm going to check the mail," Barbara announced.

"Umm . . . all right, Ma," Lisa said.

They both watched as Barbara threw open the door and walked out.

You're so beautiful! He couldn't stop looking at her. He used to watch her sleep when they were together in the cabin, listen to her breathe evenly, and think how lucky he was to be there with her . . . this woman, so wonderful inside and out.

She ran a hand over her painful head. *He's staring!* Self-consciously, she put a hand to her bruised cheek and looked away. Was she that hideous?

Speak, stunes! He scratched his head. "Well," he began, "I'm not going to stay. I just came to give you your grade. You got a B-plus."

Lame-ass excuse. She was going to get her grade in the mail, two weeks from now, like everyone else.

"B-plus," she repeated. "That's respectable."

He blushed, still embarrassed over his behavior with her in his office. "Maybe I didn't articulate this that night after class, but your children's book was excellent. It was just incongruous with the rest of the assignments you'd handed in before. You have a gift, Lisa. In the best way, you're your mother's daughter."

That didn't seem so bad to Lisa anymore. "I've decided to stop fighting it," she said. "Umm . . . listen, would you like a drink? Coffee? Tea? Soda?"

That would've been heaven, sitting with her on the couch, sharing conversation and a beverage. But he knew he had to get out of there. This was supposed to be a proper good-bye. "Can't stay," he sighed. "Got some last-minute packing."

Her heart sank. The one second she wasn't thinking about his imminent departure, she was reminded of it. She tried so hard to brighten her mood. "Yes, congratulations," she said. "When are you leaving?"

Leaving without you . . . "Next week. I'm spending Christmas with Michele and Kieran."

She was losing him, and there was nothing she could do about it. As much as it hurt, she surrendered to the inevitable. "Well, good luck," she said, choking back the cry in her throat. "We'll see you next year, then."

God, I want to hold you. "Yeah, next year," he repeated.

She thought he was about to shake her hand. The next thing she knew, she was in his arms. She held him, pressing her palms against the back of his coat. He held her carefully, buried his nose in her hair. But he knew eventually, he'd have to let her go. That was what constituted a proper good-bye.

He let her go and stared helplessly at her face. Instantly, her hand drifted up to the bruise on her cheek. That bruise did nothing to detract from her beauty. Gently, he took her hand away and held it. He looked at her unflinchingly. "I'm glad you're better," he said. "I didn't want 'I hate you' to be the last thing you heard me say."

Her hand in the warmth of his . . . all the memories came flooding back. "Hey, heat of passion," she croaked.

He closed his eyes and lovingly kissed the bruise. It may have been Lisa's imagination or the Percocet breaking into her bloodstream, but suddenly, her entire body stopped hurting. She was only remotely aware of the door opening and her mother entering the apartment.

Barbara's aura swirled around them like a malevolent poltergeist. Marc moved away to a respectable distance from Lisa and shot Barbara a nervous look. She stared at him like a mother lioness protective of her cub. "Well, I'm going to go," he announced.

Don't go! Lisa resisted the urge to clutch onto his hand. Instead, she said, "Have a safe trip."

Marc nodded in Barbara's direction, then headed toward the door. She held it open for him. He stepped into the hallway, warmed by the sunlight streaming through the skylight. He felt a rush of wind as Barbara slammed the door behind him. He thought of the last words his mother had said to him. *Well, that's that, then . . .* That was his proper good-bye.

Given her injuries, Lisa raced as fast as she could to her bay windows, which overlooked the parking lot. She saw Marc's black Jeep, parked just a few yards from her apartment building. "Careful, Melissa!" Barbara cautioned.

That was her problem. She'd been careful all her life.

Minutes later, he came into view, walking with purpose toward his Jeep. The reality of it dropped on her like a ton of bricks. He was actually going to get into his car and drive out of her life. Undiluted sorrow washed over her. Emotion, coupled with the drugs in her system, drew sobs from deep inside her. She pressed her hands against the glass and watched as he unlocked the Jeep and got into the driver's seat.

Fuck being careful! Lisa turned away from the windows and headed for the door. Barbara stared at her as if she were a lunatic. She grabbed Lisa's arm. "For God's sake, Melissa, think!" she cried. "You have no future with that man!"

Lisa eased her arm from Barbara's bony grasp. "I love him, Ma!" she wailed.

Barbara thought for a moment, then stepped aside. Lisa threw open the apartment door and lumbered through the warm hallway, pressing her hand against her throbbing side. By the time she reached the street, she was breathless and sweaty, tears pouring unabated down her face. She watched helplessly as Marc's Jeep slowly advanced from the parking lot onto the tail end of the Crescent. "Marc," she wailed. It came out of her dry throat like a whisper. "Marc!"

Marc turned onto the street and looked in his rear-view mirror for oncoming traffic. *Shit!* His eyes widened.

She was standing in the very same spot where he'd clocked Bryan-fucking-Livingston. She was crying, shivering in the freezing cold like a leaf. Instead of turning right, he whipped the steering wheel left onto the street and gunned the car in her direction.

Fuck road rules. He stopped the Jeep in the middle of the street, and, leaving the motor running, he threw open the door and sprinted to her. He stared at her teary face, and his heart squeezed in his chest. "Marc!" she sobbed with relief.

Marc tore the coat from his back and draped it around her shoulders. She opened her arms to him, and he pulled her close, resisting the urge to mold her against him. "I don't want to hurt you," he laughed happily in her ear.

Lisa wrapped her arms around his waist, pulled up his sweater, and pressed her hands against his cotton shirt. "You're so warm," she whispered.

Just then, Lisa looked up at her bay windows and saw Barbara, looking down at them . . . *on* them. The blinds dropped down in front of the window then, obscuring Barbara's face. Lisa closed her eyes, savored the smell of his aftershave, basked in the warmth of his body against hers. "It's just us against the world," she thought out loud.

Careful of her injuries, Marc wrapped his arms around her waist. She felt so good against him. He wasn't going to let her go ever again. He pressed a kiss against her cheek. "That's all we need," he said in her ear.

Epilogue

On the deck of their condo, Lisa abandoned the preliminary sketches for her new book and stared out at La Jolla Cove at sunset. Distracted from her deliciously gossipy conversation on the cordless phone, she watched the seals cavorting on the rocks, as they soaked up the last rays of the sun that slashed the brilliant blue sky. The world seemed bigger, more beautiful that day . . . all because she had a secret.

"Are you listening to me?!" Ione cried from the other end of the phone. "I can hear you detaching, Melissa."

Lisa came back to earth. "Of course I'm listening to you," she lied. "I was looking at my view. Girl, it's so beautiful out here! You've got to come out for a visit."

"How are you *really*, Lisa?" Ione asked.

Lisa giggled, still marveling at how one life could change in so little time. The day Marc had come for her, they went upstairs where he asked Barbara for Lisa's hand. Permission which Barbara begrudgingly gave. However, because both Marc and Lisa were divorced, they were forbidden to marry in the Catholic church. One week before Christmas, the civil service calendars were packed. So, Lisa and Marc ran off to Las Vegas. In front of Adam and Doug, Nina and Tim, and Barbara, Haley Melissa Martin became Haley Melissa Guerrieri, locked in wedded bliss by a young Elvis.

"I've never been happier," Lisa said simply, and it was the truth.

"That's great, Lisa," she sighed. "I'm glad. Remember what I said to you that day in the bar? About you being married and pregnant in a year? You laughed at me. Now you see I'm halfway right."

Lisa just laughed. Ione didn't know just how right she'd been. "Well, A.J. says, and I quote, 'to tell you and the White Devil hello,' " Ione said. "I think that's her way of making up."

Even A.J.'s militant stance couldn't dampen her day.

"Tell her that *Mrs.* White Devil sends her regards," she chuckled.

They giggled like they used to. "Well, I'd better go," Ione sighed wistfully. "I'm going to take you up on that visit soon."

"I'll have your room ready, sweetie," Lisa promised.

They hung up, and Lisa, grinning from ear to ear, looked out at the seals.

Marc slipped his key in the lock and entered the condo. He'd driven like a bat out of hell on the I 5, just to be here. Home. Music from the SOS Band filled the minimalist living room.

Then he saw her, on the deck. A shiver sliced through him. The slight March breeze blew her hair back from her face, made the diaphanous dress cling to her body. *Damn, that body.* Their wedding night was the first time they'd been together since the cabin. He was careful not to be overzealous, just in case she hadn't completely healed from the car crash. Just to be with her again, skin on skin, making love with his wife. And lying there with her afterward . . . talking, laughing, not having to be anywhere but there, cloaked in the sanctity of their commitment. His groin throbbed just from him thinking of it.

He snuck up behind Lisa and slipped his arms around her waist. He felt her laugh against him. "I was missing you all day, Mrs. G.," he said with a naughty grin.

Mrs. G.! Maybe it was the novelty of it, or her love for him that was bigger than the oceans—whatever the reason, she still beamed when she heard it. "Ditto, Dr. G.," she laughed.

Marc ran his hands over her hard nipples, which protruded through the silkiness of her dress. He resisted the compelling urge to step out of his trousers and satisfy that old familiar itch. More for himself than for her, he moaned, "We've gotta get dressed if we're going to make it to L.A. in time for dinner."

She laughed. She turned in his arms. His curious blue eyes contrasted sharply against his tanned, strikingly handsome face. She wanted to see that face when she divulged her secret, remember his expression for the rest of her life. "Hey, guess what?" she said.

Completely unsuspecting, he asked, "What?"

She held his face in her hands and leaned in. "The stick turned blue," she whispered.

The stick turned blue? Then he put two and two together. Adrenaline coursed through him. *Oh my God!* "No shit!" he exclaimed, jubilant.

His blue eyes looked questioning, hopeful. She was ecstatic that this time, they both would get what they wanted so desperately. She raised her right hand, like she was swearing an oath. "No shit," she promised.

It sank in. He was going to be a father. She was the mother of his child, incubating his seed. The sheer weight of it hit home. He stared at her, disbelieving his own good fortune. Emotion overcame him. He blinked away tears and savored the expression of pure joy on her face. "I love you," he said, his voice raw.

She kissed his mouth. She doubted she could convey everything she felt for him with words, but she would try. "Oh, sweetie," she sighed. "I love you so much."

Just as Marc reached for her, the phone rang. He took her hand and held tight as she switched on the cordless phone and put it to her ear. "Hello?" she said, then her eyes widened, and a smile of pleasant surprise touched her mouth. "We're fine, thanks."

He gave her a look, like *Who is it?* She squeezed his hand. "Sure, he's right here," she said. "Just a minute."

She handed Marc the phone. "It's for you," she announced.

Warily, Marc took the phone. "Hello?" he said tentatively.

"MarcAntonio, it's your mother," she finally announced across the wires.

A heady mix of emotions flooded through him ... nostalgia, anger, fear of rejection, love. After all, he was a part of her; he and Lisa had made a part of her. "Ma," he said quietly.

"I got your number from Adam," Rosalie announced. "It's good to see you're alive and well."

More than alive and well. Marc looked down at Lisa's curious, beautiful face. "We're great," he declared.

"Well, I won't keep you," Rosalie said. "I just wanted to see how you and your ... Lisa were doing."

So, he wasn't disowned. She loved him after all. "Everything's great, Ma," he said. *Should I ... ?* "As a matter of fact, Ma, Lisa and I are expecting a baby."

For the first time in forty years, he heard his mother giggle with unadulterated joy. "Oh, MarcAntonio!" she cried. "That's wonderful for you. I mean, for you and Lisa."

He couldn't hate her. After all, she was trying. "Thank you, Ma," he said, all shy. For a second there, he was a little boy again, craving her approval.

"MarcAntonio," Rosalie said, and she sounded like

she was crying. "Son . . . because of certain circumstances, your father and I couldn't give you what you needed when you were little. Your father was sick, and our only focus at the time was getting him better. After he was attacked, he was never the same. Adam helped us out a lot, but that wasn't his job. It was ours, and we let you down."

Tears trickled down his face. This was what he waited all his life to hear. He squeezed Lisa's hand harder.

"Are you happy, son?" Rosalie asked.

He snuffled, gulping air into his chest through his mouth. He looked down at Lisa, who stared lovingly up at him. "Very happy, Ma," he declared.

"Then that should be all a mother wants," Rosalie sobbed. "That's all I ever wanted for you. To be happy. Protected."

"Well, you have it, Ma," he assured her.

Marc heard her blow her nose. "Well, I've got to go. Your father's waiting for me," she announced. "We'll call you next Sunday, if that's okay."

"Sure. That'll be fine."

"I love you, son."

"I love you too, Ma."

She hung up on her end, and he clicked the OFF button on the cordless. Where there was life, there was hope.

Lisa held his face in her hands. "Are you all right?" she asked, her tone soft, concerned.

Marc took her in his arms and held her close. He buried his nose in her hair and inhaled deeply. "I'm the luckiest man in the world," he sighed, over the sound of the ocean crashing over the rocks.